MARY LARKIN

SHADES OF DECEIT

sphere

SPHERE

First published in Great Britain in 2013 by Sphere
This paperback edition published in 2014 by Sphere

A CIP catalogue record for this book is available from the British
Library.

ISBN 978-0-7515-5165-5

Typeset in Sabon 11.25/14.5 pt
by Palimpsest Book Production Limited, Falkirk, Stirlingshire
Printed and bound in Great Britain by Clays Ltd, St Ives plc

Papers used by Sphere are from well-managed forests and other
responsible sources.

MIX
Paper from
responsible sources
FSC
www.fsc.org FSC® C104740

Sphere
An imprint of Little, Brown Book Group
100 Victoria Embankment
London EC4Y 0DY

An Hachette UK Company

www.hachette.co.uk
www.littlebrown.co.uk

Also by Mary Larkin

The Wasted Years
Ties of Love and Hate
For Better, For Worse
Playing with Fire
Best Laid Plans
Sworn to Secrecy
Painful Decisions
Suspicious Minds

I dedicate this book to my good friend, Theresa, for her guidance during the times when I suffered mental block.

Author's Note

The geographical areas portrayed in *Shades of Deceit* actually exist, and any historical events referred to in the course of the story are, to the best of my knowledge, authentic.

However, I wish to emphasise that the story is fictional; all characters are fictitious and any resemblance to real persons, living or dead, is purely coincidental.

Belfast

1920s

1

Louise McGuigan glanced nervously at her reflection in the wide shop windows as she stepped out briskly along Castle Junction towards Ann Street. She was reassured by what she saw. She looked confident – more so than she felt – her blonde curly hair falling to her shoulders and catching the faint rays of a weak sun. Her slim figure, in the new black suit bought especially for the occasion, looked good. She definitely appeared at her best. On her way to one of the large bookshops in the city centre for a job interview, she was glad her prayers had been answered. The morning had dawned bright, though rather chilly, and the dark clouds that gathered low in the sky were holding themselves at bay. With a bit of luck she might make it to her destination without looking like a drowned rat in her new outfit. That was all she asked: to arrive dry. The rest of the day could look after itself. It could then snow for all she would care.

It was a big step to take from working in the mill to joining the staff in one of the big book outlets and she quailed at the very thought of it. It was something she wouldn't have had the courage to do off her own bat, but, unknown to her, her brother, Johnnie, had set up this interview.

The previous week Johnnie had been talking to a customer outside the shop he part-owned on the corner of Crocus Street. Louise had waved across to him as she hurried by on her way home from the Blackstaff mill during her lunch break. The man he was conversing with had turned and, catching his eye, she had given him a broad smile and nod of acknowledgement. She recognised him as the father of an old school friend.

That night Johnnie had come to her house and gleefully announced that he had managed to get her an interview for a job in the the city centre. In shock, Louise had slumped onto a chair and gawped at him in disbelief. He explained that the man she had seen him talking to earlier that day, Stan McDade, had admired her good looks and attractive smile. Johnnie had then confided in him how clever Louise was, adding that she was wasting her time in the mill. But, he went on, it was so hard for her to get a job in the present climate and she was losing

4

all hope of ever bettering herself. He didn't mention to Stan that Louise wasn't trying particularly hard to look for alternative employment outside the mill. That was best left unsaid. In his opinion his sister needed a push in the right direction and he had decided that he was just the one to do it.

Stan told Johnnie that his daughter who worked in Eason's bookshop was leaving at the end of the week, having obtained a position in an office as a trainee typist and bookkeeper. He said he was quite friendly with the manager in Eason's and surprised Johnnie by saying that he would have a chat with him and perhaps influence him to see Louise. If she managed to get the job it could also be a stepping stone for her into office work, as it had been for his daughter. Which couldn't be bad in the long run, Stan jested, obviously very proud of his daughter. Johnnie fervently agreed with him and silently added, it would be bloody marvellous!

The interview was the result. Stan had later called back to the shop to tell Johnnie that Al Murray, the manager of Eason's, had agreed to see his sister on the following Saturday. Louise quickly worked out that she had five days to prepare herself. New clothes were essential if she wanted to create a good impression. She only hoped it would be all worthwhile. She didn't want to squander precious money by taking time off work and spending her hard-earned cash just for a few minutes' talking to some man in a suit-and-tie position, about a job that was probably already promised to someone in the know. She knew that positions had to be advertised in-store, so it seemed futile to her.

But then again . . . neither did she want to throw her brother's kindness back in his face. So she decided the least she could do was to pull herself together and make the effort. And her motto for the day: nothing ventured, nothing gained.

Taking Wednesday afternoon off work, she went shopping. Thank heavens for good old Joshua Kelley Waddilove, she mused, the insurance agent who, during the course of his work, had seen at first-hand how a lot of working-class families struggled to pay for essential items such as clothes, footwear, furniture – even food. Joshua knew that once the resources of the pawnbroker had been exhausted, many of these less fortunate people had only the local moneylenders to turn to in their hour of dire need, who would charge extortionate rates of interest on their loans.

Joshua, realising that something could and must be done, had had the foresight to devise a system to ease these poor families' hardships. He came up with the brilliant but simplest of plans, by which he would provide vouchers that people could exchange in local shops for what they needed. They could then repay the amounts owed in small, affordable weekly instalments, which would be collected by the company's door-to-door agents. Word soon spread and demand grew for the vouchers, which were later to become popularly known as Provident cheques. And thus a thriving nationwide business was founded. Joshua Waddilove also got his just reward as its growth expanded among the poorer communities.

Louise had taken out some of these cheques to tide them over Christmas. Paying them off at a weekly rate, she should be able to renew them in time to get some Easter treats for the family. Thanks to the cheques, she had been able so far to leave her own little nest egg intact. But now she had no choice but to break into the meagre amount she managed to put away from her wages each week to save for her marriage to Conor O'Rourke. She begrudged using this money, certain that a mill girl wouldn't stand a snowball's chance in hell of ever being employed in a bookshop. Not that she wouldn't be capable of doing the work. She was aware that she was intelligent. Hadn't the nuns wanted her parents to send her to college to further her education? At the time, however, financial circumstances had decreed that she leave St Vincent's School and go to work in the mill. As far as she could see, she had missed her chance for good of anything better.

Still, she had to give it a try, feeling she must put her best foot forward. Needing to look competent and as personable as possible to have any chance that the interview would go in her favour, she had planned accordingly. She had read somewhere that first appearances and attitude were the most important factors for a successful interview: that she had to sell herself, if she were to progress.

Ever since her mother had packed her bags and left to go and live with her fancy man, Bill McCartney, a foreman fitter who also worked in Blackstaff mill, money at home had been tight. First, there had been the shotgun wedding and the loss of Johnnie's weekly contributions to the family coffers once he married Mary Gilmore, then her mother's wage had gone when she had. Harry had looked for a job for months after leaving school. Peggy had only recently finished her education, so there had been no help there. To begin with, her father had expected Louise to work miracles on what he gave her weekly, along with her own wages.

Thank God, though, Harry had finally obtained employment in a newly opened branch of Kennedy's bakery over on Beechmount Avenue. Also, Matthew McFadden had taken Peggy on full time in the family grocery shop, of which Johnnie was now a partner. This meant they were now both contributing to the household budget, which was a big relief for Louise.

Thinking about the outlay that this interview had

cost her, Louise could only hope her extravagance would pay dividends. Realising she had reached her destination, she came to a halt and stood gazing blindly through her reflection in the window at the profusion of books in the shop, endeavouring to calm her racing heart before entering.

Once inside, she hesitated and peered around to get her bearings. It was a big place and very busy, with people of all ages browsing through the books and magazines. Colourful posters advertising well-known as well as new authors covered the walls, and books of all descriptions – thrillers, romances, war and history, science fiction and fantasy – were ranged on stands or laid out, row upon row, on the floor space. She was mesmerised as she walked along the aisles, seeking a notice directing her to the manager's office. Feeling out of place, she knew she must look completely lost among all this literature.

A pretty assistant approached her, a beaming smile on her face. 'Can I be of any assistance?' she enquired politely.

Louise turned to her gratefully. 'Oh, yes, please. I've an appointment with Mr Murray.'

'Is it about the sales position?'

'Yes, it is,' Louise confessed.

'Come, I'll show you where to go. I'm Deirdre Walsh by the way.'

'I'm Louise. Louise McGuigan.'

'Well, don't look so worried, Louise McGuigan,' the girl chided her gently. 'Mr Murray is a very nice person, you'll get on great with him.'

With these words of encouragement, Deirdre led her to a door near the children's book section, opened it and stood back to allow Louise to enter a small room. 'Good luck.'

To Louise's consternation, two other girls were already sitting primly on chairs close to another door marked 'Private'. Guessing she wasn't the only one after the vacancy, she thanked Deirdre for her help and sat alongside them.

The door closed on Deirdre and Louise covertly eyed the competition. They were attractive-looking girls, one a redhead and the other a blonde like herself, and probably about the same age as Louise. Both were well turned out for the occasion. After a cursory glance and nod in her direction, they avoided her eyes. They seemed tense and Louise guessed that they were every bit as nervous as she was. She felt as though she had butterflies fluttering about in her stomach and was a bit nauseous.

A young woman dressed in a neat, dark-green suit came through the door marked 'Private' and, reading from a clipboard in her hand, glanced at the girls. 'Josephine Devlin?'

The redhead jumped nervously to her feet as if stung.

'That's me,' she gasped.

Businesslike, the woman smiled and, leading her into the other room, closed the door behind them.

Fifteen minutes must have passed before Josephine reappeared. She gave no indication whether or not she had made a good impression and without a word or backward glance left via the entrance to the shop floor.

Another name was called. 'Rita Morris?'

The same procedure ensued. More time elapsed and when Rita reappeared, she was no more forthcoming than Josephine, giving Louise a nervous little smile as she passed so she wasn't in any way enlightened. Had either girl succeeded in obtaining the job? Sure that Rita must have been successful, Louise was a bundle of nerves when her turn finally arrived. By now her internal butterflies were rampant. Nevertheless, determined to put on a good show, she rose, smoothed her slim-fitting skirt about her hips, straightened her shoulders and, when her name was called, went to meet her destiny.

The woman in attendance ushered her into the room and, leaving her standing in front of a desk, took a chair at a table to one side of it, on which sat a typewriter and a large black telephone. Louise stood waiting, silently eyeing the man seated behind the battered desk. He looked quite young for a managerial position. Somehow, she had pictured Mr Murray as a middle-aged family man, but Louise surmised he would be in his mid-twenties.

11

He continued shuffling through papers for some moments, then, lifting his head, motioned for her to sit down.

Glad to get the weight off her shaking legs, Louise sank gratefully and, she hoped, gracefully onto the chair in front of the desk and gave the man a speculative look.

His gaze had returned to the papers in front of him, which he now boxed together and put to one side. 'Can I see your references, please.' Without lifting his head he held out his hand across the desk.

Louise was nonplussed. No one had mentioned anything about references to her. Getting no response, he lifted his head and looked down his nose at her.

'I beg your pardon?'

'Your references, I need to have a look at them,' he said, somewhat impatiently.

Louise gazed blankly back at him. 'I didn't know I'd need any references,' she managed to splutter.

He frowned and looked at her as if she were an idiot. 'You always need references. Didn't you need them when you started your previous jobs?'

Confused, Louise felt colour rise up her neck into her cheeks like mercury in a thermometer. She felt so stupid. He obviously didn't know she was a mill worker. She had assumed that Mr McDade would have explained the circumstances to this man. But perhaps he had thought that he had better not say anything about her present employment. Why then hadn't she been warned? Was she supposed to keep dumb? Not say where she worked? Johnnie had not mentioned anything about it either! In a quandary, Louise was speechless for a few moments. Then tossing her head she gazed at him defiantly. This was not her fault and she had nothing to be ashamed of.

'I started work in the Blackstaff mill straight from school and I've worked there ever since. If I recall rightly, I didn't need any references then.' She hadn't planned to be so curt but that was the way the words came out and she inwardly squirmed at her indiscretion.

He was silent so long – at least it seemed long to her as she impatiently waited, head bowed, hands clasped tightly on her lap, for him to reply – that she thought she must surely have blown it. At last, forcing herself to meet his eye, she rose slowly to her feet.

'I apologise for wasting your time, sir. It appears I am here under a misapprehension. And I thank you for taking the time to see me.'

She was almost at the door when his voice stopped her. He pointed to the chair, and said sternly, sounding just like one of the nuns in St Vincent's School, upbraiding a wayward pupil, 'Sit down, please.'

She paused a moment, but then slowly obeyed him.

13

'Are you always so touchy?'

She drew back, insulted. How dare he speak to her like this? 'I beg your pardon?'

A slight grimace crossed his face. 'I said, are you always so touchy?'

'Excuse me? . . . I was told to come here and see you, Mr Murray. I thought you would know all about me. I'm sorry that I have no references to offer but I didn't know that I would need any.'

He sighed and relaxed a little. 'Sorry. That's my fault. I should have introduced myself, Miss McGuigan. Unfortunately Mr Murray cannot be here today. I'm standing in for him. He probably knows all about you, but I don't. You see, your name is not on my list of interviewees.' He nodded towards the papers he had searched through in vain and placed to one side. 'Let me introduce myself. My name is John Bradford. I apologise for the misunderstanding, but I wasn't made aware of your circumstances.' He frowned briefly across at the other woman. 'That's why I appear to be at a bit of a loss here.'

Oh, you're not the only one, Louise wanted to say, but managed to hold her tongue. 'What happens now?' she asked quietly. 'Do I come back another time? Or have you already selected one of those other girls?'

'Actually, I am not in a position to dictate whom we employ. Mr Murray attends to that. He wasn't

14

feeling too well. A bit of a cold, I believe, and probably didn't want to spread any germs about. Hence his absence. I'll pass on my notes to him when he comes back to work, but he is the one who makes the final decision, not me. You will be notified by post as to the outcome of this meeting.'

She was on her feet again. 'Well then, since you can't interview me I may as well go. Thank you for your patience, Mr Bradford.'

He leaned forward, arms on the desk, hands clasped in front of him, with an expression of derision. 'Feeling sorry for yourself? Poor little you, having to work in the mill, eh? There are thousands like you, you know, but I've never met one with such a large chip on their shoulder.'

She blinked with astonishment, then without thinking rose up out of the chair, pitched herself forward on her hands, leaning across the desk into his face and hissed, 'How dare you poke fun at me. I didn't come here to be insulted. What would someone like you, a white-collar worker, with everything probably handed to you on a plate, know about working in a mill, eh?'

He lounged back in his seat and laughed at her audacity. 'Actually, I know quite a lot about mill workers and, in my opinion, they're the salt of the earth.' Louise opened her mouth to speak but he overrode her. 'My father worked in the flax store in Grieves Mill since he was no age. He died last

15

year at just fifty-five. Dust in the lungs was the cause of his premature death, his, and those of many before him and since. And do you know how he got that? Poor ventilation, that's how! A couple of windows might have kept him alive that bit longer, but they would have cost money and big firms don't squander profits on trivial things like windows. I remember him coughing his guts up every night. It was a sorry sight and it broke my poor mother's heart. But he never once complained. It was his job and he just got on with it. So, yes, I do know something about mill workers. And I'm always glad to hear of people getting away from the mills . . . bettering themselves.'

He paused for breath, annoyed at himself. What was he ranting on about? This girl had managed to get under his skin, and he had got on his bloody high horse; he hated the way the mill workers were treated. Still, she had every right to sit there and gape at his antics.

Quieter now, he said, 'Believe me, you're not the only one born at the wrong time in the wrong place. When only mill work was available to the poor, they had no choice but to accept it or live in poverty. However, my father made sure none of his children followed in his wake.' He gave her a rueful smile. 'Now, do you still want to apply for this job or not?'

Somewhat surprised at his outburst, Louise

16

accepted the implied apology and sat down again. 'Sorry. Yes, please.'

'Then let me get some personal details from you.'

He took her name and address, date of birth and brief details of her work as a weaver. Then reaching across the desk, he offered her his hand. 'We will be in touch soon, Miss McGuigan. Sorry for ranting on like that. I'll put a good word in for you.'

With a nod of farewell to the woman who had taken a keen interest in all this intercourse, Louise left the room, head high. John Bradford cast a shamefaced glance towards his colleague at the table, hiked his shoulders and grimaced slightly, knowing that he had been out of order. Al Murray's secretary gazed sternly back at him, unimpressed by his handling of the situation. The girl had come here today obviously unprepared, through no fault of her own. John Bradford had no right to reproach her like that. As a matter of fact, he had been downright insulting to the poor thing.

After all, he was only a glorified clerk himself, recently brought in from another shop. She could have conducted the interview better herself. She decided that she would inform Mr Murray all about it and, the next time he was unavailable, perhaps he would leave things in her capable hands instead of bringing in someone still wet behind the ears.

2

Her thoughts in a whirl, Louise hurriedly left the shop. Flustered and upset, she paused outside to collect herself, facing the shop window again, only this time to hide her distress from passers-by as she strove to calm her jangled nerves. With fingers pressed tightly against her mouth to smother the sobs that threatened to burst from her throat, she finally gained control and, with a frustrated shake of the head, started to walk along Ann Street. She needed time to think things through before going home. How could she face her brother? Unconsciously, her feet led her towards a café near Cornmarket that she sometimes visited when shopping in the city centre. Seated at a corner table, she picked up the menu and gazed vacantly at it, unable to take in the contents.

In a daze she flailed about, thinking of ways in which she might have provoked John Bradford's behaviour but found none. There weren't any . . . but she must have said something to antagonise him, mustn't she? Why else would he have subjected her to that long tirade about his father and the mill? Did he think she was too ashamed to admit that she worked in a mill and was he putting her in her place? Had she been the one in the wrong? Yes! She must have been! No getting away from it. Sitting there expecting that man to know all about her. Who did she think she was? Some celebrity? Would it have been any different if Al Murray had been there? Perhaps. He might have been more understanding. That young assistant Deirdre had mentioned Mr Murray's name. She can't have known that he wouldn't be present at the interview.

Discovering that she had unconsciously crumpled the menu out of shape, with an embarrassed glance around she smoothed it out flat on the table. What on earth had made her go on like that? Why let that man wind her up? And lucky him! Neither her mother nor her father had made any effort to keep her out of the mill. She cringed inside with shame as these unsolicited thoughts invaded her mind. Now she was whining to herself. Her mother had needed the extra money she brought in, full stop.

When Louise had just left school, Johnnie had been thrown out of the shipyard because he was a Catholic and her mother had had to make up for the loss of his wage. So Louise had been sacrificed. Not that she had thought so at the time, but now she realised that she had indeed been the loser. The sacrificial lamb.

People might believe that she was ashamed to be working in the Blackstaff mill but this just wasn't true. She was happy enough there in the weaving shop. If Conor O'Rourke's mother wasn't such a snob, Louise would have gone on as before. It made no difference to Conor that she was a weaver, so why worry about his mother or anyone else? So long as Conor loved her and wanted to marry her, who or what else mattered?

The hours worked in the mill were long and hard but the workers in the Blackstaff were, as that rude man had so rightly stated, the salt of the earth. They had been understanding and supportive to her when her mother had packed her bags and run off with Bill McCartney. Except for the odd few, principally the women who had felt the scorn of Nora McGuigan's tongue lashings when they had dared to play fast and loose while their husbands were away at the Somme, fighting for their country. And who could fault them for showing their scorn of Nora? Certainly not Louise, who felt let down by her mother's betrayal. She did not blame them in the slightest for getting their dig in when given half a chance. Now she felt as if she had betrayed her friends at work, those who had remained loyal to her.

And Johnnie . . . She squirmed slightly. What would his reaction be? There was no way she would be offered the sales position now. Not after all that palaver back there in Eason's. Imagine forgetting her manners to that extent. She couldn't get over her stupidity.

Conor's mother, Cissie O'Rourke, was a hypocrite through and through. Louise shouldn't let it bother her that Cissie thought her not good enough for her son because she was a mill worker. But deep down it hurt. It was the cause of all Louise's insecurity.

Eventually, Cissie, with all her highfalutin airs and graces, had been exposed for what she was: a downright liar and an unmarried mother into the bargain. It was disgraceful the way she had kept her son in the dark about his parenthood, leading him to believe that his father had deserted him. Bearing this in mind, Cissie should be glad that Louise still wanted to marry her son. All the same, Louise was far from being a snob and it would be nice to make a friend of one's mother-in-law, in fact, easier all round.

Of course it might still happen. Opinions sometimes changed drastically. Before Johnnie's shotgun wedding to Mary Gilmore, Nora McGuigan had been devastated at the very idea of Johnnie, the apple of her eye, having to marry a girl he'd made

21

pregnant. Although she had put on a good front, Nora had blamed Mary for ruining her son's life. However, as it turned out, everything had panned out well for Mary and Johnnie. And now, due to the circumstances surrounding the birth of Nora's own baby, called Lucy after Nora's mother, Grannie Logan, Nora and Mary were as thick as thieves.

Cissie O'Rourke was the least of her worries, Louise decided. To be truthful, she could do without an interfering mother-in-law and she imagined that was just what Cissie O'Rourke would be. Always poking her nose in where it wasn't wanted.

Conor hadn't known that he was illegitimate at the time he proposed marriage to Louise. It wasn't until the year before, when Cissie had first heard of his intention, that she had arranged for father and son to meet, hoping Conor's father would advise him against marrying a mill worker. A reluctant Conor had travelled to Birmingham to discover that although Donald McAteer was his biological father, Conor hadn't even been given his name. O'Rourke was his mother's maiden name. He even found out that he had two half-brothers, Andrew and Josh, older than himself and a half-sister, Joan, just a few months older.

Conor had been deeply ashamed to learn the truth about his mother's deceit. For a while he had broken off with Louise, afraid to tell her the result of his visit to his father, afraid that she would never marry

22

a bastard. Men could be so stupid at times. He had caused her untold pain and unwittingly driven her into the arms of another man, George Carson.

After a lot of misunderstanding and anguish, he had eventually picked up the courage to tell Louise what he now knew about his mother's betrayal. Since then their love had been stronger than ever. Cissie must really think so very little of Louise to have risked sending Conor to meet his father. Louise could only thank God that it had backfired on his mother.

Suddenly aware that the girl behind the counter, with whom she always had a friendly word, was eyeing her in concern, Louise flashed her a false smile. Today she was in no mood for idle banter, but rising reluctantly to her feet she went over to give her order.

'I'll have a pot of tea and—' Louise glanced along the counter and, seeing a plate of assorted cakes, said, 'a slice of shortbread, thank you.'

As she filled the teapot, Jean Garland spoke tentatively. 'I don't mean to be nosy . . . but are you OK?'

'Just a bit of a headache. A cup of tea will, I hope, soon shift it.'

More concerned now, Jean said with a wave of her hand, 'Away and sit yourself down and I'll bring this over.'

The café had been almost empty when she arrived but now, it being the lunch hour, customers were drifting in. Glad of the excuse, and with a nod towards the door, Louise gently chided her. 'Don't be silly. You'll be up to your eyes in a minute. But thanks all the same.'

She waited for her tray, paid the bill and, with a big grin to convince Jean that she really was feeling all right, thanked her, then went to a table at the window where she could sit and pretend an interest in passers-by. The tea did help somewhat, and as she relaxed she went back over the interview, word by word. No matter how she looked at it, it appeared that she had ruined any chance of getting employed at Eason's. A favourable outcome was out of the question.

When she left the café the weather had changed. The dark clouds were now brooding low over the rooftops and rain seemed imminent. It was much colder. Her neck was bare, so, hiking her shoulders up as close to her ears as possible for warmth, Louise hurried up Cornmarket towards the tram stop at the bottom of Castle Street. As she turned the corner, a cold wind was gathering speed and gusting along High Street, nipping at her ears and cutting through the fine material of her suit. The tram queue on Castle Street was long. Pushing tortuous thoughts to the back of her mind, she joined the discontented people grumbling about the sudden change in the weather and acting just the way she felt. She folded her arms tightly across her chest, hugging herself for warmth, and prepared for a long shivering wait.

It was some time before, chilled to the bone, she at last clambered on to the tram's platform and sidled into the lower deck. Gratefully grabbing on to the last remaining leather hand strap that hung from a brass bar running the length of the vehicle's ceiling, she clung on tight, glad to be inside where it was warmer. Not much warmer, she admitted, but at least the heat of bodies crowded together helped, even if a mixture of unsavoury odours permeated the air.

Staring blindly through the misted windows, she hung on to the strap and swayed with the rocking motion of the tram until it reached the Grosvenor Road junction, where she quickly alighted. Crossing the Falls Road, she started on the last lap of her journey up Springfield Road towards home.

On the tram she had planned what she would say to Johnnie. Should she try putting it over as one big laugh, pretend that she might still be in with a chance and hope he would never be any the wiser? No! That wouldn't be fair. She owed it to him to be honest and direct about it. As she walked, she had spent the time trying to find an easy way to break the bad news but on arrival at the shop she was no further forward. She still hadn't a clue what to say. Her brother and sister were serving customers, so with a wave of acknowledgement Louise went straight through into the office and put the kettle on. Soon she was joined by Johnnie.

Aware that all was not well, his glance was apprehensive. 'How did it go?' he asked tentatively.

'They said they'd be in touch. I'll get a reply through the post.' She grimaced and, deciding to get the bad news over with, added, 'But I'm not feeling very optimistic about it.'

A frown gathering on his brow, Johnnie queried, 'Why not?'

'Well, for a start it wasn't Al Murray conducting the interviews, and of course, I didn't have any references. Nobody mentioned I'd need them. And there were two other girls already waiting to see him when I got there. It seems Mr Murray called in sick and a young man called John Bradford was standing in for him. We weren't on the same wavelength, and I'm afraid I let him get under my skin.'

Johnnie's frown deepened. This sounded ominous. 'That's not like you, sis, when you knew what was at stake.'

'I know and I'm sorry.' She shrugged.

'Ah, Louise, you didn't make a mess of it . . . did you?'

Hanging her head in shame, she nodded. In spite of all her endeavours to hide it, her unhappiness hung in the air between them like a cloud.

Concerned now, he stepped closer and gently took her in his arms, holding her close. 'Shush now, surely it can't be all that bad. What happened to leave you in this state?'

His kindness overwhelmed her and, afraid of breaking down, she said abruptly, 'Look, Johnnie, I'm sorry I've let you down, but if you don't mind I'm too upset to talk about it just now. Later, perhaps?' Pushing herself away she headed for the door. 'There's a customer waiting, Johnnie,' she called over her shoulder as she rushed through the shop, in an attempt to stop him from following her. With a final nod of the head, she hurried through the side door that opened on to Crocus Street.

Ignoring her reference to the customer, which at any other time in Johnnie's book would have been a sin, he followed his sister outside, but she had already crossed Springfield Road and was turning down Springview Street. Johnnie returned indoors and, apologising profusely, attended the woman who was waiting to be served.

On the hall mat Louise was delighted to find two letters, one from Conor and the other from Cathie Morgan, her best friend. Scooping them up, she rained kisses on each envelope. They were something she would relish later on when the evening meal was over and she could read them in private without any interruptions. Feeling much better at this prospect, she climbed the stairs to put away her new suit. Hanging it on a clothes hanger, she held it aloft, admiring the cut of the hip-length jacket and slim-fitting, wrap-over skirt.

Made of fine wool, it really was beautiful. She had spent more of her savings on it than she had intended. It was the most expensive item of clothing she had ever bought and with hindsight she now realised that if she had chosen a brighter colour it could have been suitable as her going-away outfit. But black had seemed more appropriate for an interview. Perhaps now that the ice was broken there would be more interviews on the horizon. She hoped so, which would mean it wouldn't be such an extravagance after all. It was up to her to make things happen, not have people feeling sorry for her and trying to organise her life. She must think positively. Planting more kisses on the letters, she placed them carefully under her pillow and headed back down the stairs to make a start on the evening meal.

Putting all thoughts of her failure to one side, Louise set about lighting the kindling in the grate that her father had laid before going off to work that morning. In spite of her mental turmoil, the picture of her father doing this made her smile. Tommy McGuigan was a changed man these days. He handed Louise money for the upkeep of the household each week, not as much as she would like, but she was working on that. He even did menial jobs about the house, something he had refused to do in the past. Louise often wondered whether, if her mother had been a stronger-willed woman, their marriage would have survived. If she had challenged him now and again, put her foot down, was there a chance that things might have turned out differently? That was something she would never know.

The rest of the family seemed to have come to terms with her parents' break-up. Now and again Harry took his sweetheart Hannah McFadden to visit their mother and Bill at their lovely new house up Glen Road, and Harry was full of praise over it. Then, Peggy was forever trying to persuade her sister to let bygones be bygones. When her mother gave birth to Lucy, Louise had bought a small present for the baby but passed it on via her sister. She knew her mother was very hurt at her lack of response to the many invitations sent to her, but Louise couldn't help that. Her mother was settled and apparently very happy and, whilst Louise didn't begrudge her her good fortune, her concern was now for her father, Harry and Peggy whom her mother had deserted. Not that Louise and her da had ever been very close but he was still a comparatively young man and had been so down in the dumps lately.

She felt heartsore for him and worried about what would become of him. He pretended not to care what was happening to his wife but Louise knew that the birth of baby Lucy, fathered by Bill McCartney, of all people, had devastated him. Watching him withdraw more and more into himself, she wanted to weep. True, he had not been the ideal husband and father. However, it was his wife who had made the break. She was the one who had walked out on her family, leaving all her responsibilities behind. The burden of looking after the home had fallen on Louise's young shoulders, so she felt justified in rejecting all offers of reconciliation.

The vestibule door burst open and Peggy breezed in. Hands on hips, she stood facing her sister. 'What on earth happened?' she demanded. 'Johnnie isn't very happy with you at the moment. He's in such a dither . . . dreads seeing Stan McDade. Not that I think Stan will care one way or the other.'

She paused for breath, allowing Louise to butt in. 'Listen, Peggy, I don't want to talk about it at the moment. And I don't want you mentioning it in front of me da, do you understand?'

Peggy opened her mouth to object, just as Tommy's step sounded in the hall.

Throwing her a warning glance, when the vestibule door opened, Louise greeted him, 'Hi, Da,' before retreating into the sanctuary of the scullery to finish off the meal she was preparing. A subdued Peggy followed her. After washing her hands at the sink she silently assisted her sister by getting the plates and cutlery ready.

Peggy, who was the youngest, had been spoiled whilst her mother was at home, being treated as the baby of the family, although Peggy had always scorned this idea, insisting that she had missed out on many things. Leaving school shortly after her mother had run off, she had been fortunate when Johnnie had been able to get her started full time in the grocery shop where he was then manager. Under his management the shop had thrived and Johnnie was overjoyed when Matthew McFadden had offered him a partnership. Matthew had helped Johnnie in every way possible to achieve his life's ambition, even acting as guarantor for a bank loan. Johnnie would never forget his great generosity.

At first, at a loss without her mother and resentful at having to help out with the housework, Peggy had fought against all the changes that had to be made in the disrupted household. Now, with some money of her own coming in each week, she had settled down and threw her weight into helping to keep the house running smoothly. For this Louise was grateful. It certainly eased her burden a lot.

Louise threw some lard into the pan and was about to add three pork chops to the sizzling fat when Peggy gave her a sideways glance. 'Aren't you forgetting about Harry?'

'As if I would. Remember last night, didn't Harry say he was going to Hannah's for his tea?'

'Oh, I forgot all about that. They're as thick as

31

thieves, them two! I hardly ever see Hannah outside the shop these days. When she's not at home helping her mother, she's out gallivanting with our Harry.'

'But you've lots of other friends, haven't you? Surely you don't mind if Harry courts Hannah. They seem to be well matched.'

'She was my best friend, until that Harry fella started following us around,' Peggy insisted stubbornly. 'It's not as if Mrs McFadden will ever hear tell of her Hannah marrying our Harry. She's far too possessive, so she is. Especially since Mr McFadden passed away. Our Harry should wise up and set his cap elsewhere.'

It had been a terrible shock when about six months earlier Matthew McFadden had suffered a massive heart attack. His wife, Liz, had always been a frail woman, and the shock had almost finished her off. She was still recovering from the aftermath of her husband's sudden death and all the turmoil of the funeral. Johnnie had been a tower of strength during this terrible time. Indeed, there was every chance that Mrs McFadden wouldn't have survived the intense pressure without his help. Now she lived like a recluse, refusing to leave her home and depending more and more on Hannah.

Although she was inclined to agree with Peggy, Louise retorted, 'Time will tell. Who knows what's in store for them.'

Once the meal was ready, the two girls served it and joined their father at the table.

'This smells delicious, so it does, Louise,' Tommy enthused as he poured gravy over his chop. 'That's one thing we've got to be grateful for. You're a grand wee cook, so you are. Your mother trained you well, Louise. Do you think she knew that one day she'd up and leave us?' He stopped momentarily as if overcome and Peggy shot her sister a covert glance. Surely that wasn't a muffled sob she had just heard coming from her father. Wonders would never cease.

Ignoring Peggy, Louise tossed her head and threw him a scornful look. 'I'll tell you this much, Da. If I'd had as much as an inkling of what she intended doing, I'd have been gone before her. I never dreamed that she'd take herself off like that.'

'You don't really mean that, Louise,' her father reproved her. 'You'd never leave us in the lurch in the way your mother did. Would she, Peggy?'

'I certainly hope not, Da. Because if you were depending on me to keep the house running, we'd all starve to death, so we would.'

'Ah . . . don't you believe it,' Louise assured her. 'If it came to pass you'd soon learn quick enough! Do you think for one minute that I like being in charge here? Do you? Why, I'm nothing but a glorified slave . . . just like me ma was and I'll be glad to wipe the dust off my feet when me and Conor can afford to get married.'

33

Tommy considered his words before answering. 'I hope you don't have to eat those words, my girl.'

'What on earth are you talking about? I know Conor won't let me down. I wish I was just as sure of getting into heaven.'

Carefully wiping the last of the gravy from his plate with a piece of pork, Tommy looked embarrassed. He chewed slowly before replying. 'All I'm saying is, there's many a slip twixt cup and lip.' Still chewing on the pork, he rose from the table with a contented burp and gently ruffled her hair. 'Take no notice of me, lass. That was a lovely dinner. The chop was nice and tender, just as I like it, and the gravy was as good as your ma's ever was. Thanks, love.'

Gathering up his dishes, he headed for the scullery, saying over his shoulder, 'I promise I won't be too long in here. I'll be going down to the pub for an hour or so.'

Peggy gaped after him in amazement. Then she giggled and nudged her sister in the ribs with her elbow. 'Do you know what? For a moment there I thought he was going to offer to do the dishes.'

'Chance would be a fine thing.' Louise's answer was automatic. She was trying to figure out what her father meant. Just what was he hinting at?

Following him into the scullery, she said, 'What did you mean out there, Da?'

'Ah, take no notice of me, love. I was just

34

thinking of your mother. I was every bit as sure as you are of Conor, that your mother would never leave *me*.' He held out his arms, palms held up. 'And look what happened. So don't give all your heart away – eggs in the one basket as it were – keep a piece back in reserve in case you're ever let down. You know what I mean.'

'Look, Da, Conor is in an entirely different class from you. He would never lift a hand to me for a start. Or taunt me the way you did me ma. I trust him implicitly.'

'I know I wasn't the perfect husband, Louise. But I never looked at another woman. Ah, no. That's one thing I can never be accused of. Your mother was the only woman for me, and I never touched another. And that's more than can be said for your mother. She didn't get pregnant holding Bill McCartney's hand, now did she?' Tommy barked with laughter at his own wit. 'Or anything else for that matter.'

Louise grunted in disgust. 'No! You were too busy gambling and drinking away all the spare cash. And that reminds me. I'll need some extra money from you every week from now on. Everything keeps going up except the housekeeping money.'

His brows bunched together. 'Well, I can tell you this now, my dear. It won't be much.' Giving her a gentle push out of the way, he closed and barred the scullery door, leaving Louise to glare at it, none the wiser.

3

A disgruntled Johnnie shuffled around the shop, checking windows and doors and making sure everything was secure. Heaving into his arms the paper bag of groceries he had packed earlier, he set off for home. He was annoyed that Louise had apparently fluffed her chance of getting the job as saleslady in that shop, but he was also concerned that the interview seemed to have knocked the stuffing out of her, lowered her morale and made her decidedly unhappy. And that wasn't like his sister. This guy must have really got under her skin because his Louise could give as good as she got. But then, he mused, perhaps she had overreacted.

As he walked along Springfield Road to his home in Violet Street, he was still worrying. He paused at the police station across the road from Springview

Street and gazed at his feet, debating what to do. He was in two minds. Should he go over and check that Louise was all right, find out just what had happened today? Or . . .

He glanced up at the watchtower of the police station. Better move on in case the sentries thought he was behaving suspiciously. Especially with him carrying a large bag in his arms. They should know him well enough by now, but one never knew when there might be new policemen on duty who did not know him. Still deep in thought, he walked slowly, shaking his head in frustration. Better not to go over. His da would be there at this time of day and Louise wouldn't thank him for coming while Tommy was present. They couldn't say a civil word to each other.

He and his father didn't see eye to eye these days. Never had, if truth be told. But ever since that night when Tommy McGuigan had tried to persuade his son to neglect to do his duty by marrying Mary Gilmore, they had hardly exchanged a word. When Mary had dropped the bombshell that she was pregnant, it had come as a great shock to Johnnie, but his amazement had known no bounds when his da had offered to borrow the money for him to run off to England and shirk his responsibilities. Tommy had wanted him to stay across the water until the dust had settled.

Tommy had pointed out that Johnnie was not

yet nineteen, for heaven's sake, and he mustn't let that slip of a girl ruin his life. Johnnie had stubbornly stuck to his principles. He had enjoyed the pleasure and now he was prepared to pay the penalty. He had to do the decent thing and marry Mary. Not let her down. He wouldn't have been able to live with himself otherwise.

Because they had broken up for a short time before Johnnie had become aware of Mary's condition, Tommy had even had the audacity to suggest that Johnnie might not be the father of Mary's child. And if Johnnie held off for a while, Mary just might come up with another name to saddle the infant with. Johnnie was speechless with rage. He had expected ructions for getting Mary pregnant in the first instance; had, indeed, feared that his father would throw him out of the house; had expected him to rant and rave about the way he had brought disgrace down on the family. But he had never in his wildest dreams imagined that his da would come up with something of such magnitude. To leave Mary in the lurch? That was something he couldn't do. He might be only coming up to nineteen but Mary had yet to reach her seventeenth birthday. He had actually felt insulted at the idea that his da could think so little of him as to believe him capable of such treachery.

After failing to convince his son to even consider his advice, Tommy had washed his hands of them and, in spite of all the pleas from his wife and family, had even declined to attend the wedding ceremony. He had never once to this day acknowledged his daughter-in-law or his grandson. It was as if they didn't exist. As far as he was concerned, they were no kin of his and Johnnie had never spoken a friendly word to him since.

In spite of their many hardships, misunderstandings and trials, Johnnie and Mary had managed to struggle through. And although he wouldn't for one second admit it, Johnnie had been relieved that when his son was born, he was the spitting image of himself. There could be no doubt now who had fathered the child. Ashamed at the relief he felt, Johnnie had silently apologised to his wife for the insidious doubts, planted by his father, that had festered in his mind for some months prior to the birth. He was delighted nevertheless that his son had inherited his good looks. Just to prove to his da how wrong he was, of course!

What annoyed him most at the minute was the fact that Louise was acting as if their da was the victim of the piece. The way Johnnie saw it, their mother had just cause to run off with Bill McCartney. After his return from the Somme, when the children were still at school, for many long years Tommy had led his wife an awful existence. Once he had recovered sufficiently from his war wounds, except for a slight limp, Tommy was welcomed back into his old job in the tram depot, held open for him while he was away fighting for his country. It was permanent employment with a good salary. Belfast had thrived after the war and with higher wages now being paid to the lower-class workers, families had a chance of buying their own houses. There were plenty of properties on the market at reasonable prices. The world was their oyster. Or so Nora had thought.

She was to be sadly disillusioned. Instead, as time passed, as a young lad Johnnie had helplessly watched his da squandering the money his ma had scrimped and saved whilst he was in the trenches. Instead of living on the army pay as others were doing, she had slaved in the mill as a doffer, working herself up into the position of spinner, hoping this would lead to the chance of a better life. Her dream was to buy a house somewhere away from the troubles with a bathroom and a garden for the kids to play in. And she had, by living sparsely without any luxuries, saved enough money to give them a good start. In spite of all her pleas, her husband had turned a deaf ear on her. The conquering hero had spent all his wife's precious savings on booze and horses. Buying pints for the hangers-on who would listen with rapt attention to his stories of the war, and betting on horses that never won.

In Johnnie's opinion his ma, given the chance,

had every right to go off with Bill McCartney who sincerely cared for her. She deserved a bit of pleasure. Besides, what else could she do once a baby was involved, eh? The baby! That was the deciding factor. Never in this world would Tommy McGuigan have reared another man's child. A Protestant's child, to boot. He was already the laughing stock of the district. To capitulate and take his wife back, carrying another man's child, was unthinkable. Tommy's pride meant too much to him.

However, Johnnie wasn't blind to his mother's faults either. Ah no, Nora was by no means lily-white. She had committed adultery, brought great shame on the family, and was the talk of the Blackstaff and surrounding district. And she had broken her eldest daughter's heart. In a very short time she had gone from the pious Mrs McGuigan, respectable but put-upon wife, to wayward, defiant adulteress and lover of a Protestant man. Nevertheless, it had worked out for her and Bill. They were obviously very much in love and the birth of young Lucy was a bonus that had cemented their love, pregnancy being so unexpected at his mother's time of life. Louise should be happy for them, forgive and forget like everyone else. Family was family, after all, and life goes on, no matter what disasters strike.

* * *

Daylight was fast fading and the rain, which had started as a fine drizzle, now belted down, exacerbating the gloom. Johnnie shrugged deeper inside his jacket in an attempt to escape the worst of the heavy downpour and quickened his pace, continuing on down the street, completely preoccupied. Head bent against the driving rain, he was almost at his front door before he noticed the car parked outside. There weren't many cars round about here and he approached it warily. One never knew what to expect, what with the police station at the corner of their street. It would not be the first time a car bomb had been left near by. With security being so tight most suspect vehicles were usually quickly discovered and a cordon thrown around the district until ownership of the vehicle was confirmed and whether or not it posed a threat.

Another thought entered his head. Had Mary's brother Liam done something stupid again?

Liam Gilmore, his brother-in-law, was an unwelcome guest in Johnnie's house. Johnnie still smarted with anger each time he thought of how Liam had trapped Louise in the backyard of Mary's home, where her parents were holding a wedding reception for their daughter and Johnnie. Liam had seen Louise go into the scullery, probably heading for the outside toilet in the backyard, and had quickly followed her, securing the door behind him. A shiver had run down Johnnie's spine as he recalled the whole unsavoury incident. God alone knew how things would have ended if Johnnie, who had been keeping an eye on Liam, had not noticed him following Louise out of the house. Finding the door barred on the scullery side he had run to the next door neighbour's house and with a quick apology asked if he could use their toilet. Once out in the yard he climbed over the dividing wall.

Liam Gilmore had Louise pinned against the wall, one hand over her mouth, and she was struggling to escape his other groping hand when Johnnie grabbed him by the hair, yanking him roughly off his sister, and proceeded to give him a thorough thrashing. Blood had poured from Liam's busted nose, splattering both of their clothes. Liam Gilmore got what he deserved that day and a bad feeling of animosity remained between them.

Then there was the time when he had been so jealous of Conor O'Rourke walking out with Louise that he had accused Conor of being a grass, and with his mates had given Conor a beating, supposedly at the hands of the IRA, that had put Conor in the Royal Hospital.

On closer examination Johnnie realised that the little Austin car belonged to Bill McCartney and he came to a halt in consternation as memories assailed him.

He had completely forgotten that Mary had invited his mother and Bill to tea tonight. Examining the car, Johnnie thought it looked in great nick. He was surprised; Bill was taking a hell of a chance bringing it to the Springfield Road. It was easily recognisable and some lads would be only too glad to see Bill get what they might see as his just deserts for luring away from the family nest the wife of conquering hero, Tommy McGuigan.

Mary had warned Johnnie to be sure to come home early tonight. This was the first time Bill had been invited to accompany Nora to their home, and Mary had stressed that he must be made to feel welcome. He was family now, she had pointed out. And overwhelmed with worries about Louise, Johnnie had completely forgotten all about the visit.

Drawing a deep breath, he paused to shake rain-water from his clothes and hair before entering the house. Putting what he hoped was a warm, welcoming smile on his face, he opened the vestibule door and stepped into the hall. A glance into the parlour, where their visitors were usually entertained, showed him that it was empty. He proceeded past into the living room, apologies dropping sincerely from his lips.

'What an awful night it's turned out. Sorry I'm late, folks. Some stock arrived as I was about to leave and I had to help unload it.' He thrust out his hand to Bill. 'Glad you could make it, Bill.'

Bill had seen very little of any of the McGuigans

44

on their home ground since the disruption he had caused when he had at last persuaded Nora to flee the family home. He was not sure whether he was really welcome or was just being tolerated. Not that it really mattered. But it would be a lot easier all round if they all got on with each other. He eyed Johnnie closely for any signs of hidden innu- endos. Finding none, he grasped the proffered hand in a warm clasp. 'Thanks for inviting me, Johnnie.'

Bending over his mother, Johnnie patted the head of the baby she held on her lap. Mary saw to it that he was often in the company of his mother and his baby half-sister, aunt to his son Michael. That's how he'd recognised the car. Bill was forever dropping Nora and Lucy off at the shop. It was a perfect starting point for Nora to keep in touch with her own mother, Lucy Logan, who lived in Oakmount Street.

'My, but she gets bonnier every time I see her,' he declared and chucked the child under the chin. 'Aren't you just lovely, Lucy? Mmm?' In return he received a wet gurgle and a show of gums. With a laugh of delight he gazed fondly at his mother. 'She's lovely, Ma. A real credit to you and Bill. And I don't need to ask how you are. You look blooming, so you do.'

'Thanks, I'm fine, son. Couldn't be better, all thanks to Bill.' A warm glance was thrown her embarrassed lover's way.

Drying her hands on the edge of her apron, cheeks becomingly flushed from toiling over a hot stove, Mary came to the kitchen door to greet her husband. 'Hi, love.'

Her hair was tousled and her skin glowed. To him she looked beautiful and his eyes told her so, making her cheeks become redder still. 'Sorry I'm late, pet.' He hastened to her side and Mary relieved him of the paper bag of goods he carried.

'Hang that wet coat on the back door,' she said, motioning him into the kitchen. She nodded towards the draining board. 'I've indulged in a nice bottle of wine,' she whispered in confidence. 'You pour Nora and Bill a drink, Johnnie, and entertain them while I finish off in here.'

'You sure you can manage on your own?' Having her attention, he mouthed the words, 'I completely forgot they were coming. Sorry!' Raising his voice, he said, 'Where's our wee bundle of joy?'

'I put him down for a nap. I want him to be on his best behaviour. Make a good impression on Bill. He has yet to meet our Michael, you know. When you pour the drinks you can wake him and bring him down if you like.'

Nora declined the offer of wine with a hand gesture from her breast to wee Lucy. Embarrassed, Johnnie realised that she was telling him that she was still breastfeeding. Flustered, Nora asked, 'Is there any lemonade? Or a little water would do fine.'

Bill said he would have the same as Nora as he reminded Johnnie that he was driving.

Returning to the kitchen, Johnnie smiled wryly. 'So much for buying the wine, love,' he whispered, 'they prefer lemonade.'

'Hush, they'll hear you. It's not that they prefer it, love. It's the circumstances. I should have known better. I just didn't think.' She moved closer to him and offered her lips. 'All the more for us later on, eh, love.' Johnnie snatched the offer of a quick kiss before pouring the drinks and, returning to the living room, prepared to entertain their guests.

Sipping her glass of lemonade, Nora asked, 'How's the rest of the family faring, son?'

'Fine. No complaints as far as I know.' Johnnie crossed his fingers out of sight as he told this lie.

He needn't have bothered; Nora McGuigan was no fool. 'Mmm, is Louise still not feeling any kinder towards me, then?'

'Give her time, Ma. She'll eventually come round, so she will.'

'How much longer will it take, do you think?' Nora's voice was sad. She fretted about her eldest daughter, whose attitude was cutting her to the core. They had always been so close. She had thought that Louise, above all others, would side with her, rather than with Tommy. Her daughter knew better than most just how she had suffered under her husband's roof. What on earth had gotten into the girl?

Seeing tears gather in his mother's eyes, Johnnie said quickly, 'Only time will tell, Ma.' Feeling awkward about the turn the conversation was taking, Johnnie changed tack and addressed Bill. 'Hear you've changed your job, Bill.'

Bill responded to his show of support. 'I have that, Johnnie. And very much for the best, mind you. More money, healthier surroundings and away from all the elbow nudging and snide remarks every time I had to attend to a loom, or a broken pulley, or a spinning frame. Has the gossip settled down any since we left? Or is Louise still having to bear the brunt of it?'

'Not really, she has plenty of friends there and she ignores the ones who still snipe at her. Still, I'm trying to get her to look for other employment, so I am. Make a break from where everybody knows her business. But she seems content enough to stay in the Blackstaff. You yourself didn't move very far, Bill. Across the road to Mackie's, eh?'

Bill laughed. 'That's right. But it's a whole new kettle of fish. I'm contented with my lot. How are things for you since Matthew McFadden died? His death must have come as a terrible shock. I didn't like to impose at the funeral.'

'Aye, there was a big turnout, but I saw you there. Thanks for coming. It was an awful shock.

That goes without saying.' Johnnie bowed his head a few seconds in sorrow. 'It nearly killed his wife, God bless her, but she eventually rallied round. Sadly, now she wants shot of the shop. Wants it sold yesterday, as it were. It holds too many memories for her. Unfortunately it's a bit too soon for me to ask for another bank loan. I'm doing all right, mind you. But I still owe a whack of the money I borrowed when Matthew offered to make me a partner. I only hope I can persuade her to wait until I can extend the bank loan. I'd hate to share the business with some stranger.'

Bill lapsed into silence for some moments. Puzzled, Johnnie waited him out.

'Johnnie, I think you already know I was an only child . . .' He looked to Johnnie for confirmation that he was aware of this fact and, receiving a nod in reply, continued, 'Well, when my mother died some time ago the house became mine and I've rented it out. Mam was also very careful where money was concerned and she left me a tidy sum and she was also well insured to cover the funeral expenses. She was a wonderful woman, a great saver, as was my father before her.' Bill laughed, obviously self-conscious. 'Will you just listen to me. If I keep on like this I'll be writing a book. Anyway to cut a long story short, if need be I could let you have a loan, if that's any good to you. And there would be no hurry paying it back.

We could arrange for you to repay it at an agree-able amount each month.'

Taken completely unawares, Johnnie was sitting open-mouthed when Mary's voice hailed him from the kitchen. 'Johnnie . . . I hear Michael. Better go and lift him before he starts giving off.'

Snapping his jaws closed, Johnnie stuttered, 'Thanks very much, Bill. I'm flabbergasted, so I am. I'll be only too happy to discuss it with you. Come to some agreement.'

'Once you've found out how things stand, if I have enough, I'll be only too happy to oblige. At a profit, of course,' Bill warned him, with a little laugh.

'Of course. That goes without saying.' A wail filtered down the stairs, slowly gathering momentum.

Mary's head popped in and out again as she warned, 'Johnnie, you had better get Michael down. You know what he's like; doesn't like being ignored.'

Johnnie was only too pleased to fetch his son down. He was so proud of him and he hummed to himself as he mounted the stairs. Imagine Bill having that type of cash stashed away. That was a turn-up for the books.

Bill had also been in active service in France but had been sent home in the early stages, with shrapnel injuries. Disappointed to be found not fit enough to return to the front on medical grounds, he managed to get his old job back as a foreman fitter in the

Blackstaff. He had befriended Nora and had some-times taken her and her four children on outings whilst Tommy was still away fighting the fight. Bill had been very good to them but when his feelings for Nora got the better of him she had spurned his advances. She was afraid of her own feelings towards him and sent him packing some time before Tommy returned home from France, an injured and embit-tered man. Shortly afterwards Bill had got a job on the other side of town and did not return until some years later, after his mother died.

This whole period had been a particularly diffi-cult time for Johnnie. Having been forced into a shotgun wedding, he had moved into rented rooms next door to his parents. However, Mary had found this situation unbearable so shortly afterwards she had asked him to move out.

It was all too much for Johnnie and he feared for his sanity in a world that was teetering out of his control. He'd had no one to turn to, to discuss his troubles with. His mother was still at home at the time but she was too wrapped up in her own private affairs, of which at that stage Johnnie had had no inkling, and it would have been easier talking to the kitchen wall than to his father.

It was Matthew McFadden who had rescued him from the brink of despair, helping him and Mary get a house. Once he and Mary had been reconciled, she had explained to Johnnie that she hadn't wanted him to feel trapped into marrying her, but her mother, guessing that Mary was pregnant, had forced the issue.

To top it all, Matthew had offered Johnnie a partnership in the shop. His cup overflowed. What more could a man ask for? He would be forever grateful to Matthew McFadden for his understanding, advice and great generosity. He felt his loss so deeply.

Here now in this reunion with Bill he discovered that he liked the older man and felt that they could become good friends. They shared a lot of common interests and found plenty to talk about. The offer of a loan was the icing on the cake. The evening was a great success and, all too soon, tired whingeing from the restless children brought an end to the visit. Nora and Bill prepared to leave.

'You'll have to come back soon,' Johnnie said warmly, and, happy that the two men had gotten on so well, Mary seconded it with a warm glance at Nora.

'Not unless you come to our house first. What about Sunday lunch?' Nora eyed her son. 'Or are you afraid of offending our Louise?'

'Don't be silly, Ma. Me afraid of me sister? Catch yourself on.'

'Then we'll expect you next Sunday. Say about one o'clock? Is that all right with you, Mary?'

'We'll be there, Nora. You can count on it. Come rain or shine.'

Bill had been completely won over by the antics of young Michael and had played ceaselessly with the youngster. He gave him an extra-long hug before handing him over to Johnnie. 'That's a fine young lad you have there, Johnnie.'

His eyes twinkled as he added, in a loud aside, 'Maybe next year Nora will give me a wee brother for Lucy.'

Amazed at the cheek of him, Nora snorted, 'I heard that, Bill McCartney! You should be so lucky. Remember, I'm no young hussy any more.'

Bill continued to tease her. 'Well, you never know what's ahead of you and I think you could have a couple more babies, if you put your mind to it.'

'Just you count your blessings that you've got a lovely wee daughter,' she warned him, with a playful punch on the shoulder and a loving glint in her eye. Inwardly she silently prayed, *Please God, let Bill be Lucy's father*. 'Best see if the car's still out there, or we might have to start walking.'

Startled into action at the thought that their car might have been pinched, Bill hastened to the door. He returned with a sheepish grin. 'It's still there. Come on, let's get a move on.'

Once Louise had the house to herself she quickly cleared up and retired upstairs to her room and her precious mail.

Piling the pillows against the headboard, she sat

cross-legged on the bed and leaned against them. Leaving Conor's letter to one side, she opened Cathie's first. It was the third letter she had received from her friend since Cathie had defied her parents and, against their wishes and her close friends' advice, had left behind her old life and taken the ferry over to Scotland to elope with her Protestant sweetheart, Trevor Pollock. When Cathie had started seeing Trevor, she had had to keep it secret from her family, knowing they would not have approved of her getting involved with a Protestant. As Cathie had never mentioned them getting married, Louise was fairly sure that they were living together outside of wedlock.

A glance at the address on the top of the page told Louise that Cathie had moved house yet again. They had been living in Stranraer for a while, then Dumfries and now they were in Carlisle. Using the word 'house' was putting it grandly. So far, grubby bedsits had been all they could afford and, sensing her friend's misery, Louise's heart had ached for her. She started to read, hoping this letter held some good news for a change.

Dear Louise,

    I hope you are well. You'll be glad to hear that you can reply to the above address as I think we'll be here for some time to come. Third time lucky, I hope. (Fingers crossed.) I would never have dreamed that Trevor would have trouble getting a job, what with his education, but at last he has started work in a factory. On the night shift, mind you. Imagine! I can feel his despair, it's eating away at him, but he's bottling it all up. He says he's all right, that so long as we're together that's all that matters. But I'm beginning to doubt it. We hardly see anything of each other these days. When he is coming in from work, I'm on my way out. Like ships passing in the night. It's awful, so it is. I'm getting into such a state over it that I want to cry all the time.

As you know I've been working in a hotel and the money isn't great. It's my wages that has kept us going since we arrived in Scotland. I was happy enough there but now here in Carlisle I'm working in a factory. I'm pressing trousers all day long and I hate it. We had to move again to be nearer Trevor's workplace and it's all I've been able to get, so far. I must confess that I can see my parents and you and everybody else's point of view who took it upon themselves to tell us that we should wait and not rush into things. You were all so right! I wish now that I'd listened to you. However, I've made my bed and I must sleep on it.

I feel so lonely here, Louise. Me ma

hasn't bothered answering any of my letters. I suppose me da won't let her. You know what he's like. But it's breaking my heart, so it is. Please write soon, Louise. I'm longing to hear all the news from back home. Pages and pages of it. Tell me all about Conor and how things are working out for your ma and Bill McCartney. What does your wee half-sister look like? Have you seen anything of George Carson since we left? How are Jean Madden and Joe McAvoy getting on? I want to hear about anything and everything, no matter how trivial. I miss you so much!

    Love and kisses,
    Cathie xxxx

Tears streaming down her cheeks, Louise folded the sheets of notepaper and pressed them tightly against her chest. She couldn't believe what she had just read. Cathie's former letters had been quite cheerful and bright, full of hope. It must have been one big act. What was going to become of Cathie and Trevor? Would they stay together? Would Cathie dare return to Belfast? Would her parents let her come back to their home? Questions! Questions! Questions!

    She put the notepaper back in the envelope and reached for Conor's letter. From start to finish this was more heart-warming. A glance at the address showed her that he was still living at the family home in Birmingham.

My darling Louise,

Great news! I'll be home on Friday night for the weekend. That's why I'm a bit late answering your last letter. I wanted to be sure I would be coming home, courtesy of my dad. He's providing the boat fare. There's talk of a strike at Liverpool so I'm taking no chances. Dad is running me over to Holyhead – that's in Wales – and I'll be able to get the boat to Dun Laoghaire or Dublin from there. The journey will be longer but at least I'll get home. I don't know what time I'll land in Ireland, I'm not sure of the times yet, but once I'm there I'll be on the first train up to Belfast that I can get on. Just expect me to arrive at your door sometime late Friday.

I'm so pleased that I can't stop grinning and my sister is teasing me something awful. She says that you must be some girl to get me so excited and I've assured her that you really are something to write home about (excuse the pun).

My new family are lovely. They are all going out of their way to make me feel at home. I was at a concert last night with Josh and it was fantastic. Actually two of the turns were from Belfast.

I don't know just how my family visualise Belfast, but going by his comments I fear Josh thinks that I am straight out of the sticks. He doesn't realise that in spite of the troubles, Belfast is a capital city, with all that that implies regarding entertainment and so on. I'll say goodnight now, my lovely Louise. Roll on Friday. I can't wait to see you.

All my love and plenty of kisses. I expect you to give me all the kisses back when I see you.

Yours for ever and ever

Conor

x x x x x

Although he was far off across the water, Louise thought Conor's grin must be contagious, because she found herself smiling widely as she returned the letter to the envelope and carefully tucked it away under her pillow. All her worries faded as she pictured herself being able to confide in Conor. She wanted to be able to tell him everything and be sure of his ability and willingness to share her trials and tribulations. Louise, thinking about her own life, sometimes wondered what had got into her, getting involved way back then with George Carson, what with him being a Protestant just like his friend Trevor – and look how difficult that had made life for Cathie. Louise and George had gone out as a foursome with Trevor and Cathie, in that short period when she and Conor were no longer seeing one another. Even though she'd liked George, even been attracted to him – she blushed to remember their antics on Cave Hill that day – the fact of his religion had been inescapable. In the end they had parted as friends – and thank goodness Conor had come back on the scene. Then, gathering together the writing materials she would need, she started to answer Cathie's letter. She wrote industriously and at length, bringing her friend up to date on all quarters as far as she was aware. Urging her to keep her hopes up, she signed off with promises to try to see Cathie's mother and give her all the latest news of her daughter. Sealing the envelope, she descended the stairs and put it in her coat pocket to post next day. Downstairs, she attended to her ablutions and retired early to bed before the rest of the family bustled in for the night.

4

Conor O'Rourke glanced irritably at his watch for the umpteenth time. On the last leg of his journey from Dublin to Belfast he had been sure his train would reach Great Victoria Street station in ample time for him to get a tram home before the curfew of half past ten. He had obviously been mistaken. This train was certainly no express. It stopped at every station and people seemed to take for ever either getting on or off. There was lots of bustle, but no speed. His frustration increased by the minute.

The last tram would be off the road by ten o'clock during the curfew and, at the rate the train was going, the curfew would be in full swing before he arrived in Belfast. And unless he was lucky enough to get a lift, his only option would be to walk home to Springfield Road. There was nothing else for it! It was something he was loath to do once the police and B Specials had started patrolling the area. The Ulster Special Constabulary, commonly called the B Specials, was a part-time reserve police force in Northern Ireland set up in 1920. It was an armed corps called out in times of emergency, and was widely criticised by nationalists and the British military, who saw them as a sectarian force. At the height of the troubles, when the curfew was first clamped down on these districts, the B Specials had allegedly been accused of having itchy trigger fingers, sometimes shooting first and asking questions later. In the ensuing confusion innocent people lost their lives. As a result everybody obeyed the law, but it had caused bitter resentment and untold misery for ordinary citizens.

Even though there had been an outcry from the local clergy and the newspapers, as well as a lot of debates, no solution had been found to change the status quo. The curfew would remain indefinitely and it was deemed safer to be indoors after half past ten. It wasn't fair, but it was advisable. Except for the brave few, of course, who thought themselves invincible. They were prepared to run the gauntlet, suffering the consequences. People wondered, would life ever return to some sort of normality in west Belfast?

When the train eventually pulled into Great Victoria Street station, Conor was already on his feet, holdall over one shoulder, ready for a quick getaway. It was not as easy as he would have liked. Everybody appeared to have the same idea and with so little time to spare he fretted, doubting whether he would be able to catch a tram. Sometimes they would hang back to give late travellers a chance, but tonight was not one of those times. He soon discovered that it would have to be shanks's pony.

With a resigned sigh he made his way along Great Victoria Street to the bottom of Grosvenor Road. From there it was a long but direct walk up to Springview Street. There would be police vehicles parked on some street corners but if he stuck to the main roads and walked briskly he should just about beat the deadline.

Feeling somewhat apprehensive, he avoided the shadows, not wanting to appear furtive and attract unnecessary police interest. With a determined step he started out on the last stage of his journey home.

Louise had been on tenterhooks since early evening, waiting for Conor's arrival, ears tuned for the slightest sound from outside. She was beginning to think that he must have been delayed and had decided to stay overnight in the south when she heard footsteps pass the window and turn into the hall. She was out of her chair and at the vestibule door like a shot from a gun. Trembling with anticipation, she quickly pulled it open, only to slump back in dismay at the sight of her father stepping into the hall.

He paused, a startled expression on his face. Then comprehension dawned and he gave her a sympathetic smile. 'Oh, I forgot. You're expecting Conor, aren't you? Looks like he's not going to make it, girl, doesn't it?'

Tommy was gently nudged to one side and a grinning Conor came into view. 'Oh, yes I am. I'm here, love.'

Tommy was surprised. How had Conor managed to be on his heels when he, who prided himself on having acute hearing, had not been aware of his presence? His face cleared. He had been too preoccupied, that was why! Cissie O'Rourke had waylaid him on his way home from the pub. It was getting to be a habit, her stopping him now and again, trying to prise news from him about her son. He had been musing about their conversation as he headed on down the street. It was always the same topic: her son, and how he and Louise were getting along. Well, it appeared that she must have just missed seeing Conor by seconds, since he had arrived hard on Tommy's heels. Tommy thought it sad that the lad had so little respect for his own mother. But then again, as he would be the first to admit, there was always two sides to every story. And no one had confided any side of this saga to him.

With a fond smile he watched as his daughter was swept up in a bear-hug, pleased to note her happiness. Then closing but not barring the outer door, he sidled past them and made his way out to the yard. He remained there for some time smoking a cigarette, to let them get their greetings over with. When he returned indoors Louise was in the scullery, sorting rashers of bacon and sausages into a pan.

She beamed at him. 'Do you fancy a fry-up, Da?'

Delighted to see her so happy, he grinned in return. 'No, love, not on top of the Guinness, thanks. I'll have a bit of a gab with Conor while you make that, and then I'll have an early night.' He was discreetly letting her know that he wouldn't be playing gooseberry.

In the kitchen he found Peggy home, chatting away to Conor. A glance at the clock on the mantel-piece showed him it was almost a quarter to eleven. He asked the obvious question. 'Where's Harry?'

'He was at the pictures with Hannah McFadden tonight, Da,' Peggy volunteered. 'I suppose Mrs McFadden has persuaded him to stay overnight. She's always afraid of him being stopped by the police or, worse, by the B Specials.'

'She's right too! He's playing with fire, that one, so he is. One of these nights he'll get lifted for breaking that bloody curfew.'

Peggy laughed. 'Ah, Da, everybody does it some time or other. Most of the cops aren't so bad, you know. They're only doing their job and most turn a blind eye. It's them Specials you have to look out for.'

'And some *don't* turn a blind eye,' Tommy retorted sharply. 'And many a poor bugger has paid the price for that, by getting shot at for flouting the so-called curfew laws. And don't you forget that, miss know-all.'

Peggy rose to her feet and, going to her father, gave him a tight hug. 'If you say so, Da.' He was a different man these days, quite approachable. If only he had always been like this, her mother might never have strayed. 'Don't take it out on me,' she chided him gently. 'It's Harry who's the culprit. I'm always home in good time. Look, Johnnie wants me to make an early start in the morning, so I'm away on up to bed. Goodnight, Da.' She smiled at Conor. 'And goodnight to you, Conor. Lovely to have you home for a couple of days. I'll see you before you go back on Sunday, I hope.' He nodded his agreement. Raising her voice she hailed her sister, 'Night, Louise,' before bounding up the stairs.

'Night, Peggy. God bless.'

Tommy drew the chair closer to the dying embers of the fire and, arms on thighs, leaned towards Conor. 'How are you faring across the water, lad?'

'Not too bad, Mr McGuigan. I must confess I like the lifestyle over there. Perhaps if I was in digs I'd feel differently about it. But living with Dad and me new family, I have to admit I'm rather enjoying myself. The guys in the office where I'm training are a nice bunch, and if it weren't for missing Louise so much, I'd be in my glory.'

'I'm glad to hear that, son. I once tried to get Johnnie to go over to England, you know, but he wasn't having any of it.' He paused, wondering what version, if any, Conor would have heard about that time. Conor managed to look inanely back at him and Tommy continued, 'However, I have to admit he hasn't done too badly for himself. I hear you intend studying criminal law.'

'Well, that's what I had in mind but my father advises me to take a course in civil law, and see how I fare before making up my mind. Criminal law is a very time-consuming process and it would be a while before I could start earning good money. And, as you know, I am eager to get married.'

'I only hope you aren't planning to take Louise away from us.' Tommy raised an enquiring eyebrow at Conor. 'Surely you'll have no bother getting a job here or even down in Dublin, once you decide what branch of law you want to pursue.'

Conor twitched uncomfortably in the chair. Tommy had hit the nail on the head. He wanted to do just that: take Louise away from here to a place where there were no troubles, no curfews; where one could have a night out without looking over one's shoulder all the time; where they could live quietly together. But he had no intention of disclosing his plans to Tommy McGuigan. That's not to say that he didn't like Tommy, mind. Indeed, he was surprised just how well he got on with Louise's dad these days. When Conor had been set up as a grass by Liam Gilmore, Mary's brother, it was Tommy who had got his name cleared. However, that didn't mean he wanted to live close to him. He was inclined to think that they would get on even better if they were just within visiting distance of each other. As things stood at the moment, he very much feared that Louise might want her father to live with them when they married. That was something he would be unable to abide.

He smiled ruefully. 'Well now, it's early days. We'll just have to play it by ear. Personally, I think Louise would love Birmingham. But her wishes are my command.'

Tommy didn't like the sound of this and he leaned closer still. Lowering his voice to a conspiratorial whisper, he said, 'Your mother is worried stiff that you might want to settle in Birmingham, so she is. She seems terrified of losing touch with you altogether.'

Conor's eyes widened as he absorbed these words. What on earth did Tommy mean? How come he knew what his mother was thinking?

'I don't understand. What has my mother got to do with it?'

'Well, she has taken to stopping me out on the street now and again to see if I can give her any information on your welfare.'

Conor's nostrils flared in disdain. 'I hope you aren't obliging her,' he said through tight lips. Realising that this could be misconstrued, he blushed bright red, thinking, As if! Ma wouldn't touch Tommy McGuigan with a bargepole. No working-class man would ever be good enough for Mrs Cissie O'Rourke. Angry now, he stressed his point. '*I'll* tell her all I think she needs to know, so I'll thank you not to pass on any news at all about me or gossip about me for that matter.'

Tommy was well aware of the gaffe the lad had made and, a slight smirk touching the corners of his lips, told Conor so, making him cringe with discomfort. 'Well, son, she *is* your mother and if you and Louise ever marry we will all be family, so I have to pass myself, don't I, eh? I have to be civil towards her when we meet. You know that. Besides, she really is concerned about you. You're breaking her heart, you know.' Unaware of how Cissie had betrayed her son, Tommy pleaded her case. 'Can't you find it in your heart to give her some leeway? As far as I can see you're all the woman has.'

Conor's lips tightened but he was saved from replying when the scullery door opened and Louise beckoned him over. 'Can you give me a hand in here, love?'

Only too glad of the respite, he jumped up and went to assist her, leaving a frustrated Tommy to heave himself out of his chair. 'Well then, I'll leave you to eat in peace. I'm off to my scratcher.'

'No, Da. Hold on a minute. I've something to tell you and Conor.'

They both looked uneasily at each other and back to her. She was thrusting the plate she was holding towards Conor, her glance embracing them both as she smiled smugly. 'What do you think? I went for an interview for a job in Eason's book store in the city centre last Saturday.' She paused for effect but, receiving no comeback, with a slight frown she continued, 'And, surprise, surprise, I got a letter today offering me a position as sales assistant. I start Monday week. Isn't that great news?'

The silence was almost palpable. Completely baffled, Louise looked from one to the other. What on earth was the matter with them? Did they want her to remain in the Blackstaff amidst all the sly remarks that she'd had to endure ever since her mother's fall from grace?

With a slight stammer, she said, 'Why was I so sure that you would both be overjoyed for me? Seems I was sadly mistaken.' Her words dripped acid and her face looked like thunder. She turned aside. 'I must be daft, to think you'd be in the least bit interested.'

Conor placed the appetising plate of food carefully on the table and tried to make amends. 'We . . .' Confused, he eyed Tommy, seeking inspiration. Surely her father knew what she was on about? Tommy looked as dumbfounded as Conor felt. He pressed gallantly on. 'Well, of course I'm overjoyed for you, love. I'm just somewhat surprised, that's all. After all, you never once mentioned you were looking for another job.'

Louise nodded her agreement. That was true, she hadn't. But why was her da so displeased? What did it matter to him one way or the other? 'And what's your excuse, Da?' she enquired of Tommy.

Looking somewhat peeved, he shrugged. 'I'm wondering why you didn't tell me about it before now. Eh? Why all the secrecy? Surely you didn't think that I'd object. It's no big deal, after all. Is it?'

'It is to me. I can't believe I got the post.' Nothing could burst her happy bubble and she turned a pleased look on Conor. 'Perhaps now your mother won't look down her nose at me.' To appease her father, she retorted, 'As a matter of fact it wasn't my idea, Da. I had no intentions of leaving the Blackstaff. I've got plenty of friends there and I don't let what the others think or say about Ma get to me any more. I just blank them out. Actually it was our Johnnie who set up the interview and I didn't for one minute believe that I stood a snow-ball's chance in hell of getting the job. That's why I didn't mention it to anybody. But why are you so upset, Da? What difference does it make to you where I work?'

He shrugged. 'No particular reason. I'm not bothered one way or the other. I'm just wondering why you were so secretive about it. Anyway, good luck to you, girl. You deserve it. I wish you all the best. Well, I'm off to bed, now. See you around, Conor.'

'Goodnight, Mr McGuigan.'

The door to the small room off the kitchen, which Tommy used as his bedroom, closed on him. Louise eyed it for some moments, then without another word she fetched a knife and fork, a bottle of Flag sauce, salt and pepper from the scullery and, placing them on the table beside Conor's plate, said, 'Eat that while it's still hot, and then we'll talk.'

*   *   *

Louise couldn't take her eyes off him as he devoured the food. In her eyes he was so handsome. How she loved and trusted him. He was the epicentre of her universe.

At last, with a satisfied sigh, he pushed his empty plate to one side and wiped his mouth with his handkerchief. Once the table was cleared and the dishes washed and put away, Louise curled up against him on the settee and rubbed her face against his chest. 'It's great to have you home, love. I've missed you so much. How long are you here for?'

'I leave again about lunchtime Sunday. That gives us almost two whole days together. I can't believe my good fortune in having such an understanding father. You really will like him, Louise.'

'Your mother did you both a great injustice keeping you apart all these years,' she commiserated.

A finger against her lips silenced her. 'That's all water under the bridge now. Tell me about this job you've gotten yourself.'

'I'll just be selling books, magazines, newspapers, greetings cards, things like that, to the public . . . but I must say that I'm looking forward to it. No more slaving under whitewashed windows. No more musty-smelling clothes and hair. And no more listening to sarcastic remarks. And it's a lot quieter.'

He grinned at her enthusiasm. 'So long as you're pleased.'

She smiled and nodded. 'I am. I'm really excited. I can't wait to get started.'

'That's all that matters. Now, tell me, did you know my mother was asking your da questions about me?'

She drew back and gawped at him. 'No, I certainly did not! He never mentioned anything to me.'

Conor bit his lip. Perhaps he should have kept his big mouth shut. This could cause a rift between her and her da. After some moments of contemplation he decided that Louise had a right to know. 'I don't think it really means anything. You see, I don't mention too much to her about myself or Birmingham, so I suppose she's just doing a bit of fishing. It's only natural that she wants to know what's going on.'

'Nevertheless, me da should have said.' Louise looked worried. 'I can't understand why he didn't. It's not as if he likes her, you know. He always thought her a right snob. He's really angry that she doesn't think me good enough for you.'

Conor could see that Louise was getting anxious. He hadn't meant to upset her, especially with him being in Belfast for only a few days. He drew her close, his lips brushing her face. 'Look, I'm here for such a short break. Don't let this

73

spoil it by getting into a slanging match. You can have it out with your da when I go back. Just so long as he doesn't tell my mum anything worthwhile. Huh?'

She melted into his arms, her lips parting willingly, and all else was forgotten as they made up for lost time.

Much later Conor gave Louise one last lingering kiss and slowly rose to his feet. 'I'd better go now. I don't want to get too carried away.' He sighed regretfully. 'I'm only human, you know.'

Tentatively she said, 'I was wondering, could we not . . .'

Gathering her close, he crushed her mouth in a rough kiss. 'I promised you I'd always treat you with respect and I meant that. We'll do things the proper way or not at all.' He swung his holdall up from where he had dropped it in the hall. 'I'd better be getting off home now. See you early tomorrow.'

Troubled thoughts flailed about in Conor's mind. Temptation seemed to be everywhere over in Birmingham. He needed to make Louise really his, needed to have her firmly in his mind as if they were married, to know she belonged to him. But he had made her a promise early in their relationship and he was determined to honour it.

Opening the front door, he looked up and down

the street to check that all was clear and made a quick dash to his own house.

The key was no sooner in the lock than the vestibule door was wrenched open and his mother was hugging him fiercely.

'Mam, what are you doing up so late?'

'Tommy McGuigan said he thought you'd be home tonight, so how could I go to bed?' She pulled him into the kitchen. 'I'll put the kettle on. Oh, son, it's so good to see you.'

So much for Tommy not telling her anything. Best to make the most of it. 'I don't want anything to eat, mind. I'm too tired after that long journey. I just want to go to bed.'

'Ah, son, can you not give your old mother a few minutes of your time?'

With a resigned sigh, he sat down on the sofa. 'All right, I'll have a cup of tea, thank you.'

His reward was a beaming smile as his mother bustled into the scullery.

5

The weekend passed all too quickly. Having lived in a cloud of happiness for two days, Louise was sad after her farewell to Conor on the Sunday afternoon and was now somewhat downhearted on Monday morning as she began her last week in the Blackstaff mill. When they heard that she had obtained new employment, her close workmates were pleased for her, saying it couldn't have been easy for her, enduring all those hurtful taunts and sarky remarks over the past few months. Of course there were those who still couldn't let it pass without reminding her of her mother's shame. Nevertheless she was touched by her friends' good wishes and kindness.

Things had indeed been awkward since her mother's departure from the mill. Nora McGuigan had always been so good-living and virtuous that others were only too glad to jump on the bandwagon at her expense. During the war she had openly criticised women who carried on with other men while their husbands were away fighting for their country, pouring scorn on their excuses of being lonely. Now these very same women were only too glad to return the compliment . . . with interest!

With her departure from the Blackstaff mill under a dark cloud, they vented their spleen on Nora's nearest relation, her daughter, and Louise became the butt for their cruel remarks. When younger, her mother had been so upright that when Bill McCartney, whom in Tommy's absence she came to trust and look upon as a true friend, had dared to show a sexual interest in her, she had been scandalised, sending him packing with a flea in his ear, and leaving a vast hole in her life. She had battled on, feeling virtuous about the loss of his friendship but looking ahead to the great times in store when her husband came back from France. She had sadly lived to regret her choice. Tommy returned from the war a changed man, a bitter bully whom she no longer recognised. A sadistic ne'er-do-well who squandered their savings and slowly but surely killed her love for him.

It had come as a pleasant surprise to her when, some years later, Bill McCartney had returned to Belfast and his old job in the Blackstaff mill, still carrying a torch for her. In her vulnerable state, and without much persuasion, she had fallen for him hook, line and sinker. It had been her turn to be frowned on by her family and workmates. For a long time she had fought the strong desires that Bill aroused in her, determined to do all in her power to make a go of her marriage. But without any help from her husband, she was fighting a losing battle.

Eventually, in the face of the pleas and supplications of her sons and daughters, she left her husband and children to go and live with Bill McCartney. Of course it was only natural that she became the target for catty remarks. When the news filtered through the spinning room and weaving shop that Nora was expecting a baby, the shame and humiliation had spilled over on to the rest of the McGuigans. Louise was the prime target, as the only family member working in the mill. Nevertheless, Louise's friends had stood up for her, protecting her from most of the sniping, and between them had made her life more bearable. They were now quick to wish her all the best in her new endeavours and she was grateful to them.

In spite of all this goodwill from her workmates, Louise was far from happy. What on earth was the matter with her? She certainly wouldn't miss them all that much, would she? So that wasn't the reason for her melancholy state. Then what was it? Hadn't she just spent two marvellous days with Conor, revelling in his love and attention? They had spent every possible minute together. He had taken her out to the pictures and for a meal and generally spoiled her rotten, so why was she so despondent? As if she were missing out on something. He had loved and kissed and caressed her as far as decency allowed and she was glad that he respected her so much that he hadn't put a foot wrong. He hadn't tried to persuade her to experiment any further in their lovemaking.

Wasn't she glad? This unwanted thought brought her up short. Surely she hadn't wanted him to step over the line of decency? In the eyes of the Church, that line showed desire and love as two very different things. One, for the procreation of children, should be used only for that purpose in a stable marriage. The other was lustful passion and gratification of the body's needs. If Conor should step over this line, it would show that he didn't quite agree with the Church's teachings, that he desired her as much as she did him. But could that be so wrong? Weren't they engaged to be married? Would it make all that much difference? She shook her head in frustration, not knowing what to think any more. There were times when she didn't know what she wanted.

Then she was plagued by memories of how she had scorned her mother when she had fallen from grace and become pregnant by a man other than her husband. Nora had always brought up the family to be chaste and pure, to be good Catholics.

So Louise had been especially scandalised that her mother could sink so low: to teach one thing, then practise another. She had ranted and raved at Nora, said some hateful things to her, begged her to stay with Tommy for the sake of the family. Then Nora had told her about the baby. Louise hadn't believed her, said she was too old, had called her names and refused to forgive her.

Her mother had since forgiven Louise her offensive language, and had many times held out the proverbial olive branch, only to have it ignored. How hurt she must have been by her daughter's attitude. But to her great shame Louise was still bearing her mother a grudge because of her failing. In Louise's opinion she had every right to do so. After all, she had been the one left to pick up the pieces and hold the family together; to put her own private life on hold, as it were. So did she now want to go down that same road as her mother? A road that could lead to more shame for the family? No! Never! . . . Surely she thought more of herself and would never willingly take that risk?

Yet here she was admitting to herself that she had very much longed for more excitement in Conor's arms. Yes! She had indeed wanted Conor to seduce her, show her how much he cared. To make her feel alive and fulfilled, and to hell with respecting her. At least that was how she had felt the night before. It had seemed right then . . . but if they had succumbed to desire would she be any happier now? She doubted that she could just push the Church's teaching to one side. Look at the devastation her mother had caused. True, she appeared happy enough living in sin, showing no regret whatsoever for her actions, but that didn't make it right. And what about those she'd left behind? What about their feelings?

How would she have felt if Conor had given in to temptation? And what if she had enjoyed it? Would that have made her a slut? Or was it just that lust weakened the body to such an extent that common sense flew out the window? As she changed shuttles and kept the looms moving, she looked so vindictive, pushing away at the big combs, that Kitty, the woman whose looms were closest to her, and who had been anxiously watching her for some time, left her own looms unattended and approached her.

Startled out of her reverie, Louise gazed blankly at Kitty. 'I'm sorry, what did you say?'

'Are you all right, love?'

'Yes, yes, I'm fine. Why shouldn't I be?'

'It's just that you look all tensed up. At war with the world. Are you sure you're all right? You looked as if you were venting your spite on that loom.'

Forcing a smile, Louise nodded vigorously. 'Well, as a matter of fact I was.' Then, shamefaced, she confessed, 'To tell you the truth, I'm all mixed up, Kitty. I'm trying to sort things out in my mind.

You know, figure out how I feel. I can't think what's gotten into me lately. I don't know whether I'm coming or going these days.'

'You were attacking these looms as if you were preparing for a couple of rounds with the Manassa Mauler,' Kitty teased her. 'I hope it wasn't Conor you were thinking about when you were mentally beating someone up. Is everything all right between you two?'

Thinking that Kitty must have been able to read her mind and had somehow guessed how Louise was feeling, she blushed furiously. 'Who's this mauler you're on about?'

'You mean to tell me that you've never heard of the great Jack Dempsey, the world heavyweight boxing champion? The Manassa Mauler is his nickname. He got that name from a place in America called Manassa where he was born. I think it was in Colorado, but I wouldn't bet on it.' Perturbed now, Kitty prompted her. 'Are you sure nothing's wrong? Remember a worry shared is a worry halved.' A grimace crossed her features. 'Or so they tell me.' Her voice faltered. 'On the other hand, maybe you'd be better off not confiding in me, love. I'm a bit weak in that department and sometimes find that a worry shared can start my mouth flapping. And what I don't know I can't be accused of talking about, can I?'

Louise smiled at her honesty. 'I wouldn't know

where to start, Kitty. You'd probably end up being as confused as me. But thanks for caring. I really do appreciate your concern. And thanks for the boxing history lesson, I'll try it out on Conor. Mind you, I'll have to write that name down or I'll never remember it.'

Kitty squeezed her arm. 'You take care, love. And remember I'm here if you ever need a shoulder to cry on.' Still she hesitated. 'Love . . . I don't know how to say this, but if a man sometimes gets carried away, you know what I mean, it's not because he thinks any the less of you, you know. No, sometimes he just can't help himself. So don't be too hard on Conor, sure you won't?'

Louise blinked back tears. If only Kitty knew how strong and patient Conor was, how upright and decent, she'd be very surprised to learn that Louise was the one who was lusting after his body and longed for him to return the compliment. 'Thanks, Kitty, I'll miss you more than any of the others.'

With a final hug, Kitty left Louise to continue the assault on her looms, a ferocious frown knitting her brow.

Harry fell into step beside his sister as she hurried home from work at teatime. She smiled fondly at him and said, 'I haven't seen much of you this weekend. Hope you've been behaving yourself while I was too busy to notice.'

'When Conor's around, sis, you don't see much of anybody or anything for that matter,' he teased her.

'Well, you didn't go hungry, did you? I managed to put your meals on the table and that's what counts,' she chided him.

'I'm not complaining, love. You look after us well and I'm glad to see you so happy. Can't Conor finish his training over here? It would be so much easier for you.'

They were passing the shop. Louise craned her neck and gazed across the road to see whether there was any sign of her sister. Peggy was not to be seen, just Johnnie's head bent over the till in contemplation. That was a good sign. Johnnie was probably checking the till for the night, getting the day's takings ready to put in the safe. Once he had dealt with the final worker doing a bit of last-minute shopping, he would shut up shop for the night. Perhaps Peggy had got away early and would have the evening meal started. On the other hand she might just be in the office or the store at the back of the shop.

'He will eventually.' She answered Harry's question absently, her attention still straining across the road.

He had lapsed into silence and appeared not to have heard her. She eyed him covertly. 'Why so sad? Have you and Hannah fallen out?'

'No, nothing like that. I'm just wondering where she and her mother will end up if Johnnie gets this loan to buy Mrs McFadden's half of the business.'

Louise was quick to reassure him. 'I don't think you need worry on that score, Harry. There's not much chance of that happening at the moment. Or for some time to come, for that matter. Johnnie still owes the bank a lot of money to consider borrowing any more. He wouldn't risk taking out another loan. Besides, I doubt if the bank would let him.'

They were through the hall and in the kitchen when Harry's next words stopped her in mid-stride. 'You haven't heard then, have you?'

With a friendly wave, Louise acknowledged Peggy toiling away in the scullery. With a happy grin she removed her coat and prepared to join her, saying over her shoulder to Harry, 'Heard what?'

Harry chuckled. 'You really don't know.' He sounded bemused. He had Louise's undivided attention now. She swung towards him, hands on hips and looking askance. He giggled. 'I'm surprised, so I am. I'm usually the last one to hear anything in this house. Especially anything of importance.'

Peggy had come from the scullery and stood, arms folded, listening. 'What are you on about, Harry? What did you hear that's so important?'

His face widened into a grin. 'Now I'm really astounded. You don't know either? Hannah didn't confide in you, then.'

'Confide what? Come on, spill the beans.'

'Well, well, well! Wonders will never cease.'

'OK, Harry. Cut the capers. What's so important?'

'Bill McCartney has only gone and offered to lend Johnnie the money to buy Mrs McFadden's share of the business, that's what!' He folded his arms and smugly watched the girls' reaction to this piece of news. He wasn't disappointed.

Louise slumped down onto a chair and Peggy sagged against the scullery door jamb. She was the first to speak. 'Who told you that?'

Harry tapped the side of his nose, preparing to tease them for a moment longer, but when he saw they were both about to erupt he changed his mind and blurted out, 'Hannah! Her mother told her at the weekend. Bill McCartney is lending Johnnie the money he needs to buy her out.'

'Has Bill won the pools or something?'

'I don't know. I was sure you'd be able to tell me all about it.'

'I think Hannah must have got the wrong end of the stick. Johnnie would have confided in me.'

'Ah, but you'll be the first to admit that you were very preoccupied over the weekend. Mmm, weren't you? And I know for a fact that Johnnie and Mary had dinner at Ma's house these past two Sundays. I can only imagine they were organising the loan. What do you think?'

Louise was still sceptical. 'I don't believe a word of this. You must have got your wires crossed, Harry.'

No one had noticed Tommy enter the house and silence fell as he quietly closed the vestibule door and enquired mildly, 'Who has got their wires crossed?'

Anything to do with Bill McCartney was taboo where Tommy McGuigan was concerned. His name was never mentioned in the house.

Embarrassed eyes avoided his probing gaze as all three sought an appropriate reply.

At last Harry blurted out, 'I was just saying that Johnnie had dinner at me ma's yesterday and these two don't believe me. They think I'm making it up, so they do. Louise said I've got my wires crossed.'

It was enough to apparently bring Tommy's interest to an end. 'Huh! What about that? He's a big boy, isn't he? Can do what he wants. I'm surprised he hasn't done so sooner.' Raising his head, he threw a glance into the scullery and sniffed the air. 'Hope you're not ruining that dinner, wasting your time gossiping about your ma and lover boy.'

A slight smell indicating that the meat needed their attention became apparent and Peggy and Louise both dashed into the scullery.

Glad of the reprieve, with a sigh of relief Harry followed them and made his way out to the backyard. He admitted to himself that he had made one big mistake. He'd put his foot in it, well and truly. He should have kept his big mouth shut. His da would be the last person Johnnie would want knowing about his business, especially since it concerned Bill McCartney. But then the girls were unlikely to confide in their father, so no harm done. He hoped.

Harry was the first out of the house in the mornings to his job at Kennedy's bakery on Beechmount Avenue. He had recently been promoted to head lad in charge of the horses that pulled the bread carts around the shops and houses. After a restless night, Louise followed him down the stairs the next morning and collared him in the hall before their father got up. She needed to speak to him alone.

'What's all this about Johnnie getting a loan from Bill McCartney?'

Harry raised his hands as if to ward off a blow. 'Listen, sis, I only know what Hannah told me.'

'Then why are you so worried? Surely Liz McFadden owns her own house. And as far as I know, Matthew wasn't short of a bob or two.'

'I know she does, but she wants to leave the district. So if she can sell her half of the business she intends to put her house on the market and move out of Belfast. I think her idea is to get Hannah as far away from me as possible.'

'What has she got against you, for heaven's sake?'

'You, of all people, should understand how this feels, Louise, the way Cissie O'Rourke treats you. She thinks I'm not good enough for her Hannah.'

Louise's face reflected her amazement. To her this was a different kettle of fish. Without due consideration she blurted out, 'But she's a bit soft in the head, isn't she?' She drew back in panic as Harry seemed about to strike her.

He checked himself just in time and his hand dropped slowly to his side. He glowered at her and gritted out through clenched teeth, 'Don't let me hear you say anything like that about Hannah ever again.' His voice rose. 'Do you hear me? I love her and I know I can make her happy, just like Conor does you. Unfortunately, her mother has other plans for her. Again . . . just like Cissie O'Rourke.'

He grabbed his coat off the hanger and shrugged into it. Alarmed, Louise cried 'You haven't had any breakfast yet, Harry.'

'I'll get something at work.'

The door slammed on him and, hearing her father moving about in the kitchen, probably disturbed by all the racket, Louise headed back upstairs. She had another half-hour in bed as well as enough to think about at the moment. Harry had certainly put her in her place in no uncertain terms. Imagine his comparing her situation with Hannah McFadden's? She couldn't believe it.

6

Tuesday morning was a drag. For once Louise was grateful that the deafening noise from the looms made oral communication inaudible. The one good thing to come out of working in a very noisy environment was that you soon learned the art of lip-reading. Now, not wanting anyone to catch her attention and start a lip-reading conversation, Louise kept her head down and avoided eye contact with her neighbouring weavers. Her mind was full of anguished thoughts of her brother Harry. She hadn't realised how deep his feelings for Hannah went. He was still so young. The thought made her giggle. Now she sounded just like her parents when Johnnie had told them that he had to marry Mary Gilmore. He hadn't been quite nineteen at the time but he and Mary seemed happy enough, now that the dust had settled and they were living in their own house.

When the lunch break sounded she grabbed her coat and was off out of the weaving shop like greased lightning, followed by surprised looks and gesticulations from her fellow workers. Straight down Springfield Road she went, dangerously darting across the road, heedless of the approach of a tram, and into Johnnie's shop. The tram driver showed his anger by ringing the bell and shaking his fist at her fleeing figure.

She needed to confront her older brother, Johnnie, to hear from his own lips that Harry hadn't gotten the wrong end of the stick. That there really was cause for concern and that Harry knew what he was talking about. If possible, put poor Harry out of his misery. A startled Johnnie watched in concern as she barged through the shop and into the office at the rear without a greeting to either him or Peggy, obviously expecting Johnnie to follow after her.

He slowly finished serving the customer he was attending, his mind flailing for possible reasons as to why his sister had come and apparently in a right old mood. Knowing full well that Louise was on her lunch break and would be in a hurry to get back, he deliberately wasted some time chatting to his customer before joining her. He didn't like her attitude and felt justified in keeping her waiting. When he at last entered the office she was standing impatiently, hands on hips, on hot bricks until he appeared, a scowl marring her usually pretty face. Judging by her aggressive stance, he was inclined to think that she had actually been standing there tapping her right foot on the floor. If it didn't look so serious, it would be comical, laughable even.

'You certainly took your time,' she accused him.

'What's up with you?' he answered in a none too friendly tone.

Without any apologies or excuses for her bad manners and actions, she launched straight in. 'Why didn't you tell me that Bill McCartney was lending you the money to buy Mrs McFadden's share of the business?'

Really surprised and annoyed now, his eyes narrowed into slits, Johnnie moved closer. 'Why should I? It's none of your business.' He managed to keep his voice quiet and on an even keel but it held an unmistakable tinge of warning.

If she hadn't been so incensed Louise would have picked up on the danger signals immediately and would have known to back off. Instead she retorted, 'Because you always confide in me. That's why!'

'True. And what does that tell you?' His voice was still quiet and amenable.

Louise met his hard stare. Now he was confusing her. She blinked rapidly and stuttered, 'I-I-d-do-don't understand.'

He explained, enunciating each word slowly so that there would be no possible misunderstanding, 'That – I – don't – have – to – tell – you – everything. And when I do it's out of the goodness of my heart to keep you in the picture. Does that make sense to you?' A frown bunched his brows over angry blue eyes. 'As a matter of interest, who told you about the loan?'

'Harry! And he's terribly upset about it. So, it's true then?' A slight inclination of the head confirmed that it was indeed true and a long-drawn-out sigh escaped Louise's lips. 'Oh, God, Hannah told Harry at the weekend, and he was surprised that I didn't already know. He thought that I was holding out on him.'

Peggy's head appeared around the door. 'Sorry to break up your little meeting, Johnnie, but we've got customers waiting out here.'

'I'll be out in a minute.' Nodding in Louise's direction, he said, 'We'll have to talk about this another time, sis. OK?'

Without more ado he left Louise standing in a daze. She gazed after him in bewilderment. What on earth was the matter with this brother of hers? He was usually only too willing to tell her about everything that was going on. Even to sit down and discuss matters of a private nature with her. To share good news as well as bad. Ask her advice on occasions. Never before had he spoken to her in this abstracted manner. After all the turmoil of the last months, in her mixed-up state she wondered whether the world could possibly be coming to an end, or whether she was just losing her mind. She left the shop much more slowly than she had entered it, silent and depressed.

Johnnie was watching out for her that evening as she made her way home from work. He beckoned her over and, as she crossed the road, she reminded herself to watch her tongue. After all, Johnnie was right. He didn't have to tell her anything. It was none of her business. And considering the stance she had taken regarding her mother and Bill McCartney, he had absolutely every right to keep her in the dark about anything concerning Bill and himself. Without a word, she rested her bottom on the narrow window ledge and waited for him to speak.

Johnnie hovered over her, choosing his words carefully. He had decided that it was time his sister lived in the real world and his face was stern as he spoke. 'Listen, Louise, I usually tell you every-thing that goes on just to keep you up to date with matters, as it were. You understand?' Slowly she nodded her agreement and he continued, 'But remember this, I don't have to tell you everything! Far from it, in fact. So don't you ever upbraid me like that again about something that is of no concern of yours. Do you hear me?'

Offended, she pushed herself upright. She hadn't expected this reception and showed her irritation. Cheeks ablaze with colour, she faced him. 'Don't worry, Johnnie. I'll never trouble you again. I don't even know why you bothered calling me over. You could have just continued to ignore me. I'm not stupid. I'd have eventually got the message, you know.'

She made to go but with a growl in his throat Johnnie pushed her roughly back down. 'Behave yourself!' he warned. 'You're beginning to get on my nerves. Just what's our Harry so upset about anyway? What I do is no business of his either. Why is everyone talking about me? Why is what I do suddenly so important to you and Harry and God knows who else, by the sound of it?'

Belatedly, Louise realised that he had every right to be annoyed. With this insight, she sought to appease him. Patting the air with a placating gesture of her hand, she said, 'Sorry, Johnnie. I'm so sorry. Hannah told him and he's worried that Mrs McFadden intends taking Hannah away from the district when she sells out. He does love her, Johnnie.' She expected him to say something about Hannah's intellect but he didn't, which surprised her.

'I know he does. And she's a very lucky girl. He'll make her a good reliable husband one day and she'll make him a canny wee wife given half a chance. So what's the problem? Why does he think they'll leave Belfast?'

'Hannah told him that if her mother sells the business, she's going to put her house on the market and they'll move away from here.'

Now Johnnie was concerned. 'Why on earth would Liz do that?' he demanded angrily. 'She has no close family. Just Hannah and her. Where on earth would she go?'

'I've had a quiet word with Peggy and she thinks another lad might be involved. From what she hears, Liz McFadden is encouraging this young insurance agent, who visits her every fortnight, to take an interest in Hannah. Imagines he would be a great catch for her daughter. Peggy thinks that Hannah doesn't realise what her mother's up to. She's so . . .' Her hands played in the air. After the way Harry had rounded on her she didn't want to upset Johnnie as well. 'Well, you know what she's like, and she's easily swayed where her mother is concerned. And that's why Harry's so worried.'

Johnnie listened to all this in deepening despair. 'What a mess.' He was silent for some moments, then with a slight shrug turned aside.

'Well, there's nothing I can do about it. This is too good an opportunity for me to miss out on. Bill McCartney is willing to let me have the money I need at low monthly repayments and at a rate of interest that I can afford. I can't let a chance like this pass me by, Louise. It's almost too good to be true and, besides, it wouldn't be fair on Mary to refuse it. And another thing, I won't throw Bill's goodness back in his face.' He drew a deep breath and continued, 'It's the chance of a lifetime for me, so it is. And I won't let it slip through my fingers because of you or Harry or anyone else for that matter.'

He paced back and forth in front of her, rubbing the back of his neck for some moments, lost in thought. Then, his mind made up, he faced her again. 'I'm afraid Harry will just have to look out for himself. There's nothing else for it. I'm sorry, but that's the way it is, Louise. If I don't put in an offer, and soon . . . someone else will beat me to it. And I couldn't bear that. Having God knows who for a partner. Bill's offer is the answer to all my prayers, and I've accepted it. End of story!'

Louise needed no more convincing. 'Of course! I realise you have your own family to look out for and I'm glad for you, Johnnie.' Her shoulders drooped. 'It's just poor Harry. He'll be devastated. But as you say, he'll just have to look out for himself, so he will. I suppose he'll get over it . . . eventually.'

'Catch yourself on, Louise. Have you looked at our Harry lately? He's a fine figure of a young man. Believe me, if he plays his cards right the girls will be queuing up to get their hands on him.'

'That's not the point. It's Hannah he loves. He really dotes on that girl.'

'Listen, Hannah has always been vulnerable and naive. She is lovely looking, but a bit on the slow side, and he took her under his wing a long time ago, so that she wouldn't be taken advantage of; he was her guardian angel, if you like. He's got used to taking care of her. I imagine she's like a not-too-bright sister to him. Perhaps he's mistaking that for love. How do we know? I mean, the way I see it, Hannah will be happy enough with any man she gets so long as he treats her kindly enough.'

'And what if this man doesn't treat her kindly? Eh? What if it's her mother's money he's after? What will become of Hannah when her mother dies?' In her despair, Louise's voice had risen up a couple of octaves.

Johnnie drew back, raising his hands as if warding off a blow. 'Here! Hold on to your horses. I'm sorry, but it's not my problem . . . and it's not yours either. And remember this, Harry won't thank you one iota for interfering in his love life.' Turning abruptly on his heel, he left her staring open-mouthed at his retreating back.

Johnnie wasn't in the least bit happy about the current state of affairs. Matthew McFadden had been very good to him and he felt indebted, as if he should be looking out in some way for Matthew's daughter, Hannah. And he would do all he could to be available if Liz and Hannah ever needed his help. But if Liz thought Harry wasn't good enough for her only child, what could he do about it? He could speak to Liz but he didn't think it would do any good. And he had better watch his step. He didn't think that Harry would want him to plead his case, and he didn't want to stick his nose in where it wasn't wanted.

Why does nothing ever run smoothly? he pondered. He and Mary were delighted at the idea that he would soon own the shop, lock, stock and barrel. Their minds were a blitz of plans for the future. Well, his wife was his main priority; he had to consider her and his son. They must come first no matter how Harry was affected by his plans. There was nothing he could do about it without jeopardising the whole deal. And there was no way on God's earth that he was going to do that.

It was the time of year when all the carts in Kennedy's yard were being given their annual maintenance check, giving Harry some very welcome overtime. On Tuesday evening he had an early break for his tea and arrived home close on Louise's heels. Glad to be able to speak to him in private before their father and Peggy put in an appearance, Louise apologised for annoying him that morning. She also confessed that she had questioned Johnnie about the alleged loan from Bill McCartney, and it was indeed true. Bill was lending Johnnie the money to buy Mrs McFadden's share of the business. To her astonishment Harry was so angry he almost jumped down her throat.

He gazed at her blankly for some seconds, uncomprehending, then realising the enormity of what she had done, he bawled at her, 'How dare you! Just who the bloody hell do you think you are? My keeper?'

Taken aback by his sudden outburst, Louise was quick to reprimand him. 'Hey, hold on a minute. I thought you wanted me to find out if it were true. And you'd better mind your language in this house, sonny boy.'

He stuck his tongue out at her and pointed forcefully at it before growling, 'And what do you think this is for, eh? Do you think I can't look out for myself? Good God, Johnnie must think I'm a gormless eejit.'

He thumped the back of the sofa so hard that Louise fearfully moved back a safe distance, gasping, 'I don't believe this.'

The door opened and Peggy stepped over the threshold. She stopped and looked from one to the other of them. 'What's wrong?'

Ignoring her enquiring look, Harry glared at Louise, his face a mask of hatred. 'In future you mind your own friggin' business. Do you hear me?' Then brushing roughly past Peggy, he left the house, slamming the front door as he went. Again, without having had anything to eat. Louise felt ashamed. Twice! Twice in one day she had driven her brother away from the house without food in his belly. What kind of a sister was she? Well, she had learned her lesson, that's for sure. Never again would she try to be helpful. Never again would she meddle in their affairs. In future she would mind her own business and let them all get on with it.

Peggy was gawking at her in amazement. 'Did you hear that Harry fella swearing at you just then? You'll never learn, will you? What have you done now to upset him?' she wanted to know.

'Huh! Don't you start. Come on, let's get some grub ready before me da comes in. I couldn't bear for him to start bawling at me as well.'

The week passed slowly and when she finally received her last pay packet Louise was speechless when Mr Blair called her into his office and asked her whether she would not reconsider leaving and stay on at the Blackstaff. He said he would be sorry to lose her. That she was one of his best weavers and would be welcome back any time should she change her mind. This pleased Louise no end. It was a great comfort to know not only that she was appreciated but that should she be unable to fit into working in a shop, there would be a job awaiting her back in the mill. She thanked Mr Blair for his generosity and said she would bear it in mind, but inwardly she knew that she wanted to test her talents somewhere different; a new environment away from the mill.

Shortly before they broke up for the weekend, and before leaving the Blackstaff for the last time, Louise was overwhelmed when Kitty, accompanied by some of her fellow weavers, presented her with a small parcel, saying that they'd had a whip-round and they hoped that she would like what Kitty had chosen to buy her.

'It's not much, Louise,' she warned. 'Just a small token of our regard for you.'

Her eyes welling up, Louise carefully opened the gift-wrapped box and found a beautiful scarf in various shades of blue. 'Oh, it's gorgeous, so it is! Thank you very much, all of you. You are very kind.' Tears trickled down her cheeks. 'I'll cherish it always.'

They could see from her reception of the gift that she was truly pleased and there were smiles and nudges all round as they gathered close to wish her farewell.

Louise was indeed touched. She had never known anyone else to get a leaving present, except foremen or someone retiring from work, and she showed her pleasure as best she could, especially

to Kitty whom she presumed to be the chief insti-
gator.

She wrapped the scarf loosely around her neck
to let them see how pleased she was and they all
agreed that the colours suited her to a T.

During the week Louise had made it her business
to get in touch with Cathie Morgan's parents to
let them know how their daughter was faring in
her new life across the water. Mrs Morgan was
delighted to see her and welcomed her with open
arms, eagerly plying her with questions about
Cathie. Her husband, however, didn't seem to want
to have anything to do with Louise. Unknown to
her, Cathie had used Louise as an alibi whilst she
was going out with Trevor Pollock and her father
had been downright rude about Louise when the
couple ran away together. He didn't believe that
Louise hadn't been aware of how often Cathie was
seeing this Protestant boy, or how serious she was
about him. He thought that Louise should have
warned them of his daughter's intentions. Not that
Louise for one minute thought it would have done
any good. Cathie was besotted with Trevor Pollock.

Bella Morgan thanked her for calling and offered
to make a cup of tea but Louise, aware of Jim
Morgan's hostile attitude, declined the offer and
made the excuse that she was in a hurry. After
some uneasy, perfunctory conversation, she rose to

her feet, saying that she must be getting on her way. Under the forbidding eye of her husband, Bella offered to walk Louise to the corner and they left the house together.

Outside, Bella hastened to make excuses for her husband's bad manners. 'You'll have to forgive him, Louise. He still can't come to terms over Cathie's behaviour. Is she happy over there? I never get a chance to read her letters. Jim throws them on the fire without even opening them. I'm worried stiff about her but I don't know where to turn for the best.'

Louise brooded for some moments and then dug into her handbag and produced Cathie's last letter. Her mother needed to know the circumstances in case Cathie wanted to come home. Bella would need to stand by her daughter.

Mrs Morgan took the letter eagerly and, moving under a street lamp, silently scanned the pages, tears running down her cheeks. 'Why wouldn't she listen to us?' she wailed. 'The atmosphere in our house has been awful ever since she ran off. You could cut it with a knife, so you could. The lads' – Louise knew she was referring to her two sons – 'were so proud of her, you know. In fact a couple of their friends fancied our Cathie and I suppose they were piqued that she chose to go out with a Protestant lad after turning them down. And they won't let it lie. They keep making unkind remarks. The lads get into more than enough fights defending her reputation. I don't know where it will all end, so I don't.' She sobbed quietly into her handkerchief.

Feeling her way, Louise placed a hand lightly on Bella's arm and said tentatively, 'If she desperately wants to come home, would you take her back?'

A face ravaged with grief appeared out of the handkerchief. 'What do you mean, take her back? Is she that desperate?'

'Well, as you must see from the letter, she's a bit unsettled at the moment. If the unexpected should happen and she wanted to return, would you have her back?'

'I'd have her back tomorrow, lass, you know fine well that I would. But I don't know about Jim. He's a different kettle of fish altogether. He feels betrayed by her.' She shrugged. 'You know, at work they taunt him about not being able to control his own daughter. Not all of them, mind you, but enough. You know how it is. Some like to keep getting their dig in.'

Louise knew only too well what it was like. Wasn't she still suffering the backlash because of her own mother's carry-on?

Bella was still talking. 'And I don't blame him, you know. Cathie is in the wrong. I don't know what my Jim would do if she ever came back.' She blew her nose noisily. 'God knows where it's all going to end, I certainly don't.'

Louise squeezed her arm. 'Tell you what, Mrs Morgan, I'll keep in touch and let you know how things pan out and we can take it from there. OK?'

'Oh, that would be great, Louise. After the way Jim acted when she ran off I'm surprised you even bother about us. Thanks for caring, love.'

Not wanting to betray that it had been the desire to make sure Cathie had a home to return to that had driven her to their door tonight, Louise assured her, 'Of course I care. And I promise to keep you in the picture, whatever happens.'

Giving Louise a tearful hug, Bella Morgan ran back down Sorella Street and into her house.

Not wanting to return home too early and face subtle interrogation from her father, Louise reversed her steps up the Grosvenor and Springfield Roads and headed for Oakman Street to visit her Grannie Logan. A visit that was long overdue.

7

Easter was fast approaching and Louise was in her element. She had taken to Eason's like the proverbial duck to water, delighting in the bustle and subdued excitement of the bookworms who frequented the shop to browse and buy. Each morning saw her eagerly getting ready to go to her new job, excited at the prospect of meeting new people and the possibility of seeing some famous person or maybe even an author.

At first the family fondly indulged her as she prattled on about books, books and more books. This was followed by groans of frustration as she continued to ceaselessly ramble on, boring them to death. Now, some weeks into her new employment, she had adjusted to her new way of life and went about her business in a quiet and contented manner.

Working at Eason's had changed her whole outlook. If she worked hard she was convinced that anything was possible. She was in a position to advance to better things. Away from the mill she felt liberated for the first time since leaving school, feeling that she could do anything she wanted, achieve anything she set her mind to, in fact; convinced that she had entered a new era in her life.

Mrs O'Rourke stopped her one evening on her way home and congratulated her on her new position. 'I'm sure you're glad to be out of that mill,' she said fondly, as if she cared one way or the other.

Louise wasn't going to admit to Cissie O'Rourke how pleased she was to be free from the monotonous drudgery of the weaving shop. 'Well, it is different, I have to agree, but I miss the camaraderie of the factory. The girls were always so supportive towards each other.'

'Whatever you say.' Cissie smiled benignly at her and leaned closer. 'But then, you won't need any support in Eason's, will you? No one there knows your history, do they?' she said slyly with a little nudge of her elbow to emphasise her point.

Chin thrust forward, Louise straightened her shoulders and retorted, 'I beg your pardon? I don't have a history. At least not the kind that you're insinuating. I don't have any nasty skeletons in my cupboard. Unlike you, I'm as innocent as a newborn babe, so I am.'

Cissie acknowledged the snide remark. 'Touché. But it's a pity you can't say the same about your own mother, because, believe me, mud does stick. Even to innocent members of the family. You see, if one family member errs off the straight and narrow, people are quick to tar the others with the same brush. You mark my words, my dear.'

'That's strange coming from you, I must say,' Louise replied with a knowing smile.

She knew what Cissie was getting at in a round-about way. She was letting her know that she still didn't think Louise was good enough for her Conor, her precious son, new job or not. It was on the tip of her tongue to ask how Cissie had managed to escape all the mud-slinging over the years, considering *her* history. But then, hadn't she cut herself off from all who knew her, even close family members, to achieve some sort of anonymity? In a way one could say she had sheltered Conor from the shame of her own fall from grace. But Louise knew otherwise. It had been herself that Cissie had been thinking of all along, and in the end, in an effort to hold on to her son, it had resulted in her revealing the truth about Conor's father.

With difficulty Louise managed to bite her tongue. The neighbours still didn't know anything about Cissie's past. Conor didn't want to advertise his mother's darkest secrets. He was so ashamed of being branded a bastard that it was in his own best interest to keep the matter hidden within the family, and Louise wasn't going to let Cissie tempt her into losing her temper and exposing Conor to unnecessary ridicule.

'May I ask how you know that I've changed my employment?' Louise's voice was as sugary as Cissie's, her smile even sweeter. They faced each other like two Cheshire cats trying to out-grin each other.

'I was speaking to your father the other day and he just happened to mention it in passing.'

'I see. Well it was' – Louise paused to choose the right words – 'interesting talking to you, Mrs O'Rourke, but now I must hurry on. You see, I still have my household duties to perform.'

Unnoticed by her, her father had come alongside them. He greeted Cissie with a touch to his forelock, saying, 'Evening,' and moved on. Wishing her an abrupt farewell, Louise hurried after him.

Knowing that Cissie was watching their progress up the street, she kept her attention focused ahead as she fell into step with her father. 'Do you tell Cissie O'Rourke all our family's business or just mine?' she hissed out of the corner of her mouth.

Taking his cue from her, Tommy stared straight ahead. A slight smile on his face, he examined her indignant features with a quick sideways glance. 'What do you mean?'

'Why did you tell her I'd changed jobs, eh? It's none of her business.'

He was evasive. 'I don't recall mentioning your change of employment to her. Perhaps Conor told her, mm? After all, she is his mother. They must surely talk to each other sometimes.' He was using his own key to open the front door and once inside he strode towards the scullery, with the subject apparently dropped.

Her voice followed him. 'You're home early, aren't you?'

He reacted to the question in her tone. 'Yes, I got a pass out. I wish to make use of the scullery for a while. If that's all right with you, that is?' He turned his gaze on her and she nodded. He continued, 'I won't be here for tea tonight. I've made other arrangements.'

Removing his coat, he hung it on the rack and, entering the scullery, shot the bolt. From the sounds that reached her, she knew he was filling all the big pots and pans as well as the kettle. The scullery door opened and he entered the kitchen again. Avoiding her eye, he fetched a towel and other bathing toiletries from a shelf under the stairs. Louise watched all this in silent, wide-eyed amazement.

Wonders would never cease! Her father was actually preparing to have a bath. Or what was the nearest one could get to a bath in this house. He must be taking advantage of the fact that Peggy

111

was going to her grannie for tea and Harry was working late. He did of course bathe when he had the house to himself. But never, no, never on a Monday night. So it must be a special occasion he was getting ready for.

Louise was mesmerised; she gave this some thought. Was there a woman in her father's life now? He hadn't appeared to be acting any different lately, just his usual dour self. Surely she would have noticed a difference in him, had he been dating someone. But then, as Harry had pointed out to her, she'd had a lot on her plate lately, what with her new employment and all this concern for Harry. But if her da was courting she was all for it. She sincerely hoped he was.

If she didn't have him to worry about, she and Conor could plan for an earlier marriage. Maybe even in the autumn. They could begin to look for somewhere suitable to live when he was home at Easter. It didn't have to be anything grand to begin with, just a couple of rooms. They could start decorating right away. Ideas tripped over each other as her thoughts went into overdrive. Things were looking up. She hugged herself with joy just thinking about it.

Bill and Johnnie had tied up the loose ends regarding the loan and, in the presence of their solicitors, Johnnie had signed and exchanged

112

contracts with Liz McFadden. From now on the shop was his and his alone. He swelled with pride at the very thought of it. He had told Liz that Hannah would always have a job in the shop while he was the owner. At the moment Hannah worked three afternoons a week and could continue to do so, he assured Liz, as long as she was willing. His brother had warned him off and therefore he didn't mention Harry in the conversation, but he did enquire about Liz's plans for the future. She was non-committal, saying she had not, as yet, made any decision as to what she intended doing, if anything.

Louise was pleased for Johnnie and, to be truthful, Harry didn't seem all that bothered so perhaps Liz had decided to stay put. Not that Harry was likely to confide in Louise any more. She would just have to mind her own business and let them get on with it. She found this easier said than done.

Grannie Logan had chastised Louise for not visiting more often and with no one to prepare a meal for but herself Louise was at a loose end tonight, which was why she decided to take a walk over to Oakman Street and join Peggy. Her grannie could be depended on to wrestle up a bit extra of whatever she was cooking and they could all sit down and have a good old natter.

Shrugging into her coat, she knocked on the

scullery door to let her father know that she was off out for a while and would see him later. Leaving the house, she made her way over to Oakman Street, racking her brains as to who her father might be seeing on the sly. That is, if he was indeed seeing anyone. She cautioned herself not to jump to any conclusions.

She mustn't build her hopes too high. She knew some of the women who frequented his local, but of those who were available most were already past their best. She couldn't imagine her father being in the least interested in any of them. Unless . . . ah no, surely not. He wasn't following in his wife's footsteps, was he? He wouldn't be seeing someone already married on the sly, would he? Was there to be yet another copycat scandal in the McGuigan household? Louise closed her eyes and her mind skittered about, horrified at the disastrous implications.

She pushed these thoughts to the back of her mind. She must appear as if she hadn't a care in the world. If her grannie sensed she was worried about something, she wouldn't rest until she had winkled out of her every last little piece of information.

It was a beautiful evening, the sky pink with fluffy, sheep-back clouds, the buildings in stark silhouette beneath. An evening for walking up the mountain loaney with your sweetheart and viewing the beautiful countryside spread out below, smelling the grass and the wild flowers, listening to the birds singing and, if feeling energetic, scaling the hillside. Louise sighed. If only Conor were still in Belfast; how different life would be. With her new interest in Eason's and from listening to the other girls talking about their exploits, Louise realised how much she had been missing out. It was so different from living on the Falls and Springfield Roads with their nightly curfews, like being in a different world altogether. She wanted more out of life before she got much older. She was beginning to feel trapped.

Knocking on the door of her grannie's house, she stepped back and idly examined a car that was parked at the kerb. Car owners about here were few and far between and she pondered whom it might belong to. It must be someone visiting a neighbour, she decided. The model was vaguely familiar. Suddenly she twigged where she had last seen it and felt like making a run for it, but the door opened and her chance of retreat was gone.

A delighted smile split Nora McGuigan's face when she saw who was standing on the pavement. 'Louise! Come in, come in. Oh, but it's grand to see you, love.'

Louise dithered. As if afraid that her daughter might turn tail and run, Nora reached out and grasped her by the arm, tugging her gently into the hall. 'Oh, but it is indeed wonderful to see you, Louise.' She grimaced and sighed, as she observed the expression on Louise's face. 'I've a feeling you don't return the pleasure. You didn't expect to see me here, did you?' she said, ushering a hesitant Louise into the house.

'No, actually I didn't.' Louise sent a withering glance in the direction of her sister who was setting the table. 'Peggy never said anything about you being here tonight.'

Not in the least annoyed, Peggy said, 'Didn't think you'd be interested. Anyway, it's about time you met our wee sister.' She canted her head in the direction of the small room off the kitchen. 'She's asleep in there. Give yourself a treat,' she chided. 'Go on . . . feast your eyes.'

Nora had taken a stand between Louise and the vestibule door as if afraid she would try to escape. Now she watched warily as, removing her coat, Louise hung it up on the rack and at last looked fully at her mother. 'Let's see what all the fuss is about, then, shall we?'

In the confines of the small room, Nora looked proudly on as Louise gazed in awe at the sleeping baby. Lucy was indeed beautiful: cheeks like roses and dark curly hair and long black lashes; she looked like a porcelain doll. Louise gently touched the child's tiny fist and it automatically wound itself around her finger. She touched hair, black as coal and soft as silk. Somewhere deep inside she felt a strong emotion tug at her heartstrings.

'She's lovely,' she whispered. 'And so dark. She must take after her father.' In spite of herself Louise couldn't prevent a slight sneer twisting her lips. She knew what she was implying, aware that Nora wasn't sure just who the father was. That Tommy McGuigan might have a third daughter without knowing it.

Guessing her daughter's reckoning, Nora readily agreed with her. 'You're right! But she could lose that dark hair, you know. Some children do . . . moult . . . for want of a better word to describe it. She could go bald and grow new blonde hair. And do you know something, Louise? I fervently hope she doesn't! Or if she does, I hope and pray it grows dark again. I pray that she stays dark. To my mind she resembles Bill, but that might be wishful thinking on my part. I so want her to be Bill's child. No matter what you or anyone else may think, I sincerely hope she was born from an act of love and not duty.'

Remembering all the times her mother had railed against her father, her muffled sobs coming up through the floorboards and filling the bedroom that Louise shared with Peggy, she was overcome with shame. She clutched blindly for her mother. 'Ah, Ma, so do I. And I'm sorry for being such a bitch. I don't know what's got into me lately. I've been a real handful. Can you ever forgive me?'

Nora pressed her daughter's head to her breast and they wept together, sobbing softly on each other's shoulders, until Nora forced Louise to raise her face to hers. Giving her a gentle shake she said, 'It's all water under the bridge, love, as far as I'm concerned. I'm just glad you've come round. I've missed you so much.'

They were sheepishly wiping their tears away when the baby stirred and gave a little whimper. Louise caught her mother's eye. 'May I?'

'You certainly may.'

Grannie Logan and Peggy had stayed shut in the scullery to give Louise and Nora some private time together. When they emerged they were pleased to see a smiling Louise nursing the baby.

Grannie Logan crossed herself and cast her eyes heavenward. 'Thanks be to God.'

A knock at the door heralded the arrival of Bill McCartney who had taken a dander down to see Johnnie whilst tea was being prepared. His delight was obvious.

'Thanks for accepting our wee Lucy, Louise. You were breaking your mother's heart, you know, staying away like that. I was very annoyed with you.'

'Now, Bill . . .' Nora quickly intervened.

Shame coloured Louise's face but she faced Bill, head high. 'I'm so sorry, Bill. I've been a right fool, so I have. Can you ever forgive my ignorance?'

His laugh was deep and sincere. 'So long as we're all united at last.' He put an arm around Nora, gathering her close and ruffling her hair with his face, and to her horror Louise felt a jolt of jealousy. If only she and Conor could solve their problems and be carefree and happy like this. 'I just want your mother to be happy.'

Confused, Louise bent her head until her cheek rested on the baby's soft hair to hide her hurt expression. It was lovely to be at peace with her mother again, but in spite of her good intentions her mind turned once more to her father. What about me da? Eh? What about me poor auld da? Does nobody care how he feels? And what if this beautiful child *is* his daughter? Eh? Why, it didn't bear thinking about! She too hoped it was Bill's, because if it was ever proved otherwise, Louise knew murder would be done. Her father would not be able to contain himself. And could anyone blame him?

Conor arrived home on Good Friday for a week. Louise hugged him close and wept some tears of joy. He had been reluctant to stay in Belfast for a whole week. He had big plans of taking his beloved Louise back over to Birmingham with him for a few days to meet the rest of his family. Louise had pointed out to him that it would not be possible for her to get the time off. After Christmas, Easter was their busiest time of the year.

She would be working most of the Easter week, but later when they were not so busy she would probably get a few days off. Then she might be able to to meet his family. Feeling selfish that he was fortunate enough to get a full week's holiday, Conor let himself be persuaded to stay the week at his mother's. When he arrived at Louise's house he had no baggage with him but she didn't question him about it. He'd explain later, of that she was certain.

Her arms tight around him, she said, 'I'm so glad you'll be here for a whole week. We have so much to talk about. I'm hoping you'll be able to advise me.'

He gazed intently into her face. 'First, listen to me, Louise. You really must meet my family, and soon. They're *so* anxious to meet you.'

She burrowed her head in his chest. 'To tell you the truth, love, I'm a bit apprehensive about that. What if I don't fit in, eh? Will I have to stay at your dad's house? Any sign of a place of your own yet?'

'The family make me feel ashamed that I seem so eager to find a place of my own. They keep asking if I'm not happy with them, insisting that they want to meet you and get to know you. Once they do that, then they'll see for themselves that you're the only one for me and let me be.'

Louise felt a shiver of fear slide down her spine.

Was his family trying to convince him that she was not the right one? Not wanting to get into a confrontation on his first night home, she masked her unease with a smile and parried, 'But what if they don't like me?'

'They'll love you. I know they will.'

Still not convinced, Louise said, 'I'll come over soon. Once I'm established in Eason's long enough and can have a few days off, I'll come over and meet them. OK?'

'Promise?'

'I solemnly promise. Cross my heart and hope to die.'

'I'll hold you to that, mind.'

All else was forgotten as they made up for lost time whilst they had the house to themselves.

At last, with a sigh she released herself from his embrace. 'Time I was feeding you.' It being Good Friday and a day of fast and abstinence, she asked tentatively, 'Or have you already eaten?'

'I've had my breakfast and a meal during the day so I can have one more collation. Just a snack, mind.'

'Is bread and cheese all right, then? I got a nice piece of Cheddar today.'

'My favourite! That would be lovely.'

'You relax there. I won't be too long.'

She made for the scullery and Conor sat at the

table, drumming his fingers on the surface. He needed to talk to her too, but he'd listen to her news first and then he would talk about his plans for their future. Confess that he didn't want to stay in Belfast, that he loved the lifestyle in Birmingham. Persuade her that her destiny was over there with him.

Louise set a plate in front of him with two slices of soda farl thick with butter and a few slices of cheese. 'You can start on that while I brew the tea.'

Once they were both nursing mugs of tea, Louise sat across the table from him and eyed him covertly. She could see that he was preoccupied and before he could utter a sound she beat him to it. Dreading to hear what was on his mind, she forced gaiety into her voice. 'That's right! Let it all out.'

He drew back startled and fear gripped her. Had he a confession to make? Eyes wide, he gasped, 'What do you mean?'

Steadying her nerves, she took a deep breath and replied, 'Since you arrived I've been watching you turning something over in your mind, trying to decide whether or not to tell me, so let's hear it. What's bugging you?'

He grimaced. 'You know me only too well.' He lapsed back into silence, a slight frown on his face. This wasn't either the time or the place to make decisions. The family would be home soon. He changed tack, mentally moving on to another matter that was disturbing him. When he still didn't speak Louise patiently waited. The ball was in his court.

Raising an eyebrow, he ventured, 'Perhaps you already know?'

Louise hadn't a clue what he was talking about but was struck by a sudden thought. 'Ah, I think I know what you're on about. It's about me and Ma being friends again, isn't it? It's what you wanted. Well, we are and I must say I'm a happier person because of it. I've been an awful fool the way I was behaving.' A puzzled frown crossed her brow. 'But then . . . it can't be that. No.' She shook her head. 'You can't possibly have known about that. You'll have to enlighten me, Conor. Give us a clue. I love these guessing games.'

Ignoring the sarcasm in her voice, he went on, 'I'm delighted to hear things are all right now between you and your mother.' His face was now one big grin. 'I'm really pleased for you. But you're right, I didn't know about that. I didn't know anything about it.'

Really worried now, she enquired, 'What do you want to ask me then?'

'How's your da been doing lately?'

Perplexed, her hands flapped the air as if warding off an annoying fly. What on earth had her da got to do with anything? 'Me da?' she repeated. 'Just the same as usual. The same auld Tommy

McGuigan. Comes home from work, eats his dinner, burps, has a wash to freshen up and out to the pub. The usual routine. Well . . . most nights, that is. Why do you ask?'

Conor looked relieved; he must have got it all wrong. 'Good. We'll talk when I finish eating.'

'For heaven's sake, Conor, stop teasing me! Quit talking in riddles and spit it out.' Still his look was apprehensive. 'Come on, finish what you've started. You can't keep me on edge like this, while you scoff up that grub. I can't stand all this melodrama, so I can't. I haven't got the foggiest idea what you're on about.'

He nodded his agreement. 'Well, as you know, I always come here first but Mother was on the lookout for me today and I had to go into our house for a few minutes before coming here—'

She interrupted him. 'I guessed as much.'

His brows lifted. 'Huh?'

'You had no baggage with you.'

'Ah. All right, Sherlock Holmes. Well, while I was there, who do you think popped in?'

Finger under her chin, she pretended to give this a lot of thought. 'Well, let me see now. As it's near Easter it couldn't have been Santa Claus.' She giggled. 'It's Friday, so it could have been the milkman, or maybe the coal man?'

'No, it wasn't the milkman . . . or the coal man . . . or bloody Santa.'

'I'm afraid they're the only ones I can think of. Your mother owns the house so it wasn't the rent man. And somehow or other I can't see your mother getting Provident cheques. She'd think she was letting herself down. So it wasn't that agent. I give in, I'm afraid you'll have to spell it out for me.'

'Brace yourself then . . . it was your da.'

'Me da? I don't find that one bit funny, Conor. Why would my da be visiting your mother?'

He shrugged. 'I thought you'd be able to enlighten *me*. He was obviously startled when he saw me. It was apparent that he didn't expect to find me there. He muttered a few words to my mother, nodded at me and took to his heels like a scared rabbit.'

Louise was now sitting to attention, all ears. She was recalling how on Monday she had thought that her da might be dating someone. 'And what had your mother got to say about it? What excuse did she make?'

'She seemed as perturbed as he was. Mumbled something about him delivering a message to her. I must say it didn't ring true. I didn't believe her but I let it drop. I thought you might know what was going on.' He held her eye. 'So you're as much in the dark as I am, then?'

Louise sank back in the chair, a look of horror etched on her face. 'You can say that again. Very much so, I'm afraid.' She shook her head in frustration. 'Surely it can't be true,' she muttered. 'It just can't be.'

Conor had finished his snack and, leaving the table, gathered her close. 'What is it, love? Why, you're shaking like a leaf, so you are. Tell me what's wrong.'

'I've had my suspicions lately that me da might be seeing someone.' Her eyes wide with amazement as the realisation sank in, she gasped, 'But your mother of all people! He doesn't even like the woman.' She pushed herself away from him and gazed up at him entreatingly. 'Tell me it's not true, Conor. Tell me it's one big joke. You're making this up, aren't you?'

'Oh, my God, no!' Conor was also shocked at the idea. 'It can't be. He must have been there on an errand, just like Mam said.'

'But what if it *is* true, Conor, eh? Dear God, it doesn't bear thinking about. But stranger things have happened, mind you.'

He urged her over to the settee and they sat huddled together, comforting each other. Louise thanked God that Conor was so strong and controlled. He would be able to allay some of her fears. At least she hoped he would.

8

Shortly before ten-thirty, Conor prepared to leave. He was dog tired and longed for his bed, not wanting to get caught up in conversation with the rest of the McGuigan clan and have to sneak down the street like a thief in the night to his own home during curfew hours. As if by mutual agreement, they had pushed all their problems to the back of their minds, spending their few hours together locked in each other's arms, catching up on their news while they had been apart, mixed with sweet nothings and kisses and endearments.

Louise was in her element. She told Conor how much she loved working in Eason's shop, how happy she was about her reunion with her mother, and that her lovely, wee baby sister, Lucy, was the most adorable infant. He comforted her when she lamented about the time she had wasted and the distress she had caused by distancing herself from her mother. And all the family, for that matter.

He consoled her by insisting that she had had every right to feel aggrieved. After all, wasn't she the one who had had to shoulder the responsibility of managing the household? And what with working in the Blackstaff, she had had to face the daily snide remarks incurred by her mother's betrayal. On the other hand, her mother was lucky that she had such a tough, resilient daughter to keep the house running on an even keel while she followed the desires of her heart. Seeing Louise about to erupt, he patted her knee in a placating gesture and assured her that he fully understood that she shouldn't have had to shoulder all these responsibilities. But . . . it had happened nevertheless. However, he was glad it had been resolved so amicably and was delighted to see Louise so contented, restored to her former self.

Conor, in return, brought her up to date on how he was faring in the law office where he was starting his career as a solicitor. His eyes shone when he spoke of his fellow workers and his own progress in his training courses. She could feel the suppressed pride coursing through him as he spoke about the times he'd been to court with senior management, fighting compensation claims and representing clients in divorce cases and so on. Sometimes he felt that he should be at home, fighting for compensation for families burned out of their homes and businesses whose premises had been destroyed by bombs. He didn't mention this to Louise, fearing she might not understand. He himself didn't yet fully understand all the ins and outs of it either as he still hadn't enough training or experience. But he did feel guilty about it as if he were somehow avoiding his duty of care. Perhaps when he was fully qualified, he just might. But meanwhile he preferred life in Birmingham.

In the office he dealt mainly in domestic affairs, he explained. And this was where the bread and butter was earned. What excited him most was when someone was arrested for an alleged crime. Whether they were guilty or not, Conor relished being involved in their defence. He loved the atmosphere and everything to do with the criminal courts. He confided that one day, when they were married and settled down, he hoped to practise criminal law.

Louise heard him out in silence. It warmed her heart to hear him refer to a time when they would be married. But what worried her was that perhaps he was setting his sights too high. Would he be able to reach such heights if he stayed in Northern Ireland? It would be hard for him to achieve his ambition in the present climate, with him being a Catholic and all. Had he any chance of fulfilling these dreams if he returned to Belfast?

She knew deep down that she would be unable to up roots and leave the land where she had been born and reared. If he had to choose between her and moving to England, which way would he lean?

He went on to describe how kind his sister was, showing Louise photographs of Joan, an attractive brunette, and his two brothers, Josh and Andrew. Andrew, he confessed, was still a bit stand-offish towards him but Josh was a lovely cheerful, outgoing lad who made him feel really welcome and at home in their house. All in all, he was pleased with his good fortune and proud to at last be united with his new family. How could his mother have denied him all this happiness while he was growing up?

When she saw the photographs of the house where he now lived, Louise gawped in awe. To her it looked like a stately mansion, set in lush, well-maintained grounds, with a drive flanked by immaculate lawns sweeping right up to the big double doors. There were flower beds under the windows and bordering the hedges. It looked like something in one of those glossy magazines she'd seen in Eason's. A splendid Rover car was parked to one side of the driveway, which Louise assumed belonged to his father. Conor was obviously getting very attached to this new way of life and Louise felt somewhat apprehensive. Misgivings were eating away at her.

In spite of the doubts she felt, and perhaps as a

way of putting him to the test, she tentatively suggested that since Conor was home for a week perhaps they should start looking for somewhere to live when they eventually tied the knot. She watched him closely and thought she detected a glint of wariness in his eyes but it was gone in a flash, before she could analyse it. She convinced herself that she must be wrong. This wasn't like Conor. Why would he be wary? He had always been open and honest about everything. Now she was thinking in the past tense. Did she doubt his sincerity now? Thinking of the beautiful house where he was presently living over in Birmingham, she admitted that the thought of being reduced to two rooms in Belfast must seem somewhat daunting to him. The uneasiness she had felt earlier tingled along her spine again and she shivered slightly as if one of the boys from Milltown home had just walked over her grave.

He was sending out different signals, one minute talking of marriage, the next shying away from any hint of commitment. Had he met someone else? Sensing her unspoken concern, he gathered her close and explained that he thought it was too early for house hunting; it was better to wait until they had set a definite date for the wedding, then begin looking for somewhere to live.

He hugged and caressed her, enthusing, 'Think about it, Louise. I want the best for you. I want you to have a wonderful wedding day. I dream of watching you walk down the aisle to me, on your father's arm, in a beautiful long white dress, and a tiara on your head. We will have the reception in one of the big hotels or maybe the Belfast Castle . . . you know what I mean . . . put on a bit of a show. Perhaps we might even be able to afford the deposit on a house. Wouldn't all that be worth waiting for? Eh, love? Why, we'd be the talk of Belfast.'

Louise found herself being won over and reluctantly nodded in agreement with him, whilst thinking of the years it would take to achieve these expensive trappings. She was recalling, when she was young, listening to her mother's excited plans for the future. Nora had scraped and saved for a house with a garden and it had never materialised. Her husband had put paid to that idea, well and truly, with his drinking and gambling. Then Bill McCartney had returned to the Blackstaff and swept Nora McGuigan off her feet. No wonder she couldn't resist him. Louise would have probably done the same in her shoes.

Now that Louise had seen pictures of the family home where Conor now lived, she was dubious that he would ever settle for anything less and she grew more and more depressed. How could life in Belfast ever compete with such opulence?

The sound of footsteps outside brought Conor to his feet. 'I'd better go now, love. I'll call into

Eason's tomorrow and find out when you're free for lunch. I'll browse around a bit while I wait for you. OK?' He grinned. 'Who knows, I might even buy a book or two while I'm there.'

The idea that he was looking forward to seeing her in her workplace cheered her up a good deal. 'Great! That'll be smashing. I don't know what time I'll get off. It depends on the other girls, but I'll watch out for you.'

Harry was first through the door, closely followed by Peggy. They greeted Conor and after some desultory conversation Conor wished them all goodnight. With a final peck on Louise's cheek, he left to go down the street to his mother's house. There was still no sign of Tommy. He who was never late. He who seemed to fear the curfew as if the devil himself was roaming the streets at night. A glance at the clock showed Louise that her da still had two minutes before curfew time and, sure enough, right on the dot of ten-thirty, he pushed his way into the house, locking and barring the outer door before joining them in the kitchen.

Peggy greeted him with a giggle. 'For a minute there I thought you weren't going to make it. That would have been something for you to live down, eh, Da? It might even have made the headlines in the *Irish News* tomorrow.' She tittered at her own wit. 'Anyway, what kept you?'

133

Tommy was in good form for a change. Tapping the side of his nose, he retorted, 'Don't be nosy, girl.' He glanced at Louise. 'As a matter of fact I was talking outside with Conor for a couple of minutes. He says he's going down to see you in the shop tomorrow. I thought that as I am on the late shift tomorrow I might just go down with him. Mmm? It's about time I saw this shop you're always rabbiting on about.'

A brow was lifted in query but Louise chose to ignore it and started to clear the table. Her father hadn't shown any interest in her new job before, so why bother now? Eh? No, she decided, she didn't want him intruding on her precious time with Conor. In the scullery, as she stacked the dishes in the sink to wash, in her mind she justified her rebuffing her father. Why hadn't he come down sooner? He just wasn't in the least bit interested in her new employment, so to the devil with him.

On the other hand, she thought he might be company for Conor over the holiday period while he was home, at times when she was not available. She was well aware that there were still girls around here who would be glad to keep Conor entertained while she wasn't about, who would consider all to be fair in love and war. She would just have to play it by ear, see how things panned out, she thought listlessly.

*   *   *

Not knowing just when Conor might come into the shop, Louise was on her toes all morning, keeping a furtive eye on the door. Deirdre Walsh had taken her under her wing when she first started work in Eason's and they were now good friends, sharing their sandwiches and a cup of tea in the staff room each day during their lunch break. Louise confided in Deirdre that Conor would be taking her out for lunch today and her friend was almost as excited as Louise was, keeping an eye peeled for him. Deirdre was sure that she would recognise him from Louise's description. Not that she believed for one minute that Conor would be as handsome as Louise implied. No, she took everything her friend said about him with a pinch of salt; after all, Louise was biased. Deirdre, however, was to be pleasantly surprised.

It was shortly after twelve when she noticed a tall, dark, attractive man standing outside one of the big plate-glass windows, scanning the interior of the shop. Surely this couldn't possibly be Conor O'Rourke, she mused? On the other hand she thought it just might be. She quickly changed her opinion of Louise's description of Conor. He was even more handsome than she had expected. Much more handsome even than Ramon Novarro and much darker.

Sure that this must indeed be the wonderful Conor, she sought Louise out. Finding her about to serve someone, she excused herself to the lad and whispered in Louise's ear, 'I think your friend has arrived. You go and meet him and I'll finish this sale for you.'

Flustered and pink-cheeked, Louise thanked her and apologised to the customer. The lad straightened to attention when he saw that the lovely girl who was attending him was about to leave him. He had been standing tongue-tied, trying to think of something witty to say to Louise in an attempt to engage her in conversation. As if she could read his mind, Deirdre smiled kindly at the lad and made excuses for her friend. He accepted these with a rueful smile, his eyes following Louise's slim figure as she headed down the aisle to the front entrance.

Louise looked all around the shop floor. Seeing no one who remotely resembled Conor and thinking that her friend was having her on, she was about to go back and reproach Deirdre when she saw him push his way through the door. He caught sight of her and immediately made his way towards her. He was alone.

'So me da didn't come with you after all?' she greeted him.

'No, he thought you weren't too keen on the idea so he's meeting me later.'

Louise bit her lower lip. 'Now I feel awful.'

'You needn't be. He was very understanding

about it and could see your point of view. He said he hadn't shown any interest so far, so why bother now.'

'Exactly my sentiments.'

'When will you be free then?'

She glanced up at the shop clock. 'Another ten minutes and I'll be on my lunch break.'

'And where are we going?'

'A café where it's quiet and we can get a nice snack and talk to our hearts' content without any interruptions.'

'That sounds promising. I'll browse around here while I'm waiting.'

Spying a prospective customer, Louise was suddenly all business. 'I'll have to go. I'll see you outside shortly.'

He watched as she walked primly behind a counter to serve a young woman holding a child by the hand. Coming round the counter and stooping, she put an arm around the child's shoulders, then led her to a corner dedicated to children's books. Conor turned his attention to the large display of books in the foreign-language section.

The little girl took quite some time choosing a book: running from one book to the next and back again, changing her mind over and over. Although eager to get away to meet Conor, Louise was very patient and kind, showing her even more books and reading passages from them while the young girl listened to her in wide-eyed wonder. Louise wanted a satisfied customer and her time was not taken up in vain. Pleased at her daughter's interest, the mother bought two books. She confided in Louise that it was hard to get young Amy to read any literature other than comics. However, it looked as if Louise's patience and understanding had worked wonders and she hoped to visit again soon. Paying for her purchases, she thanked Louise again before leaving the shop.

A hasty visit to the ladies' cloakroom and a wave across the shop to Deirdre who was taking a later lunch break, and Louise was off.

Conor was lounging in the shop doorway, leafing through a book of French phrases. Louise gazed at it with raised brows. 'I didn't know you could read French.'

'Well, I did study French at St Malachy's College, but this is for Joan. She's hoping to become a foreign correspondent. She'll need to be able to speak a few languages, so this will come in handy. Meanwhile she's doing very well for herself. She's a journalist for the local *Chronicle* over there.'

At a loss for words, Louise slipped her arm through his and urged him out of the shop. Imagine being a journalist, she mused. And aspiring to become a foreign correspondent into the bargain. How clever this sister must be. What on earth must

Conor think of her excitement just because she had gotten a job in a bookshop? Somehow or other she felt deflated.

They made their way to a café in Rosemary Street recommended by Deirdre. However, once seated with their pie and chips, and a pot of tea in front of them, conversation flagged. Louise felt everything she said must sound so trivial and mundane compared to the intelligent company he now kept. She couldn't, for the world of her, think of anything interesting to talk about and she fell into a sort of wistful trance. Should she ask him if he knew who the Manassa Mauler was for the sake of something to say? No! He would probably think she was going nuts, to ask that kind of question. But knowing Conor, he would just reply, Jack Dempsey, without much thought. Maybe she could keep it for a more appropriate time.

Conor watched in silence as she aimlessly pushed chips around her plate as if she couldn't make up her mind which one to eat. What on earth was the matter with her? Reaching across the table, he put a hand on her arm, stopping her restless prodding with the fork. 'What's the matter, love? Have I done something to offend you?'

Without lifting her eyes, she vehemently denied this. 'No. Of course you haven't.' She shook her head in frustration. 'I don't know what's got into me.'

'Come on. I know something's wrong. What is it?'

Eyes like sapphires gazed into his and he was dismayed to see tears welling up in their depths. Concerned, he gasped, 'Love, what's the matter?'

'Do I bore you, Conor?'

'Never! Never in this wide world. What makes you think that?'

'I feel you've grown away from me since you moved to Birmingham and it worries me something awful. Like I'm not good enough for you any more.'

'Louise, that's complete nonsense. You've no idea how much I miss you when I'm away. My only wish is to be with you always. In fact, you're my first thought when I wake up in the morning and my last thought each night. You're always on my mind, love.'

'Oh, that's beautiful, Conor. Do you really mean it? You're not just making it up to please me, are you?'

He was startled to see the doubt in her eyes. 'Of course I mean every word of it. I'm just frustrated that you can't be with me. You know that your da and Peggy and Harry are capable of looking after each other. We could be together any time you wish. All you have to do is say the word.'

She gulped down a lump in her throat but before she could speak he was pleading with her.

'Look . . . try to get a few days off and come

back with me. See for yourself what it's like. And I promise if you don't like the idea of living in Birmingham, as soon as I'm qualified enough to get a position here, I'll pack my bags and come home. How's that?' He was sure that if he got her to accompany him to Birmingham she would want to settle down over there.

Louise looked at his earnest compelling expression and realised he had unwittingly confirmed her doubts. He didn't want to come back to Belfast to live and work.

He was continuing, 'Meanwhile, let's enjoy these few days together. Eh, love?'

9

The family assured Louise that they were quite capable of looking after themselves for a few days and insisted that she take them up on their offer to leave them to it and enjoy Conor's company whilst he was home. After some beating about the bush, to everyone's relief Louise at last allowed herself to be persuaded. Secretly, she was only too glad to take advantage of their urging her to leave them to it. It was wonderful to be free to think only of herself for a change. Every day when she finished work, she hastened home to freshen up and change her clothes to spend the evening with Conor.

As Conor wooed her he prayed she would see that she was not indispensable at home. That her father, brother and sister were adults, capable of living independently from her and looking after themselves. He kept her away from the family home as much as possible and to his relief there were no catastrophes; nothing out of the ordinary occurred. At least, nothing big enough to drag Louise from his company and send her running back home. The family was obviously able to cope with the everyday chores of cooking and good housekeeping.

A week full of treats flew past and the only blot on the horizon, as far as Louise was concerned, was that Conor must leave so soon. On Tuesday he surprised her by producing two tickets for the Grand Opera House to see a murder mystery play. She had never been able to afford to go to a live performance before and she sat enthralled as the actors brought to life a murder drama before her very eyes. She was mesmerised and excited by it all.

Still in a trance, outside she turned to Conor, stars in her eyes, and sighed. 'That was wonderful. It was so real. I've never enjoyed anything so much in all my life.'

Not caring that they were surrounded by theatre patrons leaving the Opera House, Conor pulled her close to his chest. 'Over in Birmingham we would be able to go to the theatre regularly. Think of it! You'd love it over there. Please, please, give it a lot of thought, Louise. For my sake, I beg you.'

Conor stood so long holding Louise fast, extolling the delights of Birmingham, that they became the target for some cheeky remarks like, 'Take her home, mate,' and 'Can't you wait till you get home?' These were accompanied by friendly slaps on the back.

They took it all in good spirits, the way it was intended, but as they moved on, Conor's words had dampened Louise's happiness somewhat. She wanted to point out to him that once he was earning good money, they would be able to go to the theatres here. After all, Belfast was a major city and most of its productions got rave notices. She just nodded and smiled, not wanting to go down that road, afraid of where it might lead. She might as well enjoy his company for as long as possible. To her way of thinking, the more he talked about it, the bleaker the future was starting to look for them.

The weather stayed warm and bright and each evening Conor had something different planned, some new way to entertain her.

On Wednesday they went to the Coliseum to see an old film, *The Three Musketeers*, starring Douglas Fairbanks as d'Artagnan. Louise was surprised at how closely her old flame George Carson resembled the film star. Why, it was so uncanny, he could certainly act as a lookalike if called upon. She turned to share her opinion with Conor but then thought better of it. He probably had forgotten that George even existed now, and might not like her bringing up his name in their conversation.

On Thursday, Conor had bought tickets for the variety show at the Empire Theatre, with singers and comedians. Row upon row of scantily clad chorus girls danced and sang between the main acts, even coming down the aisles between the seats and trailing their boas around men's necks. The audience loved them, but although Louise thought they were beautiful she also found their scanty costumes shameless. Why, she wore more clothes in bed than these brazen hussies had on now. A quick glance at Conor showed her he was quite happy to look at their semi-nakedness; in fact, he was lapping it all up. At the end of the evening the audience were hoarse from shouting, calling acts back for encores again and again until the curtain fell for the last time and couldn't be persuaded to rise.

Afterwards they bought fish and chips wrapped in paper and ate them as they strolled up Grosvenor Road, Conor telling her about the shows he sometimes went to now and again over in Birmingham. Passing close to McDonald Street brought Jean Madden and Joe McAvoy to mind. Conor enquired after them and Louise was only too pleased to tell him how happy they were, planning for their August wedding. She confessed that Cathie Morgan had written in her letter that she and Trevor now wished that they had waited, saving up some money before running off to Scotland. She longed to point out to Conor that they didn't really have anything to stop them from setting the date for their wedding but again something stopped her. She felt frustrated at how often she had to bite her tongue in his company now. She used to be able to ramble on about everything and anything that came to mind, but not any more. She found that she now had to pick her words very carefully. It didn't look good for any future relationship.

Finding Dunville Park on the corner of Grosvenor and Falls Roads still open, she pushed her bewildered feelings to one side. They entered by the side gate and were like children, giggling and swinging on the maypole, going down the slides and splashing water at each other from the fountain. At this hour they had the park to themselves and for a while enjoyed making fools of themselves without any witnesses, until the warden started blowing his whistle on his rounds to lock the gates, bringing an end to their frolicking. With a contented sigh, they left the park and continued on their journey home in a happier frame of mind.

All too soon the last day of Conor's holiday was nigh. The day before his return to England, the Friday of Easter week, was a day of blue skies smudged with occasional puffs of white cumulus. Although it was April the weather remained warm and the forecast was favourable. A perfect day for being outdoors in summer clothes. Louise had managed to get permission to stop work at three o'clock to spend her last day with Conor. On the dot of three he was standing inside the doorway waiting for her.

Louise eyed with surprise the haversack slung across his back. 'What on earth's in that? It must weigh a ton by the looks of it.'

He shrugged the pack higher on his shoulders. 'It does. But nothing is too much effort for your ladyship.' He gave a slight bow in her direction. 'It's such a beautiful day I decided we must go on a picnic, love. I hope that's all right with you.'

'Sounds marvellous. This is certainly the weather for it. But where to?'

Louise's attention was caught by the scrutiny of a tall, fair-haired man who had stepped back to let them out of the shop and was gazing warmly at her.

It was someone she hadn't clapped eyes on since Cathie Morgan and Trevor Pollock had absconded to Scotland and he certainly did resemble Douglas Fairbanks, except George's hair was much lighter. George Carson! Pausing, she greeted him cordially. 'You're a bit of a stranger. How are you, George?'

'Louise! I'm great. How's about yourself?' Without waiting for an answer, George Carson swung his attention to Conor. 'Conor! This is a surprise. I'm glad to see you two are still together.' His glance returned to Louise. 'Have you time for a cuppa? You too, of course, Conor.'

Nudging Louise lightly on the back, Conor urged

her forward. 'We're blocking the doorway, love.' He smiled and, nodding at George, said, 'No, sorry. We're in a hurry, George. Nice seeing you again, though.'

He didn't want to have tea or anything else in the company of George Carson, the man Louise had turned to for solace when it appeared that Conor had dumped her.

Confused that Conor could be so rude towards George, Louise called after him, canting her head towards the interior of the shop, 'I work in there now, George. Call in some day and we'll have a chat, won't you?'

George gave her the raised thumb sign to show he understood and once out of earshot Louise rounded on Conor.

'That wasn't very nice of you, Conor.'

He scowled. 'I didn't want to be stuck with him. After all, it's my last day home. I didn't think you'd mind. Do you?'

It flashed across Louise's mind that perhaps he was jealous, but why? Conor must know how much she loved him. He had no reason to be jealous. 'No, of course I don't.' Uneasy, she sought to change his mood. 'Where would you like to go?'

He grinned in anticipation. 'I thought up in the castle grounds? Eh? It should be nice up there today. We can get a tram out along the Antrim Road and take a walk around the castle grounds, find a nice spot to have our picnic. How does that sound?'

'Perfect. Let's not waste any more time then.'

She slipped her hand under his elbow and leaned close into him as they headed for the tram stop on Royal Avenue.

They boarded the tram and, it being such a fine day, climbed the stairs to the upper deck to sit holding hands on seats up front where they would have good views of the waterworks in all its glory and the splendid houses along the Antrim Road. The very houses her mother had once aspired to.

Leaving the tram at Innisfayle Park, they slowly made their way up towards the castle grounds until they found a secluded spot, choosing a place where the grass was dappled by the shade of a mature horse-chestnut tree. Close together, they rested back on their elbows and admired the view of Belfast Lough and the County Down coastline stretching out before them as far as Bangor. More at ease now, Louise chatted happily. As Conor watched all the different expressions flit across her face, he felt blessed that someone so lovely had chosen him.

A couple of hours passed quickly and Conor declared himself starving. Louise looked on amused as he unpacked the food. Everything was individually wrapped: a couple of chicken legs, some small tomatoes, a few slices of cheese, two

149

hard-boiled eggs and some buttered Hughes's baps. He had also brought a couple of bottles of lemonade and orange squash to quench their thirst. He opened the last packet with a wide grin and showed her the contents. Two thick slices of her favourite Madeira cake, for a treat later on, he warned, as he put them away again.

'Are you sure you've got enough grub there? Didn't you bring anything for yourself?' she giggled.

They fell on the spread as if ravenous and it certainly tasted great out there in the fresh air. Soon there was little left. Wiping her fingers clean on a cloth he had also remembered to bring along, Louise enthused, 'You've thought of everything, haven't you? That was delicious, Conor.' With a twinkle in her eye, she teased him, 'Don't tell me your mother prepared that feast for us?'

A frown clouded his face for a second and he shook his head. 'No, I'm afraid not. She isn't very happy with me at the moment. Complains that I'm not spending enough time with her . . .' He shrugged. 'But you know how it is, love. I've nothing to say to her. My life could have been so different had she told me the truth from the beginning. I still can't find it in my heart to forgive her.'

He bowed his head in guilt before adding, 'No, I must confess that I called into the shop and Peggy advised me what to get. She even packed it for me.

I'm quite fond of that little sister of yours, you know.'

'Yes, she's not bad if you take her in small doses. But don't you get too carried away over her,' Louise joked. 'And she's a great wee worker in the shop, according to Johnnie.'

He put his arm around her and she snuggled close. Moving slightly so that she could covertly watch his face, Louise got back to his mother and mused, 'Perhaps it was meant to be, you know, so that you and I would meet each other? I mean, if you had known your father sooner our paths might never have crossed.'

He turned his face into her hair and she thought, dear God, he's hiding his expression from me. He must agree with me. Doesn't he love me any more?

'No! You're wrong. That's the only good thing to come out of her betrayal. The only thing that keeps me returning home . . . is my love for you.'

He enjoyed living in Birmingham, so how much longer would he feel he needed to return to see her? she wondered. Did he feel duty bound? She must do something to keep his love. Cut off from the view of other strollers and ramblers as they were, Louise pressed closer against him. Maybe if they expressed their true love for each other, he would feel committed and would keep coming back to her. She moved her body in a sensual way and felt his arousal. He sought her lips and she returned his passion willingly. She felt alive. Surely this couldn't be a sin? They loved each other so much. Suddenly Conor was pushing her roughly away from him and was on his feet, his back to her, as he struggled for self-control.

Louise reached a hand out to him and said, pleadingly, 'Conor, it's all right. I love you.'

'No. It's not all right. In fact it's all wrong. Only the best will be good enough for you.'

Humiliated, and almost in tears at her stupidity, Louise turned aside and started to pack the haversack. She was right. He didn't love her after all. She had offered herself on a plate and he'd rebuffed her. She was losing him and there was nothing she could do about it. Her heart was a leaden lump in her breast.

He was instantly on his knees beside her but she shrugged him away. 'Louise, don't look like that. It's you I'm thinking of. What if you became pregnant? I wouldn't risk that. Never! Never! Never!'

'At least then you would *have* to marry me. Is that what you're afraid of? Eh? Tell me Conor, honestly. Have you met someone else and you're afraid of having to marry me?'

'Now you're being silly. Of course I haven't met anyone else, nor do I want to meet anyone else,' he said, his voice was low but vehement.

Louise continued packing the remains of the picnic, withdrawing into herself to keep the misery from showing. She had spoiled his last day at home and put a right damper on their picnic. Why, oh why, hadn't she controlled her fears and feigned innocence? Pretended she thought that all was well and there was nothing for her to worry about? That there was no one else in the picture?

Conor gripped her arms and gently stilled her feverish packing. Pulling her close, he hugged her until she calmed down.

'Listen, Louise. I love you too much for you to become the brunt of scandalous gossip. If we started mucking about you might become pregnant. Of course, if you did I'd marry you right away. That goes without saying. But there would still be talk and I couldn't stand for you to be ridiculed just because I couldn't control myself. Not after all you've had to put up with because of your mother's antics. I'd never let that happen. I won't risk hurting you through any selfishness on my part.'

He held her, whispering sweet nothings and endearments in her ear, assuring her of his undying love, until she was completely relaxed. Then easing her away from him, he jested, 'Now do you think we could manage that Madeira cake?'

Shamefaced, and with a weak smile, she nodded mutely. He started to unpack the cake on to a cloth with the remainder of the lemonade. 'Do you feel like eating this now?' he asked anxiously.

'Yes, I do feel a wee bit peckish.'

And she was. She helped him scoff off the cake and drank some lemonade. Time to wonder later if he really meant all that he was saying. Only time would tell. Perhaps there was hope for her yet.

The rest of the day passed in a flash and all too soon Conor and Louise were back home for him to say his farewells to the McGuigans. He was to start his journey back to Birmingham very early on Saturday morning and she took a tearful farewell of him that night surrounded by her family.

During the course of Conor's visit Louise saw very little of Peggy and Harry. It was whilst they were seated round the table, eating Sunday dinner, the first meal she had sat down to eat with them in a while, that she noticed how drawn and haggard her brother looked. Determined not to give him another chance to chastise her again, she had refrained from questioning him about anything regarding his private life ever since the night he had told her in no uncertain terms to mind her own business. Not that she had had much chance to notice anything when Conor had been home. She was ashamed at just how preoccupied she had been. Now, she couldn't help but eye Harry with some trepidation, appalled at his pallor. Questions of unspoken concern hovered on her lips.

Harry withstood her scrutiny for some minutes

before turning on her a look of such anguish that she drew back in her chair, shocked to the core, swallowing her dismay in a gulp. A quick glance showed her that neither her father nor Peggy – who were too busy stuffing their faces – appeared to notice the exchange between them. She decided to find out later from her sister if anything untoward had happened, whilst she had been preoccupied with Conor, that she should know about before chancing to confront her brother.

The meal was eaten in comparative silence, each of them lost in their own private world. At last her father rose to his feet and, congratulating Louise on a lovely meal, claimed he would need the use of the scullery for a short time. Peggy, with a baleful glare after his retreating figure, took herself upstairs to get ready whilst she waited for her turn in the scullery.

Harry had moved and was seated, slumped, in the chair by the fireside. Louise took the chair facing him. She had made up her mind to question him now, regardless of the consequences. What if he did bawl her out? So what? She was thick-skinned enough to be able take anything he could throw at her, good or bad. He was her brother and there was obviously something terribly wrong. She intended finding out what it was.

His eyes were closed and for a moment she thought he was asleep. His voice was abrupt when he spoke. 'I wish you'd stop staring at me like that.'

'I'm worried about you, Harry, so I am. You look bloody awful, if you don't mind me saying so. Are you ill or something? Have you been down to see Dr Wynn?'

'Thanks for the compliment. You really do know how to cheer a person up, don't you? I don't need a doctor. I'm not ill, just tired.'

'Has something happened to upset you?'

'Well, now . . . I suppose you could say that.' He hoisted himself up in the chair and, leaning towards her, confided, 'I really need someone to talk to. Help me see things a bit more clearly.'

'You know you can talk to me, Harry, and it won't go any further, no matter what. I promise.' He hesitated and she urged, 'Trust me . . . please.'

His head swayed with regret. 'I'm ashamed, so I am. After the last time you tried to help me and I nearly ate your bake off. I thought you must surely hate me. You'd have every right to gloat.'

'Never! I care too much for you. You're my brother, for heaven's sake. If I've been a bit offish lately it's because I didn't want you cutting me off altogether.'

At the sound of Peggy descending the stairs, Harry became flustered and leaned closer. 'Can we talk later?' he whispered. 'After me da and Peggy go out?'

Louise rose to her feet. 'Course we can.' She started to clear the table as her father opened the scullery door. 'You can help me wash the dishes after Peggy goes out. OK?'

Harry laughed ruefully at the cheek of her as he stacked some plates and cutlery at the end of the table for removal to the scullery. 'You're a hard taskmaster, Miss Louise.'

When the scullery was free and the other two were still within earshot, they didn't talk about anything important as she washed the dishes, and Harry dried and stacked them away in the cupboard. Louise made some tea and they sipped at it until Tommy went off to the pub or to meet his fancy woman – if there was one, that is. Louise vowed not to let her imagination run away with her. He was shortly followed out by Peggy.

An uneasy silence fell on the room with both expecting the other to break the ice. Louise patiently waited him out and at last Harry licked his lips and made a rueful sound. 'I don't know where to start,' he mumbled, flushed with embarrassment.

'Try at the beginning. It's a very good place to start. Ma always said that when I had a confession to make.' She smiled at him, trying to ease his tension. 'The best thing to do is to tell me if anything has happened since our last barney.'

'All right! I suppose you've already guessed that it concerns Hannah McFadden?'

'Well, yes, the thought had crossed my mind.'

'Well, to cut a long story short, her mother waylaid me last week on the Springfield Road and told me that a young man had asked her permission to date Hannah.' He laughed at this idea. 'I would imagine there was more to it than that. I bet he was encouraged to ask her out. Anyway, I enquired if Hannah had said anything about being interested in this *young man* and Mrs McFadden said that any woman in her right mind would be more than interested in a fine upstanding gentleman like Brian Donnelly. And do you know something, sis? To my great shame, for some seconds I was tempted to ask her if Hannah was in her right mind. What with you all implying that she's a bit on the slow side.'

Louise clapped a hand over her mouth, gasping in horror at the idea of it, and cried, 'Oh, Harry, you never did? You, of all people?'

He momentarily hung his head in shame. 'Almost. You see I love Hannah for what she is. Sweet and caring. I want to take care of her for the rest of my life. Some time ago Johnnie told me that Mr McFadden had confided in him that she is a bit slow due to an accident at birth. It's not hereditary, therefore it can't be passed on in the genes. So if she has any children, they'll be all right.'

158

Puzzled, Louise mused, 'How strange for Matthew McFadden to tell our Johnnie something so personal.'

Harry laughed outright at her surprise. 'Ah, but you see, sis, it seems he had made plans for Johnnie to marry his Hannah. What do you think of that?' He sat back and watched her intently.

He was not disappointed at her reaction. Her jaw dropped as she gaped at him. Snapping it shut, she gasped, 'I'm flabbergasted, so I am. How did Johnnie take it?'

'He nearly died when Mr McFadden told him. You see, Johnnie knew nothing about Mr McFadden's plans for him and Hannah until Johnnie told him he was getting married. It seems that Mr McFadden was very upset when he heard that Mary was pregnant, and he actually asked Johnnie if she could be bought off. Can you imagine that?'

Louise couldn't believe her ears. All this was going on and they knew nothing about it? 'How come we didn't get a whiff of any of this?'

Harry shrugged. 'I suppose we were all too engrossed in our own affairs to think about anything else. Of course, me ma knew. Johnnie had no one else to confide in, poor sod.'

'Dear God, as if she hadn't enough to worry about at the time.'

'That's what I said and Johnnie wasn't too

159

pleased, I can tell you. I must have hit a sore point. I imagine he thinks that that was the final straw where Ma was concerned. You know like . . . that's what encouraged her to run off with Bill McCartney.'

A worried frown creased her brow as Louise asked, 'Do you think it was?'

'That's something we'll never know the answer to, and I for one won't try to find out.'

'Don't worry. I'll find out. I'll ask me ma the next time I run into her.'

Harry jumped to his feet, his face blazing with colour. 'Don't you dare! Do you hear me? Johnnie told me all this in confidence. He'll kill me if he finds out that I told you.'

Louise patted the air placatingly with both hands. 'Simmer down, simmer down, I won't mention it to Ma then, OK?'

'Promise me on your word of honour that you won't say a word to anyone.' Louise hesitated and he glared fiercely at her. 'Promise me.'

Taking a deep breath, Louise said, 'I promise I won't reveal a single word of what you told me, so help me, God.'

Once more silence fell and this time it was Louise who tentatively broke it. 'Do you know this lad that Mrs McFadden thinks is God's gift?'

'No, but I've made it my business to find out something about him and to see what he looks like.'

'And . . . what's your verdict?'

Another sad shake of the head. 'To be truthful, he looks fine. Better-looking than me. Better-dressed than I am, or am ever likely to be, that's for sure.'

'Have you seen them together? How did they look?'

A shrug of the shoulders. 'You know Hannah . . . she's nice to everybody. They seemed to be getting along fine. It broke my heart seeing them together. Knowing that he had Mrs McFadden's blessing.'

'And what about him?'

Harry smiled wryly. 'If he's good to her . . . Mrs McFadden has probably done the right thing.'

'But what about you?'

'Well, as I see it, if they remain in the district, then I'll have to leave. I couldn't bear to see them together every time I go out.'

'What? Where would you go?' Louise was dumb-struck. 'Dear God, Harry, you can't leave Kennedy's. You love it there.'

'I might still be able to keep my job. You see, I've been making plans of my own, you know.'

'What do you mean, making plans?'

'I've been saving every spare penny I get my hands on, sis. When I'm on the outskirts of the town, delivering bread in the villages, I've seen some land going to rack and ruin. It has a tumble-down cottage that doesn't look too bad from the outside. But it must be a ruin or it would have been snapped up long ago. If I can get it cheap enough I think I can make something of it.'

His sister was shaking her head in bewilderment. 'Don't talk daft, Harry. What do you know about building or renovations, eh? Not only that, but if you lived there Hannah would be alone most of the day. Will she be all right on her own?'

'The land isn't big enough for building on or anything like that.' Harry was actually wringing his hands in despair. 'Look . . . after tea tomorrow could you come with me and have a look at it and see what I'm talking about? Advise me what to do. And of course Hannah will be quite happy there.'

Louise was shaking her head. 'Look, Harry, I don't know the first thing about land or property or anything like that. I wouldn't be able to advise you one way or the other. I wouldn't have even the foggiest idea where to start. I'm sorry.'

'Please . . . please, Louise? I just need a second opinion on it. I'll understand if you think I'm nuts. But there's something about this place that intrigues me.'

With great reluctance Louise agreed to accompany her brother the following evening to give her unprofessional advice on the tract of waste land, as she thought of it. Weaver, salesgirl and now a bloody estate agent. Whatever next, she mused grimly.

10

After a restless night, Louise was glad to escape the confines of the house to go to work and get some respite from probing questions as to whether or not a wedding was on the horizon. If only, she silently lamented; if only! If it were, she would have been in her glory. Instead, it seemed to her that marriage was, if anything, further away than ever. Certainly it appeared to be the last thing on Conor's mind; he was so wrapped up in how wonderful Birmingham was, but what about her? Should she give him an ultimatum? No! She must never do that. She must bide her time and hope that all would work out in the end.

In the shop, although she soon forgot the family's inquisitiveness, she discovered that it was not that easy to get away from her own misgivings.

Thoughts of Conor and Harry plagued her throughout the morning. She brooded, fearful that she might be losing Conor and dreading having to advise Harry about things she knew absolutely nothing about later that evening. Her troubled mind was on things other than her work.

To her consternation she found herself being reprimanded for standing daydreaming while customers were obviously seeking assistance. Humiliated that it was the big boss himself who had found her wanting and, to her shame, had chastised her in front of her fellow workers, she busied herself so completely, tidying book displays and in between times hurrying to assist customers, that she didn't get a minute to herself the remainder of the morning. Thus it was with a start of surprise that she became aware of George Carson standing by her side.

Realising that she must have been daydreaming again, she glanced furtively around to see if the boss was hovering near by before facing George. Not wanting him to keep her talking and bring the wrath of Al Murray down on her head once again, perhaps with the threat that she look for a new job elsewhere, her greeting to George was offhand.

George's smile faltered and a slight frown puckered his brow. He eyed her anxiously. 'I'm sorry. Did I get the message wrong on Saturday? What about that offer of a chat?'

Louise had to smile ruefully. 'You'll have to excuse me, George. Sometimes I get carried away and forget I just work here and don't own the place. So, alas, I should have made it clear that I'm free to indulge in private conversation only at certain times during my working day, like tea breaks, for instance. I'm not free now until lunchtime.'

'Well, actually, that's why I'm here. I was hoping that I could persuade you to accompany me for a cup of tea and maybe something to eat?' An eyebrow was raised in query.

A glance at the clock told her it was almost half past eleven. 'Sorry, it's been a busy morning, George, and I won't be free until one o'clock.'

With a slight nod he touched a hand to his forelock in salute. 'Will it be all right if I call back and wait outside for you, then?'

Her smile widened into a grin and her eyes sparkled like sapphires. 'I'll look forward to that, George,' she assured him.

His presence had at least put all thoughts of Conor and Harry on the back burner for the time being. She could honestly say that she hadn't given George much thought once Conor had told her his whole sorry history and admitted that he still loved her. Now she was intrigued to discover that she still found George attractive. But . . . she must tread carefully. Aware that he had cared deeply for

165

her in the past, she must not let him know that he could still arouse some emotion within her. She was badly in need of a shoulder to cry on at the moment, something that George had supplied once before when she thought Conor had dumped her. She mustn't let him get too close again. She would have to watch her step.

Louise sought out Deirdre to inform her of her change of plans. She explained to her friend that she wouldn't be joining her for lunch today as she had made other arrangements.

As could only be expected, Deirdre was annoyed to say the least and showed it. 'Couldn't you have told me earlier on and let me do likewise?' she huffed.

'Don't be cross, Deirdre, love. I've only known myself a few minutes. An old friend just called in and asked me to have a bit of lunch with him. I tried to put him off but he wouldn't take no for an answer and he's coming back at one o'clock to pick me up. I'm sorry. Really, I am!'

Deirdre looked dejected, then her face cleared. 'Oho, was it that tall, fair-haired fellow you were talking to just now who asked you out?'

'Yes, he does have fair hair. Did you notice him?'

'Who with an eye in their head could miss him? All the girls were ogling him. He comes in now and again to browse, but none of the girls have made any impression on him. I must say I was surprised that you let him get out without buying something. But then again, it obviously wasn't a book he was after.' Her shoulders slumped in a dramatic sigh. 'Tell me, Louise, how do you manage to meet all these good-looking guys?'

'All these guys, indeed. What on earth do you mean? To hear you, one would think that men were queuing up to ask me out.'

'First Conor. Now this Adonis. Where did you find them?'

'Two! They're the only two men I've ever dated and you're trying to make out that I'm some sort of Jezebel? Huh!' Louise was astounded. 'Catch yourself on!' She moved away to attend to a customer, leaving Deirdre wondering why she was offended. She wished she had two handsome men seeking her out. She would be over the moon and wouldn't care what others thought of her.

In the staff cloakroom Louise took more care with her appearance than usual, watched by a couple of the salesgirls. Once finished, she approached Deirdre, arching her eyebrows, and her friend beamed back at her. 'You look great. You'll bowl him over. Won't she, girls?' Lowering her voice, she said, 'I didn't mean to offend you earlier, Louise. You surely know that.'

'Never mind me, Deirdre. I'm just on edge today. Did you see Al tick me off earlier on?' Deirdre nodded mutely. 'Well, there you are then, you know why I'm so down. See you later.'

Joining George outside, she found him chatting away to Al Murray who was still wearing his outdoor coat, probably returning from his lunch break.

'My Uncle Al was keeping me company while I was waiting.' George looked from one to the other. 'No need to introduce you two, I take it.'

Al smiled at her. 'No, indeed. See you don't keep her late back, mind.'

George inclined his head. 'Be assured, I'll return Louise in good time.'

With a final farewell, they headed away from the shop as Al went back inside.

'That was a surprise, Mr Murray being your uncle.'

'Yes, it is a small world indeed. He's my mother's brother,' George replied. Taking her by the arm, he led her along Ann Street, then turned into an alleyway and towards a large, dark green door with a sign above. She hesitated apprehensively. 'Where are you taking me?'

'This is Joy's Entry and I'm a member of a club here.' He nodded towards the door. 'And I know we'll get something nice to eat there. Is that all right with you?'

'You know something? I've passed this entry umpteen times and I've never once taken a walk

168

down it. I know it leads out on to the High Street. Wonders will never cease. Hmm. It's time I woke up to my surroundings. I take too much for granted these days.'

From the outside, the building looked unpretentious. Louise frowned as George approached the green door and pressed a buzzer. After a few seconds the door opened and they were admitted inside by a waiter in dark suit, white shirt and bow tie.

Louise stopped, gobsmacked. This club was decked out in the best style. The bar ran the length of one wall. Every drink under the sun must have been on sale and bowls of titbits were placed strategically along the counter. A few men were seated on high stools at the bar, their feet placed on a brightly polished brass footrail that ran its whole length, helping themselves to these morsels while drinking pints of Guinness.

George was obviously a regular customer here. They were approached by a large man in a dark lounge suit, white shirt and blue tie who greeted George warmly. After exchanging pleasantries, the man, who was introduced as Frederick, snapped his fingers and a watchful waiter hurried forward.

'Joe, show George and Miss McGuigan to one of our best tables,' Frederick ordered before taking his leave with a slight bow in George's direction.

The waiter led them to a table in an alcove, which offered some privacy.

George explained to the waiter Joe that they were on their lunch break and would require fast service. He was politeness itself and told them that would be no problem so long as they didn't choose something that took a long time to prepare as all food was freshly cooked to order. Handing them each a menu, he suggested different items that could be served quickly, then asked if they would like something to drink while they chose from the menu.

George eyed Louise.

'I'll have a glass of fresh orange, please.'

When George had ordered a beer for himself and a fresh orange juice for Louise, the waiter moved off.

Taking a good look around her, Louise confided, 'Very salubrious indeed. I'm impressed. You must have a well-paid job . . .' A glance at his clothes and she continued with a nod, 'Yes, there's nothing cheap-looking about you.'

What she thought was a smug smile slipped momentarily across his face. 'I'm doing all right as a matter of fact. I work in the design office at Shorts.'

'Hmm, I am very impressed.'

'Well, I'll try to impress you some more.' He leaned forward, elbows on the table, fingers cupped under his chin, and fixed her with his eyes. 'You know that that little thoroughfare we walked along is called Joy's Entry, don't you?' Louise nodded, wondering what was coming next. 'Well, I bet you don't know how it got that name, do you?' She shook her head. 'It's named after a great gentleman called Francis Joy who came to Belfast from some little County Antrim village way back in the early eighteenth century. I think the village was Killead. Anyway, the story goes that he obtained a small printing press in lieu of a debt and used it to publish the city's first newspaper.'

Louise sat in rapt silence, listening to his every word.

'He eventually set up a printing business in Joy's Entry, producing a newspaper, and never looked back. It was originally called the *Belfast News Letter,* but as you probably know it's now known simply as the *News Letter.*' She nodded her agreement and he continued, an all-knowing look on his face, 'It was first published in 1737 and is probably one of the oldest English-language general daily newspapers in the world. There's a lot more I could tell you about Francis Joy, but it could take all afternoon and you have to get back to work.' He sat back with a huge self-satisfied grin and, spreading out his arms in conclusion, he said, 'Here endeth the lesson.'

The waiter returned with their drinks, putting

an end to any further history talks. Louise ordered a ham salad, George a sirloin steak, rare, with all the trimmings.

The meal was eaten in companionable silence. Louise felt relaxed in his company and marvelled at the depth of his knowledge of local history. Thirty minutes later, with a reminder that he mustn't get her back late and into Uncle Al's bad books, George called for the bill, helped Louise into her coat and they were ready for the road.

Outside, she dithered about whether or not to offer to share the bill, but decided against it. After all, he obviously wasn't short of a bob or two. She thanked George for a lovely lunch. 'I really enjoyed it. I didn't even know that place existed. It's very exclusive, isn't it? And expensive as well, I imagine.'

'It's for members only, that's probably why. Perhaps you'll let me take you out to dinner some night? They serve some very appetising meals.'

Undecided, Louise hesitated and, sensing her indecision, George urged her, 'Come on, I know Conor is still very much in the picture but, as you have said yourself, he's working away, and surely going out with me won't do any harm? I want to catch up with how life's been treating you.'

Louise pondered his words for a moment. There were things that she would like to find out from him too. Like, for instance, his version of how

Trevor was coping over in England. She eventually gave in to his request. 'Mind you, there's nothing very much to catch up on as far as I'm concerned, but why not? It will be a treat for me. Conor gets out and about plenty over in Birmingham so why can't I do likewise here?'

Back outside Eason's, a delighted George gripped her hand tightly and agreed with her, 'Why not, indeed? I'll call into the shop soon, OK?'

Louise nodded her approval and with a final lift of the hand he took off along Ann Street in the direction of Cornmarket. Louise entered the shop. When she was back in the staff room, the happy smile on her face brought Deirdre quickly to her side. 'You look like the cat that's stole the cream!' she said with a tinge of jealousy in her voice. 'I take it you had a nice lunch?'

'Yes. Very much so. He took me to his club in Joy's Entry.'

'Oh, very swanky. Joy's Entry? You mean that wee entry further down the street?'

'The very one. The club is halfway down the entry. It's truly magnificent, so it is.'

'By the look on your face, Conor had better watch out, you seem really smitten by that gorgeous man.'

The glow on Louise's countenance faded a little. 'Don't be silly. It was only a friendly meeting. It was lovely seeing George again after all this time.'

Deirdre looked sceptical. 'You could have fooled me. I've never seen you like this before, not even when Conor came in to see you.'

Dismayed at her friend's intuition, Louise laughed and gave her a gentle push towards the door. 'Come on, it's time we were back out there at work.' Deirdre seemed inclined to argue but, brushing past her with a flounce, Louise led the way on to the shop floor followed by her bemused friend.

Monday was the day on which Louise gathered together all the family clothes that required washing. She separated the underwear and light-coloured clothes and pushed them into the tin bath on top of the gas rings where she had water heating. Adding some Persil washing powder, she gave the clothes a good thorough prod with the pot stick, swished them about and left the bath to heat on a low light while she was out, knowing from experience it would be a long time before it was ready for the scrubbing board.

Peggy was babysitting for Mary Ellen Smith across the street and her da had left the house earlier without saying where he was going. Harry had been waiting impatiently while she finished her chores and when she reached for her coat he was on his feet instantly and, grabbing his jacket, led the way out.

'I really appreciate you coming with me, Louise. And don't be afraid to speak your mind if you think I'm being stupid. Do you hear me?'

'Never fear. I won't let you make a fool of yourself.'

Putting an arm across her shoulders he gave her a squeeze. 'I know I can depend on you, sis.'

'Remember, I'm no building expert. I can only give you my personal advice and that won't be worth much. Just where exactly is this bit of land?'

'Up past Springfield Village. Want to take a tram up?'

'No, let's walk, I'll enjoy the fresh air. We've been very lucky weatherwise this month.'

Harry laughed. 'I think the angels have answered your prayers so that you and Conor could get out and about while he was home.'

Thinking of the prayers that she had sent heavenward for good weather, Louise silently agreed with him. When they were passing by the big terraced house on the far side of the Springfield Road where Hannah McFadden lived with her mother, Harry's step faltered, causing Louise to glance across the road.

Hannah, dressed in a long, dark green straight skirt and matching jacket, set off by a cream, ruffled-neck blouse, was coming through the front door. A young fair-haired man was assisting her down the steps and she was laughing at something he had said to her. Liz appeared in the doorway to wave the couple off and caught sight of Harry and Louise across the road. Noting that her daughter wasn't aware of them, Liz gave a quick wave in Harry's direction and then ignored them, making a point of not bringing them to her daughter's attention. Harry hesitated, grunted in disgust, then lengthened his stride. For some seconds Louise had to quicken her step to keep pace with him.

She tugged at his sleeve, slowing him down. 'Harry, do you think we should go over and speak to them?'

'Why? We would be giving Mrs McFadden the chance to let Hannah see the difference between him and me. Did you see his fine clothes? I'd be too embarrassed. I'd look like a tramp beside him.'

'Now you're being paranoid. Hannah would introduce you to this lad and in future when you see them you can stop and speak and let him know that he's not the only one interested in Hannah. Besides, when you're dressed in your best you're a handsome fellow.'

Harry paused. 'Do you know something, Louise? You're right!' He gave a small laugh. 'I don't mean about me being handsome. But there's no reason why I shouldn't speak to Hannah. We've been friends for donkeys' years.' He glanced back but Liz had already gone inside and the door was now closed. Hannah and her companion were out of earshot. He sighed in relief, not really wanting to be compared to his rival in love, convinced that he would be found wanting. 'Well, too late now. Maybe some other time.'

He lapsed into a moody silence and Louise left him to brood. She had seen the hurt and anguish in her brother's eyes when he looked at Hannah and berated herself for not realising how deeply Harry loved this vulnerable girl. He was besotted with her. Why had she not noticed? Probably because they all treated Hannah as part of the family. Hindsight was a wonderful thing.

They passed an area where children were playing, known locally as the Flush because the waters from the laundry and dye-works ran into it, but really a river that was also called the Blackie. Every colour of the rainbow was reflected in the Flush, but not because it was sparkling clean. Far from it! Louise thought it was because of the run-off from the dye factory that was up behind the Springfield Park. Understanding now how polluted the water was, she cringed to remember the many hours she and Peggy and their friends had splashed about in it. How had they all survived to live this long?

The lads would skim stones across the river and, in answer to dares, would swing dangerously from a rope as far out as they could over its depths, some without much success. As well as being a favoured playground for children, in the evenings it was also a meeting place for teenagers where both religions mixed happily together. There had been no religious worries or bigotry then. The memories brought tears to Louise's eyes. Where had it all gone wrong? She wondered if today's youth still used the Flush for secret trysts.

With its bushes and dips in the ground, its lines strung between posts where sheets would be hung out to dry when the weather permitted, and with its myriad nooks and crannies, it was a great place for games of hide-and-seek. Another game was find the treasure, where they took turns to hide a trinket or some little piece of junk or other, and the others had to scramble all over in search of it, shouting out as they went, 'Am I getting warm? Am I getting warm?'

Still, she and Peggy had spent many happy Sundays there with their friends after Mass, while Johnnie and Harry played football near by with their mates to keep an eye on their sisters. She recalled the day some years ago when she had been unfortunate enough to fall in the sludge left by the bleach water and her mother had been very angry to see the state of her good Sunday coat. Johnnie had been distraught, almost in tears, saying over and over again, 'Me ma will kill me.' It had been a disaster at the time. She wouldn't have dreamed then that one day the memory would bring a happy smile to her face.

Harry glanced sideways at her. 'What are you all smiles about?'

'Oh, just reminiscing.'

Soon they reached Springfield Village. Dating from the mid nineteenth century, it was bigger than Louise remembered. Of course more houses had probably been built since she was last up here. On the outskirts of the village Harry pointed out the shop where he delivered the bread from Monday to Saturday. As they moved on, Harry took her protectively by the arm. She laughed and asked him if he thought they would be set upon.

'Everybody seems to be looking at us,' he muttered out of the corner of his mouth, as they wandered through the village centre, watched with avid interest by women standing outside their doorways, nudging each other and whispering. Louise smiled at them and received smiles and nods in return.

'That's because we're strangers. They're probably wondering who we are and who we're coming to visit. After all, there's nothing but waste land ahead. They're entitled to be inquisitive, you know. And it is their village.'

Children milled around in front of the National School, the older ones playing hopscotch and skipping, the younger ones in the forecourt with dolls and toy tea-sets. A few of them could be heard arguing over who would be mammy and who would be daddy.

Soon they reached the far edge of the village where hedges and brambles had been allowed to grow in wild disarray, so high and dense that they cast long shadows. Harry led her on for a short distance and then drew to a halt at a gate almost hidden by unkempt hedges bordering an overgrown garden. In the midst of the long grass a cottage nestled in a profusion of wild meadow flowers and weeds: buttercups, daisies, mayflowers, purple and white clover, the usual profusion of dandelions, and others they recognised but couldn't put a name to. The sweet scent of the clover was heavy in the warm evening air.

Surprised, because this was not what she was expecting, Louise eyed the cottage intently. It was a single-storey affair, built of grey stone, and the roof looked in good order. She shot a questioning glance at her brother. 'This doesn't look like any old wreck to me. Are you sure no one lives here?'

Harry grunted in disgust. 'Catch yourself on, Louise. Can you picture anyone living in there?' He had his hand on the gate. 'This gate's well bedded in. If I can't manage to shift it, do you think you'd be able to climb over? We can look through the windows and see what the inside's like. It's probably a ruin.'

To his surprise and with little effort the gate moved at his touch. A look of astonishment on his face, Harry pushed it wider until there was enough room to sidle through and motioned her to follow.

'Someone else has been here. That gate wouldn't

budge the last time I tried it.' He led the way. 'Watch out for the lions,' he joked as he waded through long grass and shrubs where a path had clearly been recently trampled up to the door.

Louise carefully picked her steps and followed him, her eyes taking in the neglected window boxes. The nets on the windows were too thick and grimy for them to see inside and Harry cautioned her, 'You stay here and I'll see what it's like round the back.'

Glad to obey him, Louise leaned closer to the window, cupping her hands over her eyes and peering inside. All she could make out were dark shapes of furniture. She leaned closer still and rubbed at the window-pane. It had little effect but suddenly the nets were wrenched apart and a man's angry face glared out at her. In a panic and completely forgetting the state of the ground around her, she yelped and lurched back, stumbling full length into the shrubs and a clump of nettles, letting out a shrill cry of distress.

Harry immediately bounded back round the corner. At the same time the door was wrenched open by the owner of the face, now concerned and full of apologies. They both came to her aid, each gripping an arm and gently pulling her to her feet.

'Are you all right, sis?'

'Yes, yes, I'm fine, I think,' she managed to splutter. 'My clothes protected me from being stung . . . that is, except for my hands.'

'Sorry for startling you like that. I thought it was them youngsters from up there.' The man canted his head towards the village. 'You're trespassin', you know. Are you sure you're all right?'

Flexing her arms and shoulders, Louise tried to reassure him. 'I think so.'

Realising that there was no real damage done, the man's voice changed, becoming cold and hard. 'Would you mind telling me what you were doing gawking through my window like that? You gave me a hell of a scare, so you did! This is private property, you know, and I won't be liable for injuries received.'

Harry had been consoling his sister, but at the man's tone of voice he stood to attention. Thrusting his hand out, he said, 'I'm Harry McGuigan and this is my sister Louise. I'm sorry about this intrusion on your property, sir, but I have often passed this house and thought it was empty.'

'Oh, and that gave you the right to snoop around, did it? Nosy bugger.'

'Of course not,' Harry answered belligerently. 'We were just interested in the condition of the house. I thought it might be up for sale.'

Louise offered her input. 'That's right! Harry knows that it's been lying empty for a long time. He asked me to come along and have a look and see if I thought it was worthwhile putting in an offer for it. He was going to find out who owned

182

the property 'cause it's obviously in good nick. Just been neglected a wee bit out here.' She nodded at the wilderness around them. 'But I assume you are the owner and it's not for sale, so please accept our apologises for trespassing.'

She offered her hand and winced when he shook it.

He was immediately alerted. 'Here, let me take a look at that.'

She turned over both hands and he examined them, watched anxiously by Harry. Her palms were grazed and bits of grit were embedded in the pads.

Harry gasped in dismay. 'Let's get you home, sis. Good evening to you, sir. Sorry for the trouble we caused.'

'No! No, that's all right. Come in and get those hands attended to first. I'll wash them and I have plasters somewhere . . . at least I think I have.' With these words he ushered them inside the house.

11

Dusk was falling when at last they left Dick Patterson's house. Inviting them in, he had introduced himself and told them to make themselves at home. He then disappeared into the scullery and, taking down a kettle from a shelf, half filled it with water. He brought it to the boil on a gas stove and returned to the kitchen with a small basin of hot water. In spite of her protestations and after thoroughly cleansing Louise's hands in the basin, he dried them and applied a pungent-smelling salve, gently teasing it into the scratches. Satisfied with his work, and very much against Louise's wishes, he produced a clean linen handkerchief from his top pocket and wrapped it securely around her left hand, exclaiming as he did so, 'There you are! That should keep you going until you get home. The other hand isn't too bad, it should be all right. That salve will take the sting out of the scratches and it won't be sticky or anything. It will also prevent any infection setting in.'

Taken aback at this stranger's kindness, Louise shyly thanked him. 'But there was really no need, you know. I'd have just washed them and hoped for the best. I hope the blood doesn't ruin your lovely white handkerchief.'

'Don't worry about that. I only use it for show. My late wife always liked me to wear a handkerchief in my breast pocket. I think she was trying to make a gentleman of me . . . without much luck, I might add.'

Louise was watching him, mesmerised, and he caught her eye and winked.

'However, one should be very careful of cuts and scratches,' he said, with a warning wag of his index finger. 'You'd never believe the different germs that are lurking out there. Always take care of anything like that. One can't be too careful. You could get blood poisoning from the slightest scratch if you don't look after it.' He rubbed his hands together and grinned broadly. 'Since you're here, you might as well have a cup of tea. Then you can tell me why you're so interested in this palace of mine.'

Harry, who had been looking around the kitchen

whilst Louise was having her cuts administered to, and longing to hear more about the cottage, nodded eagerly. Louise on the other hand inclined her head slowly. She didn't feel comfortable. She'd come up here to look over a bit of waste ground with a derelict building, only to discover it wasn't a ruin, as Harry had thought, but a fair-sized cottage in the midst of an overgrown garden . . . and occupied, to boot. Not a wreck, as Harry had led her to believe. Even if it should be up for sale, which she doubted, Louise realised that there was no way in this wide world that Harry could ever be able to afford it. Gas and running water laid on? She'd expected a ramshackle building, not this quite decent cottage. It would be far too expensive and way beyond Harry's means. She felt guilty about wasting this good man's time.

Louise was no authority on good furniture or decoration but the interior was well cared for and it certainly seemed quite solid and expensive, if a bit neglected. Perhaps because the owner was away from home for long spells at a time. The rugs that partially covered the red-tiled floor of the front room needed a good beating but looked like high-quality material. On the marble mantelpiece stood fine china figurines either side of a grand-looking clock. On the walls hung exquisite oil paintings that could be scenes from around Donegal. In a corner by a window stood a large oak bookcase, each shelf packed with books. Louise wondered if he had read every book there and wouldn't be surprised if he had. The owner must be very educated and quite well off, she surmised.

She studied him as he produced a tea caddy and fussed about making tea. He was tall and rugged-looking with dark unruly hair; she reckoned him to be in his early forties. About the same age as her da, she imagined. The thought entered her mind that his wife must have been quite young when she passed away and Louise couldn't help wondering about the cause of death.

The lack of daylight, due to the dingy curtains hanging at the windows, made the room quite dark. Dick, as he asked to be called, lit the gas-mantle and refilled the kettle. 'Those nets could do with a good wash,' he said with a frown at the windows, as if it was their fault, and admitted, 'I've been away too long this time.'

Soon they were sitting facing their host across the table, hands clasped around mugs of tea, mugs that he had taken from a cupboard. Louise was pleased to note that there was no sign of any dust on them.

With the lift of an eyebrow, Dick gestured a pipe in their direction and when they nodded their assent he commenced to scrape out the bowl with a penknife he had produced from his waistcoat pocket and emptied the burned ash into the fire. Louise, now very much aware of her bath full of clothes plumping away on the stove back home, watched him and wriggled impatiently as he started shaving pieces from a thick plug of Gallaher's Warhorse tobacco. He then proceeded to knead them in one hand with the heel of the other before carefully pressing the plug into the well-worn bowl of his pipe. She could only hope that she would not return to find some disaster. Dick was obviously fond of his pipe and treated the whole operation with great care and attention. At last, satisfied with his preparations, he lifted a spill from the hearth and, lighting it from the fire, applied the flame to his pipe. He sucked deeply a few times, patting down the burning tobacco with his forefinger, until he had it burning to his complete satisfaction. What seemed to Louise to take for ever, but in fact was only a matter of some minutes, all ended in a cloud of thick smoke. With a sigh of contentment, he sat back in his chair and gave them his full attention. It was obviously a labour of love that he performed each day.

He also had the gift of the gab and could hold an intelligent conversation on practically any subject he chose. It was almost an hour later that they took their leave.

Once clear of the cottage, Louise gripped Harry's arm and urged him quickly towards the tram stop, which was at the far side of the village.

'I never dreamed that we'd be away this long. I

hope the bath hasn't boiled over,' she cried with some trepidation. 'The scullery will be in a terrible state if it has.'

'Don't worry about it, sis. It will be my fault if it has. I'll help you clean up, so I will.'

A tram was just about to leave the stop, the conductor totally unaware of their distant figures hurrying towards him. With a spurt of speed Harry left Louise and darted ahead. Ignoring a dark look from the conductor, he grasped the pole and stood with one foot on the platform and the other on the road until a breathless Louise arrived and clambered aboard, gasping a word of thanks. This somewhat appeased the dour conductor who gave the bellrope a double tug for the driver to proceed.

Springview Street was only a few stops down Springfield Road and Louise sat, getting her breath back. Harry was in a world of his own and it wasn't until they were walking down Springview Street that he ventured to speak.

'Well, what do you think of that encounter, sis?'

'I think he must have kissed the blarney stone. He's a great storyteller, that's for sure. But I took everything he said with a pinch of salt.'

'Really? I was intrigued. The things he's seen and done, that man could write a book if he put his mind to it, so he could. He seems very knowledgeable. At least if we could believe everything he said to us.'

Harry took his key from his pocket and unlocked the outer door. Louise pushed past him and opening the vestibule door rushed for the scullery. The bathwater was bubbling away but as yet had not boiled over. They were just in time. Turning off the gas rings, she turned to her brother with a sigh.

'Thank God, it's all right.' Removing her coat, she thrust it at him. 'Here, hang that up for me, please. I'm well behind now. Will you give me a hand? Get the washboard from under the stairs and pull the mangle away from the wall out the back so I can get at it.'

'Sure, leave it to me.'

Rinsing out the sink, Louise put the plug in and let some cold water run. Then giving the clothes a final prod, she lifted some of them into the sink with the pot stick. Rubbing plenty of Sunlight soap on to each article, she began scrubbing them against the washboard that Harry had placed there for her.

Harry still hovered about but she concentrated firmly on what she was doing, guessing that he was bursting to talk about their outing. She was glad when he finally left her in peace, first telling her to give him a shout if she needed him. Once she had finished scrubbing to her heart's content, she filled the sink with clean water, rinsed and loosely wrung out the clothes, then called out to Harry for assistance.

'Will you empty the the bath while I give these a second rinse?'

He worked with a will, feeling guilty for having kept her away from the house for so long. Carefully grasping the handles of the bath, he angled it through the doorway and poured the water down the drain in the backyard, returning quickly to her side. Her urgency had rubbed off on him.

Throwing him an anguished glance, she said, 'Is the mangle ready out there?' He nodded and she thrust some vests at him. 'First of all, dry out the bath. Then as I rinse, you put those through the wringer and return them to the bath. Be careful you don't drop anything out there or it will have to be washed again.'

The mangle was kept covered under the lean-to roof their da had built years ago to protect it and the bath from the elements. Harry now pulled it closer to the scullery door. 'Don't worry, sis, I'll be careful.'

A quick glance at the clock made Louise more agitated. 'Look at the time. Da will be here soon and you know what he's like when the house gets all steamed up,' she lamented.

'My heart bleeds for him.' Harry snorted. 'Is that why you're in such a panic? Me da doesn't appreciate your worth, you know. He's lucky to have you as his slave or he really would have something to gripe about, 'cause he'd get no sympathy where I'm concerned.'

Louise rounded on him. 'Is that what you really think?'

'It's true. He cracks the whip and you jump.'

'No, I don't!' Louise was indignant but uneasy at this confession. 'Is that what everybody thinks?' she asked apprehensively.

Harry shrugged. He could see that he had upset his sister and regretted opening his big mouth. 'No, of course not, I only made that up,' he spluttered. 'I'm just in bad humour and I'm taking it out on you. Sorry!'

Guessing just why he was in such a mood and knowing how much it meant to him, she warned him, 'Harry, don't be disappointed about the cottage. If that man does decide to sell, well, to be truthful, I can't really see how you would ever be able to afford it, it's way beyond your means.' Feeling that she couldn't cope with Harry's problem at the moment, she was relieved to hear her father closing the outer door. 'Anyway here's Da. We'll talk about it another time.'

A frown gathered on Tommy's brow at the steamed-up scullery and kitchen. 'What's all this, eh?'

Still annoyed at Harry referring to her as a slave, Louise retorted with a defiant tilt of the head, 'It's what happens when you do the laundry in a confined space.'

'Your ma never got the place all steamed up like this.'

'Oh, yes, she did. Only you were never home to notice.'

Normally she would have tried to placate her father but, still smarting from Harry's words, she refused to knuckle down. 'Harry has been giving me a hand and we're just finished here. So when I hang this washing on the pulley line, I'll be off to bed.'

Changing his tone of voice, Tommy sought to appease her. 'No chance of a cuppa tea, then?'

'Not unless you make it yourself.'

Heading towards his room, Tommy said, 'I'm away on in, then.' He hesitated, waiting for his daughter to relent and even managed a sincere smile. When she showed no intention of appeasing him, he entered his room with a grunt of annoyance.

Grinning, Harry gave his sister the thumbs-up sign and mouthed the words, 'Good for you, sis.'

Louise was so weary that she actually crawled into bed. The last thing she heard was Peggy at the front door, as she fell into a restless sleep driven by dreams she couldn't later recall and awoke the next morning feeling as tired as ever, as if she had never been to bed at all.

At work next day the morning passed all too quickly and before she knew it Deirdre was pointing at the clock. It was their lunch break. As she made her way to the staff room to join her friend, she saw George Carson beckon her from the front of the shop.

Surprised to see him back so soon, she hurried towards him.

'I nipped in to see if you were free on Saturday night, Louise.'

She paused before replying. 'I think so. Yes, yes, I am as a matter of fact, why?'

'Is it all right then to book a table at the club?'

She smiled and nodded her approval.

Grinning in return, he said, 'Where shall I pick you up?'

'At the corner of Springfield Road, about seven. Will that suit you?'

'Any time suits me. Look forward to seeing you then.'

She was glad that Deirdre hadn't noticed George. She intended in future to try to keep her private business just that: private and away from the shop. No need for all and sundry to know what she got up to outside of work. The thought of going to the club with George lightened her mood immensely. Conor's letter at the weekend had been short and sweet, his excuse being he was so busy studying, which she found hard to believe. So she might as well enjoy herself. Roll on Saturday night.

Harry had lain awake late into the night, trying to convince himself that he could, with an effort, afford to buy the cottage. That is, if Dick Patterson did decide to put it on the market. Some of his workmates earned wages similar to his own and they were married. Although, to be truthful, most of them were still living with their in-laws, saving all they could in the hope that one day they might be in a position to get the keys to a rented house.

After a lot of tossing and turning, he at last decided he was deluding himself. He would be foolish to get into so much debt when he didn't even know if he stood a chance with Hannah. Tonight he would ask Louise what she thought, listen carefully and consider her proposals. She had a wise head on her shoulders, had his Louise. He would abide by whatever advice she offered.

Last night had shown him how hard his sister worked at home while holding down a full-time job at the bookshop. He realised that none of them had ever offered to give her a helping hand and decided there and then to make himself more useful in future.

With these good intentions in mind, he dutifully helped clear the plates and cutlery from the dinner table with a warning to Peggy. 'I'll help you wash these, Peggy, and give Louise a break, OK?'

Peggy opened her mouth to protest but before she could speak Harry quipped, 'When did you last help clear up in here, eh? You're out galli-vanting about nearly every night of the week, so you are.'

'Well, Louise never complained, did she?'

'No, because she's too soft. If she doesn't watch herself, she'll soon become the family drudge.'

Tommy had paused on his way to the scullery, a surprised look on his face. 'You're right there, son. We'll all have to pull our weight in this house. Louise, I'll clear out the yard at the weekend. But do you mind if I just pop into the scullery first? I'm in a hurry out.' With these words he gathered up his flannel and towel from under the stairs and hurried into the scullery.

Harry glared after him, muttering under his breath, 'You auld git.'

Louise sat, mouth agape, listening to these exchanges. She could hardly believe her own ears. Wonders would never cease. However . . . words were cheap. She wouldn't hold her breath, waiting for her da to clear up the yard at the weekend, that was for sure.

Still, she wasn't going to look a gift horse in the mouth and, rising, she said, 'Thanks for that vote of confidence, Harry. I'm glad somebody cares about me.'

Looking a bit sheepish, her brother said tentatively, 'Are you going out tonight, sis?'

Louise had seen this coming and was prepared. 'I'm going to take a walk over later and see how Grannie is. I promised her I'd call by.'

To her surprise Harry grinned at her. 'I'll be glad

to come along with you, sis, that is, if you don't mind. I've been neglecting Gran lately.'

Louise turned aside, closing her eyes in dismay. She knew why Harry wanted to accompany her. She dreaded trying to reason with him about the cottage. He could be so stubborn at times and she didn't want to get into a slanging match with him. However, she must make him see sense before he did something stupid that he might regret later on.

12

On their way over to Oakman Street, Louise felt relief flooding through her when Harry confided that he had decided it would be foolhardy for him to buy a house, even though he had been so set on it.

Louise sighed inwardly. His decision eased the tension in her and she relaxed, sensing the stress leaving her body. Harry was showing some sense at last. As he explained his reasons for changing his mind, Louise hastened to agree with him wholeheartedly, just glad that he had done so. For a start, Mrs McFadden would never hear tell of her daughter going to live on the outskirts of the village, he explained. With a wise nod of the head he added that he could understand that. It would be too lonely for Hannah. He should have realised that sooner. Besides, he didn't think he'd be able to afford the cost of owning a house anyway. He'd be skint most of the time.

Louise had been prepared to ward off any effort of his to persuade her to fall in with wild plans to buy the cottage. She had intended to be quite blunt with him and warn him that he could expect no help from her. There was no way that she could manage without his weekly housekeeping contribution as well as help him out when he ran short for essentials. Harry's change of heart took her completely by surprise.

He glanced at her and saw her emotions written on her face. He smiled wryly and paused before asking her if she would lend an ear to another problem concerning Hannah.

'If I can,' she said hesitantly, not knowing what was coming next. 'I'll certainly listen and if I can I'll offer my advice.'

'I was speaking to Hannah over in Johnnie's shop today and I thought she looked miserable. She barely registered my presence, and when she finished serving a customer she took herself off into the back office. Without as much as a glance or a word of acknowledgement, mind you. I think she was avoiding me.'

'Why? Why would she do that?'

'With her seeing this other guy, I find it difficult to talk to her.' He shrugged miserably. 'You know how it is. Things are awkward between us at present and I think she's gone off me. But Peggy says no, that Hannah's missing me and it's about time I did something about it if I don't want to lose her altogether.' His shoulders rose and fell again in dejection, but he eyed her hopefully. 'The thing is, I don't know what to do about it. Any pearls of wisdom, sis?'

'Poor Hannah. She probably doesn't know whether or not you want to speak to her, so she's playing it safe. If you're really serious about her, I think you should see her and ask her if she will go out with you as well as this other fellow. Don't give her an ultimatum or anything like that, mind. The worst thing you can do at the moment is put more pressure on her. Just convince her that you would like to remain her friend. Say that you miss the times you shared together. Ask her if she would consider being your friend again and give you the chance to renew your friendship with her.'

His shoulders slumped in despair. The sight tugged at Louise's heart.

'Ah, Louise, you know her ma is behind this whole carry-on. She would never hear tell of that.'

Leaning in closer to him, his sister hissed, 'It's not her ma you want to date, is it? For heaven's sake, wise up, Harry. Knock on the door and ask to speak with Hannah. Buy a couple of tickets for the Grand Opera House or somewhere. It might be costly, but it will show Mrs McFadden how serious you are about Hannah. That you really care for her daughter. It just might change her mind about you.'

'That's a brilliant idea, sis.' He nodded, pleased with the idea. 'I'll do that.'

'It's not always easy to get tickets for the Grand Opera House, mind. It depends on what's on. People often book in advance, so you could be lucky enough to get a cancellation, but if you can't get tickets for the Grand Opera House try the Empire Theatre. Just so long as you have tickets for a show. Her mother will be impressed and Hannah will have no excuse to refuse you.' Not that Louise thought for one minute that Hannah would do anything like that. It was Mrs McFadden who was the fly in the ointment. It's her he'd have to win over, not her daughter. But tell that to Harry and he'd run a mile rather than face Hannah's mum.

His face one big grin, he agreed with her. 'Yes, I'll do that. I'll nip down later and see what I can get. And thanks, sis.' He clasped her in a bear-hug. 'I really do appreciate all your help.'

They had arrived at their grannie's door and Harry said in an aside, 'Don't mention anything about this to Grannie. OK?'

'My lips are sealed,' his sister assured him, as Lucy Logan opened the door and greeted them with her usual warmth and hugs and kisses.

*   *   *

The rest of the week went by without any serious upheavals. The bookshop was astir with preparations for the renowned author, Joseph McGouran, coming in on Saturday to sign copies of his latest book. New titles from other authors had also been delivered and room for these had to be allocated to display them to their full sales potential.

Louise delighted in all this bustle and excitement. She couldn't get to work quickly enough each morning and the short letter she received on Friday from Conor, full of platitudes of regret about how busy he was, only made her all the more determined to enjoy her date with George Carson. She didn't believe for one minute that Conor was as busy as he was trying to make out.

Rising early on Saturday morning, with her lavender soap, talcum powder and shampoo clutched in her hands, she entered the scullery, where she had half filled the tin bath with hot water, and hung two towels ready behind the door. First she shampooed her hair and rinsed it until it squeaked when she squeezed it free of excess water. Then wrapping a towel turban-style around her head, she enjoyed a long luxurious washdown. Wrapped in a bathtowel, she emptied and dried the tin bath and hung it out in the backyard. Feeling much refreshed, she returned upstairs to towel her hair dry, grateful that it had a natural curl. Since it was a special day at work, she used a little face powder to enhance her looks.

Downstairs, she had finished making the porridge when her da emerged from his room. He appraised her with suspicious eyes. 'Why are you all dolled up, girl?'

'Well, today, if you must know, Joseph McGouran is signing copies of his latest book in our shop.' Indignant, Louise looked her father full in the face. 'It might surprise you to know, da, but I look like this every day. I've just got a little more powder on than usual for the big occasion.'

'Hmm. You're better-looking without all that muck on your face.'

Louise thumped a bowl of porridge down in front of him. 'If you want me to continue making your breakfast each morning, you'd better keep those kinds of remarks to yourself.'

Tommy gave her a baleful glare and with a snort began to eat the porridge, all the while cautioning himself, *Hold your tongue now, Tommy, boy*. He didn't want his daughter taking a leaf out of Nora's book and doing a runner, leaving him in the lurch. He depended heavily on Louise to manage the house and he would be lost without her.

Al Murray had arrived early Saturday morning looking very dapper and distinguished in a dark, pin-stripe, three-piece suit. He was accompanied by John Bradford who was dressed in a grey Harris tweed jacket with black trousers, white shirt and a fancy blue tie.

'They must be training John for management.' Deirdre nudged Louise playfully in the ribs and added, 'Maybe I should set my cap at him.'

The two men walked around the shop floor, making suggestions here and there, and Al told the girls where to be standing when the famous author arrived.

Louise and Deirdre were to position themselves near the table where Joseph McGouran would sit, but not to intrude unless he showed willing. A jug of drinking water and a glass was set ready and a pen placed beside copies of his latest novel, ready for signing when he came in at the prearranged time of one o'clock. A section in front of the table had been roped off to prevent any queue-jumping. John Bradford was given the task of looking after members of the public who wished to meet him, keeping them entertained and in an organised queue outside on Ann Street until the author himself arrived.

Deirdre suggested that she and Louise forgo their lunch break until the author had been and gone. Louise readily agreed with her. She had butterflies in her stomach and preferred to wait. They dallied near the door hoping to see what kind of car the writer would arrive in. A glance at the clock told Louise that they still had ten minutes to go. The last half-hour had crawled by and she wondered if the clock was slow.

At last a commotion outside heralded the arrival of Joseph McGouran. They hovered closer still to the door, craning their necks, but strain as they might, they could see no sign of a fancy car in the near vicinity. A tall man was conversing with John and the people at the head of the column. Louise raised her brows at Deirdre and said with a knowing wag of the head, 'There'll be a right racket if that guy tries to bunk the queue.'

'There sure will and you wouldn't blame them. Some of that crowd have been standing out there for the past hour or more.'

When it appeared that the man was indeed being given priority, the two girls scuttled back to their appointed places near the table.

John Bradford followed the man inside and stood in his shadow, all the while making hand signals at Louise and Deirdre as if expecting them to come forward. At a loss, they exchanged bewildered glances, trying to figure out what John expected them to do about this stranger. Did he expect them to toss him out of the shop?

Hesitantly, Louise went forward a few steps and caught the man's attention. He strode towards her, a delighted grin on his face, and Louise gasped as she recognised Dick Patterson. Grasping her hand, he turned it over, examined the scratches and sighed. 'Ah, they're healing well, I'm glad to see. How are you, my dear?'

Flustered, Louise was trying to manoeuvre him to one side. She was in a dilemma. Imagine him coming in today of all days to see how she was. Indeed, how had he known that she worked here? Harry must have mentioned it; she certainly hadn't said anything. She sensed a presence close behind her and turned to find Al Murray at her side. Her heart thumped against her ribs and she was sure everyone could hear it. Excuses trembled on her lips as she tried to conjure up something suitable to explain Dick's presence. There was no need. To her amazement a hand was thrust out past her towards Dick as Al greeted him.

'Sorry I wasn't here to meet you, but you are a little early.'

Apologies dying on her lips, Louise was mortified when Dick replied, 'Never mind, Al. Louise has been entertaining me.'

He winked at Louise, bringing a blush to her cheeks. She glared back at him. Just who the hell did he think he was? He would be getting her the sack if she wasn't careful. She turned to her boss. 'I'm sorry, sir. Dick doesn't know we are expecting an author to come any minute now or he wouldn't have intruded.'

Al drew back confused and looked at her with raised brows. 'Dick . . .' He turned his gaze on Dick, who hurriedly interrupted Louise's excuses.

'All my fault, Al. Louise is a friend of mine, but, alas, I have never confided in her that I'm a bit of a writer. So she is none the wiser that I go by the pseudonym of Joseph McGouran.'

Most of the staff had edged closer to hear what was going on. Louise wished that the floor would open up and swallow her.

'A friend? And she never let on? How remiss of you, Louise. Well, in that case you can help your friend while he signs the books. If you will come this way, Joseph?'

Bewildered, Louise hung back. She didn't understand what was going on. Al glanced over his shoulder and said, 'You too, Louise.'

All the built-up excitement was spoiled for Louise. Where she should have been proudly assisting the author, she felt uncomfortable, conspicuous even, standing by the table. She imagined that all eyes were on her, which was of course stupid. Who would notice her with this famous writer sitting there? It was Dick, as she still thought of him, that they had come to meet, not a common shop assistant. She greeted each customer with a smile that she hoped didn't look as strained as it felt. Taking the book, she would ask the customer whom they wanted it made out to, then pass it to the author, while avoiding meeting his eye. Joseph in turn had a friendly word and a smile for everyone and it was evident from the reception that all his fans adored him.

Feeling Deirdre's eyes on her, she glanced over, expecting a sympathetic look in return, but received a scowl and a thrust of the chin in reply. Obviously her friend thought that Louise had been holding out on her. She began to wish that she had never heard tell of Dick Patterson. She had so looked forward to this signing. Now she felt miserable.

Joseph McGouran continued to smile and sign for one and a quarter hours, at the end of which Louise thought her arm would break. It felt as if the thick, hardbacked books gained weight as the time passed. The queue at last petered out and the author rose to his feet, arching his back and stretching his tall form, giving Louise a grin. 'That seemed to go OK. Hmm?'

Before Louise could open her mouth, Al Murray immediately homed in on them.

'The staff have prepared a light snack for you, Joseph. I do hope you have time to join us.'

'I'd kill for a cup of tea right now, Al.'

Dick turned towards Louise but she was already moving across the floor to Deirdre. The hostile look she received from her friend fired her temper. 'Don't you start,' she warned. 'I don't know whether I'm coming or going.'

'Why all the secrecy? You could have told me you knew him. I wouldn't have said to anyone.'

'That's just it! I only met him at the weekend. He never said he was a writer. His real name is Dick Patterson. What on earth will Al Murray think of me? I feel a right idiot.'

John Bradford arrived at her side and gave a slight bow. He had heard her remarks and teased, 'You certainly keep the right company, young lady.'

'Whether you believe me or not I'm telling the truth.' She glared at him and he laughed.

'It's all right. Joseph has explained the situation and that you really didn't know that he was a writer. He wants you to join him for lunch.'

Louise's mouth opened in a wide 'O' of dismay and John hastened to add, 'He says to bring your friend along.'

Deirdre, all smiles now, gushed, 'We would be delighted to join him.' She squeezed her friend's arm. 'Wouldn't we, Louise?'

Without more ado Deirdre engaged John in conversation and Louise had no option but to glumly trail in their wake to the boss's office where a buffet had been laid on.

13

With the time it took helping to clear up and tidy the shop after the buffet, Louise had no time to spare before her date. George Carson had been in touch and she had agreed to him picking her up at seven o'clock at the junction where the Grosvenor Road met the Falls Road. In spite of Louise's misgivings, the buffet lunch had turned out to be a very pleasant little do, very pleasant indeed: a tasty variety of sandwiches and cakes and soft drinks. However, she noticed that in Dick's honour – or rather, Joseph's honour, or whoever he was – the men were sipping whiskey.

And although she feared provoking hostility among the staff, she was able to overcome her embarrassment when it turned out that she was actually envied by the girls because Dick Patterson spoke so highly of her. If they only knew the circumstances under which she had made his acquaintance, that she and her brother had trespassed on the writer's property, it would be a different kettle of fish altogether. Still, the craic was good and she had enjoyed every minute of the afternoon.

To Dick's credit, the trespassing incident wasn't mentioned, not even in jest. He had treated her as an old friend, speaking highly of her and Harry's friendship, acting as if they had known each other for some time, and Louise was grateful for small mercies. To crown it all Dick-or-Joseph presented her with a signed copy of his book. Louise felt as if her chest would burst with pride.

She was waiting impatiently at the bottom of Castle Street for a tram home when a large, black limousine drew up. Not knowing anyone with such a super car, she admired it furtively, examining the chrome fittings until a girl behind her gave her a nudge and motioned towards the front seat. Leaning down, Louise stared into the interior and saw Dick Patterson, a beaming smile on his face, beckoning her to get in. Without further ado she thanked the girl and joined him, sinking into the soft, comfortable leather seat with a sigh of pure pleasure.

'Wow . . . this is very posh. I thought you must have arrived by tram today. Deirdre and I were watching out for a flashy car. Mind you, we wouldn't have been disappointed.' She fingered the highly polished walnut dashboard. 'This is a real beauty. That's why, when this big fella came along on foot, with no sign of a car anywhere and I recognised you, I thought you had called into the shop to see *me*.' She bowed her head in mock dismay. 'As if.'

He laughed aloud and apologised. 'Sorry about that spot of bother I caused you. But how would I have known where you worked, eh? Tell me that!'

'I will, the same way I was supposed to guess you are a writer. And a very famous one, as it turned out,' she teased him.

'Touché. Do you forgive me?'

'Of course. You redeemed yourself.'

'Tell me, is Harry interested in my cottage or not?'

'He wouldn't be able to afford it, Dick. Believe me, it's out of the question. He had thought that it was a bit of a wreck because of the overgrown state of the front garden and he might be in with a chance of a bargain . . . you know how it is?' A slight shrug invited his understanding before she continued, 'He thought the owner might be glad to get rid of it. That's why he asked me to go with him to have a proper look around the place. But once we saw inside the house Harry knew it was well beyond his means.'

He turned his head to answer her and she winced

in dismay. She could smell the whiskey fumes wafting from his breath. They had arrived at the top of Springview Street and she quickly came to a decision. 'Let me out here, Dick, please. No need for you to break your journey.' Inwardly she was thinking, *the sooner you get home the better*.

He obediently drew the car into the kerb and turned to her. 'Will you ask Harry to get in touch with me, Louise? I've a proposition to put to him.'

Louise held his eye and said earnestly, 'Remember, Dick, he has no spare cash and no means of raising any. So don't you go putting any silly ideas into his head. OK? He's got enough problems on his plate at present without you adding to them.'

Once out on the pavement, she leaned in through the car window and cautioned him. 'A word of warning, Dick. I can smell drink on you. Be careful how you go.'

'Trust me, Louise, I'm always careful. See you again, I hope.'

'Famous last words,' she teased.

The car pulled away from the kerb and Louise watched it out of sight with some misgivings in her heart before hurrying down the street.

Now and again all the family worked late on Saturday and this was one of those days. Still quite full from the buffet, and knowing that George was taking her out for a meal later that evening, Louise didn't bother making herself anything to eat.

Instead she had another washdown to refresh herself and dressed carefully for her outing. George had intimated that they would go to his club and she wanted to look her best for the occasion. She wore her new black suit, which hadn't got aired much since she had bought it for the job interview, with a blue satin blouse that accentuated the colour of her eyes.

She was pleased with her hair. That morning it had been a mass of unruly curls but during the day they had dropped and soft, blonde waves now fell to her shoulders, just the way she liked it.

Knowing that George would feel uneasy hanging about the Falls Road in his car, she determined to be early. It was an old Austin but he took good care of it and it was his pride and joy. With a couple of minutes to spare she arrived at their designated meeting place in time to see George drawing to a stop at the corner, the car clean and shining.

'That was good timing,' he congratulated her. 'Our table is booked for eight but I thought we could have a drink at the bar first and catch up on old times. I want to hear how you've fared since I last saw you.'

'That would be great. I also long to hear what Trevor thinks of Carlisle.'

'I thought Cathie would have kept you up to date on that score?'

'She does to a certain extent, but I'm the

suspicious type. I read between the lines and came to the conclusion that Trevor isn't a very happy man. And I don't for one minute believe that Cathie's bubbling over with enthusiasm the way she makes out.'

George shifted uncomfortably in his seat but made no further comment until they arrived on High Street. Pulling into the kerb, George jumped out and assisted Louise from the car, then changed the subject. 'What did you think of Joseph McGouran then?'

'Actually, I had already met him before but didn't know he was an author. I made a bit of a fool of myself when he arrived. You see, he came into the shop a few minutes early and I thought he had called in to see me. With every eye in the shop on me, I tried to manoeuvre him to one side out of the way for this great author we were all expecting to arrive at any minute. Then your uncle Al came along and greeted him as Joseph McGouran. I found out later that Joseph McGouran was his pen name. I knew him only by his real name, Dick Patterson. I was mortified, I can tell you.'

George grinned at her delightedly. 'I'm sorry I missed out on that. I would've loved to have seen the expression on your face.'

'I can assure you that I didn't find it very funny at the time. My face must have been red as a beetroot.'

'Wow! How did you know him in the first instance?'

'Oh, that's another story. I'll tell you all about it sometime when you have a few hours to spare.'

'I'll look forward to that. It's bound to be a good one.'

They had reached the club and as George ushered her towards the entrance all else was soon forgotten. Joe, the same waiter as before, showed them to a small table close to the bar and brought a complimentary drink from the management. Taking their orders, he promised to come for them when their meals were ready.

George had ordered Louise a drink and she eyed it with a look of dismay. She knew very little about spirits, and rarely imbibed, feeling daring to even be sitting in a bar, let alone drinking in one. She was in a dilemma. Should she accept it? It was quite colourful and appealing. The rim of the tall glass had been dipped in sugar and was decorated with slices of lemon and orange. A long spoon reached through the ice cubes right to the bottom.

George watched as Louise examined the drink, a worried frown on her brow as if half expecting something slimy to crawl out of it. At last she lifted her head and looked him straight in the eye.

'What's in this?' she curtly enquired.

'It's just a fancy gin and tonic with soda water. More tonic and soda than gin, I would think. Not too strong. You can stretch it out as long as you like.' Still she held his eye.

He waited in silence and then said, 'Girls are supposed to find them very pleasant.'

'Since I don't know much about spirits or have any experience of them, I'm trusting you, George Carson, not to let me get tipsy. My life wouldn't be worth tuppence if my da ever found out.'

He laughed. 'Don't worry. I won't try to have my wicked way with you.'

'You know better.' Carefully stirring the contents in the glass, she took a tentative sip. Her widening eyes showed her approval. 'Very nice. Very nice indeed.'

His eyes twinkled. 'So I might have my wicked way with you after all?'

She blushed bright red. 'It's more than your life's worth.'

He laughed aloud. 'May I say that you're looking very pretty and elegant tonight, Miss McGuigan?'

'You may. This is my interview suit,' was her candid reply.

'It's got class. I always did think you had good taste even when—' His voice trailed off and she saw colour tint his cheeks.

She finished his sentence. 'Even when I worked in the mill?'

'I'm sorry, I didn't mean any harm.'

'It's all right, I know you didn't.'

'Besides, you'd look lovely in sackcloth.'

She beamed at the compliment. 'Now I wouldn't go so far as to say that, so I'll not risk it.' Then becoming serious, she added, 'Tell me, do you hear from Trevor very often?'

'Not very. Just the odd letter.'

'And?'

'He doesn't say much but I get the impression that he's dejected that he can't get a decent job. He's had a good education, you know.'

'That's what Cathie says. She's worried about him. I think they would like to come home but don't know what kind of a reception to expect. Do you think Trevor's parents would forgive and forget?'

A sad shake of the head answered these words. 'Forgive, yes, as I'm sure they have already. But welcome him back to the fold . . . that's another matter. You see, it's not just his parents. His father is high up in the Orange order and his position would be jeopardised. And you really can't blame him. It's his life's work. He's an upstanding member of the community and a pillar of society. One of the best. And Trevor's sister and brother have good positions. The finger would be pointed if Trevor and Cathie ever came back. Trevor would be treated like a social pariah. His life would be a living hell. I expect the family have a lot to put up with as it is. Especially now that a baby is on the way. It would be their first grandchild. Mind you, these are all good God-fearing folk I'm talking about. They just happen to be on the other side, the same side as me, as it turns out.'

Embarrassed, George wasn't looking at Louise as he spoke or he would have seen her devastated reaction at the mention of a pregnancy.

She had slumped down in her chair. 'Cathie's expecting a baby?' she gasped.

Startled, George lifted his head and gaped at her. 'Don't tell me that you didn't know?'

'No . . . Cathie never mentioned it. Are you quite sure, George?'

'Well, in the last letter I received, Trevor wrote that he was worried there would soon be another mouth to feed and one less wage coming in.'

The conversation was brought to an abrupt halt as Joe approached, smiling broadly. Picking up their drinks and placing them on a tray, he said, 'If you would like to follow me, I'll show you to your table.'

'Thank you, Joe,' George said absent-mindedly. He was helping Louise to her feet, concerned, because she looked as if her legs wouldn't support her. He wished that he had kept his big mouth shut about Cathie.

Louise was in a right state. Why hadn't Cathie told her about the baby? she silently lamented. Poor, poor Cathie. She must be out of her mind with worry.

Seeing George was distressed by her reaction to his news, Louise determined to pull herself together and smiled reassuringly at him, nodding her thanks to Joe as she took her seat at the table. The meal looked delicious. Louise had chosen lamb accompanied by home-grown vegetables, followed by apple pie and custard. George had a sirloin steak and vegetables, with bread pudding for afters.

Determined to enjoy the appetising meal and be good company, Louise managed to push all thoughts of her friend to the back of her mind. Later, she told herself, she could dwell on the baby later. She refrained from mentioning Trevor again and kept the talk going about work and trivial things like getting a signed book from Joseph McGouran. As if she thought that was a trivial matter. In fact it was the highlight of her day and she would always treasure it. The food really was superb and she was hungry, so she had no bother clearing her plate. George was interesting company and the talk flowed without any further awkward moments. Afterwards, she sat replete and relaxed. When George asked if she would allow him to get her another drink, she was happy to comply.

They returned to the lounge and, in close proximity at a corner table, George leaned over and gripped her hand. 'I'm sorry you had to hear about the baby from me, but remember, he did write that they might soon have another mouth to feed, so it probably isn't definite yet. It could be a false alarm.'

'I can't understand why Cathie didn't mention it to me.' She found herself wailing and dropped her head, biting her lower lip to gain self-control. George certainly wouldn't ask her out again if she kept giving way to her emotions like this.

His grip tightened on her hand. 'Louise, stop worrying about other people, will you? Cathie's a big girl. She chose to go off with Trevor, nobody forced her. They knew what they were doing. They'll be all right, you'll see.'

Thankfully Joe arrived with their drinks and the sad spell was broken. When he had gone, Louise slapped a smile on her face. 'Of course they will. I don't know what's come over me lately.' She raised her glass. 'Cheers.'

George silently applauded her bravery but wasn't deceived for a single minute. He touched his glass to hers. 'Cheers.'

After that the time flew by and it surprised Louise just how much they had in common. If she hadn't known that George was a Protestant, she could easily have taken him for a Catholic. She realised that the only thing separating them was religion. They were both Irish through and through but past differences in history that were way beyond their

221

control kept them apart. Why couldn't everybody agree to differ? Get on with their lives without interference?

She ventured to put in her penny's worth. 'You know, George, we all love our country, so how did the troubles get out of control? Why couldn't those in charge get their heads together and find a solution to all this bigotry? Sometimes I think it's getting worse instead of better.'

'God knows, and I do agree with you.' He shrugged, leaned closer still and, with a glance around to make sure they wouldn't be overheard, continued in a conspiratorial whisper, 'Let me tell you something, Louise. Do you remember me mentioning to you a man named Francis Joy?'

'Yes, I remember. Don't tell me you've discovered that he's one of your ancestors?' She smiled in a cheeky way and George was pleased that he had lightened her mood.

'I wouldn't mind if he was. Well, have you ever heard of Henry Joy McCracken?'

'Is this some kind of a who's who quiz? Of course I've heard of him. In fact I'd be surprised if anybody in Belfast hadn't heard of Henry Joy McCracken.'

'Ah, but did you know that he was hanged near here, on Cornmarket, in fact, in the late eighteenth century?'

In spite of her trying to appear serious, a little

imp encouraged her to remark, 'Why, was he caught shoplifting in Woolies or somewhere?'

This time George wasn't pleased at her humour and showed his annoyance with a click of his tongue. 'Don't be so silly,' he said abruptly.

She was immediately contrite. 'I'm sorry, profoundly sorry. I didn't mean any disrespect. I don't know what's got into me. It must be that drink. I told you I wasn't used to anything stronger than lemonade.'

'It's all right. I understand. It just happens that I have a great admiration for these men and I don't want you to mock them. You see, the Francis Joy I mentioned to you last time we spoke was Henry Joy's grandfather and his father was John McCracken. Hence the name Henry Joy McCracken. He got involved in radical politics at a very early age. The story goes that he joined up with Thomas Russell in forming the first Society of United Irishmen in Belfast. He was once imprisoned in Dublin for over a year because of his radical views.'

Noticing that her glass was empty, George beckoned for Joe to bring another.

Louise became agitated. 'Oh, no. No! I've had enough, thank you.' But Joe was already mixing the drink, so she gave in gracefully and accepted it.

As the tall glass was placed in front of her,

George said, 'Don't force yourself to drink it. I won't be the least offended if you leave it.'

'That's not what I'm afraid of. I've fallen in love with these tasty drinks. I could easily become addicted to them.' Not that there would be much chance of that happening if it was Conor wining and dining her. They were far too expensive. She would sip this one very slowly. Make it last.

'Three won't make you drunk. Maybe a little relaxed, but not drunk.'

Seeing she was contented enough, he rambled on. 'When the Irish Rebellion broke out in 1798, Henry Joy was made general of the forces mustered at Donegore, which then attacked Antrim town. They were defeated by government troops and McCracken went on the run. After a month or so he was captured at Carrickfergus whilst trying to get a boat to escape to America.'

George leaned back in his chair and drained his second pint of Guinness. He caught Joe's eye and gestured for another, giving Louise a big grin. 'Well, what do you think of the story so far?'

'As history goes, it's very intriguing.'

'I'm not boring you, am I?'

'No! Far from it. In fact, I'm mesmerised that you know so much about him. Do continue, please.' This appeared to be said tongue-in-cheek but George wasn't sure. Afraid of boring her further, he said, 'Well, to cut a long story short, the bold Henry Joy

McCracken was tried for treason and hanged in Cornmarket on the same day: 17 July 1798.'

Spreading his arms wide, he gave Louise a smug, all-knowing look and said, 'Here endeth the history of Ireland – part two. Oh, and before I forget, the best part of the story is . . . Henry Joy McCracken was *not* a Catholic as a lot of folk think. Oh, no. Believe it or not, he was a staunch Presbyterian. Now, what do you think of that?' He sat back, waiting expectantly for her reply.

Louise straightened in her chair. 'Now that's something I didn't know. A United Irishman a *Protestant*? I don't believe you. You've got to be joking!'

'No. It's the God's honest truth, so help me. How did it all go so wrong when they all wanted the same thing?'

It was shortly after ten when they eventually left the club. Louise asked that George drop her off at the Springfield Road junction since she felt just a wee bit tipsy. This warned him that he needn't stop anywhere along the way. He smiled wryly, not believing she was tipsy but respecting her wishes.

'I'll call into the shop some day. OK?'

Leaning across, she gave him a kiss on the cheek and got out of the car. She nodded and lifted her hand in farewell, then crossed the road without a backward glance.

*   *   *

She dawdled up Springfield Road, her mind in a whirl. Not once had she given Conor O'Rourke a single thought tonight. Not once! Not even when she was getting ready to meet George, when she would normally have felt some pangs of guilt, had Conor entered her mind. She had been looking forward to seeing George so much, and then the news of Cathie expecting a baby had threatened to spoil their evening. But George soon put things in perspective and the night had been a very enjoyable one. In fact they had gotten on so well that she now doubted the wisdom of seeing George. Religion still played a big part in relationships in Belfast. She agreed wholeheartedly with her da where that subject was concerned. People should stick to their own kind unless they were looking for trouble. And a good example of that was the predicament Cathie Morgan was now in. God help her, she sighed.

Turning the corner, as if her thoughts had conjured him up, she caught sight of her father further up the street and slowed down in confusion. He certainly hadn't been on the Springfield Road; she would have noticed him before this. All the shops were closed at this late hour and the only people in front of her as she walked up the Springfield Road were Mary Ellen Smith and her husband Paul, and a couple of teenagers on the far side of the road, walking quickly to get home before the curfew started.

So where had Tommy McGuigan suddenly popped up from? Mrs O'Rourke's? That was her first thought; she shook her head in denial. She must be wrong. Her da and Conor's mother? No! She had to be wrong. But wasn't it beginning to look that way? Hadn't Conor all but implied that his mother wouldn't touch Tommy McGuigan with a bargepole? And Louise had been in agreement with him because she believed that her da couldn't even stand the sight of the woman. It didn't seem possible, but she began to have an uneasy feeling about them.

She continued on past her own front door and made a detour down Waterford Street, along the Falls Road and back round to her own front door again. Walking round in circles, she was giving her da a chance to be back in his own room before she went into the house, otherwise she might say something she would later regret. She needed time to give this latest bit of intrigue some thought. A lot of thought, even.

Peggy was leaving Mary Ellen's house where she had been babysitting and had crossed the street to join her sister. They entered the house together. Of Tommy there was no sign.

In the close proximity of the hall Peggy's nose twitched and she turned on her sister, an expression of alarm on her face. 'Have you been drinking?'

Louise gripped her arm and tried to urge her towards the stairs. 'Mind your own business.'

'Let go of me. I need to use the toilet. And you *have* been drinking, haven't you? I can smell it.'

Louise glared angrily at her. 'Why don't you shout out a bit louder? I don't think Mary Ellen heard you the first time.'

Peggy's demeanour changed and she apologised. 'I'm sorry, Louise. I just didn't think. It's just that I'm surprised at you. You've never done anything like that before, as far as I know.'

'It's all right. Just be quiet. Don't give him a chance to come out and start ranting at me.'

'Sorry.'

'And don't spend all night out there. I want to go too.'

14

After Sunday Mass, Harry walked home with Louise and Peggy. He had not been home the night before. Liz, much to his surprise, had invited Harry to stay the night rather than take the chance of breaking the curfew. Hannah's mother was still not too happy about this new arrangement but Hannah had been insistent that she be allowed to court Harry and that had settled the matter.

As soon as they were through the door, he grabbed Louise in a bear-hug and twirled her around the kitchen, watched by a baffled Peggy.

'Thanks, sis. You were right! Mrs McFadden has deigned to let me go out with Hannah again.' His face scrunched up at these words as if he were sucking on a lemon. 'Mind you, she's still not very happy about it but doesn't want to upset Hannah any more than necessary. But with my charm and personality, I'll soon win her over to my way of thinking.'

'You shouldn't have to grovel to Liz McFadden. It's Hannah you want to take out, not her mother,' Louise exclaimed in disgust. 'Just who does she think she is?'

'Never mind.' He continued cheerfully enough, 'I did what you said and got tickets for the Grand Opera House. There was a musical show on and Hannah was thrilled to bits. So thanks for your advice, sis. We had a great time last night and Liz, as she asked me to address her, made me stay for supper and then gave me the use of the settee to sleep on.'

'You were at the Grand Opera House with Hannah McFadden?' Peggy gasped.

The look on her face was comical. Tweaking her nose, Harry confessed, 'I was indeed . . . nosy.'

Still she gaped at him. 'You must really want to impress her *and* her mother. It must have cost you a week's wages for the tickets.'

'Don't be daft, Peggy. I only took her to the Grand Opera House. It's not quite as expensive as you think. So shut your gob, OK?'

Peggy smiled knowingly. 'Ah, you took her up to the gods'.' These were the cheapest seats in the theatre although quite comfortable.

Harry was quick to deny this. 'No, I did not.

We were in the stalls and the seats were lovely, thank you very much. And we had a perfect view of the stage.'

'Here now, that's enough, you two,' Louise interrupted, not wanting a slanging match over something as trivial as to where they had been sitting. 'Watch your tongue, Harry, and apologise to your sister. As for you, Peggy, mind your own business.'

'Sorry, Peggy.'

'I'm sorry too, Harry. It is none of my business. But can I be bridesmaid?'

'Here, hold on a minute! Who said anything about marriage? I'm only allowed to take her out, not walk her up the aisle.'

'The way you two are going on, it looks like I might beat you both to the altar.'

Their heads swung round in Peggy's direction. Louise was the first to find her voice.

'Are you seeing someone?'

'What difference does that make? The rate you're going at, I'll be married while you two are still thinking about it.' With a flounce she started up the stairs.

Harry and Louise eyed each other then burst out laughing. Harry squinted at his sister. 'She's right, you know.' He held her eye. 'Any sign of a ring for you yet?'

A sad sigh escaped Louise's lips. 'Do you want the truth? I don't think Conor and I will ever marry.'

'What?' Her brother gasped, obviously dismayed. 'He's one of the best. What happened? Have you met someone else?'

'Well, it's like this. Conor wants to settle over in Birmingham.' She grimaced and shrugged. 'I don't want to leave Belfast. I love it here, even with all the troubles.'

'Did Conor say he wants to stay over there? Did he? He's daft about you, you know that. He'll do whatever you say.'

'Not any more, apparently. People do change. I suppose it was only a matter of time. So much for absence making the heart grow fonder,' she said with a grimace. 'It seems to be making ours grow colder.'

'Ah, sis.' He reached for Louise and gathered her close. His kindness overwhelmed her and the tears ran unheeded down her cheeks. 'Don't cry, sis. I'm sure you're mistaken. I know he's still mad about you. You can see it every time he looks at you.' He pushed her gently away so that he could see her face. 'What about you, eh? Have you met someone else?'

Rubbing her eyes hard with her knuckles, she sniffed loudly and released herself from his embrace, even managing a timorous smile. 'I imagine Conor is meeting some lovely girls over there, so why do you think I'm the culprit?'

'Because I know that Conor cares about you . . . a lot.'

'If you say so. Anyway, time will tell.' She quickly changed the subject. 'Oh, I nearly forgot. I've a surprise for you.'

His eyes questioned her and she confided, 'You know that author who was doing a signing in our shop yesterday?'

Harry nodded. 'Yes, Joseph McGouran. What about him?'

'Well, that Joseph McGouran is none other than our very own Dick Patterson.'

Harry gazed at her, a puzzled frown on his face. Then comprehension dawned and he sank down on to a chair, his jaw dropping with amazement. 'I don't believe you. You mean to tell me that the Dick Patterson we met up at Springfield Village is also the famous author, Joseph McGouran?'

'As I live and breathe. Why would I lie about something like that?'

'Strange. You'd think he would have mentioned it to us.'

She pouted at him. 'Why? We were just a couple of strangers to him, after all. I don't suppose for one minute authors go about boasting, "Hi, look at me. I'm a writer." Now would they?'

He laughed wryly. 'No. Especially under the circumstances we met him.'

'Exactly!'

'Did he recognise you?'

'Of course he recognised me. Remember, we

weren't wearing masks and striped jerseys,' she jested.

'And how did he react?'

'A lot better than me, I'd say. He was charming. Acted as if we were old friends and even enquired after you. I'm glad to say that he didn't mention how we met. From what I gather he's a very successful author and quite rich too.'

'Lucky so-and-so. That's a turn-up for the books, pardon the pun, isn't it, sis? Remember I suggested that he could write a book?' He was still shaking his head at the wonder of it all. 'I'm not a bit surprised, mind you.'

'Huh! You could have fooled me. Your chin almost bounced off your chest when I told you just then.'

Still dazed, Harry said, 'He certainly looked the intellectual type. And remember that big bookcase, it was jam-packed with books. I remarked on that, didn't I? Never was a truer word spoken in jest. Eh? Imagine, him an author.'

'And to think that I failed to believe your words of wisdom,' she said with downcast eyes and mock awe. 'In short, he gave me a lift home and he sent a message for you.'

'What?' Harry showed his dismay. 'Surely you told him that I couldn't afford the cottage, didn't you?'

'Never fear. I made that very clear. Crystal clear,

as a matter of fact. Nevertheless, he said to ask you to get in touch with him. Said he has a proposition to put to you.'

'Did he give you any clues what it's all about?'

'No. But be very careful, Harry. Don't let him put any big ideas into your head. Remember you'll need all the money you can save if you want to marry Hannah McFadden.'

'Don't worry, Louise. I won't do anything silly.' He started towards the scullery but retracing his steps said diffidently, 'Louise, I know it's Sunday . . . but could you find it in your heart to iron a shirt for me?'

'Look, Harry, I wish you well with Hannah but I'm not going to start ironing your shirts on a Sunday.'

He turned away crestfallen but when she called out his name he swung round with a grin on his face. 'I knew I could depend on you, sis.'

'Don't! This is not going to become a habit, so it's not,' she warned.

'I promise it won't.'

'What time are you going out?'

'I'm picking up Hannah at four. We're going to the Botanic Gardens, then probably take a walk round the museum while we're there. I won't be home for tea. Liz has asked me back to their house for supper if you please.'

'Liz?'

'As I said earlier, she asked me to call her Liz, so I'm starting as I mean to go on. Everybody else calls her Liz, so why not me?'

Louise's face was a picture. With a cheeky wave he entered the scullery and she heard him bolt the door.

Louise reluctantly spread a thick blanket on the table, to save if getting marked by the hot iron. If she was quick she might get finished before her da put in an appearance. He would raise the roof if he caught her ironing on the Lord's Day.

Conor's letter was quite flimsy when it arrived on Monday. Louise fingered it and immediately thought, he's going to break it off. He's fed up with pretending and making excuses for not getting home more often to see me. It will be full of kind remarks and lamentations that he loves me but that Birmingham has got a grip on him.

Glumly she tore open the envelope. There was a single sheet of notepaper inside.

My dear lovely Louise,

I hope you are well and still enjoying your new job. I know you must like it as your last letter was so full of it, I could almost feel your excitement. It has been too long since I last saw you, so I have wangled a few days off. I miss you so much and can't wait any

longer to see you again. I'll be home late
Wednesday to Belfast. I have to return again
on Sunday. Isn't that great news? Three whole
days? You and I together. I can't wait.

All my love,
Conor xx

No kisses rained down on it as was usual with
her. As she recalled the flash of emotion George
Carson had provoked in her on Saturday night,
guilt consumed her. She wished the letter had been
full of regrets and empty promises. Then she would
have felt it was acceptable for her to encourage
George's attentions. With a sigh, she folded the
sheet of paper and returned it to the envelope.
There was no letter from Cathie. Tucking Conor's
letter into her pocket, she removed her coat and
headed for the scullery with a frown. She wondered
why Peggy was late tonight again; she was beginning to make a habit of it. Louise would have to
put her in her place. She couldn't be allowed to
come and go as she saw fit.

It had been a slack day in the shop and with
time on her hands Louise's thoughts constantly
lingered on her Saturday outing with George. He
had aroused feelings in her that she had not
experienced for a long time. She had thought that
she was just responding to kindness because it

had been so long since Conor had held her close and caressed her. She was starting to delude herself that she and George were enjoying a platonic friendship. They had gone out together when she had mistakenly thought that Conor had dumped her some time ago, no strings attached. Now she realised that a platonic relationship was out of the question, no ifs or buts about it. She was attracted to him too much, wanted him to kiss and caress her, make her feel wanted. They could not continue as 'friends'.

Well, now she had a genuine excuse not to lead him on. Conor was coming home for three days and she must explain to George that she would have to end their brief relationship before it even got off the ground. She could not see him any more. So why did she feel so glum? Wasn't she seeing Conor, the love of her life, for heaven's sake? She should be excited and happy at the thought of being with Conor for three whole days. If he still loved her, perhaps he would buy her a ring. Nothing too expensive, but it would let her know where she stood.

She should be pleased at the very idea. Yet here she was in a quandary, not knowing what she wanted for the best. Could she possibly be losing interest in Conor? No, she had been truly worried about his intentions . . . but maybe that was just a matter of pride. It was embarrassing with everybody enquiring when the big day was going to be. Why couldn't people keep their noses out of her business?

She had another change of heart. Now she would rather he didn't mention anything about getting engaged. There was something amiss in their relationship even if she couldn't put her finger on anything specific and say with some conviction, 'That's it.' So if he offered to buy her a ring she would suggest that they wait a little while longer, no matter what others thought.

She realised that even if Conor and she did break up, it would be unwise for her to keep seeing George Carson. She could never marry a Protestant, not that it was ever likely that he would marry the likes of her. She was between the devil and the deep blue sea.

It was her father who brought the news home. A broad grin on his face, he burst through the door. 'Johnnie's wife has another baby.'

'She can't have. She's still got another month to go,' Louise cried.

'Well, I got it from the horse's mouth. Johnnie himself asked me to tell you. Mary was taken into the Royal early this morning. He's just back from there. It was all over so quickly that he hadn't the chance to let anyone know.'

'That must be why Peggy was late. And I thought

she was skiving. She must have been minding the shop. Are Mary and the baby all right?'

'Johnnie says they are both fine. It's a wee girl and Johnnie is over the moon about it.'

Louise was surprised that her father seemed so pleased about the baby. Johnnie's first child, Michael, was such a bonny lad that she got the impression that her da regretted cold-shouldering him and Mary. He had never taken any notice of them before or made any effort to invite them into his home. It was so silly. The child was a grandson that anybody would be proud of. Maybe this time things would be different and this new baby would unite her da with the rest of the family once and for all.

15

On Wednesday evening, knowing that Conor would be arriving soon and without any hints from Louise, the rest of the family made themselves scarce, saying they would be home late. When the remains of the evening meal had been cleared, the dishes washed and put away, the others quickly got ready and took their leave, even her da showing some consideration for a change.

Grateful that there were no sarky remarks about rings and confetti and things like that, Louise took stock of how much time she had left to prepare for Conor's arrival. A glance at the clock on the mantlepiece showed her that she had at least an hour to make the most of her looks before he reached the house, probably longer. He was taking what was colloquially known as the 'banana route', as the trams as often as not were noted for coming along in bunches and it depended on which end of the bunch you caught. Peggy had thoughtfully left the kettle on a low light on the stove and soon Louise had a soapy basin of scented water ready for her ablutions.

Upstairs she towelled her hair and, while it dried out, she carefully applied the little face powder she wore. Glad that she had natural blonde curls, and her hair was rarely a problem, she twisted strands around two of her fingers and brushed and worked at it until it fell to her shoulders in soft waves. Standing in her camisole and slip, she examined herself in the full-length wardrobe mirror and sighed. She didn't think of herself as a beauty, far from it, but the image reflected back at her told her she didn't look too bad either; that she was far from being a plain Jane. Carefully removing from the wardrobe the new outfit she had bought during her lunch hour on Saturday, she held it against her body and turned this way and that. She was pleased with what she saw.

Hanging it on a hanger over the top of the door, she appraised it, nodding with pleasure. It still looked as good to her now as when she had first set eyes on it in the shop and worth every penny. Sometimes she bought things in the sales that she regretted spending the money on, but not this suit. It was perfect in every way. Guilt began to sneak into her mind but she resolutely pushed it away. Conor never mentioned how well his savings were going towards their wedding so why should she worry when she bought something she liked but thought a mite too expensive? After all, the wedding seemed as far away as ever. If at all!

Actually she had got a bargain. She and Deirdre had heard that a shop said to specialise in clothes for the upper classes, at the bottom of Ann Street, was having an end of season sale. Hope in their hearts, they had walked down the street and stood outside the premises. It had a small frontage with a Dickensian-styled window either side of the door. One window was graced with a beautiful white bridal gown, displayed to full advantage with all the trimmings. In the other a bright red classical evening gown with matching shoes and handbag was on show. There was no sign of a price tag to be seen.

Louise whispered in Deirdre's ear, 'They don't show the price tags. Afraid we'll run a mile if we see them. Do you think we should even bother going in? It'll probably cost an arm and leg to buy anything in there.'

'The owners probably don't want to scare off us working-class people.' Nodding towards the coming and going through the door, Deirdre said, 'Seeing as we're here we might as well join them. We can always look but we don't have to buy, do we?'

Inside, they were surprised at how far back the shop extended. Neither of them had been in here before because they knew that the prices would be well beyond their pockets . . . but during a sale, who knows? With a bit of luck they just might pick up a bargain.

There were rows of rails with cut-price outfits. Ignoring the beautiful new arrivals, they made their way along to the sale rails at the far end of the shop, their eyes nearly popping out of their sockets at the quality of the clothes and how much they had been reduced. None of your old rubbish here. The shop was packed, and no wonder. Items were disappearing from under their very noses even as they stood contemplating them and queues were forming outside the changing rooms. It was as if Christmas had come early.

Deirdre reached for a skirt to look at, but an arm thrusting between her and Louise grabbed it before she could make up her mind, causing her to nudge her friend and hiss, 'If you see anything, anything at all, that you fancy, just grab them and if they're suitable we can try them on and decide which we like best. Otherwise we'll get nothing here.'

Louise laughed aloud when her friend pushed a girl to one side and practically lifted a dress from under her nose.

Deirdre turned fiercely and snapped, 'What? If

we don't push and shove like the rest of them all the good stuff will be gone and we'll get nothing.'

In the face of her wrath, Louise took a backward step, inadvertently landing on the toes of someone behind her.

'Alright,' she gasped. 'You lead the way and I'll follow.'

Over her shoulder she apologised to the owner of the trampled toes and received a dirty look for her trouble.

Now, smiling happily, Louise fingered the material of the skirt. She knew little of quality clothes but to her it felt like what she imagined a fine worsted material would feel. Whatever, it was certainly the latest style in the spring collection, and with the uncertain Irish weather, and the cut of the outfit, it would be suitable for some time to come. Furthermore it was the colour that suited her best, a pale jade.

Two buttons that could have passed as items of jewellery, they were so ornate, secured the front of the waistband where the skirt wrapped snugly around her small waist and hung perfectly on her slim hips when she secured the buttons. The matching top was a fine lawn material with long sleeves and small buttons to match those on the skirt. Lawn she did recognise; at one time she had thought it was solely used for the making of handkerchiefs. Far from it. Bill McCartney had bought her mother a lawn blouse for Christmas. Louise had been green with envy, thinking how lucky her mother was with this new man in her life, and her new baby, while Louise had to content herself with running the family home her mother had deserted. Life was so unfair, she thought. Now she was the proud owner of this classy little number.

When Louise next looked in the mirror dressed in all her finery, she gasped with delight. She looked so different. The pale green colour made her skin glow and the style suited her to perfection. She looked so elegant. As she stood there gazing at her image, George Carson came into her mind and she wished she was going to that club in Joy's Entry with him. This suit was tailored for showing her off in all the right places. It was so flattering. Instead she was sure that Conor and she would settle down on the settee at home and strive to keep up a sensible conversation. Why had she bothered going to all this trouble just to sit all night on a bloody sofa? The excitement of what lay in store for her was almost unbearable, she thought bitterly.

Everything was so different from what it used to be like. At the beginning she and Conor could talk all evening without getting bored and there would be plenty of cuddles and kisses in between. Nothing to worry about but enough to keep their love for each other alive and ticking over nicely.

Now, Conor would spend the whole evening afraid of giving her a good old-fashioned kiss in case they got carried away. Why was the onus always on her? Why did she feel ashamed for wanting more?

A knock at the door brought her out of her reverie and she slowly descended the stairs, straightening her skirt as she went. A smile on her face, she opened the outer door as she tried to compose herself. Conor was beginning to get on her nerves the way he was acting lately and she didn't know how to greet him any more.

Conor was picking up his holdall from the pavement as he raised his eyes to hers. His mouth fell open as he drew himself upright and gawped at her. He stood there motionless, rooted to the spot, until her voice welcomed him in.

Pleased at his reaction, Louise said, 'For heaven's sake close your mouth, Conor, and come in. You look like the village eejit standing there.' Maybe the effort was worthwhile after all, she thought, if it can have such an impact on him. He really did look bowled over.

Conor slowly crossed the threshold, kicking the outer door closed behind him. Feeling unusually nervous, she moved to stand in front of the fireplace. His bag dropped heavily to the floor and Conor slowly approached her, his eyes roaming all over her body. Placing a hand on each shoulder, he gazed into her eyes.

'You look beautiful, Louise. And that blouse really becomes you.'

'Thank you, kind sir,' she said demurely and released herself from his hands, expecting him to hold and kiss her. A chaste kiss, mind. But no! Well, at least he liked the blouse. She supposed that was something to be grateful for. Moving away, she said, 'Sit yourself down and I'll make you something to eat. You must be starving after that long journey.'

Still in a daze, he watched her head for the scullery, then with a raised hand called out, 'Hold on a minute, love.'

She turned and stared at him, eyebrows lifted. 'Yes?'

'You can't cook and sit about in all that finery. It wouldn't be right. Or am I jumping the gun? Have you something planned for this evening?'

'No.' She laughed. 'I just want to show off my new outfit to you.'

'Is there still a dance on Wednesday night over in St Paul's Hall?'

Her heart fluttered. How she would dearly love to go to a dance, even one in the parish hall. Her nod said that, yes, there was.

'Do you fancy going over for an hour or so?'

'I'd love that very much, so I would. I'll fetch my stole.'

Without more ado she raced upstairs and in a

few minutes reappeared with a soft crocheted stole. It was the one her grannie had crocheted for her when she had been bridesmaid at Mary and Johnnie's wedding. No way was she going to wear her old coat over her beautiful new outfit. Besides, it was a lovely evening and they hadn't far to walk.

As usual the hall was quite crowded. The dance there was a favourite midweek break for the youth of the parish. Louise handed her stole into the cloakroom and obtained a ticket for it. She noticed that Peggy was there with Rose Smith and, trailed by a proud Conor, she headed towards the girls, who were seated against one wall. They were discussing some boys across the dance floor when Peggy looked up to see her sister and Conor approaching.

Jumping to her feet, she cried, 'When did you get that suit? It's gorgeous, so it is. Could I borrow it next week, Louise?' she asked with a sly little smile, knowing full well she had a better chance of borrowing the crown jewels. But then again, nothing ventured, nothing gained.

Knowing that she was becoming the centre of attraction, Louise did a little pirouette, causing more friends to come over and admire the suit. Conor couldn't hide his resentment and Louise was pleased at the way he glared when some of the lads she knew smiled and flirted with her.

As far as dancing was concerned, Louise could do no wrong in Conor's arms. He was a terrific dancer, even more so since he had moved to Birmingham. Aware that Conor was probably regretting his impulsive offer to take her to this dance, Louise felt somewhat guilty at all the attention bestowed on her. She'd had her fun, pleased at the effect her suit had caused, and suggested that they could leave early and call in to see Mary's new baby on the way home. Conor agreed a bit too eagerly. Although he wouldn't admit it for the world, he was extremely jealous of all the attention Louise was getting and was only too happy leaving the dance earlier than anticipated.

They strolled arm in arm along Cavendish Street to Violet Street where her brother lived. The parlour light was on and, with two young children in mind, Conor ignored the knocker and tapped lightly on the window. The blind was lifted slightly, then they heard someone enter the hall and the outer door opened.

Johnnie greeted them quietly and ushered them inside towards the parlour. 'Mary's upstairs with Michael but the baby's in here.' He turned his head and gave them a warning look. Not knowing what this meant, Louise entered the room with a puzzled frown. Once in the parlour she soon found out the reason. They had picked the same night to visit as Mary's brother.

Louise glanced at Conor for direction. He had vowed that he would never stay under the same roof ever again as Liam Gilmore. He avoided her eye. Louise wanted to turn and leave, but didn't want to offend Johnnie. After all, it wasn't her brother's fault. They had arrived without any warning.

Watched anxiously by Johnnie, she nodded, acknowledging Liam. Taking his cue from her he rose to his feet and introduced his companion. 'Louise, Conor, this is a friend of mine, Brenda McIlroy.'

They both nodded. Brenda rose and, smiling pleasantly, offered her hand to Louise. 'Nice to meet you, Louise.'

Louise returned her warm handshake. 'Same here, Brenda.'

Aware of Conor's reluctance, Liam's face showed some relief at Louise's coolness. He was quick to inform Louise that Brenda was one of the best. 'I can't believe she's willing to put up with me.' Obviously Brenda didn't know anything about Liam's past, or his assault on Louise. She was looking warily from one to the other of them, thinking that she had missed something. 'I'm a changed man these days, Louise.' Liam's voice held a plea.

Although Conor had remained silent during this exchange, he had no intention of being civil to

Liam Gilmore. He had been the cause of too much damage and pain in Conor's life, especially when he and his cronies attacked Conor, leaving him hospitalised.

The baby chose that minute to make herself heard and Louise moved swiftly to the cot.

'Oh, she's beautiful. Come and take a look at her, Conor.'

Glad of the chance to ignore the couple, Conor joined her by the cradle and leaned close to see the infant. Louise took the opportunity to find out what he would like to do. 'It's your call, I'll go along with whatever you decide,' she whispered.

'I'd like to leave now, Louise. I'm sorry but I can't tolerate that reprobate.'

'Don't worry, love. I understand.'

The baby continued to cry and Louise lifted her gently from the cradle. 'Hush, my wee, angel, hush,' she crooned. Over the child's head she caught Conor's eye. 'Her name is Angela. Isn't that nice?'

'She'll probably be a real tomboy,' he jested.

More cries erupted and Johnnie carefully took the baby from Louise's arms. 'I'd better take her up to Mary.' He shushed the baby and said, 'She obviously needs a feed. Mary must have fallen asleep up there. She was dead beat. I won't be a minute. Sit yourselves down. Or put the kettle on and make a cuppa, Louise. You know where everything is.'

Conor quickly interrupted him. 'Thanks, but we won't be staying, Johnnie. I'll call in to see you and Mary before I go back. Goodnight, everyone,' he said suddenly to no one in particular and stepped into the hall without a glance in Liam's direction. Making her farewells, Louise was quick to follow.

Louise clung to Conor's arm as they made their way home. 'I'm sorry. I had no idea Liam Gilmore would be there tonight. I haven't set eyes on him since that time at Johnnie's wedding reception when he attacked me out in the backyard.'

'I suppose we should really forgive and forget, but for the life of me, I can't stand the man. I can't even bear to be in his company; I don't even want to be in the same room as him. And I don't see why I should, just to please others.'

'You're right, love. I've managed to avoid him all this time. Mind you, he suffered for his assault on you and his father has, I think, kept a tight rein on him ever since. Mary actually thought big Mike would have thrown him out of the house, but I expect Mrs Gilmore wouldn't hear tell of it. He's the apple of her eye, you know. Some apple, eh?'

'Aye, probably a crab apple,' he retorted with a titter.

Conor slowed his step and turned her to face him.

'Listen, Louise, there's no need to make excuses for that piece of trash. If I do decide to settle down here I suppose I'll have to learn to pass myself in his company if he happens to be there. Until then I won't give him the time of day.'

'Actually, I was surprised to see him there tonight,' Louise confided. 'Our Johnnie can't stand him either, but he is Mary's brother – blood and water and all that – and her mother and father have been so good to them. Johnnie has to put on a show for their benefit. To be truthful, from what I hear Liam is a changed lad these days. I think he bit off more than he could chew when the boyos found out that they were being blamed for something he and his cronies did. They all deserved the hiding they got. They won't do anything like that again in a hurry.'

'I was very lucky the lads found out that they were getting the blame or my life wouldn't have been worth living. *Me* a grass? I ask you.' He smiled at the thought. 'I still think that Liam is a bad apple and I want nothing to do with him. Leopards and spots come to mind.'

The words 'settle down here' warmed Louise's heart. Surely this was a good indication of his future plans. He cupped her face in his hands and kissed her tenderly. Eagerly she kissed him back and they continued on their way home. At her door when Louise unlocked it, Conor said, 'I'd better not come in tonight, love. It's late and your ones will be here soon and I'm very tired from travelling all day. You don't mind, do you?'

Turning her face away to hide the hurt she was feeling, she managed to keep her voice light. 'Of course I don't mind. You must get your rest. See you tomorrow.' She swung suddenly away from him and, pushing the door open, stepped into the hall.

'Hey, hold on a minute. What time tomorrow?'

Afraid of losing her self-control she surged ahead, opening the vestibule door and abruptly saying over her shoulder, 'Whatever time you can manage to fit me in. But remember, I've to go to work. I can't afford to take time off when you decide that we must spend some time together.'

Conor stepped back on the pavement, startled, as the heavy outer door was slammed in his face. He gazed at it for some moments, then giving it a kick looked furtively around to see if anyone was watching. The street was empty.

Anger shot through him as he headed back to his own house. What the hell was wrong with her now? What had he done wrong? He loved Louise but didn't know how to please her any more. It was getting to the point where he wasn't looking forward to coming home for a few days. It was more like an endurance test. He shouldn't have bothered his head. However, with the temptations he was experiencing in Birmingham, he needed to remind himself how much he loved Louise, that she was the only one for him. His head down deep in thought, he almost blundered into Tommy McGuigan as he barged down the street.

Tommy reared back in alarm, his arms raised to save himself. Then grabbing hold of Conor's forearm, he cried, 'Conor! Have you gone blind?'

'Sorry, Tommy. I didn't see you there. I was in a dream.'

'More like a bloody nightmare with that scowl on your face if you ask me. You're sure in a terrible hurry. Is my Louise coming after you with a rolling pin or something?'

Conor was in no mood for debating with Tommy McGuigan. He gave him a sickly smile. 'Yeah! Something like that.'

They exchanged a few words and went their different ways. It was only when Conor entered the house and his mother was plumping up the cushions and fussing about the room that he began to wonder just where Tommy McGuigan had spent his evening.

Meanwhile Tommy was thanking the Lord for his close shave. Cissie would never forgive him if Louise heard about their carry-on before he and Cissie had a chance to explain their new-found friendship. However, Conor didn't appear very astute at the moment. He was unlikely to twig that Tommy had just left his mother's house.

* * *

Deirdre couldn't comprehend why Louise was so grumpy next morning at work. Hadn't Conor got home? Hadn't she asked for Friday off this week so that she would have two whole days with him before he returned to Birmingham? Had he perhaps been delayed? Louise hadn't given her a chance to question her, bustling about as if the shop was on fire and the books needed instant evacuation. She hadn't even looked her straight in the eye all morning.

First chance she got, Deirdre tentatively questioned her friend. 'Did Conor get back all right yesterday?'

Louise tossed her head, squinted at her and curtly replied, 'Yes! Why shouldn't he?'

'I thought maybe because you've been in such a foul mood all morning that he hadn't made it,' Deirdre snapped back. 'Pardon me for showing some friendly concern.' She turned abruptly on her heel and walked the length of the shop, looking for a customer to attend to.

Louise sighed as her eyes followed Deirdre's progress. There had been no need for her to rush away like that; two assistants were already down there. Louise hadn't meant any offence. She would make it up to her friend at lunchtime.

As they ate their sandwiches in the staff room, Louise filled Deirdre in on the happenings of the previous night. She described how she had dressed up in her new suit to impress Conor and that he had taken her to the dance in the St Paul's Hall. Relieved to hear that Conor was home, Deirdre became more interested in the impact of Louise's new suit.

'That was kind of him. Did your suit go down well?'

Glad to change the subject, Louise gushed, 'Great! I love it! I felt like a model and Conor was really bowled over with it. As I said, we went to the dance over in St Paul's because he said it wouldn't be right to be all dressed up to just sit around at home. Everybody was looking at us. Peggy had the gall to ask me if she could borrow it next week. The cheeky bitch. And I think Conor got a wee bit jealous of all the attention I was getting.'

'Surely not. He must have been proud as Punch.'

Deirdre knew nothing about the things that had happened to Louise and the McGuigans; of the time her mother had betrayed them and ran off with Bill McCartney, long before Louise joined Eason's. Not wanting to let out secrets that were best kept in the family, she finished her tale on a flat note. 'He didn't come in with me last night. Not even a goodnight kiss at the door, so to be truthful, Deirdre, I don't know where I stand with him at the minute. Perhaps taking me to the dance

258

was a way of softening me up. You know, to let me down gently.'

'Are you seeing him tonight?'

'That's just it. We didn't even make any arrangements.'

'Oh, come on now, Louise, you must have done something to annoy him, surely.'

'Nothing that I'm aware of. But how's about yourself? Have you had a chance to wear your new dress and shoes?'

'Alas, I haven't had anywhere special to go to yet. But I don't mind waiting. I'm delighted with them, so I am.'

'Ah well, time to get back to the grindstone.'

'Never worry. He'll be here before the day is over.'

Louise hoped her friend's crystal ball was crystal clean.

16

Thursday was usually a slack day in the shop, the calm before the storm, leading up to the hustle and bustle of the weekend. Slack or not, Louise always found something interesting to do. She never tired of sorting out books into alphabetical order after they had been left lying haphazardly about by browsing customers, trying out different arrangements on the shelves. She was very artistic and had a natural flair for it. Al Murray, who missed nothing that went down in his store, was aware of Louise's remarkable aptitude for this work without supervision and had put her in charge of arranging and ordering the bookshelves. She soon became known by the endearing sobriquet 'the arranger'. But today time seemed to stand still as Louise worked with one eye on the clock, hoping that Conor would put in an appearance. At half past three, doubting that he would come so late in the day, she was amazed when out of the blue she saw George Carson push his way through the front door and gaze around. He didn't often visit the shop midweek and she wondered if he had called in to see her. It would be so infuriating if he had plans to take her to the club; what with Conor being home, she would have to decline.

She was immediately ashamed of herself. Conor had made a point of coming to visit her, enduring that long and wearisome journey just to spend three days with her. Whether to keep their romance alive or to call it off, she wasn't sure, but whilst he was here she must give him her undivided attention, find out what his plans were. He had seemed overwhelmed to see her last night, telling her she looked beautiful in her new suit, but then he had spoiled everything by leaving her standing frustrated at the door. So who knew what was going on in his mind? And so far today he still hadn't put in an appearance. Was he holding a grudge against her? She hoped not. Things were awkward enough between them at the moment.

Catching sight of her, George smiled and raised a hand in greeting. 'Good afternoon, Miss McGuigan.' He grinned when he reached her and fluttering her eyelashes she smiled demurely back.

She curtsied and said, 'What can I do for you, sir?'

Taking his cue from her, he pretended to remove a top hat, hold it against his chest and bow slightly in her direction. 'I ordered a book by Louisa May Alcott. It is titled *Little Women*. Would you be so kind as to see if it has been delivered yet,' he said politely as if she didn't already know all about it. Hadn't she helped him choose the book?

'If you'd like to walk this way, sir, I'll check for you.' So this was the reason why George was here today. Silly her.

'If I walked that way people would start talking about me.' He tittered.

Ignoring his gag, Louise went to the place where reservations were kept and soon she was holding the book up for George's inspection.

He nodded and dropping the act she laughed. 'Follow me and I'll wrap it for you, George.'

He followed closely behind her to another counter where fancy wrapping paper was displayed to tempt buyers. 'As it's a present, George, would you like to purchase a nice sheet of wrapping paper?'

'It is, yes. And yes, I'll have a sheet of that paper with the pink dots. As you already know it's for my god-daughter and pink is her favourite colour.'

'It is a lovely story. She should enjoy reading it.'

'Yes, I think she will.'

Anxious to know if he had any news from Trevor

262

Pollock, she changed tack. 'Have you heard anything from Trevor since we last spoke?'

He looked uncomfortable. 'No. He only writes now and again. We're not like you women, you know. I for one find writing a right bind. I never know what to put in a letter.'

Suddenly George paused. Louise looked up to see what had caught his attention and he said quietly, 'You never said that Conor was home.'

'Eh?' Then following his gaze she saw Conor near the door. Flustered, she snapped, 'Why should I?' She immediately regretted her curtness.

He straightened up and his voice was clipped. 'True, why should you indeed.'

'I'm sorry.' She made to touch his arm but quickly withdrew her hand, afraid Conor would see and misunderstand. 'Well, I haven't seen you since I learned that he was coming over. He only arrived late last night.'

George noted the gesture and his lips tightened in a straight line. 'I was going to ask you out to the club tomorrow night. It's a special gala night and there will be a cabaret on. A terrific singer will top the bill.' He grimaced. 'I suppose that's now out of the question.'

George paid for the book and thanked her. Louise's heart sank as she saw her chance of showing off her lovely suit at the club go up in smoke.

One eye on the advancing Conor, who was taking his time, stopping to look at books and idling about, George asked, 'How long is he home for?'

'Three days.' Conor caught her eye and she could see that he was upset. 'Please go now, George. I don't want to give him anything to gripe about.'

George scowled at her from under gathered brows and, turning abruptly away, did as she requested without as much as a thank-you or a goodbye.

The two men met in the middle aisle, watched by an agitated Louise and half the staff, it seemed to her. Deirdre could hardly serve her customer, she was so agog. There were times when Louise couldn't see her friend far enough. She was so transparent, just hadn't a clue how to be discreet.

Louise saw another customer enter the shop and head for the children's corner near her. Al Murray had come onto the shop floor and, glad not to be caught out standing twiddling her thumbs, she went to greet the new customer.

It was some time before she was free. Conor, who had been prowling about, came quickly to her side, a book in his hand. He glared at her and seethed. 'Does he come in here a lot?'

Taking offence at his attitude, she said, 'Who are you speaking of?' She hoped she had gotten her grammar right. Lately, sometimes it was hell on wheels talking to Conor. He knew it was a sore point with her but he still continued to correct her speech, making her feel inferior. The girls over in Birmingham must be beautiful English speakers. But who would expect an Irish ex-mill girl with no great education to get her grammar right and pronounce her words correctly? Who indeed?

'You know who I'm talking about!'

Worried that she might indeed have gotten her grammar wrong, and not wanting to show any signs of discord, with Al Murray on the prowl, she reached over and took the book he was holding. For the benefit of those watching she tapped it with a finger, pretending that was what they were talking about. 'If you mean George Carson, yes, he does. As you may recall his uncle is manager here and George buys a lot of books.' She nodded towards the book. 'Now do you intend buying this or should I just stand here hugging it?'

He nodded and for the first time seemed to notice her grim attitude. 'Am I annoying you, Louise?'

'Not at all.' She was now examining the book. Another foreign language book, only this one was German and very expensive. 'I see you're treating your sister again.'

He looked startled, caught on the hop as it were. She didn't usually ask leading questions and he hadn't meant to buy the book. He stuttered a bit and admitted, 'Ah. Ah . . . A friend asked me to get it for her.'

Her lips tightened. She must be a very close friend if he was willing to buy *her* such a costly gift. He should be saving his money for an engagement ring if he intended marrying her. Filled with indignation, she said brusquely, 'Sorry but I can't let you have a discount on it. Pity, since it's so expensive.'

'Did George get a discount on his?' he retorted slyly.

'His wasn't as expensive as this one. Besides, he buys a lot of books but refuses to ask for a discount on any of his purchases on account of his uncle being the manager. He doesn't want to start tongues wagging and put Mr Murray in a difficult position.'

'I'm surprised. But then, I suppose it's easy to be extravagant when you're rolling in it as he seems to be.'

Conor was on the point of picking up a sheet of silver giftwrapping paper but ignoring his effort Louise stuffed the book in a paper bag bearing the device of Eason's and pushed it across the counter to him. She was livid with him for slighting George. Wasn't he buying some girl an expensive book? The look on her face warned him not to argue. Without another word he reached into his inner pocket for his wallet and extracting some money handed it to her.

She counted the change deliberately out into his hand, coin by coin. 'Thank you, sir. I hope your friend appreciates this lovely gift. It's not many that are talented enough to read German.' Then she got a sly dig in. 'But then, you probably know your friend well enough to be aware of her talents. Now if you'll excuse me there is another customer waiting to be served. Good afternoon, sir.' Leaving him standing open-mouthed, she headed for a woman with a young boy, browsing in the children's corner.

Conor couldn't believe his ears. She had been deep in conversation with Carson, and kept right on talking to him even though she knew he was pottering about in the background waiting. And now she couldn't spare him a minute. What did she take him for, some kind of eejit? The book had been a spur-of-the-moment idea while he was keeping an eye on George Carson. His sister's friend had asked him to check the prices over here and he had intended getting Louise's opinion on it. Now he was landed with a pricey book that he could barely afford and which Louise obviously thought he had bought for another woman. With a baleful glare in her direction – which went unnoticed as she was busy with the lady customer and her child – he turned on his heel and left the shop.

Louise fretted the rest of the afternoon. There could be no going back now. She had cooked her goose well and truly. Conor was unlikely to ask her out again. Who knows, she thought, perhaps it would be for the best and she wiped a defiant tear from the corner of her eye.

As she left the shop with Deirdre at closing time she got a shock to find a sheepish-looking Conor waiting outside for her. He was so stubborn and proud at times that she had doubted he would ever show his face again, but was relieved that he had. Deirdre, who had been fishing for information about the day's shenanigans, now slowed down alongside her but with a warning glance Louise bade her farewell and waved her on her way. With a snort, Deirdre stalked off, her bad humour apparent.

Approaching Conor with a wry smile, Louise said softly, 'Sorry about that carry-on earlier, Conor. I'd no control over the situation, you know. After all, I only work there, and am duty bound to serve whoever comes in.'

'No, it's I who should apologise. I shouldn't have loitered about when you were serving George Carson. It must have been uncomfortable for you. Although, I must confess, I was intrigued at how deep you were in conversation with him. Was it anything important?' He stepped back, hands spread wide, palms down, gently patting the air as if trying to take off, and bit his lower lip. 'Excuse me. There I go . . . being nosy again. Please forget I said that, Louise.'

For a moment her mind went blank and she couldn't even think what she and George had talked about, then Trevor sprang to mind. 'George was saying that Trevor hinted that Cathie might be expecting a baby and I was devastated that she hadn't mentioned it to me in her last letter.' Louise knew this wasn't true as George had already discussed this with her in the club. But she had to say something to Conor.

Conor relaxed. News like that would explain their apparent closeness when he entered the shop before they were aware of his presence. Louise still worried about her friend.

'That's awful news. Or . . . perhaps they're pleased about it?'

'If Cathie had been pleased I'd have been the first to know. Trevor told George that they didn't know for sure but that Cathie is late. She must be in an awful state with nobody to turn to over there.'

'Well, one makes one's bed and one must lie on it.' Loath to waste time talking about Cathie, he quickly changed the subject. 'Where would you like to go this evening?'

Louise hadn't been giving their outing much thought, what with thinking Conor would not want to bother with her any more. 'I've heard the Coliseum has a good film showing. *The Ten Commandments*. Theodore Roberts plays Moses and Estelle Taylor plays his sister Miriam. It should be great with those two in it.'

'Yes, I know. I saw the poster from the tram on my way down the Grosvenor Road. It should be good. It's directed by Cecil B. DeMille,' Conor replied.

'And the accompanist in the Coliseum is smashing as well,' Louise gushed. They had reached Castle Junction and Louise glanced down High Street at the Albert clock. 'We'll have to hurry if we don't want to miss the start of the film. Then we'll have a couple of hours to ourselves afterwards.'

Conor was silent and Louise covertly watched him from the corner of her eye. She could almost see him struggle to find words to say. Did he not want to spend any time alone with her? She decided to help him out of his quandary.

'Look, Conor, I won't mind if you want to go home early to spend some time with your mother.' It seemed ludicrous to her, knowing how he felt about his mother, that he could possibly agree but she was giving him the excuse to back out of coming back to her house after the film.

He swung round, forcing her to stop abruptly and face him. 'No! No. You've got it all wrong. You see, Mother wants me to bring you in tonight for tea.'

Louise knew that her jaw had dropped and snapped it shut. 'Why?' she cried.

'I have no idea. But if you could see your way to humouring her, it would get her off my back for the rest of the week.'

Louise was shaking her head violently. 'No, I'm sorry, Connor, but no.'

'Please, Louise?'

'Conor, you don't have to go to these extremes to avoid being alone with me. Just don't bother coming near me again. OK?'

He had eased her into a shop doorway at the bottom of Castle Street to make his plea but she thrust herself free and stamped towards the tram stop, cheeks crimson with mortification at the way people in the queue, having nothing better to do, were staring at her.

Conor joined her and stood at her side, silent. When the tram came, they managed to pile on to the platform and hung on as it moved off up Castle Street. People shuffled inside to make room for them but she still refused to meet his eyes as he willed her to look at him. Leaning close, he whispered for her ears alone, 'I'm sorry. I didn't think you would mind. A half-hour will do, I'm sure. Please, Louise.'

She ignored him and he lapsed into stony silence until they reached their destination. She surged ahead of him off the tram, almost coming a cropper in her haste to get away. He gripped her elbow firmly to steady her and assist her across the road.

At the corner of Springview Street he stopped and brought her roughly to a standstill.

'Louise, none of this is of my choosing. Mam was insistent and I thought you would be pleased if she had a change of heart towards you. I said I would bring you in for a short while, but since you're so against it I'll make your excuses. Just don't let it spoil our bit of a break, please?'

'I don't know what your mother's playing at, Conor. She still thinks that I'm not good enough for you. It will remain the same even if we do eventually get married. I really do think we should call it a day.' She glanced down at her hands and rued that she hadn't even got a ring to throw at him. Not that she would throw it. No, she would hand it to him like a lady and then walk away, head high, with her dignity intact. Well, she could still do that. She turned and stalked up the street, her head in the air.

In spite of nosy neighbours, he quickly followed her and pulled her back and into his arms. 'Don't say that! Forget I ever mentioned my mother wanting us to call in tonight. When we get married we will buy a house on the other side of town. Maybe the Shore Road or somewhere, OK? I'll see you to your door and I'll pick you up at half six. The big show starts at seven.'

Louise was bemused as they walked the rest of the way. Those marvellous words 'When we get married' had worked their magic. Outside her door she relented and lifted her head. 'I'll come in tonight . . . but don't you think I'll make a habit of it, Conor O'Rourke.'

His relief was so heartfelt it was almost palpable and she was glad that she had relented. 'Thanks, love. See you later.' A peck on the cheek and he was gone.

Pleased to be reprieved, Conor hurried back down the street to grab a quick bite and get ready for his night out.

His mother was in the scullery. 'I've the pan on. Sausage, bacon and egg, and a couple slices of soda, all right?'

'Fine, Mother.'

Cissie came to the scullery door. 'Did you manage to persuade her to come in for a cup of tea tonight?'

'Louise. Her name is Louise, Mother. Yes, I did. And why are you so persistent? You never bothered before.'

'I have something important to tell her and I know she will be pleased. Everything will be different from now on. Trust me, Conor.' She disappeared back into the scullery.

He watched her retreating figure and wished with all his heart that he could trust her but he had long ago found out that his mother was very unpredictable. He couldn't even think of anything she could do or say to win Louise over; he could but hope.

As expected, the film was outstanding and the organist played his part well: either great dramatic passages or sad emotional ones, whatever was needed. However, with the worry of dropping in for tea with Conor's mother Louise could not give the film the attention it deserved. She sat in the doldrums, wondering just what Cissie O'Rourke had in mind. It would be nothing pleasant, she could bet, unless Cissie had had a sudden change of heart and for the life of her Louise could not image this being the case. Would whatever Cissie had planned come between her and Conor? Possibly. She hoped not, not now he was talking about marriage.

During the film Conor sat holding her hand, aware of her distress but finding no words to ease her anxiety. He could only pray that his mother was not going to create a scene. That was something she was very good at! What she could possibly say that would please Louise was beyond his ken. She had never once tried to get to know Louise.

They left the cinema in silence. It was a dry night, the sky above a clear dark blue dotted with stars, and they decided to walk home, both wanting to delay the inevitable visit to his mother's house.

When they eventually arrived at the door, Louise turned to him.

'I'm dreading this, you know. So don't be surprised if I should suddenly jump up and run out of the house.'

'To be truthful, so am I. I'm quaking in my boots. But please take anything she says with a pinch of salt.'

Straightening her shoulders, Louise sighed and nodded at him. 'Let's enter the lion's den.'

Cissie answered their knock immediately as if she had been already standing behind the door waiting for them. 'Louise, come in, dear. Nice to see you. You look lovely. Thank you for coming to see me. Conor, please take Louise's coat.'

Pulling her coat closer around her, Louise said, 'No thank you. If you don't mind I'll keep it on. I won't be staying too long.' Louise didn't want to be hanging about waiting for her coat if she should need to make a hasty escape.

Cissie had an occasional table pulled forward and chairs arranged within reach of it.

Louise noted that as well as a plate of sandwiches and another of biscuits, four cups and saucers were set out. Her eyes met Conor's and canting her head towards the table she mouthed 'four'. He followed her gaze and shrugged. He had no idea there would be another guest.

'The kettle is boiled but I'll wait until Tommy

comes before I make the tea. Is that OK with you?'

Cissie kept her head down and tried to hide the smile that played around the corners of her mouth. She could imagine only too well what a bombshell she had just delivered.

Louise opened her mouth but no sound came out. It was Conor who got his vocal cords working first. 'You don't mean . . .' His voice trailed off in disbelief.

Cissie beamed at him. 'Louise's father? Of course I do. What other Tommy do we all know? I told you I had some good news for you.' A footstep in the hall and a tap on the door caught her attention. 'Ah, that will be him now. Come on in, Tommy. We've been waiting for you.'

The door opened wider and Tommy McGuigan, taking off his cap, stepped into the room. He gazed at the figures, frozen like a tableau in stone. Cissie, with a big wide smile on her face, seemed in command. As for his daughter and Conor, they looked totally flabbergasted and eyed him as if he had two heads and horns.

His gaze returned to Cissie. 'What's going on here, eh?'

'Nothing. I asked Conor to invite Louise in for a cuppa so that we could have a chat. I haven't said anything yet. I wanted you here to back me up. Make yourselves comfortable while I brew the tea.'

With a nod of acknowledgement at the silent couple, Tommy disobeyed her order and, following Cissie into the scullery, closed the door behind them.

Stupefied, Louise leaned close to Conor and hissed, 'Do you know what this is all about?'

He still looked in a state of utter shock and could only manage to shake his head.

In the scullery another heated conversation was taking place. Keeping his voice low, Tommy said fiercely, 'And just what do you want me to back you up on? Eh, woman?'

'Why the plan you and I discussed the other evening. I thought that since Conor was home, now would be as good a time as any to tell them.'

'Tell them what? I don't know what the bloody hell you're talking about.'

'We sat out there the other night and I said wouldn't it be great if you were able to move in with me. And you smiled your agreement.' Cissie glared at him. 'Don't you dare deny it, Tommy McGuigan.'

'I remember saying that.' Tommy did indeed recall it, as he had been hoping to have his way with her as a result. 'What has that to do with Conor and Louise?' He was at a loss to comprehend what she was ranting on about.

'Don't you see, Tommy? Now that we're having a relationship it is the right time to make arrangements.'

'What kind of arrangements are you talking about?' Tommy's heart dropped to his knees. 'I hope you haven't said anything to anybody about us?' His voice rose in horror at the thought and Cissie shushed him.

She was beginning to realise that she was making a mistake, forcing him to come out into the open about their affair. 'Just that we had something to tell them. I'm sure they'll be glad to know that they can get married and live in your house.' Cissie had lifted the kettle and was pouring water into the teapot whilst she argued with him. 'Here, make yourself useful. Carry this tray in and we can talk things over.'

'Oh, no you don't.' Tommy leaned into her face and shook his head angrily. 'I'm not ready to move in here. Let's settle for what we've got, Cissie. There's no need to rush things. My Louise will go bonkers if I leave the house. Think of the scandal, woman!'

Cissie drooped against the cupboard like a wilted flower. 'But I have already said we were making plans.'

'While we are having this bloody tea that you must have insisted they come in for, let me do the talking. Do you hear me? I won't be tied down before I'm ready. And that's final.'

Tommy opened the scullery door and picking up the tray laden with teapot, milk jug and sugar bowl, with a warning glance at Cissie, he returned to the kitchen. Somewhat crestfallen, she followed him.

His mind in a whirl, trying to figure a way out of this mess Cissie had landed him in, Tommy set the tray on the table and lifting the teapot made to pour the tea.

Cissie's voice caused him to pause. 'I'll do mother,' she said sharply.

Tommy's lips tightened but setting the teapot down he let her take over.

Louise sat, hands clasped tightly in her lap, wishing she hadn't allowed herself to be cajoled into coming here. But now she had to find out what was going on before she left. She had never in her life before known her da to be so embarrassed. Cissie had opened Pandora's box; now Louise wanted to see just what nasty secrets would be exposed.

17

Harry came through the door on Friday at teatime with an armful of lovely mixed flowers. He had bought them from the shop Johnnie's wife had worked in before their marriage. Situated on the corner of Milligan Street, it was noted for its wonderful floral displays and he had spent some time choosing them. He had come out of the shop still admiring their fragrance and colour, as well as much lighter in pocket than he expected. He then realised that he would have to walk up the Falls and Springfield Roads carrying them. Trying to look as inconspicuous as possible, he marched forth. He was fortunate enough to meet only a few of his mates who, as he had imagined they would, took the mickey out of him. Bearing the brunt of their barbed gags with as much dignity as he could muster, he carried on regardless. Finding Louise in the scullery, he held them up to get her attention.

'Hi, sis. I didn't think you'd be home yet. I was going to put these in water.' He glanced around the kitchen. 'Where's Conor?'

She came forward, wiping her hands on her apron. 'Oh, they're lovely, Harry. Are they for Hannah? Conor is calling for me later.'

Thrusting the flowers towards her, he mumbled shyly, 'No, they're for you, sis. Just to say thanks for all your help.'

Overwhelmed by his generosity, she took the flowers carefully from him. 'Ah, Harry, you shouldn't have. You'll need to start saving every penny you earn if you intend getting married. But thank you. Thank you very much. I really do appreciate them.' She sank her face close to the blooms and inhaled their perfume. 'They're gorgeous, so they are.'

'Oh, it will be a while yet before I can even think of marriage. I'm keeping it under my hat so don't you say anything to me da or Peggy. I don't want any sarky remarks from them. Besides I've still to win Liz round first.' His look became anxious. 'You were in bed early last night. Conor and you haven't fallen out, have you?'

'No, you're right there, Harry. That's something I've found out to my cost. The less anyone knows about your private business, the better. And no,

Conor and I are just fine. Don't you worry your head on that score.'

Not satisfied and sensing something was amiss, Harry sidled closer to Louise. 'Is anything wrong, sis?'

Louise had decided to keep quiet about the spectacle their da had made of himself last night. Half the time she hadn't been able to make head nor tail of what he was saying anyway. She realised that she shouldn't have bolted out of Cissie's house as she had, but the thought of another McGuigan scandal in the making didn't bear thinking about. They were still only now coming to terms with the last one.

She began remembering the upheaval caused by her mother's fall from grace and she felt consumed with worry. It had been a terrible time for all the family. They couldn't go through all that again: the shame, the spiteful gossip, the heartbreak. No, it would be intolerable.

Last night when the tea had been poured and Cissie had been coaxing them, in vain, to have a sandwich, Tommy had cleared his throat and in a voice that Louise barely recognised said, 'Tell me, what silly rumours has Cissie been filling your ears with?'

Cissie, her face like a beetroot, cried in denial, 'Come off it, Tommy, I haven't said anything untoward to them. And they aren't rumours. I was just going to tell them the truth. Explain how things stand between you and me. Is that so wrong?'

Coming out of her stupor, Louise managed to get her tongue working and cried in alarm, 'Are you trying to tell us that you two are having an affair?' Humiliated, she glared at Cissie. 'I don't believe you. Me da thinks you're a stuck up auld so-and-so and he wouldn't touch you with a bargepole. He said so himself. Didn't you, Da?' When her father failed to respond, she insisted, 'Admit it. It's the truth, isn't it? Didn't you say that, Da?'

Tommy, looking mortified, flailed about for something to say and save the situation, but before he could open his mouth, Conor beat him to it. Cissie was his mother after all and Louise was, in this instance, in the wrong. He wasn't pleased at the idea of Cissie and Tommy together but it takes two to tango and if they were indeed having an affair, then Tommy shouldn't welsh out on it and make a liar of his mother. Tommy should back Cissie if she was telling the truth. As far as Conor could see, his mother had done no wrong. Heaven knew she was no saint but he believed what she had just said and he felt duty bound to support her. With trepidation, he tried to reason with Louise.

'Here, hold on a minute. What if they are, eh, Louise? They're both consenting adults and free agents after all. It's none of our business what they get up to.'

Louise couldn't believe her ears. Conor was actually siding with them. 'No they're not! My da might be a consenting adult but he certainly isn't a free agent, so he isn't! Far from it. And what's more as a Catholic he can't get a divorce. And what about the rest of our family if he moves in here? How would I be able to keep a house going on our small wages?'

Glad of the chance to air her opinion, Cissie said, 'That's just it! You and Conor could live in your house. Think of it . . . you could get married sooner than expected.'

'We wouldn't want to live there! We would want a place of our own.' She refrained from adding, far away from the rest of you lot.

Affronted that Cissie and his daughter were taking things into their own hands, talking over him as if he wasn't there, Tommy rose to his feet. This was getting out of control. 'Look, girl, I can do anything I like!' he admonished Louise. Then, facing Cissie, 'As for you, it's not your decision.'

Seeing the chance to make her da see sense, Louise taunted him, 'You would be opening a can of worms, so you would. Think of it, Da. All the scandal about me ma and Bill McCartney would be raked up again and all because of you and her this time.' She nodded towards Cissie. 'I thought you hated this woman. You said so yourself. How would we be able to show our faces in public again, eh? Tell me that, if you moved in with her?'

'Look, Cissie is mistaken. I've no intention of causing a scandal. And I won't be moving in here or anywhere else for that matter. And we will continue to be very discreet as, you must admit, we have been so far, since there has been no talk about us. Has there? There's no need for anyone to know our business if we play our cards right.'

Louise was incredulous. 'I'm not going to stand here listening to any more of this drivel. I'm ashamed of you, Da, so I am.'

Three steps took her to the door and out through it. She raced up the street as if the devil himself was after her, hoping against hope that Conor would follow suit. He didn't.

She couldn't believe that Conor had stayed behind. Her face was awash with tears as she arrived at her front door and there was still no sign of him. Conor should be showing his allegiance to her. The house was empty. Once inside, running straight up the stairs, she undressed and shaking like a leaf got ready for bed. Imagine . . . she had never been to bed this early since she was a child. Sure in her heart that Conor would eventually show up, she kept her ears pricked. Not that she had any intentions of letting him in. Indeed, no!

But she needed to know that he cared for her; after all, she depended on him to support her. They needed to sit down and talk, and sort out this latest family saga between them.

In a way it was her own fault. There had been warning signs that her da was seeing someone and she should have made it her business to find out just who the mystery woman was. If she had, then she would have been prepared and could have nipped it in the bud. She would have tried to put a stop to it before Cissie O'Rourke got her claws into him well and truly.

How would this affair affect her and Conor? Her da had said that they would be discreet, so that meant he had no intentions of giving Cissie up. Maybe Cissie would show her da the door now that he had revealed how little he thought of her. Louise heard him come in a bit later, go into his room and quietly close the door. Shortly afterwards Peggy and Harry arrived home together. Louise had left her handbag hanging on the stair banister where it would easily be seen by whoever was last in so that they would know she was home and lock up for the night. Conor did not put in an appearance. Disappointment eating away at her, she curled up into the foetal position and pretended she was asleep when Peggy came to bed. But sleep eluded her for a long time and she was glad that she didn't have to get up for work the next morning.

And the rest of them could see to their own breakfasts for a change.

Harry watched with apprehension as different expressions chased each other over Louise's face. Alarmed at the apparent depth of her misery, he reached out and gripped her arm. 'What's wrong, Louise? Why are you so upset?'

She shook her head and managed a weak smile. 'Sorry. I was lost in a world of my own there.'

'I could see that. So tell me, what's happened to make you so miserable? Is it anything to do with Conor?'

'Not Conor. His mother.' Pulling herself together, she said, 'The others will be here soon. I'll tell you some other time. The dinner's ready. Sit down and I'll lift yours if you want to get away early. Meantime I'll put these lovely flowers in a vase.'

She reached over and kissed him on the cheek. He opened his mouth to speak but she was already heading for the scullery.

Conor was also down in the dumps. Reluctant to leave his mother alone with Tommy, and not wanting any more upsets, he had forced himself to stay behind and nibble at a sandwich and sip some tea while making desultory conversation. Once things had calmed down somewhat and he was sure it was safe to do so, he escaped upstairs to his bedroom. He had heard raised voices and sat perched on the edge of the bed in case he needed to intervene. The voices dropped to a mere indistinct murmur and shortly afterwards he heard Tommy leaving the house. Conor debated whether or not to go and see if Louise was all right but decided against it. She mightn't thank him for it. They could sort all that out tomorrow when they were alone.

Conor felt that he had let Louise down; that he should have sided with her. What must she be thinking of him? She would think that he was under his mother's thumb, that's what she'd think. A proper little mammy's boy. However, he knew that Tommy McGuigan had been abusive towards his wife, Nora, during their marriage and that was what had eventually driven her into the arms of Bill McCartney. The state Tommy was in tonight, there was no way he would leave his mother alone with him. In fact he was very much against Tommy McGuigan moving in with his mother, but that was out of his hands.

He would be at Louise's door first thing in the morning to eat humble pie and explain his reason for staying behind when she had stormed out of his house. He would try to make matters right between them.

After a lot of tossing and turning in bed he awoke with a blinding headache, probably caused by the tension of the previous night; it certainly wasn't a hangover. Huh! He should be so lucky. He washed and shaved before his mother awoke. When he heard her moving about upstairs he prepared a soft-boiled egg, tea and buttered a slice of bread. He was ashamed at her obvious gratitude when she came down the stairs and found her breakfast already on the table. Why had he never thought to make her breakfast before? Because he was a spoiled brat and she had no one to blame but herself for that. She never allowed him to do a hand's turn in the house. He would be no gift for any girl, let alone his Louise.

Sitting at the table, he furtively watched his mother as in silence she tentatively dipped a piece of bread in her egg. Granted, she was no oil painting but neither was she ugly. He would describe her as maybe just short of being pretty if he were asked. He wouldn't have thought her to be Tommy McGuigan's type but then again wasn't Tommy a changed man these days? How had she and Tommy ever gotten together? he mused. And how come those ever nosy neighbours, who could sniff out the least hint of a scandal a mile off, could not see what was going on on their very own doorsteps? Either way, it made no difference to him. He had no intentions of rushing into marriage and living in Springview Street. His ambitions were set a damned sight higher than that.

* * *

Louise overslept on Friday morning. She tumbled down the stairs in great haste but the house was empty. There was one place set for breakfast and a note was propped against the milk bottle.

Hope you enjoyed your lie-in, sis. Have a good day.
Left you something to eat. It's in the cupboard.
Harry

Feeling in a happier frame of mind after a good lie-in, Louise smiled at her brother's thoughtfulness. Harry was growing up into a lovely lad and she hoped he knew what he would be taking on should he ever marry Hannah. Her mother, Liz, would be forever hovering about in the background, sticking her neb in where it wasn't wanted. He deserved a lot better than that.

Not having eaten since teatime the night before, she found two cheese sandwiches in the cupboard as directed by Harry and making herself a mug of tea she sat at the table and devoured them. She had just finished and was wiping breadcrumbs from around her mouth when there was a knock on the door. Reluctantly, she rose to her feet, wondering if it was Conor and what he would have to say for himself as she opened the door.

They faced each other, Louise straight and proud

looking, and Conor drooped and miserable. Some moments passed. Taking pity on him, she opened her arms and he was inside the hall instantly. Kicking the door shut with his foot, he gathered her close.

'I'm sorry about last night,' he muttered into her hair. 'I feel I have betrayed you.'

All the bitter resentment within her melted at his abject humility. 'It's all right, love. Once I had time to think, I realised you were in a bit of a predicament. Of course in the circumstances you had to back your mother.'

'Still . . . it wasn't fair on you.' He looked down at her. 'But, believe me, please, I had no idea whatsoever that your father was courting my mother.'

She giggled. 'Is that what they're calling it now?'

He opened his mouth to speak but she pushed past him into the kitchen. 'Sit down. Give me a chance to get ready and we'll go out as planned. OK? I took today off so that we could have some time together and I'm not wasting another minute sitting here trying to right things we have little control over. As you have already pointed out, they are adults and have a right to please themselves, no matter who suffers the consequences.'

Relieved to postpone any criticisms of their parents' antics, Conor removed his coat and reaching for Thursday's *Irish News* sat down to wait.

18

The weather forecast on the wireless that morning had promised good weather during the day with light showers later in the evening, so Louise suggested that they should have a lazy day out in the fresh air and perhaps go to the Clonard picture house in the evening. First they went over to Johnnie's shop for some fruit and lemonade to take with them. Peggy pointed out to her sister some groceries that looked fresh enough but that were going cheap to make room for new produce. Delighted at the chance to save a bit of money on the housekeeping, Louise chose some of the food-stuffs that she would use over the next few days. Peggy filled one of the paper sacks and left it to one side, saying that she would take it home during her lunch break.

Peggy brought her sister up to date on how lovely their wee niece was. She said that she would be proud to be godmother to Angela on Sunday morning. 'I only wish I had something new to wear,' she moaned.

Guessing what was coming, Louise said, 'Believe me, Angela won't even know what you're wearing. Just make sure that you don't drop her.'

'I just want to look my best for her, so I do. She's a beautiful baby,' Peggy said wistfully.

'Catch yourself on, Peggy. No one will notice what you're wearing. They'll be far too busy gazing at Angela and making a fuss of her.'

When Louise still didn't take her up on the hint she was throwing, Peggy sadly said, 'Is there any chance of you letting me wear your new suit?'

'Yes, a snowball's chance in hell.' Peggy's face dropped and Louise insisted, 'It wouldn't fit you, sis. I know it won't.'

'I'm sure it would. We're about the same size, aren't we?'

'In your dreams. I'm much slimmer than you.' When Peggy still pouted, Louise said, 'All right. Be my guest. Try it on. But it won't fit, I know it won't.' Louise believed that because Peggy was heavier than her, she would look ridiculous in the suit. She was therefore secure in the knowledge that her suit was safe from her accident-prone sister.

Getting her change from her purchases and a profusion of thanks from Peggy, Louise left the shop and linked arms with Conor as they headed up the Springfield Road. The conversation touched on every subject except Cissie and Tommy.

As they passed the McFadden house, Louise told Conor in confidence about Hannah going out with a new boy and how hurt Harry was about it. Harry had blamed it all on Liz McFadden for trying to turn Hannah against Harry, but after a bit of friendly persuasion Liz had eventually consented to let him court her daughter as well.

Conor looked incredulous. 'Do they still do that . . . you know, ask permission of the parents? I thought it was only the aristocracy who did that because they didn't want their offspring marrying beneath them. If you like someone you ask them out and then it's up to the individual couples whether or not they get engaged. Not their parents. Well, that's what I think, for what it's worth.'

'You're right, but Hannah is a vulnerable young girl, and Mrs McFadden is very old-fashioned about such matters. She's very protective of her daughter and it's so much easier to go along with her whims and keep the peace.'

Conor kept a straight face as he looked seriously at her. 'Are you trying to tell me that we might have to fight Harry to get your da's house? Mind you, Louise, I'll be terribly disappointed. I thought

294

that you being the eldest we would be first on the list. I was so looking forward to coming home soon to set up house there.'

Startled, Louise stepped back, her face a conflicting mass of emotions. 'I . . . I don't understand?'

When he remained straight-faced and silent, she became agitated. 'I'll have you know, Conor O'Rourke, that when I eventually get married there is no way in this whole wide world that I'd continue to live in the same street as your mother. Not even if I was paid to do so. So there! You can just stay over in Birmingham for all I care.' She actually stamped her foot like a petulant schoolchild, so enraged was she at the very thought of it.

Conor threw his head back and laughed at her antics. 'If you could only see your face.'

In uncontrolled fury she flew at him, pounding his chest with her fists. It was only then that he realised she really was upset and grabbing her wrists he pulled her close. 'Here now, I was only having you on.'

It was her turn to get her own back. 'Just remember what I said and make up your bloody mind what you want. Me or Birmingham.' Gulping air into her lungs, she added, 'I mean that, Conor. Don't you ever joke about anything as important as that again or I won't be responsible for my actions. Do you hear me?'

He backed off, holding up his hands in mock defeat. 'Loud and clear. Loud and clear.'

They passed the Flush in strained silence, Louise still fuming. Soon the edge of Springfield Village came into view. Conor, like herself, had not been up here for some time and he was bemused at the changes that had taken place. Being older than her, he remembered things that she hadn't even known about. To regain favour with her he told her his memories of the gas pipes being laid. He supposed the water supply being piped by workmen was from one of the freshwater springs that were dotted about.

Louise gave a little laugh. 'Now that's something new I've learned today. I didn't realise there were any springs hereabouts.'

'Why do you think so many streets begin with "Spring"? Even this place is called Springfield Village, isn't it?'

Ashamed of her ignorance, Louise brought to his attention the National School where children were playing. Their mothers were taking advantage of the good weather to give their rugs and mats a thorough beating on the clothes lines while keeping an eye on their offspring.

Not wanting to pass Dick Patterson's house, she took a path around the outside of the village where she vaguely remembered having been when she was very young. Once they were clear of the overgrown hedges, tangled brambles and clumps of nettles, the land stretched out before them in a sea of long grass, of undulating shades of green and silver shimmering in the breeze.

Conor gasped aloud. 'What a view! It's lovely. I never dreamed of it being like this. How come we didn't come here when we were kids?' He turned to her in wonderment. 'Did you know about up here?'

Her brow furrowed in contemplation, Louise thought back to her childhood days. 'I remember being warned not to go any further than the village. And, mind you, the village only consisted of several rows of houses in those days. There was the laundry and the bleach mill providing work for the villagers and the school for the local children. So we were never tempted to go any further. It was a big enough adventure playing at the Flush. Then as we got older we started saving jam jars and lemonade bottles to get into the afternoon matinée at the Diamond and the Clonard picture houses. And in another year or so our parents thought we were old enough to catch a tram into town. We felt all grown up then and with our new independence the Flush became a thing of the past, but we never did get to wander beyond the village. We were too scared to venture any further in case the bogeyman jumped out on us.' She walked on until the grass was blowing around her legs and, taking deep breaths of the fresh-scented air, she enthused, 'It really is beautiful, isn't it?'

'I'm surprised nobody has bought this land. I'll get my father to make a few discreet enquiries about it when I get back. Land is worth a fortune over in England. I'm sure it's no different here.'

'I'm sure someone does own it,' Louise argued.

After a short distance the grassy plain gave way to a more rugged landscape. They sat with their backs to a boulder to rest and drink their lemonade and gaze in wonder about them. It was while they were eating their apples that a dog came bounding towards them.

'I hope we aren't trespassing.' Conor quickly rose to his feet when the dog's owner came into sight.

Louise, still sitting, arched her neck and saw Dick Patterson striding in their direction. He lifted his hand in welcome when he recognised her and she did likewise.

Surprised, Conor whispered out of the corner of his mouth, 'Do you know this guy?'

Smiling broadly, Louise assured him, 'Don't worry. He won't bite. He's that author I wrote you about.'

Louise was on her knees playing with the dog, a black Labrador, which was really little more than a pup. She rose to her feet when Dick reached them and offered him her hand. 'Nice to see you again, Dick. This is my good friend, Conor O'Rourke.' She canted her head towards Dick. 'Dick Patterson.'

The men shook hands and Conor asked anxiously, 'Are we trespassing here, Mr Patterson?'

Dick rubbed his chin and pondered for a moment as he glanced around. 'Yes, I suppose you are at that. Though I'm not quite sure just where my bit of land ends. I know that I rent this field to that farmer over there.' He pointed and in the distance they could make out a scattering of farm buildings. 'But no matter. I forgive you anyway. It's not unusual for Louise to trespass on other people's property. I suppose she has already told you about our first encounter?' Dick raised an enquiring eyebrow.

'She did mention about an author signing books in Eason's, if that's what you mean.'

Dick's eyes narrowed. 'You don't live near by then?'

'My mother does but I work away. I stay with my father in Birmingham. I am home for a few days to see Louise and visit some friends.'

'I see. So Louise is not spoken for yet? I wondered about the lack of a ring on her finger. The lads about here must be blind.' Dick directed his attention back to Louise. 'Come back with me for a cup of tea?'

She sensed that Conor had not taken too kindly to Dick and hesitated.

'Come on, keep an old man company for a while.'

She gave his shoulder a playful push. 'You're not old. Far from it.' But still she paused. 'What do you think, Conor?'

He reached for her hand as if to claim possession and said, 'I don't mind.'

Perturbed as to why Louise hadn't mentioned this man to him, Conor left all the talking to them and couldn't get over how familiar they were with each other. This man was old enough to be Louise's father . . . surely he hadn't designs on her? He shook his head in disbelief. But doubts niggled away at him. Why then had she not said anything about him?

When they arrived at the cottage, Louise stopped in wonder. 'My, but you have been busy.'

The cottage now nestled in a chocolate-box setting. It was unrecognisable from her previous visit. The paintwork on the window frames had been touched up and new snow-white nets could be seen through the shining glass window-panes. The long grass had been cut short and the window boxes painted and planted with new blooms.

'It's beautiful! It does you proud, Dick.'

Dick had watched her inspection of his homestead with a pleased smile on his face. 'I must confess it's not my own work. I hired a woman to make the indoors habitable and a handy man to attend to the outside of the house and the outhouses and gardens. They did a grand job of it, I must say.'

He released the dog and let it run ahead of them, then ushered Louise through the gate and followed her, leaving Conor to bring up the rear. He did so reluctantly, feeling left out of it and something else as well. Could he possibly be jealous of this older man?

Inside, clapping his hands with a single smack, Dick Patterson said, 'Right then, make yourselves at home. I'll put the kettle on.' He had tethered the dog outside and added, 'I'll get Spark some fresh water first.'

Louise sat on the small sofa while Conor debated whether to join her or take an armchair. He chose one of the armchairs but later was to regret it.

'Can I give you a hand, Dick?' Louise shouted through to the scullery.

'No, I'm almost ready, thank you.'

He came bustling in with a tray bearing a plate of biscuits and three china mugs. 'I'm sorry that this is all the fare I have to offer. You see, except for a bowl of porridge in the morning and tea and biscuits in the evening, I have a meal out every day and that saves me from doing any cooking.

I'm not too keen on burned offerings.' He smiled and winked at Louise.

He emptied the tray on to the table and returned for the tea, saying, 'Do you take sugar, Conor? I forgot to ask.'

'No. Just a little milk, thank you.'

When he came back with the teapot and a jug containing milk, Dick motioned for Louise to make room for him beside her.

'Will you do mother, Louise?'

'Of course.' There was plenty of room for two on the sofa and she inched over to let him sit down before reaching for the teapot.

Using the tea strainer to catch the tea leaves, she filled the mug in front of him with tea, and reached over to pour Conor's then her own, telling them to help themselves to the milk.

They quietly nibbled at their biscuits and sipped their teas. It was Dick who eventually broke the silence.

'Did you remember to tell Harry I wanted to see him, Louise?'

'I did, Dick. I told him that evening when he came in from work.'

'If he is not interested in listening to my proposition, will you tell him to let me know? You see, I'll have to make other arrangements.'

'Dick, I already told you he can't afford to buy this cottage.'

'I've decided not to sell the cottage. It's something else that I want to talk to him about.'

'Oh, that makes a difference then. It's awkward for Harry at the moment. You see, as well as working long shifts he has a girlfriend to consider now.' She paused for thought. 'Perhaps he could bring her with him if that's all right with you? Her name's Hannah McFadden.'

'That would be fine, Louise.'

Conor had sat listening to this conversation, feeling he was on the outside looking in. It was like a play being acted in front of him when he had missed the beginning of it. It was obvious that Dick Patterson was no stranger to the McGuigans. How come Louise had never mentioned meeting him before and not just at the book signing? And now Harry buying a cottage like this; he found it all hard to take in.

A lull fell over them and Conor decided it was time he joined the party, albeit as a gatecrasher. Clearing his throat, he said, 'Did I pick you up right? Was Harry really interested in buying your home, Dick?'

Dick glanced at Louise. 'Is it all right to discuss Harry's plans with Conor?'

Louise felt colour redden her cheeks and Conor thought, *You may well blush. You have left me feeling like a right eejit since we met this man.*

'Well, as you already know, Conor, since you

303

arrived home I haven't had much time to bring you up to scratch on what's been happening lately, or you would already know what Dick is talking about.' She gave Dick the nod to go ahead. 'Of course Harry won't mind Conor knowing about his business, Dick. After all, he's almost part of the family.'

Dick nodded and turned his attention to Conor. 'After my wife died I travelled a lot and due to my negligence the cottage fell into a state of disrepair. Harry noticed it when he was delivering bread to the village and thought it was derelict. So hoping that he might be on to a good bargain, he brought Louise up here to get her opinion of it. By coincidence I had arrived home the day before and when Louise tried to look into the house through the dirty windows I thought it was some youngsters from the village and snatched the curtain back quickly to scare them off. In doing so I nearly scared the life out of her. That's how we first met. Is that about right, Louise?'

'And she didn't realise that you were the author who was coming to do the signing at Eason's?'

'I don't write under my own name so she didn't make the connection. My pseudonym is Joseph McGouran. I'm sure she at least told you what happened when I arrived at the shop . . .' He broke off. 'I digress. That's another story.'

Conor was becoming more confused than ever and he lapsed into a sullen silence. He couldn't believe that Louise had put him in this predicament. A glance at her showed him that she was embarrassed over the whole episode and, not wanting to cause a scene without giving it some thought, he was on his feet and making excuses to leave. Let her remain if she wanted, he'd had enough. He had to get out of this place before he made a spectacle of himself.

Looking at the clock on the mantelpiece he pretended shocked surprise. 'Good Lord, is that the time? I'm afraid I forgot to say, Louise, but my mother is expecting me back soon. I didn't think we would be away this long.' He paused, waiting for her to say she would come with him.

She opened her mouth to speak but Dick beat her to it. 'You don't have to go now, Louise. I'll give you a lift down later, if you like. I'm enjoying our conversation, as always.'

Angry at Conor's attitude towards this benevolent man, she dithered.

Conor took the decision out of her hands. 'Don't bother, Louise. I'll see you later. Good day to you, Dick. Perhaps we will meet again. I'll see myself out.'

From where she sat Louise watched him stride down the garden path and it was obvious from his stance that he was in a right old temper. He pulled the gate closed behind him without so much as a backward glance.

*　　*　　*

Conor stalked through the village and, bypassing the tram stop, stomped his way quickly down Springfield Road. His mind was a maelstrom of conflicting dark thoughts. Before he knew it he had reached the corner of Springview Street, his nerves still strung as tight as a drum.

If he went home his mother would interrogate him as to why he was back so early and what could he tell her? Some holiday break, he fumed. He was now regretting ever coming home. Obviously Louise wasn't missing him; she seemed to be having a whale of a time with the great Dick Patterson, or was it Joseph McGouran? He couldn't care less what he was called.

He continued on down Springfield Road. He would sit in Dunville Park for a while and try to figure out in his mind what the hell was going on.

19

Louise let the silence hang in the air for some moments after Conor left the cottage. She felt so depressed, not knowing what to say to excuse Conor's behaviour. She looked so forlorn and sad that Dick sat looking at her, his forehead knotted in a frown, then remarked, 'Why so down, Lou?' He raised his hands in a placating gesture. 'Sorry, I'm sure you don't like people shortening your name.'

She brushed the air with her hands to show indifference to his remark and groped in her pockets for a handkerchief. Dick thrust his into her hand as the tears started to fall.

'Thanks.'

In spite of her best endeavours a sob escaped her lips as she roughly rubbed one cheek after the other. Dick moved closer but refrained from touching her. He was finding his admiration for her changing into something more emotional and it disturbed him. He needed time to think about what was happening to him. This was something he hadn't foreseen. He had never been affected like this before, except with his wife, and was afraid of it getting out of control. After all, he was old enough to be this girl's father. Well, maybe not quite; but still much older than her.

He cautioned himself to be careful. He didn't want to give this young girl cause for concern. She had enough on her plate at the moment, worrying about Conor, who was behaving like a callow youth. He would gladly throttle him if he thought it would be of any benefit to this lovely girl.

With a final sniff and blow into his handkerchief she tucked it away in her pocket. 'Thanks, Dick. I'll wash it for you and return it later.'

With a grimace she continued, 'It's like this . . . Conor and I don't seem to have very much to say to each other any more. One thing after another has cropped up since he came home on Wednesday. Things I should explain to him as we go along . . . but before I get a chance to say anything, through no fault of my own, something else happens. The result is that Conor doesn't know what to think. He must believe that I'm holding out on him. Deliberately keeping him in the dark. I'm not trying

308

to put the blame on him by any means, mind you, although he hasn't been very helpful. To tell you the truth, it's been awful.' She paused and seemed to lose the thread of the conversation.

Dick gently prompted her. 'What happened?'

'One misunderstanding after another, that's what! At one stage I actually told him to choose between Birmingham and me and now I'm afraid he might just do that and I'll be the one to lose out. We came out for a walk today to talk and clear the air and, as you know, instead we ended up here and yet again nothing has been resolved. In fact he must be even more bewildered than ever. Wondering how I know you so well and he has never heard tell of you . . . except as Joseph McGouran the author. He will be thinking we're carrying on behind his back.' She managed a wan smile and a sad shake of the head at this ridiculous idea.

Dick hoped she didn't notice the hot colour that he felt burn his face. 'If he loves you there is no way he will choose Birmingham before you. He would be mad if he did,' he quietly assured her.

'Why?' she trilled loudly. 'Eh? I bet he meets plenty of really attractive girls over in England. Girls with no past history holding them back every time they meet, no scandal hanging over their heads. You see, Dick, my family has been the cause of a lot of scandal and malicious gossip these past few years and just last night I learned of more to come. So why should Conor bother his backside about me? I'm really the only thing keeping him here. And believe it or not, I'm quite happy in Belfast. You see, I don't want to live anywhere else. In my heart I know it wouldn't work out if I had to leave my family and friends and move away across the water.'

Relieved to hear this, Dick put his arm across the back of the sofa and leaned closer. It was hurting him to see her so upset. He was aching to take her in his arms and comfort her, but didn't dare. 'You are beautiful,' he declared. 'I have met all kinds of girls in my travels around the world, and believe me, you are one of the beautiful ones.'

She clicked her tongue in disapproval and shook her head in disbelief.

'You are! You are also so natural and kind. You have an incredible personality. It would be hard for Conor to find anyone better than you.'

To his relief she started giggling. 'Oh, Dick, give over. Would you listen to yourself. Anyone would think you were putting me forward for canonisation. Blessed Louise McGuigan. Far from it. Although,' relaxed now, she jested, 'I must say, it has a nice ring to it.' Impulsively she put her hand on his thigh. His breath caught as he felt a shock, as if a bolt of lightning had shot though him. 'Thanks for listening to my tales of woe, Dick.'

When she removed her hand and delved into

her pocket to retrieve the handkerchief again to scrub away the tears from her face, Dick was glad of the respite to gain some self-control.

With a sigh she admitted, 'Before he went away I thought Conor and I were made for each other and nothing could ever come between us. Now I'm not so sure. You see, I find myself quite strongly attracted to someone else, so maybe it would be better if Conor and I took a break from each other until we are both sure in our minds as to exactly what we want.'

Surprised at this frank confession, Dick queried, 'Does this other man feel the same way towards you?'

'I think so. He's Al Murray's nephew and we do get on quite well together.'

'George Carson? Yes, I've met that young man. Did you meet him through your work?'

'No. We became friends some time ago. Conor and I had our differences in the past before he went across the water. He dumped me. Or so I thought at the time. Anyway, I got the impression that he didn't love me any more. My friend Cathie Morgan was dating George's mate Trevor Pollock, and I made up a foursome with George for a short time. He was very kind and gentlemanly towards me, although we both knew it couldn't come to anything, what with him being a Protestant. We were just good friends. Then Conor came home and sorted everything out between him and me, and Cathie ran off to Scotland with Trevor. I never once set eyes on George again until lately, when he walked into the shop one day. Conor was home at the time and George had called in to take me out to lunch.'

'Have you seen George since?'

'Yes. I've even been out with him a few times, just as a friend, you know? But I've grown to like him a lot. Surely I can't be in love with Conor if I enjoy another man's company so much?'

'Sometime when we are focused so completely on one particular person, we don't give others a chance to get to know us. It's as if we are wearing blinkers all the time. But perhaps, as you say, a break from Conor might show just where your true feelings lie.'

Louise turned her head to say that he might be right but the words died on her lips when she realised how close he was. Dick's arm was now across her shoulders and feeling the heat of his thigh resting against hers she straightened up and cautioned herself. *Beware! If I stay here any longer he'll think I'm looking for comfort or something and with my quick temper God knows what could happen should he make a wrong move towards me. I'll probably hit him.* She became flustered. *I had better get out of here*, she thought, *while the going's good.*

Easing her body away from his, she rose to her

feet. 'I'll have to be making a move, Dick, before it gets any later.'

Aware of her sudden unease he smiled and rising he faced her and put his hands on her shoulders. 'First let me make you a fresh cup of tea before you go.'

'No. No, I'm fine, Dick. I have to get home to make the family dinner.'

His closeness was affecting her in a way it hadn't before; she was now aware of him in a way she had never dreamed possible. She shrugged his hands off her shoulders and reached for her handbag. 'I really must go now.'

He picked up her coat and held it till she put her arms into the sleeves then, before she could move, he returned his hands to rest on her shoulders. His expression remained stoic as he gazed intently into her eyes. 'Have you ever thought that you might be better off with an older man? Someone you would have no qualms about? Who would make it his life's mission to care for you?'

Her eyes widened and confused thoughts darted about in her mind. Does he mean himself? Don't be silly, she chastised herself, of course he doesn't. But then his hands came up and cupped her face. Startled, she made to free herself but his hold tightened. 'Stupid fool that I am, I have only today realised how much you've come to mean to me, Louise.' Slowly he placed his lips against hers; just a short but meaningful kiss. 'Given the chance I can do better than that and you would be safe and secure with me. Think about it, my lovely.'

She stood mesmerised. He slowly relinquished his hold on her and, deciding not to risk any more chances, he said, 'I'll drive you home.'

'No, no, there's no need. I'll walk, it will help clear my head.'

'I said I'd see you safely home and I intend to do just that. Come on, let's hit the road.'

Unable to think of anything to say, Louise sat gazing out of the car window on the way down Springfield Road. At the corner of Springview Street she put her hand on the door handle as she got ready to get out but Dick indicated that she remain where she was.

'I'll see you to the door.' His tone brooked no argument so she let go of the handle and sat quietly back in her seat.

He drew the car to a halt when she indicated her home and turned round in the seat to face her. 'Please don't let anything I've done or said today put you off me entirely. I hope to remain your friend no matter what happens. OK?'

Anxious to get out of the car and escape his worried eyes, she nodded.

'And I would still like to see Harry and his girlfriend tonight, if possible. Will you try to arrange that?'

Again she nodded and at last felt free to get out of the car.

She stood on the pavement shaking like a leaf, not caring that curtains were twitching in the windows across the street as nosy neighbours watched the goings-on. This would give them plenty of ammunition to gossip about. It would become an unspoken contest as to who could find out first who the gentleman in the big shiny car was. Louise could imagine them rubbing their hands in glee.

She watched as the car turned up Springfield Road, then with a pointed glare across the street she let herself into her home. What on earth was she going to do now? Who would have thought that Dick Patterson, of all people, fancied her? Or was it all in her mind? Was her imagination running away with her? Dear God, please protect me from doing anything stupid, she prayed.

One thing was for sure! Conor mustn't get wind of this or he would probably throw a tantrum, dump her right away and run as fast as his legs would carry him to the boat. That was what he was good at. Especially if he guessed that she really liked Dick in a friendly sort of way and knowing that she wouldn't want to lose his friendship. Conor would never believe for one minute that their relationship was purely platonic.

*　　*　　*

Dick drew the car to a stop outside Barney Hughes's bakery. He hands were shaking on the steering wheel. Distressed and angry with himself, he recalled what he had said to Louise. How could he have been so stupid? He had behaved like an adolescent boy with her. What on earth had he been thinking of? Dick Patterson . . . always so sure of himself, blurting out his feelings like that. But then, he really had no other option. He had already stayed in Belfast too long. His business down south could not be neglected any longer. Although he had a good staff looking after it, he didn't believe in taking chances and being absent long-term at any given time. He liked to be in the thick of things.

Well, no real harm done. Louise had eyed him as if he was a nutcase. He could only play it by ear, and see what came of it.

Harry was pleased to hear that Dick had invited him and Hannah to visit the cottage tonight around seven. Very intrigued as to what he wanted to confer with him about, he assured his sister he would be very careful and remember that no matter what Dick might hint at to the contrary, he couldn't afford to buy the cottage. He said that he would go as soon as he had eaten his dinner, had a wash and collected Hannah, in that order.

'It's a bit short notice. It will probably be later

than seven, by the time we get there. Do you think that will be all right with him?'

'I would imagine so. Now remember to keep your wits about you. Dick is a man of the world and he's very shrewd. If you're not sure of anything he puts to you, just say you'll think about it and get back to him. Take all he says with a pinch of salt.' She was glad to see her brother look so happy.

When Tommy came in he sat in silence at the table and scoffed up his dinner in record time. It was obvious that he didn't want last night's revelations brought to the notice of Peggy and Harry. Louise didn't want to start anything either and was only too glad when he got up from the table without a single word of thanks and went into the scullery. Harry's mouth dropped open as he looked from one sister to the other, ready to give off, but a warning shake of the head from Louise silenced him before he could utter a word. Trust his da, he brooded. Where could he be going this early in the evening that was so important? He could have asked if any of us were in a hurry out, he mumbled to himself. After only a matter of minutes in the scullery Tommy emerged and, with a farewell wave to no one in particular, made his way out of the house.

Conor had not been in touch with Louise since leaving Dick's cottage. Not sure whether or not he would show up for their meeting, she had never-theless prepared and served the dinner and, with a no-nonsense attitude, told Peggy to wash the dishes and clear up. Ignoring her sister's exaspera-tion, she was ready and waiting at seven o'clock. She wasn't disappointed. Conor did arrive as usual at seven on the dot. Shrugging into her coat and picking up her handbag, she went straight out the door to meet him.

Conor stood looking shamefaced. 'Hi. I didn't know if you would still want to go out with me tonight.'

Louise shrugged. 'Why not? It was you who ran off in a huff, not me.' Although she was feigning indifference, she was so pleased that he had turned up, she wanted to hug him.

'Are we still on for the Clonard, then?'

'Unless you have somewhere better in mind?'

As the wireless forecast had predicted, the weather had taken a change for the worse and a light drizzle was falling. 'I suppose it would be better than walking about in this. That is, as long as it's all right with you? We can go further afield if you like?'

Taking the scarf from around her neck, she covered her hair with it and tied it under her chin, then pushed her hand under his elbow. 'The Clonard is fine. But . . . remember, Conor, we must clear the air before you go back to Birmingham.'

'I agree wholeheartedly, Louise, but not now. Tonight we just relax and try to enjoy ourselves. OK?'

'If you say so.'

In the warmth of the picture house, with his arm around her and her head resting against him, Louise felt contented, but was ashamed to find she couldn't keep her eyes open. Soon, after a feeble fight against it, she allowed herself to be lulled into a light slumber. The next thing she knew, the really loud tone of the organ at the finish of the Keystone Kops awakened her with a start and she was in time to see the credits roll up the screen.

Conor was smiling tenderly at her. 'You must have been exhausted, poor dear.'

She knuckled the sleep from her eyes and bit her lip as she admitted, 'I was very tired, but that's no excuse. I'm so sorry, Conor, for being such poor company. I hope at least the film was good. Did *you* enjoy it?'

'Well, when I said relax I didn't mean it quite literally. We've seen the film before so you haven't missed anything. I did enjoy watching you sleep, though. It's a sight I'd like to wake up to every morning.'

She held her breath; was he going to commit himself? She closed her eyes and sent a prayer heavenward. But no, he was helping her on with her coat. Outside the rain had stopped and the air felt cool and fresh.

Louise came to a decision, to get whatever was between them out into the open and settled, so that she could enjoy Conor's last day home tomorrow without a cloud hanging over them. 'Let's go for a walk up the Falls Road as far as Beechmount and take the long way home, eh, Conor? It will give us a chance to talk.'

'If that's want you want.'

As they walked close together, holding hands, clearing her throat, Louise began. 'I'm going to try to explain all that has happened since I last saw you. It's all mixed up, so please bear with me.'

Holding nothing back, she revealed her going out with George Carson the Saturday before Conor came home and how he had come to the shop on Wednesday to invite her out again on Friday night. 'I had every intention of telling you about it on Wednesday but, as you are aware, we went to the dance, which, by the way I enjoyed very much, thank you. I thought you also enjoyed yourself, although I know that Liam Gilmore gives you the pip at the best of times, but, again, I thought you handled that admirably. As for Dick Patterson—' Finding she was unable to talk about Dick, she paused momentarily. 'Well, that's a long story and you'll get a good laugh when you hear it. He's already told you how we met, but I'll fill you in on the whole story later.'

She glanced up at his stern profile and he said through clenched teeth, 'I really can't stand that Liam Gilmore fella.'

'I know that, but—'

'There's no buts about it. That's one of the reasons I don't want to live here in Belfast.' He hesitated. 'Tell me, Louise, would you have gone out with George Carson on Friday night had I not come home?'

Taking a deep breath, she confessed that she would have.

'Ah, . . . I see.'

'Well, you can't blame me, Conor. For one thing I was anxious to show off my new suit. And I don't believe for one minute that you are sitting all alone at home, over there, dreaming about me. You are out with your sister and brothers, meeting all their friends and having a good time. I trust you. I haven't any choice. However, I do expect you to trust me in return.'

'And what about Dick Patterson?'

Still embarrassed by her last encounter with Dick, Louise immediately became nervous. Praying that her voice wouldn't betray her, she asked innocently, 'Dick Patterson? What about him?'

'Do you see him often?'

She drew away from him. 'Now you're insulting me. He must be old enough to be my father.'

'I'm asking if you see him often. How is that insulting you? Unless . . .'

Now her back was up. How dare he question her like this? 'I'll have you know that I've never been out with that man, if that's what you're on about.'

She hurried ahead and he quickly followed her. He was uneasy and wanted to see her face when he questioned her.

'Forgive me, Louise. It's just that I'm jealous as hell. I need you to be honest with me. If that's not asking too much.'

She gaped at him in confusion. 'I'm always honest with you. How can you think otherwise?'

'Look, love, why not humour me, please? Why don't you come back with me and see what you think about Birmingham? Give me a chance to show you what a great place it is. Meet my family and see what a nice bunch they are. Please? Will you?'

'I can't at the moment.'

'At least promise me that you'll think about it. And mean it this time. We must come to a decision about where we go from here. I can't go on like this. It's driving me crazy.'

She slowed down and took a deep breath. 'You see? This is what always happens every time I try to tell you how things are when you've been away. You've only one thing on your mind and that's

322

trying to get me over to Birmingham. You won't try to see things from my point of view. We can't have a sensible conversation any more. I think we find each other boring and irritating and I've come to the conclusion that it is best if we go our own separate ways. Call it a day.'

Conor stopped and swung her roughly into his arms. 'Surely you can't mean that, Louise?'

'And why not? We're only getting on each other's nerves. Aren't we?'

'Because I love you and I think you love me.'

'I'm not so sure about that any more. I think we've drifted too far apart and it would be best to break it off now before one of us gets hurt.'

Louise couldn't believe she was saying these things. Hadn't she been hoping all along that he would ask her to marry him and settle down in Belfast? Now here she was, giving him the perfect excuse to make a clean break from her and return to Birmingham with a clear conscience.

He gazed intently at her for some moments as if trying to read her mind. At last, with a frustrated shrug he said, 'All right then. If that's what you want. We'll leave things as they are for now but we are wasting time that we could be spending together. So it's up to you.'

Her heart plummeted to her very feet. He was accepting her ultimatum. Well, what had she expected? Lord knows, she had goaded him

323

enough. Should she eat humble pie? Never! Never in this whole wide world would she crawl to him. He had revealed his true colours. Let him do what he really wanted to do: run back to Birmingham.

They had reached Oakman Street and, afraid of breaking down in his company on the rest of the walk home, she came to an abrupt halt. 'I'm going to call in and see Grannie, so goodnight, Conor.'

He opened his mouth to say he would come with her but she had already crossed the street and was knocking on Grannie Logan's door. Hands clenched into tight fists and his face a grim mask, he stamped on down Oakman Street, in a furious temper.

To hell with this, he fumed inwardly. How could she do this to me? Well, I'll set off early tomorrow morning and save her the bother of dumping me. She has at last convinced me we are not meant for each other, so what would be the point of seeing her tomorrow? Yes, that's what I'll do. Get away early and avoid another confrontation, he thought with a stubborn determination.

He tossed and turned most of the night, wondering what to do for the best, but crawled out of bed on Saturday morning tired and none the wiser. Louise had always been the only girl for him. True, he didn't deny that he had looked and wondered about the girls he had encountered across the water. And if he were truthful with himself, there were times when he had been sorely tempted.

All the thoughts he'd had the evening before appeared idiotic in the light of day. He decided that he might as well spend his last day home in Louise's company. He had a wash and dressed quickly. Before he had breakfast he'd call down and eat yet another bit of humble pie. Then he'd ask Louise to accompany him to the Grand Opera House tonight, that is, if he was lucky enough to get two tickets.

20

Hannah was tickled pink to hear that she was going to meet a real live author. She skipped down the steps to meet Harry and clung to his arm as they made their way up Springfield Road, chattering away more than usual. Harry was happy to see her so exuberant. He had found her somewhat distant when she was involved with the other lad. Had she known that it was her mother who had kept Harry from asking her out? Or did she think that he had ceased to care for her? Even when Liz had changed her tune and had given them her blessing, Hannah had seemed somehow different. She was more reserved for a start, less talkative and prone to going off into a world of her own, wool-gathering. And no matter how hard Harry tried, he couldn't get her back on the easy, happy-go-lucky footing they had once shared.

She shook his arm excitedly. 'Tell me, what's he like . . . this author?'

'He's a great bloke. Although he seems to be well heeled and has written some books, there are no airs or graces about him. None whatsoever.'

'How many books has he written?'

'I don't know. When we first met, we didn't even know that he was an author. Remember I told you how we met him?'

She giggled and nodded, having heard about this hilarious episode when Harry could stop laughing long enough to string two words together. 'You were trespassing on his land, weren't you?'

'That's right. Of course he was annoyed at first but ended up inviting us inside and introducing himself as Dick Patterson. He cleaned the scratches on Louise's hands. Made a good job of it, too. She only found out he was an author when he turned up to sign books at a signing session next day at Eason's. I've already told you that he writes under the name of Joseph McGouran.'

Although she had heard all this before, Hannah still hung on to every word Harry uttered. 'How old is he?' she urged.

Harry's face screwed up as he gave this some thought. 'I don't really know. I reckon he's about the same age as me da or maybe a bit younger.

I'm no good at guessing people's ages. In his early forties maybe.'

Hannah drank in everything he said as if memorising it. People thought her a bit slow on the uptake but Harry knew her better than anyone. He was aware that she took everything to heart and stored it away in her memory bank. She was maybe a little hesitant but always sure of anything she said. That was Hannah! She thought before opening her mouth. She was a great cook too and could follow recipes to a T. He had enjoyed many a tasty meal prepared by her when invited to dinner by Liz. If she had any fault it was being too trusting; she could find no fault in anyone. She thought everyone was good like herself.

He loved this girl with an all-abiding love and didn't know what he would do with himself if Liz got her way and forbade them to marry. Her mother was Hannah's only surviving relative and she was devoted to her. He couldn't see Hannah leaving Liz on her own. Would Hannah side with her mother if she had to choose between her and Harry? If she did, Harry's life wouldn't be worth living.

Now he tightened his hold on her. 'We're almost there, sweetheart. You'll soon see for yourself what he's like.'

Hannah stopped in admiration when the cottage came in sight. 'Why, it's beautiful, so it is.'

'It sure is. Wait till you see the inside. You'll fall

in love with it. But remember, if your mother eventually gives her permission for us to marry, I won't be able to afford anything as grand as this. It's way beyond my pocket.'

She paused and stared intently up at him. 'Do you really want to marry me, Harry? You could have any girl you wanted, you know.'

He laughed at the idea. 'That's very flattering of you to say, Hannah, but you're wrong there. I couldn't. It's only you I want to spend the rest of my life with. No one else.'

Her lip trembled and her expression was forlorn when she said, 'You're sure? You honestly mean that, Harry?'

She looked so unconvinced that he sought to reassure her. Concerned, he tightened his grip on her hand to encourage her as they walked up the path to the cottage. Relaxing, Hannah exclaimed at the wonderful shrubs and plants, deeply inhaling the perfume of the flowers in the window boxes.

Before they reached the door it was pulled open and Dick stood there, hand outstretched to greet them. 'Come in, come in. Glad you could make it.' He clasped Harry's hand in a firm grip and turned to Hannah. 'This must be Hannah. I'm very pleased to meet you, my dear. You're a sight for sore eyes.'

Rosy-cheeked from his admiration, she said shyly, 'Hello, Mr Patterson.'

'Please call me Dick. Everyone else does.'

He ushered them through the hall and into the front room. Here Hannah forgot her shyness and, clasping her hands to her bosom, gasped in sincere admiration.

'This is beautiful.' She turned to Harry. 'Mum would love this.'

'Thank you,' Dick said, humble at such genuine praise for his decor. 'Make yourselves at home, I won't be a minute.'

He went into the scullery. Harry's ears pricked when he heard what sounded like footsteps on stairs. Then he recalled Dick pointing out a small flight of wooden stairs near the back door when he had first showed him and Louise around the house. Those lead up to the loft, he had told them, which is absolutely crammed with rubbish. My wife threw nothing away. I think she was a bit of a jackdaw, the way she hoarded things.

When Dick returned to the kitchen he was carrying a cardboard box and a scrap of cloth. Sitting facing them in the armchair, he carefully dusted the box with the cloth and set it on an occasional table near by.

'Now to get down to business and discuss my proposition with you.' He caught Harry's gaze and held it. 'I'm aware that you occasionally do shift work and some of your weekends therefore are not free, right?'

Harry nodded in agreement, more intrigued than ever.

Dick continued, 'Times are changing, lad. Not just here but all over the country. Life was different when I first came here. I fell in love with this area almost at the same time as I did my wife, Rosemary. I bought the land hereabouts shortly after I got married. I met Rosemary in a library in Dublin when I was researching my second book and I fell totally and utterly in love with her. Her dark-haired, blue-eyed beauty was breathtaking. To my great delight, she confessed to similar feelings for me and although she was, in my opinion, in a class above me, she took me on. I considered myself the luckiest man in Ireland.'

He leaned back in his chair for a long time, reflecting on the memory he had just shared with them. After what seemed like ages he suddenly leaned forward and broke the silence. 'Right! Enough is enough. Perhaps you would like a cup of tea or a drink of lemonade before I go into all this rigmarole,' he said, nodding towards the box.

Caught up in the story of Dick's life Harry declined but glanced at Hannah with a raised eyebrow. 'Perhaps, love, you'd like something to drink?'

She quickly shook her head. Moving the table until it was between them, Dick opened the box. It was full of old parchments and papers. Harry thought straight away that they must be deeds and important legal documents.

'I haven't looked at these in years.' He shook his head at his own stupidity. 'I've been terribly remiss about important things like these. Anything could have happened to them. A fire, a burglary, and I would have had a lot of trouble replacing them or proving ownership if it ever came to that. So there you have it. I just want you to see the deeds for the cottage and the plans to show the extent of my land here in the village.'

Harry was confused. Why was Dick Patterson, author and landowner, disclosing all this to a mere lad, he wondered?

Dick grinned across the table at him. 'You must be wondering why I'm telling you all this.'

Harry laughed. It was as if Dick could read his mind. 'You know, the thought had occurred to me.'

'Well, Harry, the long and the short of it is, I would like to offer you a part-time job if that's all right with you.'

Harry was more puzzled than ever. A frown knitting his brow, he said, 'What kind of work have you in mind? I honestly can't see how I could be of any use to you, whether it be part time or full time.'

'For a start, you would have to live here on the weekends you were free and keep the place in a good state of repair. I've decided to retire here eventually and I don't want to come back to a tumbledown wreck.'

Harry sat open-mouthed. Hannah was watching him with bated breath to see what his reaction would be.

'You could of course live here full time if you wish. Whatever suits you best.'

Harry was leaning towards Dick, his arms resting on his thighs, a sceptical look in his eyes. 'Tell me this, Dick, why would a man of your wealth not just bring in someone who knew what he was doing? Like a handyman, for instance. You know, a jack of all trades. I'm just a labourer. I have no school certificates or apprenticeship training documents to show how smart I am. We have just recently met. I could be the biggest crook in the whole of Belfast for all you know. So why me?'

'I pride myself on being a good judge of character, son, and I feel I can trust you. So why should I employ a complete stranger if I can have you? Huh?'

Harry still couldn't comprehend what was happening. Somehow or other it didn't quite ring true.

'Is this some kind of a joke, Dick? Are you taking the mick?'

Dick was taken aback by Harry's crass remark. 'No! No, no, I'm very sincere. Why can't you believe me?'

'Because I'm no fool. You're obviously a man of the world. You've done well for yourself. Why should you trust the likes of me?'

'Listen. If you so wish I'll have a contract drawn up, stating that you would be in complete charge of this cottage, and my whole estate in fact. Would that suit you? It will be a legal and binding document. There will be no hidden agenda. As I said, it will be a clear-cut and precise contract. And I will pay you a monthly wage to be discussed and agreed between us.'

Harry suddenly remembered. 'Hold on a minute. Didn't you tell me you let the pasture out to a farmer for grazing?'

'Yes, I did, and Jimmy Doherty pays me through our banks. It's a mutual business arrangement that suits us both very well. So don't for one minute think I would expect you to collect any rent on my behalf. No, your job would entail keeping the cottage clean and tidy and managing the gardens. I'll introduce you to my solicitor and he will advance you the money for any repairs or decorating as required and requested by yourself. Obviously, with him being a solicitor, he'll require proof of purchase in the form of cash receipts for any goods you buy for the estate. The only other thing I ask of you is that you make sure Mr Doherty, or anyone else for that matter, doesn't start planting corn or barley or whatever on my land. And keep an eye out for squatters. Now, is that absolutely clear? Any questions?'

'And how am I supposed to prevent squatters moving in, eh? I wouldn't be allowed to carry a shotgun. Not that I would ever want to. People might get the wrong idea.'

'Of course not, Harry. That would be unheard of. If you discover anything that looks in any way suspicious, you phone my solicitor immediately and he will take care of it. It will be out of your hands. That way you won't have to involve yourself in anything risky. I only want you to keep an eye out for me. Be my lookout, as it were.'

'Let me get this straight. I could stay here any time I'm available. Keep things up to scratch and look out for intruders and watch that that farmer doesn't sow any cereals. But how am I to know if he does? I don't know the first thing about farming.'

'Very simple. First he'd have to plough the pastureland before he prepared the ground for seeding. That all takes time. You would be able to spot it right away and take the necessary steps that I've already explained.'

'Well, Dick, there's something that sticks out a mile to me and I can't make any sense of it.'

Dick quirked a brow at him.

Harry continued, 'Why now? Eh? You say you've owned this cottage for years and bought the land shortly after you married; you've come and gone, leaving it vacant for long stretches at a time. So why are you being so cautious now?'

Dick grinned warmly at him. 'See . . . you've just proved my point that you are no dozer, son. The reason I want you to keep a lookout for me is that land is increasing in price by the year. Some people think that they have a God-given right to just stick up a tent or move in a couple of cows or goats to graze and after a length of time they can claim ownership. Or, as you might already know the term, "claim squatters' rights".'

'Like some people do with empty houses?' Hannah blushed as she dared to interrupt the conversation.

'There you go. Just like Hannah said. So are you game to watch out for me? Be my eyes and ears?'

Harry looked at Hannah and beamed. 'Well said, love, I couldn't have put it better myself.'

He then sat in silent thought for some time until Dick prompted him. 'What do you think?'

Remembering Louise's advice, he replied, 'I'm sorry, Dick, it's too much to take in all at once. I need time to think it over and get some advice on it.'

'Of course you will. That goes without saying. I wouldn't expect an answer right away. I'm going down south for a couple of days and then I'll be back here for about a week. Think you might be in a position to let me know by then?'

Harry nodded. 'Yes, if everything's as clear-cut as you've said, there should be no problem.'

Rising to his feet, Dick clapped his hands together, then reaching across for Harry's hand he shook it heartily. 'This calls for a celebration drink. I have a nice bottle of wine. Will you both join me in a glass?'

Hannah at once declined and Harry said, 'Let's wait until we have something positive to celebrate, Dick. Anyway, it's time I was seeing Hannah home.'

'You will let me know as soon as you've made up your mind, Harry?'

'I will. You've certainly given me a lot to think about. I'll hardly be able to sleep a wink tonight,' he replied with a smile.

They said their farewells at the door and headed back down through the village. Hannah was in a very pensive mood. She was aware that she was regarded by some people as being somewhat slow, which made her hesitant about asking questions in case she made a fool of herself.

She covertly watched Harry out of the corner of her eye. Different expressions clouded his face. He was locked in a world of his own, his mind flying all over the place, trying to find faults in Dick Patterson's proposal. It seemed to Hannah that he had always treated her with the greatest respect, talking everything over with her. Was she wrong to believe that? Did he now think her too backward to discuss this business proposition? If so, how would she be able to confide in him? Would she be able to explain to him what had happened to her? And, most important still, would he understand and forgive her?

At last he came out of his reverie and caught her eye. To her relief he asked her what she thought of Dick Patterson; did she think that he was on the level?

'Yes, I do. He seems a very decent man.'

Harry laughed and hugged her close. 'My love, you are so trusting.'

She bowed her head. 'You're right. I am, but I've learned to my cost that not everyone can be trusted. I've been so stupid.'

He slowed down and tilted up her chin to face him. 'What's happened? Did someone insult you or say anything to you?'

'No, no.' Quickly changing the subject she went on, 'Tell me, what do you intend doing about Dick's offer?'

Harry had a vague feeling that she was putting him off. No matter. His prime concern at the moment was to find somewhere quiet and secluded where he could think this offer through without any undue distractions before going over it with Louise. He looked intently down into Hannah's face. 'You're sure you're all right, love?'

'Yes. I'm fine, Harry. Have you decided what you're going to do?'

There it was again. That feeling that all was not hunky-dory. 'First I'm going to talk it over with our Louise, and maybe Conor. I'll listen to what they have to say, and if necessary I'll see a solicitor. Surely it can't cost all that much for a bit of advice? Eh?'

'I wouldn't think so. But wouldn't Conor be able to advise you? After all, that's what he does for a living, isn't it?'

'Good Lord, I never thought of that. Of course, you're quite right. You've saved me some cash already,' he said with a grin.

Something was still niggling at the corner of his mind, but he couldn't bring it into focus. He shrugged mentally. If it was all that important it would soon surface.

Louise lay awake from six o'clock on Saturday morning – wakened by the mental alarm in her head. It was her usual time for rising to see to the breakfast and get ready for work. However, she hadn't to get up early today. She had taken the day off to spend it with Conor. Remembering her ultimatum and Conor's agreeing with her that they would be better off parting company, she very much doubted that he would put in an appearance. He could only be expected to take so much and no more, she mused despondently.

A timid knock on the front door caught her attention. Puzzled, she carefully eased herself out of bed, not wanting to waken Peggy. Gently pulling the net curtain slightly to one side, she was astonished to see Conor standing on the pavement, looking up at the window. She motioned to him that she was coming down and to wait there.

Grabbing a cardigan, she pushed her feet into her slippers and quietly descended the stairs. Afraid to open her mouth, beckoning Conor into the hall, she pulled her cardigan tightly around herself and, folding her arms tight across her chest to hold it in place to ward off the chill morning air, waited for him to say something. She didn't know what to expect. Had he come to say a final goodbye before he took off or had he something else in mind?

He loudly cleared his throat and with a finger to her lips she shushed him. 'Do you want to waken the whole street? Anyway, I thought we said all we had to say last night, or am I missing something? What are you doing here at this unearthly hour, huh?'

'Well, since you have taken the day off work I thought it would be an awful shame to waste it and I hoped you might consider going out with me today. I promise not to upset you. Surely we can at least be friends for one day. I can't picture life without you, Louise.'

She stood tight-lipped as if pondering over his offer. 'On one condition,' she said a bit too abruptly.

'What's that?' he asked anxiously.

'We don't argue or grumble or rake over old ground. I think we could have a nice day together as good friends if we don't bother to make promises that we can't keep. OK?'

He eagerly nodded his head. 'I promise. No sarky remarks. No bickering.'

'Away you go then. Come back at a reasonable hour, say about eleven, and I should be ready to go.'

She shooed him out the door, and quietly shut it behind him. Closing her eyes, she leaned against the cool door, thanking God and all the saints for giving her another chance and asking them to guide her to do the right thing this time. If she couldn't bite her tongue and be more agreeable, then all would be lost as far as Conor was concerned. It was her last chance to put things right between them.

21

On Saturday morning, Harry joined Louise in the scullery while she was stirring the porridge. She glanced over her shoulder at him, at his big smile, happiness exuding from every pore in his face, and her gloom lifted a couple of notches as she found herself smiling back at his infectious grin. 'You look like the cat that stole the cream.'

He laughed uproariously. 'I feel like it too.'

Placing a finger to her lips, she shushed him, nodding towards the wall behind which their father slept. 'Then your meeting with Dick Patterson went all right, I take it?' she said softly.

Harry lowered his tone to suit his sister's. 'You could say that. But I just need some advice, so I do.'

'Well now, I can't help you there, I'm afraid. If it's expert advice you want, you—'

He interrupted her. 'No. No, it's nothing like that. I certainly want to hear your opinion of Dick's proposition, but I also want Conor's advice on it.'

'Now? You mean, like today?'

'Yes, if that's possible.' He looked taken aback. 'He is off back to Birmingham early tomorrow, isn't he?'

'And you're working this weekend, aren't you? So when do you propose talking to him?'

He looked crestfallen. 'I was hoping he'd spare me a few minutes. I'm working from twelve today until twelve on Monday with the usual breaks. Is there any chance of seeing him before you two go out today?'

Louise was glad now that Conor had dropped by earlier to talk to her, and she wouldn't have to explain to Harry that they wouldn't be going out together any more, that they had decided to go their separate ways. She could tell him about that some other time when she had gotten used to the idea herself. Certainly not now. Harry would learn soon enough that it was over between them.

Meanwhile she said, 'You're in luck. If you can be here at eleven today you might see him. He's picking me up then.'

The door to Tommy's room opened and he came out into the kitchen. Hands on hips, he stood at the entrance to the scullery and scowled at them. 'What's all the noise about?'

343

'What noise?'

'You two were kicking up enough racket to waken the whole street. Is that porridge nearly ready?'

'You're up earlier than usual, aren't you? Guilty conscience or something?' Louise enquired. 'Sit down and I'll lift yours now.'

'Sarky bitch! I heard your voices through the wall and thought that I had overslept,' he growled by way of an excuse. 'The pair of you were shouting at each other, so you were. I thought you were having a bit of a barney. What has you up so early anyway? Considering you have the day off and he's on the weekend shift? What's going on then?'

'Nothing that would interest you, Da.'

Disgruntled, Tommy went and sat at the table and Louise said softly to Harry, 'Ignore him if he starts asking any questions. He's just being a nosy auld bugger as usual. We weren't making any noise. Shouting indeed! We were speaking too low for him to hear and that's what got him out of bed so quickly. He was afraid of missing out.'

Remembering his outburst of laughter, which had been loud enough to waken the dead, Harry felt guilty but tentatively agreed with her.

Ladling some porridge into a bowl, she carried it to the table and placed it in front of Tommy, saying sweetly, 'Were you afraid of missing out on something, Da? Would you like us to repeat our conversation for you?' These words were said tongue-in-cheek and she paused, as if waiting for an answer.

A baleful glare was his only reply and she berated herself. She had better mind her Ps and Qs or he might go and move in with Cissie O'Rourke just to spite them.

Harry had been to the newsagent and was coming up the street as Conor was leaving his home. Harry paused to pass the time of day with Cissie O'Rourke who was standing, arms folded, in the hall. Then he and Conor strolled up the street and entered the house together a few minutes before eleven.

Conor greeted Louise. 'Hi, love. Harry's been telling me that he needs some advice from me.'

'Indeed he does.' Louise glanced at Harry. 'Da's gone out, so we have the house to ourselves. Do you want to talk to Conor in private, Harry?'

'No, Louise, I want your opinion as well as Conor's advice so please stay.'

The three of them huddled round the table as Harry began to relate Dick Patterson's offer, explaining in as much detail as he could what had been discussed the night before. 'I don't think I've left out anything of importance, but I might have omitted some small details that are of no consequence. It was a bit much to take in all at once.'

When Conor realised that it was not off the top

of the head advice that Harry was after, he asked for some writing paper and, taking a fountain pen from his breast pocket, prepared to listen attentively, occasionally making notes. Harry finished his narrative, raised an inquisitive eyebrow and looked expectantly at Conor.

'I think I've covered just about everything significant. And I did take your advice, Louise, and told Dick that I would need some time to think it over before committing myself to anything. He agreed. What do you think, Conor?'

'What time do you start work today, Harry?'

'Twelve o'clock.'

A glance at the clock on the mantelpiece showed Conor that it was just after half past eleven.

'It's time you were on your way, then.' With a frown, he quickly scanned the notes he had made. 'I wish I had known sooner about this, Harry. There isn't much that I can do today. It could all be pretty straightforward, but then again it could be a right pig in a poke, if you know what I mean. Like an awful lot of trouble for you. Before I commit myself I'd need to see that written contract you mentioned. Just to make sure there is nothing hidden in the small print that could possibly tie you up contractually and maybe even financially. You never know. You mentioned that it would be a legal and binding document. Well, you know the old adage, "Act in haste, repent at leisure," so

346

don't you sign anything until I've had a chance to look it over. Is that absolutely clear now?'

Louise bristled with indignation. 'Dick Patterson is too decent a man to do anything underhand, so he is.'

Conor's head shot up and he caught her eye. 'How can you possibly know that? Eh? Didn't you say you have only recently met the man? Isn't that right?' His glance turned on Harry. 'Or Perhaps Harry has known him longer than I am aware of?'

Harry puffed out his cheeks with some exaggeration. 'No, no, I just met him last week with Louise.' He turned to Louise. 'I agree with Conor. He's right, Louise. Although I find him nice and agreeable, Dick is practically a stranger to us. We don't really know him, do we?'

Conor had watched changing expressions flit across Louise's face and guessed that she didn't agree with her brother. Now he prompted Harry. 'Are you willing to take a chance? Or are you prepared to wait, Harry? Otherwise I'll not be able to advise you of what's in your best interests. If you can't wait you'll need to get someone in town to handle it for you.'

'Oh, I'll take your advice and wait, Conor. After all, I only spoke to Dick last night, you know. There is no great hurry. I'll see if I can chase up that contract. Make sure everything is above board.'

'Well, it looks as if you won't get it today, or tomorrow, it being Sunday. And I'm off again early in the morning. So if you like, you can post it over to me when you get your hands on it, and I'll get back to you as soon as I can. Is that all right with you?'

'That would be great, Conor. At the moment I honestly don't know what to do. I'll make up my mind when I have the contract. Dick's going back to Dublin today for a couple of days and then he'll be back here for a week. It's more than likely I'll get the contract when he's back in Belfast. Louise and I will have a look at it and then I'll post it over to you. That would be the quickest thing to do. I'm assuming that Louise has your address.'

'Of course I have,' she butted in crossly. 'How do you think we communicate with each other, eh? Carrier pigeon or something?' she said sarcastically.

'All right! There's no need to get on your high horse. I was just making sure. This is a very serious matter for me, so it is.'

'Sorry, Harry. Of course it is. I didn't mean to snap at you.' She glanced at Conor. 'I've got a lot to think about at the moment. Look, you had better go or they'll be sending over to see if you intend coming in to work today, and you don't want that. I'll see you tonight.'

Clasping Conor's hand in a firm grip, Harry

shook it. 'Thanks a lot, Conor. I'm much obliged. I'll be in touch with you as soon as I can.' He quickly left the house and took Springview Street at a run.

Alone at last, Louise didn't know what to expect. She turned in Conor's direction and found him eyeing her covertly.

'What's on your mind?' she asked. 'Have you decided you would prefer not to spend the day with me after all? Don't be afraid to say. If you're having second thoughts I'll understand.'

He began to fluster. 'No. No, nothing of the kind. What makes you say that?'

'The fact that you can't look me straight in the eye for one thing. I thought perhaps you had changed your mind about us going out together today.'

'Far from it. I have all kinds of treats planned for you.'

'I'm relieved to hear that. I thought that you might be a bit short of money.'

Knowing that she was harping on about the language book he had bought in Eason's, Conor debated whether to have it out with her. He decided against it. Maybe he would get a chance later. He laughed instead. 'I think I'll just about manage to get by.'

Louise watched him playing with ideas. When he wasn't forthcoming, she said, 'I'm ready. I just have to change into some decent clothes. I'll be about ten minutes. Then we can take the town by storm.'

It was a warm day with the sun trying to push clouds aside and come out in all its glory. Convinced that it would eventually manage to do so, Louise dressed carefully. Determined to look her best, she chose a pale-primrose-coloured dress.

Made of fine cotton, it was high at the neck with a neat collar, small white pearl buttons that she left undone, and a white satin band encircled her slim waist. The fine material clung to her hips and flowed gracefully around her calves. Having brushed her hair until it shone and fell to her shoulders in blonde waves, she powdered her nose and examined herself in the mirror. Pleased with her reflection, she took her best white woollen cardigan from a drawer and swung it loosely around her shoulders before descending the stairs.

Conor heard her coming and rising to his feet he watched the vestibule door. Overcome by her fresh beauty, he made to approach her but stopped himself in time. He had agreed to their parting the night before and it wouldn't be right to take her in his arms now for a hug. She might not reciprocate and that would be a bad start to their outing. 'You look a picture. Will I have the pleasure of your company for the whole day?'

'If you so wish.'

'I certainly do. I've been thinking. Since the weather is fine I would like to treat you to lunch, anywhere you like . . . your choice. Then we'll go wherever you want and enjoy each other's company without any interference. And to crown it all we'll have dinner in some grand hotel this evening. How does that sound?'

Louise smiled wryly. 'Like a fond farewell, if you ask me. Still, I'm glad you want us to break up in a blaze of glory. But can you afford all these lovely treats?'

More at ease now, he fixed his eyes on hers, holding them intently. 'I tossed and turned, couldn't sleep a wink all night tormenting myself about everything. I don't really think that we're doing the right thing, you know. We still need to talk this through. OK? I can't bear the thought of you with anyone else. It's driving me to distraction.'

'Last night we decided to go our separate ways, remember? No more quibbling. This morning we agreed to spend time together as friends.'

Louise took a determined stand, but he responded with an emotional plea. 'Then how will we be able to resolve our differences?'

'Let's just take things as they come, eh? See if we can be friends without any bickering for once. Then decide what's best. Believe me, otherwise we'll be just wasting our time. So what's it to be?'

With a shrug he gave in gracefully. 'So be it.'

22

Peggy attempted to crawl stealthily from under the bedclothes on Sunday morning to avoid waking Louise, only to find her feet entangled in the sheets. She fell off the bed onto the linoleum with a resounding thump, rousing Louise from a deep sleep. 'Sorry, sis,' she gasped. 'I was trying so hard not to disturb you.'

Pulling the blankets back over her with an irritable grunt, Louise gave a start and squinted at the bedside clock. 'What time is that?'

Peggy was all apologies. 'I'm sorry, sis. I really am. It's only half past seven. It's early, you lie on for a while. I'll be as quiet as I can.'

'You quiet? You don't know the meaning of the word. You're like a bull in a china shop.' Rubbing the blear from her eyes with her knuckles, Louise groaned and made to sit up but flopped back down again as a sudden thought struck her. 'Are you right in your mind? This is Sunday.' She squinted at her sister. 'Isn't it?'

'I know it is and it's also the day that Angela gets christened, remember?'

'Not until twelve o'clock Mass she doesn't. Get back into bed for a while. It won't take you nearly five hours to get ready.'

'I want to have a bath before me da gets up and then I'm going to put some of those ribbons in my hair to try to get it to curl. You know, the way you used to do it.' The 'ribbons' were strips of cloth that Louise had cut from an old dress for that express purpose.

Wide awake now, Louise sat up. 'What do you want to do that for? Your hair is lovely as it is.'

'Remember you said that I could wear your new suit?'

Louise nodded apprehensively, not knowing what to expect. With all the happenings of the last couple of days she had completely forgotten about it. She waited with bated breath to hear what her sister had to say. Surely she wasn't able to squeeze into that suit?

'You'll be pleased to hear that you were right and it is too small for me . . . but . . . now please don't shout at me. I didn't think that you would mind . . . I also tried on your black interview suit and,' she paused dramatically, 'it does fit. Honest. Cross my heart and hope to die. It's not tight enough for me to do any damage or stretch the seams.'

Louise smiled at her. 'I know, it's a different style. The loose-hipped jacket and wrapover skirt will suit you fine. Yes, I'm sure it will look good on you.'

'And you don't mind if I borrow it, then?'

'So long as you take care of it. Remember, Angela may be lovely but she spews just like any other baby and it stinks just as bad, so be very careful how you hold her.'

'I will, I promise. So what do you think? Advise me, please. I thought perhaps if I curled my hair I'd look different, you know, more mature-looking, especially as I will be dressed in black.'

Louise was dismayed to hear this and crossly objected. 'Why on earth would you want to do that, eh? Don't put years on yourself, love, you'll be old soon enough. You're lovely as you are. Besides, you've never curled your hair before and God knows how it will turn out. What if it's a mess, eh? Then what will you do?'

Peggy looked mutinous. 'You used to curl your hair with strips of cloth and it was always lovely.'

'I know I did, and it was an awful nuisance to do it! It took so long. I discovered it was easier just to curl it round my fingers while it was still damp and work on it.'

'It's all right for you to say that. You've a kink in your hair and it curls even if you don't twist it around your fingers, so don't patronise me.'

'Tell you what, go and take your bath and I'll have a go at curling your hair, since you're so set on it.'

'You really mean that?'

'So long as you don't blame the outcome on me if it doesn't meet with your approval. Away down and get bathed before me da takes over the scullery. You'll find the cloth strips I used in a box under the stairs.'

'Thanks, Louise. You're the best sister in the world.'

Peggy scooted downstairs and Louise sank back against the pillows, a satisfied smile on her face.

Whilst Peggy was attending to her toilette, Louise lay snug and happy in the big double bed. She was in her glory. The time spent with Conor yesterday had been the most enjoyable day in a long while. They had just followed their inclinations and after a dander around the shops along Royal Avenue they had stopped at a café on York Street attached to the Co-operative store. The top floor was used as a dance hall – the Orpheus – on Wednesday and Saturday nights, but during the day it was used as a café and was always worth a visit. It was bright and clean, with a good selection of delicious snacks and pastries. Over lunch they talked and teased each other. It was as it used to be when they first went out together: no long silences or hurtful remarks, or looking to find fault in each other's words.

Afterwards they had a walk around the vast store itself. The Co-op, as it was locally known, was a large department store and sold just about everything under the sun. Louise was enchanted with the china department and the furniture department sent her into a state of raptures.

'Oh, to be able to buy a three-piece suite like that.' She pointed to a settee and two matching chairs, loaded with cushions in exquisite colours. They were arranged around a circular, highly polished table on which stood a figurine of a Grecian-style lady holding an urn on one shoulder.

Conor's eyes twinkled as he cast a sideways glance at her. 'What good would it do you?'

Louise drew herself up to her full height. 'What good? It would make me feel like a princess, so it would. What good, indeed!' she scoffed, as she elbowed him in the ribs.

'Well, for a start, where would you put it?'

She looked at him in bewilderment, then the penny dropped. 'Don't be stupid. I'd need a big house as well.'

They had paused by the suite. Sitting on the settee and putting an arm around her shoulders,

Conor pulled her close. 'Louise my love, how I wish I was in a position to buy you a beautiful home and that suite and everything else your heart desires.'

She looked into his eyes and confessed shyly, 'I don't need a big house. All I need is love.'

'Well, that's not a problem. You should know by now that I love you.'

'Do you, Conor? Do you really love me? Are you quite sure about that? Or are you still in love with the past when we were foolish enough to think we could change everything to suit ourselves?'

He was startled at this disclosure. 'How can you even think like that . . . unless you're having second thoughts.' He was gazing intently at her, a concerned glint in his eyes. 'I do love you. Really. Surely you know that by now. And I want to give you the best I can. Within my capabilities, that is.'

'Shush, Conor. Remember you promised we were not going to rake over old ground. Please let's forget everything for a few hours. OK?'

Realising she was right and that they were about to fall into the same old ruts, he nodded his agreement. 'My lips are sealed.'

'Good! Then we'd better get up off this sofa before someone throws us out.'

Even if they couldn't afford these beautiful things, it was lovely seeing how the other half lived.

Conor led her to the floor above, devoted to

ladies' and gents' clothing. The furniture was quickly forgotten as Louise became enthralled by the vast variety on display. Conor surprised Louise by buying her a jumper that she had gone into raptures over and had obviously fallen in love with. It was a fine, soft knitted mohair in a beautiful shade of pink and was a bit on the expensive side. In spite of all her attempts to put him off the idea, he kept insisting until at last he wore down her resolve and she relented, humbly accepting the beautiful gift. She paraded around, proudly holding the paper sack with Co-op emblazoned across it for all to see.

As they left the store, still troubled, and with a nod towards her present, Louise said, 'Are you sure you can afford this, Conor? It is very expensive. I can still take it back, you know. You're not leaving yourself short, are you? Or . . . have you come into some money lately?' Her eyes widened in anticipation. 'Or better still, have you won the pools?' she said with a giggle.

Pleased that she was worrying about the state of his finances and obviously didn't want him to run short, he smiled fondly at her. 'Afraid not. I've been saving all my spare cash to treat you and I had enough to buy that gift,' he nodded towards the carrier bag, 'thank God. I'm just glad to give you something you really like.' His voice was heartfelt as he looked at her, eyebrow raised.

Although nothing was said, this was a reference to the book she had resented his buying for another woman and she felt ashamed. She knew that she had been most unkind towards him that day, when he was already smarting at finding her locked in deep conversation with George Carson. Worse, she had left Conor standing around whilst she prolonged the chinwag. Doubt set in. Was that why he had spent so much money on her? Not wanting to start fault-finding, she turned away from him in confusion.

Conor knew her well enough to guess that she was still aggrieved about his purchasing the book. At the risk of stirring up any more bad feelings, he said softly, 'With your permission I'd like to clear the air about something.' Seeing that he had her full attention, he continued, 'Cast your mind back to that day I purchased a language book in Eason's for a friend.'

Undecided, she looked at him in silence for some moments. 'Not just any old book, but a *very expensive* one if I may say so.' She emphasised the words 'very expensive' to make sure he got the message. She didn't want to hear any lame excuses from him.

'Yes, an expensive book it was, that I admit. When you told me the price it practically took my breath away. But you see, that's when everything went pear-shaped. I had no intentions of buying the damned book. I only wanted your opinion on it.'

Louise's mouth formed in a soundless O. Then she made as if to interrupt but a raised hand stopped her before she could find her tongue.

'Please hear me out. I had been asked to find out the price of that particular book by my sister's friend, so she could compare the price with those in the Birmingham shops. She wanted to buy it for a friend as a birthday present. But to my great surprise, and before I could get a word in edgeways, you had it wrapped up, telling me the price and saying you couldn't allow me a discount on it. I was completely gobsmacked.' He paused, a sad expression on his face. 'I bet that Deirdre girl was wondering what was going on. She was watching us like a hawk.'

Louise grimaced. She remembered her friend's avid interest in their proceedings. And who could blame her, the way they had been carrying on?

Seeing that he had made his point, Conor continued, 'One thing led to another and before I knew it, and to my great dismay, I must admit, I found myself paying for a book that I didn't even want. Receiving my change from a haughty-faced young woman I didn't recognise as my girlfriend and in a matter of minutes I was standing outside the shop, embarrassed and confused.'

Colour had crept up Louise's neck as he explained

the unwanted purchase and she cringed with shame. 'I'm sorry, Conor. I didn't know. Honest.'

'I know you didn't.'

'I am very, very sorry. I really should have known better.'

He puffed out his cheeks in an exaggerated sigh. 'That's what I thought too. However, I was later more upset by the thought that you were annoyed that I had called in and caught you deep in conversation with your old flame George Carson. I just want you to know the truth. Now that's me finished. Hopefully we can enjoy the rest of the day out.' He looked troubled. 'That is, if you believe every word I told you?'

'I do, and I'm ashamed of myself. I might be able to get it changed for you or maybe get your money back.'

'He shook his head. 'No! There's no need to do that, but thanks all the same.'

Again Louise made to speak and again he raised his hand. This time he gently touched her cheek and gave her a quick kiss. 'No more recriminations. What do you say we take the tram to Greencastle and paddle in the sea for a while? If the tide is out we can walk along the beach to Whitehouse and up the Mill Road. Then along Whitewell Road to Floral Park and on to the Antrim Road. From there we could get the tram back into the city centre. We have enough time and we would certainly be ready for our dinner in the International Hotel after all that walking.'

'That's a wonderful idea, Conor. You really know how to treat a girl, don't you? I was hoping that you would suggest something like that, but are you sure of those directions? We're not going to get lost, are we?'

'Your wish is my command. Trust me, we won't get lost.' He clicked his fingers. 'And lo and behold, here's a tram coming to collect us.'

Grabbing her hand, he ran her to the nearby tram stop outside the Co-op and bundled her on to the platform and upstairs to the upper deck. Louise giggled the whole time. Conor was delighted to be in the clear as far as the awkward saga of the book was concerned and hoped that all was now well between them.

Peggy, coming upstairs wrapped in a bathtowel, the box of ribbons clutched under her arm, brought Louise back to reality. She got out of bed and pulled on an old cardigan and her slippers because even in warm weather the linoleum was cold to her bare feet.

'Put on something warm, Peggy, and let's get that hair sorted out.'

Once they were settled, Peggy sat on the only chair in the bedroom so that Louise could work her magic. Louise straightened the tangles in her sister's hair and voiced her surprise at just how long it had grown.

'Actually it's about the right length at the moment for curling. So here goes.'

Separating fine strands Louise wound them round a long piece of ribbon-like material and, tightening it up close to the head, secured it in place. It took about a half-hour to complete the whole process and Louise eventually finished with a long audible sigh of satisfaction.

'You know something, Peggy? I think this is going to turn out all right. It's easier working on someone else's hair rather than your own. I used to feel all tied up in knots when I'd done mine.'

'Thank you, sis. I'll come down and help you with the breakfast.'

'That'll be a first,' she snorted. 'But there's no need. You have a wee lie-down. I'll shout up when it's ready.'

Downstairs, instead of going into the scullery, Louise took a chair with a view from the window. She wanted to watch out for Conor, who was popping in to say farewell before heading off back to Birmingham. The night before, they had dined at the International Hotel. The meal was scrumptious and, replete, they moved from the restaurant into the lounge. They sat side by side on a comfortable sofa, sipping orangeade and talking until it was time to catch the last tram home, where they had a kiss and a cuddle saying their goodnights.

She saw Conor pass the window now and had the front door opened before he could raise his hand to knock, to avoid waking her father. He entered the hall, eased his holdall to the floor and closed the door gently. He was delighted to note by the silence in the house that her da apparently wasn't yet out of bed. Taking her in his arms, he devoured her with his lips and whispered endearments in her ear, his hands caressing her body while she feverishly urged him on.

This was different from the usual Conor; there was no holding back. He had never allowed himself to lose his self-control to this extent before. But why now? Had he made up his mind to marry her and get a position in Belfast? Or was he running out of patience and taking what he could get, while it was available?

She was not to find out. Tommy McGuigan made a lot of hawking and coughing noises to make them aware of his presence when he left his bedroom and entered the kitchen. With a heartfelt sigh and a final lingering kiss full of passion, Conor reluctantly let go of Louise and was out the door in a trice. He was in no fit frame of mind to face any aggravation from Tommy McGuigan.

Conor headed up the street towards Waterford Street and cut through to the Falls Road. His mother had insisted on rising early and making a fry-up for him, this being his last morning at home. She wanted answers as to what Louise and he intended doing. And he knew that she thought he was lying when he told her that he didn't know. So he avoided passing the door again in case she collared him, hoping to get a last shot at him.

Peggy was almost ready for the christening. She sat on the chair in front of the wardrobe mirror from where she could see Louise unroll and remove the ribbons from her hair. Dismay furrowed her brow as she anxiously watched a corkscrew curl escape each piece of cloth. At last all her hair was free and she gaped in horror at the tiny tight curls sticking out all over her head.

Her wide dark-blue eyes welled with tears as she reached up and pulled at the curls; just to see them bounce back to her scalp like a coiled spring. 'It's awful,' she whimpered through trembling lips, 'Oh, I wish I'd listened to you, sis. I can't go out looking like this.'

A bit overwhelmed herself at the sight of Peggy's hair, Louise sent a silent prayer up to her favourite saint, St Theresa, who had never let her down before and, gripping her sister's shoulders, gave her a gentle shake. 'Behave yourself! I'm not finished yet.'

Curl by curl, she loosened each one with her

fingers, pulling it taut until it dropped significantly. Feeling more confident now, she wound the strands of hair around a finger, loosening the curls, coaxing them into shape. Then she brushed the hair from the roots to the ends, smoothing and fingering it around Peggy's head until it formed a bright halo. Whilst this was going on Peggy's eyes remained shut tight, her face screwed up, and Louise made tsk-tsking sounds with her tongue as if she wasn't having any luck. Then finally with a smile of triumph on her face and a quick thank-you to St Theresa she said, 'There you go. It's much better now, so you can open your eyes.'

As if against her will Peggy forced her eyes open and gazed at her reflection. Then straightening up in disbelief, she exclaimed, 'Is that me?' Her glance shot from the vision in the mirror to her sister and back again. 'I don't believe it! I don't believe it!'

'Well, if it's not you, then who do you think it is?'

Slowly Peggy rose to her feet and approached the mirror as if in a trance. Her head felt like air. Curls clung close to her skull and the light streaming in through the bedroom window turned them to gold.

'I don't believe it,' she kept repeating like some mantra. She touched the softness with fingers that trembled; it felt like silk. Close to tears, she spluttered, 'It's beautiful, so it is.' She was overcome with emotion and Louise felt a pang of guilt. Peggy was so easy to please; in future she must spend more time with her sister. Treat her like the adult she was and not as a child.

'Wait till me ma sees you. You look absolutely gorgeous, Peggy. She will be so proud of you.'

Peggy always championed her father when given the chance. 'And me da?'

'And me da. He'll be delighted. If he recognises you, that is. Away you go downstairs now and put on your jacket and shoes and give me a chance to finish getting ready.'

Peggy planted a kiss on Louise's cheek. 'If you need any help, give me a shout.'

The front pews were reserved for the parents and family of the child to be baptised. As family members arrived, they each fawned over the baby, saying how beautiful she was and gazing in wonder at Peggy's transformation, their faces bestowing more compliments than words could ever convey.

Nora couldn't believe her eyes and hugged Peggy tight. 'My baby has grown up.'

Not to be outdone, Bill whispered, 'I always said you were a dark horse. You look beautiful, Peggy.'

'It was our Louise who did my hair. She deserves all the credit.'

'No! The beauty was always there. Louise just brought it to life.'

The bell tinkling in the sacristy sent warning tones that the Mass was about to start, causing everyone to scuttle for their seats as the priest and altar boys took up their positions.

The baptism itself was to take place when the Mass ended. Family and friends remained in the pews and waited until the noise and bustle of the congregation leaving the church had subsided. Then Father Connelly stood by the holy water font and greeted the parents, godmother and family friends. You could hear a pin drop as the christening began. It went over a treat, Father Connelly congratulating Johnnie and Mary on having produced such a lovely, contented baby. Young Angela Margaret McGuigan made not a sound when the holy water was poured over her head and a little trickled down her cheek. She just lay on Peggy's arm, her eyes watching every movement, and gurgled happily as Peggy held her over the holy water font.

When they left the church, outside family and friends had gathered around Baby Angela Margaret and Peggy to wish the baby all good luck for the future and to offer silver coins as was the custom. Peggy nearly outdid Angela as everybody admired her new hairdo and costume, while Johnnie and Mary stood back taking it all in, grinning from ear to ear with pride.

It was Louise who noticed her father lingering

at the top of Grosvenor Road from where he could see all that was going on. She was in a quandary. They were all going back to Johnnie's house where a buffet and drinks were being laid on to wet the baby's head. Should she ask her brother to invite their father to join them? Then her eye fell on Liam Gilmore who was there with his mother and father, the happy, doting grandparents, and she knew it was too soon. Liam was Mary's brother but it would be many a long day before enough water passed under the bridge for the families to be united . . . if ever. Her father would never forget Liam's cowardly attacks on his Louise and Conor O'Rourke.

23

The first thing Deirdre did on Monday morning when she came into the staff room was rush to Louise's side. Lifting her friend's left hand, she gazed in mock dismay at her bare fingers. 'I was sure you would have a ring to show off this morning.' Unceremoniously she dropped Louise's hand and, with a look of scorn, eyed her accusingly as if her friend had committed some great crime. 'Shame on you, girl.'

Louise grinned at her. 'Just goes to show, eh? You'd have had me married off long ago if you had your evil way. Afraid of competition or something? Is that it?' Sadly shaking her head, Louise confessed, 'Far from getting engaged, Conor and I have decided to cool things off for a while and see how it goes. Not that it's any of your business, of course.'

'You mean *you* decided!' Deirdre paused as if to gather her thoughts. 'So, he won't be coming over to see you any more?' She sounded incredulous. Taking an exaggerated step back, one hand on her hip, she said, 'I don't believe you. You're having me on.' Louise was smiling and Deirdre, not so sure now, gasped, 'Aren't you?'

'He will be coming over as usual to keep in touch with his mother and we shall go out as friends . . . sometimes. That is if we both feel like it. And with your blessing,' she added with a hint of sarcasm.

'And you agreed to that?'

Louise nodded. 'Yes. Why not? It will leave both of us free to go out with others should we feel that way inclined. It will certainly suit me better. I'll be able to go where I want, with whomever I want, instead of sitting at home wondering what Conor's up to.'

'Just who do you think you're kidding?' Deirdre's look was contemptuous. 'Eh? You . . . sitting at home twiddling your thumbs? Come off it, Louise McGuigan. Do you think I'm an eejit or something? What about George Carson, eh? You've been leading him on no end. Are you going to give him the push as well? Huh, it's the money that has put Conor's nose out of joint, isn't it? George has turned your head by taking you to all them fancy clubs and splashing money about. That's what it's all about! Isn't it?'

Louise was hurt and outraged at these insinuations. How could Deirdre think so little of her? 'George and I are just good friends, nothing more,' she huffed. 'And yes, I do enjoy going out to clubs with him and I'm glad he is not stingy with his money. If he continues to ask me out, I'll go willingly, without any feeling of guilt. But there is nothing going on between us. Now that I'm a free agent I can go out with whomever I want. And I'm not a bloody gold-digger if that's what you're hinting at.'

Deirdre threw up her hands as if in defeat. 'I'm only giving you a friendly word of advice. You're taking one hell of a chance, aren't you? Conor is a very handsome lad and a good catch. Many a girl will be giving him the eye once it gets around that he's free of you.'

However, Louise was not to be appeased. 'I'm sure a lot of girls are doing that already. If we're meant for each other, nothing untoward will happen. If it does,' she shrugged, 'then we'll know that we're not fated to be together. Better to know sooner than later.'

'I hope you don't live to regret it, girl, that's all I can say.' Deirdre shook her head mournfully. 'Talking of George . . . he's been in a couple of times while you were off. Had a look round and left before anybody could approach him. What do you think of that?'

'By anybody, I take it you mean yourself. Before you could collar him.'

Deirdre laughed outright. 'Aye, something like that,' she admitted. 'When I caught his eye he was off like a scared rabbit.'

'Obviously he didn't want you giving him your sales patter, trying to sell him a book.' Glancing at the clock, she said, 'Come on, it's time we were getting out on the shop floor.'

Deirdre's parting shot as she headed for her allocated station was, 'Most likely, George was hoping to see you.'

Although she had enjoyed the days off, Louise really had missed going to work in the shop. Glad to get back into the swing of things after her short break, she worked hard, looking for tasks to do, like tidying shelves and putting books back in alphabetical order. She kept busy and the morning flew by. At lunchtime Deirdre cried off, saying that she had asked the boss for permission to go on a later lunch break that day as she was meeting her current suitor. Not that she had mentioned this reason to the boss.

Louise rolled her eyes. 'I wonder how long this one will last. You're just too fussy, you know. But enjoy yourself, after all, you're only going out for lunch.'

'Well, you never know. Perhaps he'll be Mr Right,' Deirdre replied with a smug smirk.

*   *   *

As Louise was about to step out through the door on her lunch break, the sight of George Carson gazing at men's clothes in a shop window across Ann Street brought her to an abrupt halt.

He was so absorbed in conversation with an attractive girl by his side that he didn't notice Louise. She hovered inside the bookshop, undecided what to do while examining his companion. She had a mane of beautiful auburn hair and a figure that would turn heads for a second look. Her clothes were obviously expensive. A long cashmere coat draped her slender body, with a pale primrose silk scarf thrown casually around her neck, highlighting her clear complexion. Stylish brown boots gave her added height.

Louise decided that she could do without being compared to this beauty. It would have been bad enough if she had been all dolled up and looking her best, but dressed as she was in her work clothes?

She dithered. What to do? Could she get away by pretending not to notice them and slip down the street and around the corner while they were engrossed in each other? She would certainly try. Awaiting her chance, she stole out of the shop at the same time as two other women and tried to appear to be with them; keeping her head turned, she passed the women, excusing herself and commenting on the weather. She made her way to the corner and turned into Cornmarket with a swift glance over her shoulder. George and the girl were still deep in conversation. With a great sigh of relief, she headed in the direction of her favourite café.

So much for her not wanting to speak to George. More fool her. He obviously had no intention of talking to her. Perhaps she was getting a bit above her station, thinking he might still be interested, indeed. Was that maybe why he had come to the shop looking for her when she had time off: in case she heard about his lady friend from someone else? He was a decent enough bloke and would try to save her any embarrassment.

But then, why had he brought this beautiful girl down to wait across the road from the shop with him? Whatever else he was, he wasn't spiteful. Could she be a relative? Louise toyed with this idea. She could very well be, she mused. Still, Louise wouldn't want to meet her, relative or not, in these circumstances.

Thank goodness Deirdre had asked to take a late lunch break today. Her friend would have been unable to stop taking the mick, and would certainly have called attention to the couple. At least Louise had been spared that ordeal. A confrontation in front of her friend? God forbid! She shuddered at the very thought of it.

However, she knew she would miss the visits to his club and other places of entertainment that were well beyond her pocket. George Carson was opening up a whole new world to her and that was what attracted her to him. She was nothing more than a gold-digger and should be ashamed of herself. George had probably worked out just how shallow she was and was giving her the cold shoulder. Well, if that were the case, she was certainly getting the message loud and clear. But still, she admitted to herself, it had been very nice while it lasted.

To get away from all this worry and confusion, her mind turned to the letter she had received this morning from Cathie Morgan. It was still in her coat pocket, unopened. Why was she so reluctant to read her friend's letter? Because she was afraid it would contain more bad news. What would happen if Cathie was expecting a baby and them not married? Her father would never let her return to the family home. Surely, in dire straits such as this, Mrs Morgan would overrule him?

She pushed open the door of the café, her taste buds watering at the lovely aroma of baking. It was busy and she joined the queue at the counter, scanning the room for an empty table, but there wasn't one vacant. She would have to take a tall stool at the counter along the wall, worse luck. Jean Garland made small talk as she served her, her attention elsewhere as her eyes roamed all over the café.

Pushing her tray towards her, Jean leaned over the counter and spoke in a low tone, 'Quick, Louise. A table has just been vacated. You can pay me later.'

Louise didn't waste any time. With a swift 'thank you,' she picked up her tray and hurried in the direction Jean had indicated.

Stirring sugar into her tea, she sipped it, then made herself comfortable and took Cathie's letter from her pocket. Opening it, she spread it out on the table beside her plate and, biting into the tasty ham sandwich she had bought, started to read, noting that Cathie's address was the same as before.

Dear Louise,

Just a short note to let you know the latest. I am expecting a baby. I was devastated at first, worrying about how on earth we could possibly survive with only Trevor's meagre wage coming in. Then our prayers were answered . . . at least I sincerely hope so.

You see, Trevor had confided in Alan Wright, a lad he is friendly with at work, about the baby and the state we were in. Alan couldn't understand how a lad with his education was doing labouring work, stacking shelves at night. He must have been discussing Trevor's situation at home with his father. Anyway, he came in to work the other day and said that his father had told a friend of Trevor's educational standards and suggested that he might want to interview him for a position that would soon become vacant in his building firm. And the outcome is that Trevor has to go for an interview on Friday. Please say a prayer for him, Louise, then maybe if he gets the job we'll be able to afford to get married.

I've no more news at the moment. All I can think about is this job interview. I do hope it works out. Give my regards to all back there.

Lots of love and God bless,
Cathie x x x

Louise squeezed her eyes shut to stem the flow of expected tears and sent a prayer heavenward to St Theresa, beseeching her intercession. She would write to Cathie tonight and try to cheer her up. Tomorrow she would call in to St Mary's on Chapel Lane during her lunch break and light a candle for them.

Deirdre came back from lunch with a wide grin on her face and stars in her eyes. A good sign! She and her latest conquest must have hit it off. That meant that she would have less time to poke her nose into Louise's affairs, as she would be too busy looking after her own. Later in the afternoon during a slack period, after first making sure none of the managerial staff was lurking about, Deirdre sought out Louise.

'Where on earth did you get to this lunchtime?' she demanded. Without any preamble she went on, 'George Carson came into the shop to see what was keeping you. I don't think he believed me when I said that you had already left. Couldn't understand how he'd missed you.'

Confused, Louise frowned. 'I wasn't supposed to meet him today. He must have gotten his wires crossed.'

'He had a very attractive girl with him. You should have seen her, Louise,' Deirdre gushed. 'Like a film star, she was gorgeous, so she was.'

Glad of her facial control, Louise smiled cheerfully and enquired, 'Did he say why he wanted to see me?'

'No. He said he was sorry to have missed you but would call in later today if at all possible, or one day this week.'

Louise shrugged as if she couldn't care less. 'I won't hold my breath.'

Disappointed at the reception her news was receiving, Deirdre said, 'Guess what? I'm going out again tonight. You know, this just might really be the right fellow for me.'

'How often have I heard that? Listen to me, Deirdre, and this time pay heed. Enjoy yourself.

Pretend you couldn't care less and see what happens. Most men enjoy the chase.'

'You think so?'

'I know so. Let *him* do the running for a change.'

'I think I'll try doing it your way. It seems to work where you're concerned. Oh-oh, here comes Mr Murray, talk to you later.'

George Carson didn't put in an appearance that afternoon and Louise breathed a sigh of relief. She felt drained and didn't want any more confrontations for the time being.

She hurried home from work, knowing a bigger load of washing than usual awaited her attention. If you take a break, she mused, the work just piles up on you. Sometimes she felt like an old married woman. By the time she got the tea over with, it would take her the rest of the evening to clear up the washing and hang it on the pulley line. In fact maybe some of it would have to wait until Tuesday.

Her da would go out as usual, his excuse being his need to get away from the steamy atmosphere in the house. Not that he'd be much use anyway; he would just sit there complaining as usual. Peggy was babysitting for Mary Ellen Smith tonight so she wouldn't be of any help. Feeling disgruntled, she opened the vestibule door and stopped in amazement.

Thank God for Harry. He had stopped his weekend shift only at midday, yet here he was, standing in the kitchen with a welcoming grin on his face. The smell of bacon and sausages filtered through from the scullery. After a few hours' sleep, he had dressed and got ready to go out, then started the tea: sausages, bacon and eggs, with two plates of crusty bread cut and buttered, the table set and the kettle simmering away on the stove.

'I hope this is all right, Louise. I didn't know what to make. Will I open a tin of beans?'

Planting a kiss on his cheek, Louise held him close and thanked him sincerely from the bottom of her heart. 'Thank you! Thanks very much, Harry. I owe you one. You sit down now. I'll finish off here.'

'Ah, give over, sis. You've helped me no end. Hannah and I are going up to the village later on to see if Dick Patterson is home from Dublin yet.'

'I hope he is. The sooner you get that contract over to Conor, the better. But I think you're being a bit premature. After all, he only left yesterday morning and as far as I know he has other business to attend to.'

'No matter, it's a nice evening and the walk will do us good. I'll let you know how I get on.'

On Tuesday morning, Harry told her that Dick wasn't home yet but he would take a stroll up there again tonight and maybe he'd have better luck then. There was a spring in his step and Louise was pleased to see him so happy.

At teatime on Tuesday evening, Dick Patterson's car drew up alongside her as she waited at the tram stop at the bottom of Castle Street on her way home. He greeted her with a warm smile. Without more ado she clambered into the front passenger seat, breathing a heartfelt sigh of pleasure as she sank into the soft leather. The thought struck her how great it would be to own a car. I could very easily get used to this and all it entailed, she mused. She was off again on one of her 'if onlys'.

Dick's voice invaded her thoughts. 'It's great to see you, Louise.'

She smiled back at him but felt a little uneasy at the expression in his eyes. She didn't deserve such kindness from this caring man. Was she maybe jumping the gun? Perhaps his feelings for her were like those of some fathers for their daughters? To be honest, taking her own father as an example, she didn't think so. But then again, everyone wasn't like Tommy McGuigan.

Perhaps she was imagining things, but after the remarks Dick had made to her before he left for Dublin, which she had found a little unnerving, she was beginning to feel somewhat ill at ease.

She quickly regained her composure enough to speak. 'Thank you for the lift, kind sir,' she trilled, then squirmed in her seat, knowing she hadn't got the tone quite right.

Aware of every move she made, of every inflection

in her voice, he wondered why she was fidgeting so much. Was she planning on letting him down lightly? Had she no feelings at all for him? Best take it slowly, he determined. One step at a time.

'I've had that contract drawn up for Harry, I'm glad to say. I'm pleased with the wording, nothing too deep that Harry won't be able to understand. Do you think he could come up tonight and we could go over it together?'

'Dick, I know for a fact that he would be delighted to.'

'Will you accompany him?'

She raised her eyebrow at him. 'Somehow or other, I think Hannah will be with him. They are both very excited about it all. They've been patiently walking up that road to your house this past couple of evenings to see if you were home yet. Everything seems to be working out well for them and I'm not one to play gooseberry.'

He drove in silence for some moments. 'Tell me, Louise, may I have the pleasure of your company some evening? Could we perhaps go to the Grand Opera House?'

She gave him a sideways glance. 'Why me? I mean—'

He interrupted her. 'Because I enjoy your company so much, of course.'

'Dick, I don't know what to say. I'm at a loss for words.'

'Say yes and I will call at your house for you and, if possible, I would like to meet your father.'

Louise wriggled uncomfortably. 'Dick, somehow or other I don't think that would be a very good idea,' she managed to splutter.

'Why not? Tell me . . . truthfully now. Do you find me so obnoxious?'

'Don't be silly. Of course I don't.'

They had arrived at her door. He warned himself to take it easy but crashed on regardless. 'Shall I come in and meet your father now? I'd really like a chat with him.'

'No! He won't be in at this time. He's on the late shift today.' She knew this to be untrue but hoped her father would not arrive and prove her a liar.

Dick submitted gracefully although he thought she was telling him a wee fib. She was becoming a little agitated and he didn't want to upset her any more than necessary. 'Perhaps another time then.'

Anxious now to get away, she said, 'Look, if you really want me to come to the Grand Opera House with you, let me know when you get the tickets and I'll meet you at the corner. It's best that my father doesn't know all my business. He'd never stop questioning me. Is that OK with you?'

He was somewhat relieved that she had at least agreed to go out with him. 'Whatever you say. I'll call into Eason's and confirm our date. Would tomorrow night be too soon? It's easier to get tickets for midweek shows than weekends.'

'That would be fine, Dick.' She was already outside the car and on the pavement and spoke over her shoulder. 'Thanks for the invitation.' In a flash she was inside the house.

Louise relayed Dick's message to Harry when she saw him. Her brother was overwhelmed with excitement.

'Sis, all this seems too good to be true. You wouldn't believe the plans Hannah and I are making. We might even get married sooner than anticipated. Liz has hinted that she will put the wedding over for us.'

Louise was perturbed by his enthusiasm. 'Be very careful, Harry,' she cautioned.

'Of course I will. I'll get your opinion on the contract tonight and if it passes your scrutiny I'll post it over to Conor tomorrow morning and see what he has to say.' He rubbed his hands together in glee. 'I'm thrilled to bits, so I am.'

'I can understand your exuberance, Harry, but don't rush into anything. Stop and think before making any rash decisions you might later regret. You're still too young to get married and Mrs McFadden can be quite intimidating. Don't let her try managing your affairs. Surely you can wait another year or two? And . . . don't ever forget the old adage, "If something looks too good to be true, it *is* too good to be true." So be warned. If in doubt, kick it out.'

'Your pearls of wisdom, eh, sis? I understand. But believe me, I'm determined not to let that happen. So stop worrying. I can't wait to get my hands on that contract. I only hope that Conor doesn't find any hidden pitfalls in it.'

24

Tommy sat on the easy chair by the hearth, reading *Riders of the Purple Sage*, a western by the popular writer Zane Grey. He and his friend Bobby down the street always exchanged western novels and Zane Grey was his favourite author. Louise was ironing Monday night's laundry and eyeing her father furtively, willing him to retire before Harry came back from his visit to Dick Patterson. She was looking forward to hearing Harry's news and have a good browse over the contract, without any nosy interruptions from her da.

She frowned as Tommy inched his chair even closer to the fire. He looked as if he was settling down for a good read, so that hit on the head the idea of a quiet chat with Harry. Once her da got his nose stuck into a Zane Grey book, he could become lost in it, staying up late many a night to finish it. That, however, didn't stop her da from homing in on a conversation if anything out of the ordinary was being discussed by the rest of the family. He never missed a thing. It was uncanny how he could be lost in a book one minute and yet the next be aware of all that was going on around him. She certainly couldn't. Harry wouldn't keep his da in the dark for long. No, he would soon put him wise once it was all signed, sealed and delivered.

Tuesday morning had started off bright and clear with a stiff breeze buffeting white clouds across a pale blue sky. Before leaving for work, Louise decided to take a chance on the weather and had managed to get the washing, still wet from the night before, out the back and on to the clothes lines. She'd made dire threats to Peggy to keep an eye out for the weather. If there was any sign of rain at all, she was to run home and bring the clothes in or her life wouldn't be worth living. The wireless forecasts were usually fairly accurate but one couldn't always depend on the meteorological men to get it right. So on Peggy's head be it.

That morning she had also lit the fire and banked it up with dampened slack to keep the house warm. That way, if all went well weather-wise she would be able to get the clothes aired in front of the fire as she ironed them. To her relief the rain hadn't materialised and the laundry was ready for ironing. Now she would be able to get everything cleared away before she retired for the night.

She continued to watch with chagrin as her da was obviously making himself comfortable for a long night's read. She'd show him! Stamping over to the shelf where the wireless sat, she switched it on and started fiddling with the knobs until she hit on a music station. Tommy's glare in her direction didn't pass unnoticed. She covertly watched his reflection in the mirror and was pleased when he marked his place by turning down the corner of the page and, closing the book, rose to his feet. Thank God for small mercies, she thought gleefully. Her da was about to retire. That settled that!

The smug look on her face quickly changed to one of utter dismay when, setting his book on the arm of the chair, he said, 'I'll put the kettle on and make us some toast. Eh, Louise? You deserve a wee break from that ironing, so you do.'

He must have twigged what she was up to. What else could she do but scowl and mumble crossly that it was time he made himself useful. He entered the scullery and there were a few thumps as he filled the kettle and put it on a low light on the stove to boil. Then, well pleased with himself, he returned to the fire with a toasting fork and a plate of cut bread. He poked at the hot embers and then, with a thick round impaled on the fork, he held it close enough to the embers to get the best result without actually burning it.

In a fit of anger, Louise got on with her ironing as if her life depended on it, surprised at the amount she accomplished as she was spurred on by her bad temper. Some time later her da, putting the fork carefully to one side on the hearth, rose from his seat with the toast piled on the plate. With a grin in her direction he made his way towards the scullery.

'There now, that didn't take too long, so it didn't.'

Breathing in the warm aroma of fresh toast made Louise feel rather peckish and her bad temper mellowed somewhat.

'I'll brew the tea now, shall I?' Tommy's voice reached her from the scullery. 'Are you going to take a break and join me?'

'I suppose I may as well. It's not too often that I get a cuppa handed to me.'

'You'll enjoy this toast, so you will. It's light and I've spread plenty of butter on it. The way you like it.'

Louise had to admit to herself that her da was certainly aiming to please. She wouldn't have expected him to know how she liked her toast done and her good humour slowly returned. Placing the hot iron on the hearth, she sat down opposite her father's chair and accepted the cup of tea he carried in to her, helping herself to a slice of toast from the plate.

Biting into it, she admitted, 'This is delicious. Is there much bread left?'

'About half a loaf. Why, would you like some more?'

'No. Just checking there's some left for the other two when they return.'

Tommy joined her by the fire and they ate in silence for a while. When he cleared his throat, Louise knew that he was getting ready to interrogate her.

'Tell me something, Louise, what would you think if Cissie O'Rourke and I were to get together?'

Louise almost choked on her toast as she spluttered, 'What do you mean by getting together? Like living together? Well, if that's what you mean, I wouldn't like it one bit, that's for sure. And, to be truthful, I think you'd be doing the wrong thing. I think you would live to regret it.'

His brow furrowed and he scowled at her. 'Just hear me out for heaven's sake, will you?'

'You can't change my mind, Da, no matter what you say. She and I don't get on and she's certainly not my idea of the ideal stepmother. In fact, far from it. She's a troublemaker, that one and, once you were married, I wouldn't risk living in the same street as her.'

'Now you're being silly. She is just a lonely

391

woman and I'd make sure to keep her on a tight rein.'

Louise actually laughed aloud at the idea of her father thinking that he could control Cissie O'Rourke. 'You've got to be joking.' She turned away in disgust.

'No. You're wrong. See here, I'm the one who will make the rules. Cissie knows where she stands with me. There would be no nonsense. And remember, you and Conor would get this house, so you would. I'd give a backhander to the rent man and get your name put in the book. Think of it! A rented house? They're like gold dust round here these days.'

'And two lodgers with it? No, thank you very much, Da. If and when I do eventually get married I won't stay here, you can bet your life on that. I'll want a house of my own.'

His eyed widened with surprise and he urged her, 'You're being very silly about this. Think about it, Louise. A rented house! That's something that isn't to be sneezed at around these parts. Won't you even think about it?'

'Well, as a matter of fact, I don't have to give it any thought at all. And you can save your breath on that score, Da. Conor and I have decided to go our separate ways for a while. So I'm not in the least interested in this house or any other house for that matter.'

To put an end to the conversation, Louise rose to her feet and took the empty dishes into the scullery.

Tommy gazed after her, open-mouthed. He raised his voice to make sure she heard him. 'What do you mean, "go your separate ways for a while"? I thought you were engaged.'

Without turning around, she waved her left hand in the air. 'Can you see any ring? Have you ever seen a ring on this finger, Da? It was all in the mind, nothing binding. It's just as I say. We're both going to see other people, see if we meet someone we like better. Enjoy ourselves while we're young enough. Got the message, Da? We've discovered that the world out there is a big place. And we want to learn more about it before we tie ourselves down to marriage.'

Alerted by sounds of revellers outside returning home from places of entertainment, and knowing that her brother and sister would arrive soon, she said, 'Listen to me, Da, we haven't told anyone else about this. It's nobody's business but ours. So mum's the word. Please?' she begged.

With a disgruntled snort, Tommy picked up his book and headed for his room. His daughter had given him a lot to think about. He wasn't all that keen to move in with Cissie O'Rourke, not if it wasn't going to change anything. He would rather stay put. The whole idea of moving in with Cissie was a feeble attempt to keep Louise and Conor on Irish soil.

A few minutes later Harry and Peggy got home. After a quick glance around, Harry nodded at Louise and mouthed the words, 'It looks good, sis.'

Louise smiled in return and gave him the thumbs-up.

This miming was behind Peggy's back. 'Is me da not home yet?' Peggy asked as she shrugged out of her coat.

'He went to bed not long ago. And keep your voice down so you don't disturb him.'

Peggy showed her surprise with raised eyebrows. 'Early, isn't he?'

'Not early enough,' Louise muttered softly with a grimace at Harry. She had finished ironing and, after putting the iron out of harm's way in the scullery, she piled the clothes into different lots ready to be taken upstairs.

Peggy sniffed the air suspiciously. 'Have you been treating yourself to some toast, girl?'

'No. Actually, me da made a cuppa tea for us.'

'He might have waited for us to come in,' Peggy said with a sulky pout.

Harry placated her. 'Never mind, Peggy. You get the pot and cups ready and I'll toast some bread.'

'Thanks, Harry. I'll go up and change into my nightdress first. I won't be long.'

Harry moved closer to Louise when their young sister left the room and, keeping his voice low, said, 'Everything looks great, Louise. I'm very pleased with the contract. I'll keep it until you get a chance to read it and then I'll send it over to Conor and if he gives it his approval . . . I'll be earning a fair bit of extra money every month. It's hard to take it all in. It's like some kind of dream that I hope I don't wake up from.'

Humming 'Danny Boy', he turned towards the scullery but Louise stayed him with a hand on his arm. 'If you're happy enough that it's all right, don't bother about me. Send it over to Conor tomorrow. The sooner he gets it the better. If he gives it the go-ahead then Dick can set the wheels in motion before he goes back to Dublin. I can see the contract any time. And, after all, you know that I'm no expert on anything like this.'

'Sure?'

She gave him a reassuring thump on the arm. 'Yes, I'm sure. This is your business, Harry, and I sincerely hope it works out for you. Conor is good at what he does, so you have that in your favour. Besides, he has the backing of his office at his disposal, should he need any advice.' She gave him a slight push. 'Go on, bring another fork and I'll help you toast the bread, before I go up to bed.'

'Thanks again, sis.'

* * *

It was near lunchtime when Dick Patterson came into the shop on Wednesday. Of course, being a celebrity, he was the focus of all eyes. Unconcerned, he ignored all the attention and browsed a bit in the history section, then selecting a book on Irish history, he took it over to Louise's counter.

Keeping his voice low, he said as he handed over his purchase, 'I managed to get two tickets for the Grand Opera House tonight. It's a drama. Do you like thrillers?'

'To tell you the truth, I have developed a liking for all stage productions. I love the theatre, real live people on the stage weaving great stories. I think they are wonderful actors and so talented, even the ones with small parts to play. Nothing is left to chance. They are all very professional. I feel a great admiration for them.'

He smiled at her enthusiasm. 'Good! That's good to hear. Then does tonight suit you?'

She nodded and he proffered his payment for the book. Putting it in a bag, she gave him his change with a 'Thank you, sir,' keeping it on a formal basis to foil any eavesdroppers.

'I'll pick you up tonight then, at the corner?'

He raised his eyebrows and she knew that it was a question not a statement. 'OK. At seven o'clock.'

'Now that that's all settled, will you let me take you out for a bite of lunch?'

Louise glanced over at the clock. How the morning had flown by. 'You certainly can. I didn't realise it was that time already. I'll just powder my nose and meet you outside. And thanks for asking, Dick.'

With a little salute, he said, 'See you outside then.'

She watched him walk to the door, a happy smile on her face. It slipped a bit when she turned to find George Carson awaiting her attention. He greeted her, head tilted to the side. 'You're a bit of a stranger.'

Aware that he must have seen Dick, Louise became a bit flustered. 'Deirdre mentioned that you were asking for me the other day.'

'Yes, I was indeed. How you got past me I'll never know. Are you avoiding me, by any chance?'

With a puzzled frown, Louise replied, 'Excuse me if I've got this all wrong, but did we arrange to meet on Monday?'

'You're right, of course we didn't. You see, my cousin is home from Canada for a holiday and he brought his fiancée over with him. He went to visit his old workplace on Monday and she didn't want to spend an afternoon stuck in some office with a bunch of strangers, so I brought her downtown to meet you and to ask if you'd like to join us for a drink.'

His cousin's fiancée. All was explained. 'It must be nice for you to see them, I'm glad for you.'

'Will you come out with us tonight? It will be just the four of us.'

'I'm sorry, but I have already made other arrangements for tonight, George.'

'How's about Saturday night? There is a great turn on at the club. Would you care to join us then?'

'I'm sorry, but I have already made plans for Saturday night also.'

He showed surprise. 'Are you having me on?'

Offended, Louise straightened up. 'I beg your pardon?'

His jaw dropped and he looked at her in amazement.

Louise responded to his surprise. 'What? You think Conor is my only friend and now that he's gone back to England I'll sit at home, hoping that you'll ask me out? Have a titter of wit, George. I already have a date for Saturday night.' Inwardly, she was asking God to forgive her for her outright lie.

George's face went beetroot red. He was all apologies. Embarrassed, he eventually managed to find his tongue. 'I think nothing of the kind. A lovely girl like you could have any man you wanted if you put your mind to it.'

'Not quite. I'm very choosy, so I am. You won't

find them queuing up at my door. Nevertheless some men do find me attractive and enjoy my company, believe it or not.'

He was flabbergasted. 'What brought all this on? I thought we were friends. I certainly meant no offence.'

'Yes, and I hope that we can remain friends, but, as I say, I am booked for tonight and Saturday night. Look George, I can't stand here gossiping all day. I'm meeting someone for lunch and I'm already late. Can I get you anything before I go?'

Without looking, he picked up a newspaper and handed it to her, fumbling in his trouser pocket for loose change.

She smiled inwardly when she saw it was the *Irish News* he had inadvertently picked up. He would kick himself when he realised his mistake. He'd never live it down if his Protestant friends ever found out that he had bought the *Irish News*. But that wasn't her problem.

'Sorry, but you'll have to excuse me.' She folded the newspaper and handed it back to him with his change.

He still looked stunned. 'When will I see you again?' he asked tentatively.

'Not any time this week, I'm afraid. Anyway, you know where to find me if you still want to take me out.'

She said an abrupt goodbye and hurried to the

staff room, inwardly laughing at his antics. That'll show George Carson not to take her for granted in future. Shrugging into her coat, she powdered her nose and picked up her handbag. Earlier, while talking to George, with a shake of the head to let her know that she was not coming, she had waved Deirdre on out. Her friend had probably assumed that she was going out to lunch with George.

Soon she was joining Dick outside. Her steps slowed when she saw that George had beaten her to it. The two men were deep in conversation.

As she approached them George eyed her intently through narrowed lids. Mindful that she had told him of her interest in George Carson, Dick was loath to ask him to join them.

Louise saved him from committing himself and smiled at George. 'Is this as far as you've got?' Without waiting for an answer, she turned her attention to Dick. 'Sorry for keeping you waiting, Dick. We had better get a move on or my lunch break will be over before it even starts.'

Dick quickly picked up on her cue. 'Nice to see you again, George.'

Louise didn't meet his eye when she said, 'Bye for now, George.' She was very much aware of his displeasure.

They walked off along Ann Street, while George stood for some time gazing after them. To say he was stunned would be putting it mildly. Wily old

Dick Patterson. Imagine him getting his oar in. Surely Louise couldn't contemplate going out with the likes of Dick Patterson? Why, he was years older than her. I'll make it my business to get to the bottom of this, he thought ruefully. Perhaps he *had* been taking it for granted that if ever Conor O'Rourke was out of the picture, he would be there to step in and enjoy seeing Louise without her having any expectations of marriage. Hadn't she made it quite clear that she would never marry a Protestant? That it would cause too much trouble for her and her family? Still, one didn't need to have marriage in mind to enjoy each other's company. They could carry on as before – in a purely platonic relationship.

So much time had been wasted that lunch was a hurried but enjoyable affair. Dick was a wonderful companion and pointed out things to her without being patronising. Even while listening to him, she picked up words that she knew but hadn't had the education to use in the right context. Nevertheless she was totally relaxed in his company and looking forward to accompanying him to the Grand Opera House that evening.

Harry had posted the contract off to Conor that morning and was going about in a dream. People had to speak to him twice, maybe three times, before getting his attention. Louise noticed that her da was eyeing him suspiciously. She wondered what he would have to say about Harry's plans.

Warning the family that she was going out and that she would be the first to use the scullery after they had eaten, she took the warm plates from the oven and served the dinner, ignoring her da's reaction to the portions of champ and sausages she doled out – it was all she had had time to cook. She also warned that she had no intention of washing the dishes before she went out so someone else would have to clear up. With a threatening glower at his younger sister, Harry immediately volunteered, saying he and Peggy would see to everything, while Peggy grimaced with distaste.

The meal over, Louise collected her towel and toiletries and was about to bar herself in the scullery when her father cornered her. 'Can I have a private word with you, Louise? I won't keep you a minute.'

Tight-lipped she let him into the scullery. 'You'd better not.'

'I can never manage to catch you on your own,' he grumbled. 'Is it true what you told me about you and Conor?'

'Keep your voice down,' she whispered. 'Why would I say so if it wasn't the truth, eh?'

'Cissie will be devastated when she finds out.'

'Huh, like I care what she thinks? I don't think

so. She'll not lose too much sleep over it, if I know that woman. She was only using me as a means to an end and her ruse has failed. She might even send you packing when she hears that Conor might not be returning to work in Ireland.' She was nudging him none too gently out into the kitchen as she spoke.

Suddenly enlightened, he cried accusingly, 'You're seeing some fella tonight, aren't you?'

'I thought you would never guess.' With a final shove, she closed and barred the door behind him.

As she approached the junction of Springfield Road and Falls Road, Dick's car drew alongside her at the kerb.

Once again she sighed as she sank into the soft leather upholstery. 'Do you know something, Dick? You are so lucky to have a car. Especially one as lovely as this.'

She failed to notice the satisfied smile on Dick's face as he savoured her words. Louise liked her comforts; that was something in his favour. 'I worked very hard to get where I am today,' he assured her. 'I wasn't handed anything on a plate.'

'I can well believe that. It's obvious that you're a hard worker. There is something decent and steadfast about you. I think you would be trustworthy. But tell me, why have you never remarried?' Suddenly flustered, she said hurriedly, 'Oh,

I'm sorry, Dick. Please forget I said that. It's really none of my business.'

'You can ask me anything you like, Louise. The truth is, I courted one other woman since my wife died but it didn't work out. So I kinda lost interest in the opposite sex.'

'That's a shame. You might have had a son by now who would eventually have taken over your business.'

He gave a light laugh. 'Oh, I haven't given up all hope entirely, you know. I've recently met someone I care a lot for, so who knows what might come out of it?'

Louise could not understand why these words were like a blow to her solar plexus. Why did she care if he had met someone? Why did she suddenly feel uneasy? Wasn't that what she wished for: to see him happy? Did she fear losing him as a friend? Surely not. She had known him only such a short time. Managing to conceal her dismay, she said, 'I'm so glad to hear that, Dick. You deserve a companion for your twilight years.'

These words mystified Dick. Was she deliberately misreading his insinuations? Or was she warning him off as gently as possible?

'Twilight years indeed! I'm not all that old, Louise. I'm probably not as old as your father . . . and I'm still young enough to start a family, you know.'

Louise thought of her father moving in with Cissie O'Rourke and maybe starting a family. Surely Cissie was a bit past it. Or could she still conceive? Weren't they the very same thoughts she had entertained about her own mother when Nora had disclosed that she was pregnant by her boyfriend Bill McCartney? Louise had been devastated by that disclosure as had everyone who had heard the news. Was Cissie pregnant already? It didn't bear thinking about. 'Is Cissie pregnant?' She unconsciously voiced her thoughts.

Dick had found a spot to park. His voice was clipped and cold when he assured her that Cissie and her father couldn't be further from his mind. And if Cissie was pregnant he knew nothing at all about it. After all, he had never met either of them.

Weighed down by her thoughts, Louise remained silent until they were entering the Grand Opera House. The silence remained unbroken while he ushered her through the chattering, jostling throng to the auditorium.

It was all so exciting that she forgot her anxieties. A delighted smile on her face, she turned to him as she sat down. 'These are great seats.'

His face lit up with pleasure. 'Only the best for you.'

She moved closer so that her arm was against his and reaching over with her other hand squeezed his forearm. 'Thank you very much, Dick.'

Not one to miss an opportunity, Dick quickly covered her hand with his and squeezed back. 'I'm glad you're pleased.'

He made no effort to release her hand and she felt that she had made a mistake. What must he think of her for being so forward?

Aware of her unease, Dick sighed inwardly and removed his hand. He expected her to move away but she remained leaning close against him. The lights dimmed and for a moment he was tempted to put his arm around her. He decided against it. He didn't think she would want a man in his twilight years, as she so nicely put it, cuddling her, especially in public.

The stage was set to look like the inside of a very old haunted house and the play had spiritualist overtones. Louise sat in rapt wonder when at one point, with the audience tense and on the edge of their seats, a ghostly figure floated across the back of the stage. It was so expertly done that it caught the audience unprepared, eliciting a lot of loud gasps and some suppressed screams. Louise reached instinctively towards Dick. He clasped her hand reassuringly.

The moment passed but she continued clinging on to his hand, her heart thumping in her breast. He shifted his body until her arm was through his and he hung on grimly. She made no effort to remove it. It was a long time since Dick Patterson had felt so happy in the company of the opposite sex.

At the interval he suggested that they stretch their legs and go to the bar for a drink. It was packed but Dick found a stool for her and joined the crowd at the counter to place their order.

Louise was startled when, above the babble in the lounge, a voice rang in her ear. 'Well, well, well, look who's here.'

A glance over her shoulder revealed George Carson, accompanied by the lovely redhead and a tall dark-haired man.

'Here, Louise, let me introduce you to my cousin,' he canted his head towards the man, 'Gordon and his lovely fiancée, Gabrielle. Who, by the way, prefers to be addressed as Gabby.'

Hands were shaken and pleasantries murmured about the play.

'Are you enjoying the show, Gabby?' The girl paid Louise no attention, smiling brightly over Louise's shoulder. Louise turned to see what had caught her attention and discovered that she was looking at Dick who had returned with their drinks. George made the introductions and the talk became general until George happened to mentioned that Dick was a famous author. At this revelation Gabby made it her business to sidle over beside Dick and engage him in conversation. It was obvious that she was well read. Louise was jealous as hell to see Dick so interested in everything Gabby said. She envied this girl her confidence and ability to keep a conversation flowing with these three men, while she sat sipping her drink in silence like some interloper who had no right to be in their company.

The barman announced it was five minutes before the play was due to restart and that patrons should return to their seats as quickly and quietly as possible. Dick was at her side immediately, smiling down at her, offering his hand to help her down from her stool and ushering her towards the door.

'Won't you join us for a drink afterwards?' It was Gabby who issued the invitation and it was directed at Dick.

'I'm afraid not. I'm driving and Louise has to be up early in the morning to go to work. Another time, maybe?'

'If you're not busy tomorrow, Dick, would you like to join Gordon and me? We intended going to Bangor but we can change the location to suit you. Can't we, Gordon?'

Gordon's eyebrows rose in enquiry, but whatever he read in Gabby's expression, he gave an abrupt nod and turned away.

'Thank you, Gabby, but I am very busy at the minute. I have a lot of paperwork to catch up on. But thanks all the same for the kind offer.'

Back in their seats, Louise said, 'Gabby was very forward, wasn't she?'

'I've met her kind before. Besides, she wasn't wearing a ring.'

'Nevertheless, she's supposed to be Gordon's fiancée. I must say I was surprised that he didn't rebuke her. He seemed quite spineless to me.'

'They probably have an understanding.'

The curtain-up put a halt to their conversation. Confused, Louise kept her distance during the second half of the play, and Dick silently berated George Carson for interrupting their enjoyment.

25

As the drama continued to unfold before them, there were more than a few frightening surprises in store. A ghostly apparition hovered behind the heroine before disappearing towards the back of the stage. Soon after, a shapeless form swooping over the audience, wailing like a banshee, brought many an involuntary scream from the women and stifled gasps from some of the men. It all seemed so real and so scary that Louise unconsciously edged closer and closer to Dick for protection from the ghouls. Nothing seemed to unsettle Dick and he took the opportunity to gently pull her hand under his arm and clasp it tight against his side. She didn't retract it and he sat contented, watching her out of the corner of his eye. In the dim light her skin glowed as she apprehensively followed every movement on the stage with wide-open eyes. That was one of the things he loved about her. She didn't realise just how lovely she was, nor put on airs and graces. He hoped she would remain unspoiled.

Louise gradually relaxed contentedly against him and, to Dick's great delight, remained there until the end of the play when the curtain fell on a hushed audience. Then, the acting having been so real, the audience surged to their feet in a standing ovation, applauding to show their appreciation. The curtain rose and fell over and over again, the cast bowing and waving, before it slowly came down for the final time.

Dick silently prayed that they would not see George or his friends as they left the Grand Opera House. To avoid anyone catching his eye, he bent his head and gave all his attention to Louise as they were jostled by people eager to leave the building. His prayer was answered; they escaped without another encounter.

Louise was locked in her own thoughts during the journey home. She was trying to imagine herself seeing someone she took a fancy to and being so brazen as to show her interest, as Gabby had done, especially if a male companion was with her. She just couldn't comprehend how any woman could behave like that.

On the other hand, Gabby couldn't be further from Dick's mind as he debated whether to ask Louise to go out with him again. He felt like a teenager on his first outing with someone he fancied and desperately wanted to see again. Drawing the car close to the kerb at the front door of the house, with a deep sigh he came to a decision and turned in his seat to speak to Louise. At that same moment Louise faced round to thank him for a lovely evening. Before she could open her mouth, he spoke.

'Louise, will you come out with me again on Saturday night?' He dreaded her refusal, not knowing how he would be able to persuade her to change her mind if she did.

Confused, Louise slumped back in the seat with a loud sigh and he prepared himself for the worst. 'Look, Dick, I don't know what to say. I'm afraid of spoiling your chances to meet other women you might want to get to know better. I couldn't fail to notice that you and that Gabby girl got on like a house on fire during the interval. I'm surprised her friend didn't say something.' Dick had to smile at how indignant she sounded. She was still giving off. 'I thought that Gabby was going to gobble you up, she was so blatant, and her with her fiancé. I honestly don't know how Gordon managed to control himself.'

Did he detect a hint of jealousy there? Dick

hoped he wasn't imagining it and considered his words carefully. 'I would be delighted if you said "yes", you would be happy to accompany me. That is, unless you find the idea distasteful. I am not in the least interested in Gabby or any other woman but I really do delight in your company.' There, he had made it clear who he was interested in. Louise still looked baffled and Dick's heart sank. What else could he say to convince her? Tentatively he said, 'But perhaps I bore you?'

'Oh, no. No, never. I enjoy going out with you, Dick. I just don't want to waste your time bothering about me. You could be courting someone you could really care for and want to marry. Someone who will give you children. You yourself told me that, and whoever she may be, she might not like you pandering over the likes of me, even if she lives in Dublin.'

Now Dick was puzzled. What on earth was she talking about? 'Did I say I cared for someone in Dublin?'

'No . . . but I can't remember you showing interest in any particular woman here in Belfast. So I assumed there was a lady in Dublin who had caught your attention. I thought you only asked me out to pass the time because you were at a loose end while waiting to return to Dublin.'

She was looking at him with a bewildered frown. He snorted in exasperation. 'Let's clear the air here,

Louise. The only girl I'm interested in is you and I'm only asking you to give me a chance to show how much I care for you. There! I've admitted it. I just want to join the queue behind Conor and George. That's all I ask, a chance to be with you. How about it? Will you come out with me on Saturday night?'

She couldn't take it all in. It was unbelievable. Surely he couldn't be serious? Attracted to him as she might sometimes feel, he was still old enough to be her father. Glancing about as she tried to think of how she could let him down gently, in the car's wing mirror she caught sight of her father coming up the street. Without more ado, she made a sudden decision. 'Perhaps you should meet my father after all. Here he comes now.'

Startled at the sudden turn of events, Dick watched her climb out of the car. Then as the realisation of what she had just said dawned on him, he hurriedly followed her example and joined her on the pavement, anxious to meet Tommy McGuigan in the flesh.

Louise remained standing outside the house until her father reached them. 'Da, this is Dick Patterson. The author who did a signing at Eason's not so long ago . . . remember I told you about the occasion?'

Tommy nodded, recalling all the excitement at that time. But what was this man doing with his daughter? The men took stock of each other. About the same height, dark-haired, why, they could pass for brothers, Dick thought in dismay.

'Dick, this is my father, Tommy.'

Dick reached for Tommy's hand and grasped it tightly. 'I'm pleased to meet you, Tommy.'

Tommy, still bewildered, shook Dick's hand warmly. 'Likewise, I'm sure.'

'Da, I've invited Dick in for a cup of tea.' She had her key out and was unlocking the door. 'Would you like a cuppa?'

Still mystified, Tommy said, 'Why not? It'll be nice to chat with someone my own age for a change.'

Embarrassed, Louise said warningly, 'Mind your manners, Da.'

She left them to it and going into the scullery closed the door behind her. Her mind was in a tumult. She couldn't comprehend just what Dick Patterson was up to. She hadn't thought of him romantically, considering him too old. Sure that her da would send him away with a flea in his ear, she waited for loud voices giving off, but it didn't happen. She took her time brewing the tea while striving to eavesdrop on what was going on. She could hear their voices but not what was said. When the tea was ready she made a big issue of opening the scullery door, loudly clearing her throat to let them know that she was coming in.

They broke off their conversation as Louise pushed her way through into the kitchen, carrying a tray with three mugs of tea and a plate of Rich Tea biscuits. Dick rose to his feet and taking the tray from her he placed it on the small occasional table within their reach.

Her father was reclining in his usual chair, a bemused look on his face. He honestly didn't know what to make of this man his daughter had brought home. Dick had spoken to Tommy, man to man, telling him how much he cared for Louise and saying that he hoped Tommy would give him his blessing as he tried to win her affection. He explained that he realised he was a good deal older, but was comfortably off and knew he could make her happy.

Avoiding Louise's eye, Dick took his mug and waited for Tommy to speak. His fate was in this man's hands, as it were. He had expected to dislike Tommy McGuigan but to his surprise he found him pleasant enough. But, after all, he didn't have to live with him. However, in the little time they had been together he had felt they shared a mutual respect and he had come to the conclusion that Tommy would not stand in his way.

Louise glanced from one to the other, trying to read their expressions. 'You two seemed to be getting on well enough while I was in the scullery, but now you appear to be struck dumb. Did I interrupt something?'

Still Dick waited for Tommy to break the silence and reached for a biscuit. He had made his intentions plain, but would the age difference put the other man off?

Clearing his throat, Tommy caught his daughter's eye and said, 'This gentleman has asked me for my permission to walk out with you. What do you think of that, Louise?'

She glared at her father and, with an exasperated sweep of her hand, said, 'I hope you told Dick that I'm old enough to decide whom I see and that you don't influence me either way.'

Then she rounded on Dick. 'And as for you, my man, anything you choose to say must be said to me and only me. My father is not my keeper.'

Dick sat gazing at her in speechless wonder, thinking how lovely she looked when angry. Her eyes sparkled like sapphires and her sensuous lips trembled. He flailed about for something nice to say, anything that would appease her and dampen her spleen.

Hands wide apart in a gesture of sorrow, he explained, 'I'm sorry, Louise, if I've done the wrong thing, but I can't get you to take me seriously.'

Tommy sat mute, looking from one to the other, not knowing what more he could say to improve the situation. He considered himself a good judge of character and he thought Dick was all right. His Louise could do a lot worse for herself.

'Look, Dick, thank you for a lovely evening. And since you're so set on asking me out, please pick me up on Saturday evening about sevenish. You may as well come to the house for me, seeing as you're so insistent. Now please finish your tea and I'll see you to the door.'

Dick finished his biscuit, quickly drank the tea and was on his feet in double-quick time.

'Thanks for your advice, Tommy. And I'll bid you goodnight.'

In the privacy of the hall, with a twinkle in her eye she smiled broadly at him. 'That didn't go too badly then, did it?' Reassured, he lifted her hand and kissed it. A laugh in her voice, she teased, 'I'll tell you something, Dick Patterson. I hope you can do better than that or you're out on your ear.' It never ceased to amaze her how she could be so at ease with him. If only he were a bit younger, she thought.

Overcome with happiness, Dick gently cupped her face in his hands and kissed her softly on the lips. 'I mean to take things slowly. I'll show you the respect you deserve. Goodnight, love. You have made me one very happy man.'

'Well, I don't know about that. I have sent the other two off with a flea in their ears and whether or not they come back is up to them. I really did enjoy your company tonight but it will take more than a few evenings out to make us a couple. Goodnight, Dick, I'll look forward to seeing you Saturday night.'

Delighted at the sudden turn of events, Dick said, 'Is there anywhere in particular you'd like to go, Louise?'

'Surprise me.'

Climbing into the car, Dick flashed her a beaming smile and with a salute pulled away from the kerb.

Her father was still sitting, mug clasped in his hands and deep in thought, when she returned to the kitchen. 'You know, you could do a lot worse, girl, so you could. That Dick Patterson seems a fine man.'

Louise pursed her lips and said, 'I thought you'd think him too old for me.'

'Well now, I must admit he's no spring chicken. But if you'd told me about him before this I might have been up in arms and suggested that he was a cradle-snatcher. Having met him, I think he's all right and he certainly would look after you. But . . . what about Conor? Eh? Is he definitely out of the picture? You two have been through a lot together. I always thought that he was the one you'd marry.'

Settling on the chair facing him, Louise replied, 'Look, Da, I never thought I'd see the day I'd be asking you, of all people, for advice . . . but I've no one else to turn to.'

'Well, if it makes you feel any better I promise not to repeat anything we discuss here tonight.'

She looked him straight in the eye and said, 'Can I really trust you, Da? I don't want anyone gossiping behind my back.'

In his efforts to reassure her, he reached across and patted her knee. 'I swear I won't let you down. Please believe me, Louise. Give me a chance to show that your future means a lot to me. There are times when I don't show it but I do love you, you know.'

'I know you do, Da, but what about Cissie? Eh? You tell her everything.'

Pleased at the chance of showing her that he could be trusted, Tommy said, 'I won't any more. Not about you or your personal life. I promise.'

'Well, it's like this, Da. I'm all mixed up.' She sighed and leaned towards him, her hands clasped in her lap. She was having second thoughts now about encouraging Dick Patterson. 'You see, since I started working in Eason's my whole outlook has changed. Before, all I wanted was for Conor to get a job here, marry me and we'd live happy ever after. Like every fairy-tale ending. If I had stayed in the mill, I would have pestered Conor until he bought me a ring and started planning the future with me, just to get away from here and have a place of my own.'

She looked up briefly at Tommy and he

responded, 'I can understand that. So, what's changed? Have you really broken off your relationship with Conor?'

'No. That's just it, Da. Conor wants us to keep on as before but I'm inclined to think that he also has some doubts. I know that if we still felt that we were meant for each other, he wouldn't be able to stay away. He would insist on getting a position here and come home for good. Marriage preparations would be in full swing. But now I feel that's not going to happen.'

Tommy looked confused. 'Do you not think that perhaps it can still happen?'

She shook her head sadly. 'No, I think that we should be so committed to one another by now that we would be going full steam ahead, making plans to settle down. That is, if we were meant for each other. The way I see it, if anything, we are steadily drifting further apart. As far as I'm concerned, it's all over between us.'

Tommy was nodding his head in agreement. 'I see what you mean. I know when your mother and I first met we couldn't get married quickly enough.' He noted the change in his daughter's expression and guessed she was thinking, *And look how that ended*. He hurried on, 'It was my fault that your mother left home. Mine alone. Conor would never, I'm sure, do anything like that. I was a swine, so I was. It nearly killed me when your mother took off like that, especially when I heard that she was carrying Bill McCartney's child. I was sorely tempted to top myself but I found out I was too big a coward even for that.'

He was becoming upset and she hastened to reassure him. 'I know that you would never commit suicide, Da. Your faith is too strong. I'm not asking for guidance here, Da . . . just running it by you so I can see things more clearly in my own mind, but I do trust your advice.'

'Well . . . if Conor and you hadn't been so close I would be urging you to give Dick Patterson a chance. I feel he would make you happy. I think you should keep your options open and see what happens. You're still very young, you know. You don't have to rush into anything.'

'Thanks, Da. You've made up my mind for me. I didn't want to appear to be leading them on, but they both know the score and, as Grannie Logan would say, let's wait and see how it pans out.'

A loud knock on the door made Tommy and Louise look apprehensively at each other. Gesturing for her to remain where she was, Tommy went to see who had delivered such a heavy-handed knock. The voices were muffled but Louise thought she recognised Harry's slurred tones. Surely he hadn't been arrested for being drunk and disorderly or something? Not their Harry; she had never seen him the worse for drink. Rising slowly to her feet, she walked to the vestibule door, a worried frown puckering her brow. Her da and Harry were in the hall, with a scared-looking Peggy standing unnoticed on the pavement behind two police constables.

Harry was battered and bruised. There were bloodstains down the front of his white shirt. His speech was slurred because his mouth was swollen and bloody. He looked as if he had been hit by a lorry. Concerned, Louise grabbed him by the arm and pulled him into the kitchen. Then she beckoned to Peggy. 'Come in, Peggy,' she said with a wrathful glare at the policemen.

They had been unaware of Peggy hovering behind them and were all apologies for blocking her out.

Ignoring them, Louise was gazing in horror at her brother. 'What on earth happened to you? Were you knocked down?'

He was holding a handkerchief to his mouth and she could see that his lip was split open. She waved her hand, conceding that he would be unable to answer her. 'Never mind, you can fill me in later. I'll heat some water and clean you up.' She gave him a gentle push down onto the settee. 'Sit down. Peggy, make him a strong cup of tea and put four spoonfuls of sugar in it.'

Glad to be given something useful to do, Peggy

hurried into the scullery. Tommy was still at the front door, talking to the policemen. At last they heard him wish them goodnight. 'Thanks for bringing my son home, officers. I'll see he goes to the station in the morning to make a statement.'

Louise gently bathed Harry's face. His lip was badly cut and one eye was starting to swell. Unable to control her curiosity any longer, she cried, 'What happened? Who did this to you?'

'I ran into a brick wall.' He tried to grin but winced as his face hurt. 'You should see the other guy,' he mumbled.

'This is bad. You should sue whoever did this to you.'

'He's already suing me for assault.' Harry closed his eyes. 'I'm so weary. Can we leave all explanations until the morning, sis?'

She was bathing his grazed knuckles now. 'No we can't. I wouldn't get a wink of sleep. So tell us what happened.'

Peggy came to his rescue. 'Here, Harry. Drink this, it will make you feel better and take these two aspirins.'

'Thanks, Peggy.'

Tommy, who had been standing behind Harry, waiting until Louise had finished bathing his wounds, added his concern to the others'. 'Tell us, son, what happened? Who threw the first blow?'

'I did. And do you know what? I think I broke

his jaw and I'll be glad if I did. He deserved everything he got. I think I'd have killed him if his pals hadn't pulled me off.'

Astounded at this outburst, Tommy came closer and stood looking down at his son. 'Why? In the name of God, why? Have you been drinking?'

'Da, don't tower over him like that. Sit down, you're making him worse. When he tries to speak that cut on his lip starts bleeding again. I think it will need a couple of stitches.'

When Tommy didn't move, Louise tried to elbow him to one side, but he remained steadfast.

'I'm not moving until I hear the ins and outs of this. Whoever he hit is pressing charges of assault against him. He could do time for this. End up with a police record.' He glowered angrily down at his son. 'Is that what you want?'

Harry had had enough. All he wanted was to close his eyes and blank out the other man's face. He had probably injured him badly.

'Come on, Harry. Who is this other guy and why did you hit him?'

With his eyes still closed, Harry said, 'Look, I'll give you a quick run-down on what happened and then I'm off to bed, all right?'

The three of them nodded and hung on to his every word.

'This guy I had the scrap with used to go out with Hannah. I only found out tonight that he

425

made a pass at her. Touched her up, you know what I mean?'

Shocked to the core at these disclosures, Tommy cried, 'Are you telling us he raped—'

Harry raised a hand to stop his father. 'No, Da, I'm not. It didn't go that far but he fondled her and, you know, touched her. Hannah was very upset when she told me. You see, tonight I asked her to marry me. She said that she couldn't because she had let another man touch her.'

'If he didn't molest her, son, are you not just overreacting a wee bit? Many a lad chances his arm and it's up to the girl to put him in his place if she isn't interested. When did this happen?'

'I'm not sure. I think about six weeks ago.'

Tommy looked more frustrated than ever and Louise was inclined to agree with him.

'And you're only retaliating now?' she gasped.

Harry defended himself. 'Like I've already said, I didn't find out until tonight. Didn't I?'

'Why tonight, eh? You're not making sense, Harry.'

'Are youse listening to a word I'm saying? Hannah only told me about it tonight. I asked her to marry me. She said she couldn't unless she told me the truth.'

'And you think that you were justified in attacking this lad *six weeks later*?' Tommy shook his head in disbelief. 'What has got into you?' He

426

sank back in his chair, puffing out his cheeks in exaggerated exasperation.

'Da, this lip needs stitching. Will you help me walk him over to the Royal? We can sort all this out in the morning.'

By now Harry had fallen into a light doze.

With a weary sigh, Tommy raised his head and spoke in a low voice. 'According to the police the other lad is in a worse state. They think his jaw may be broken. Who would have thought that our Harry would be capable of doing something like this?'

'I know, Da, but he thought he was defending Hannah's honour.'

Tommy looked at her intently. 'Do you think he was right?'

'No. Like you I think he was overreacting.' She glanced at Harry to make sure he was still asleep. He appeared to be but nevertheless she shushed her father.

Not to be deterred from getting his penny's worth in, Tommy lowered his voice further and whispered, 'Do you think that Hannah was egging him on?'

Louise gave a soft laugh. 'Not for one minute would I think that. Hannah is so honest I don't think her capable of telling a lie, never mind falsely accusing someone.'

'Why now? Why decide *now* to ask her to marry him? Has he won the pools or something?'

Louise chewed her bottom lip. All this confusion

was getting her down. 'It's a long story, Da. You'll hear all about it in due course. Now can we please get him over to the Royal before it's too late to try stitching that cut, otherwise it will leave a permanent scar.'

'OK then, let's get moving.'

Shaking Harry roughly by the shoulder and ignoring his pleas not to be taken to the hospital, Tommy got him to his feet.

Unable to comprehend what was going on between her father and Louise, Peggy, who was standing looking at them with a bewildered frown, asked tentatively, 'Can I come too?'

'No, Peggy, love. You'll have to get up as usual for work in the morning. Johnnie will be depending on you. I'll take the day off, and me and me da will look after Harry tomorrow. Try to get some sleep, love.'

With a gentle push Louise sent Peggy on her way to bed.

It was a struggle getting Harry down the Springfield Road and over to the Royal. Once there a nurse dressed Harry's wounds and the injection she gave him was taking effect. It lessened the pain and he was much more aware of what was going on around him. The journey back home was easier. They were fortunate to return without running into any police patrols.

The following morning when Peggy broke the news to Johnnie he left her in charge of the shop and rushed over to see if he could be of any help. Louise asked him if he could get word over to Kennedy's bakery to let them know that Harry had had an accident and wouldn't be in for a couple of days.

Johnnie said he would see to it and when he learned that his brother had to make a statement at the police barracks he offered to accompany him.

Tommy was relieved when Harry accepted his brother's offer. 'Then if you don't need me, I'll go on in to work and try to get away early this evening in case I'm needed then. Will that be all right?'

He was assured that it would be fine. Relieved, Louise went into the scullery to make up his sandwiches. She was glad her father was going to work as usual. He had been like a cat on a hot griddle all morning.

She was pleased too that he had been able to hold his tongue for a change. She herself wanted to rant and rave at Harry, but knew that it would be to no avail. The damage was done and Harry would have to accept his just deserts. She wished Hannah had kept her big mouth shut.

While the two brothers were at the Springfield Road police barracks Louise helped Peggy in the shop until they returned. She could not help

429

worrying. Harry had never been in any kind of trouble before. As it was his first offence, would he escape a prison sentence? She knew very little about the ins and outs of the law and had never been near a courtroom in her life. She had heard of a few families who had sons and even daughters locked up, but it was because they had committed some serious crimes. She suspected that Harry would have to go before the magistrates court.

The morning seemed never-ending but at last she saw her brothers walking up Springfield Road from the barracks. She had just finished serving a customer and, following her out the door, went to meet them. Johnnie stilled her questions with a finger to his lips.

'We may as well keep this in the family, sis.' Peggy had come to the door of the shop and he addressed her. 'Get the kettle on, Peggy, please. I'm parched.'

Johnnie attended to a customer while Louise helped Harry into the office. 'How did it go?' she asked anxiously.

Harry silently pointed to his stitched lip and shook his head, indicating that he couldn't or wouldn't speak.

Johnnie, entering the office, answered for him. 'The other lad is still in hospital. His father was also at the barracks with a solicitor but we didn't get a chance to speak to them. The duty sergeant was very helpful and a bit on the sympathetic side. He said that as it was Mr McGuigan's – that's our Harry – first appearance in this police station, he didn't think it would be an indictable offence – that's committing a serious crime. But that wasn't for him to decide.'

Johnnie paused to accept a mug of tea from Peggy. 'Thanks, love. I really need this,' he said, taking a few long slurps from the mug before continuing.

'The sergeant pointed out that that was only his personal opinion after many years in the force and should only be taken as such, and not to build up our hopes. Anyway, if it goes against Harry a summons will be directed to him, requiring him to appear before the Belfast magistrates court. He will be informed by official letter one way or the other. The sergeant also said that, having spoken to the plaintiff, he was of the opinion that it was a case of six of one and half a dozen of the other. In other words, he didn't think it would go any further. But then again he repeated that that was only his humble opinion for what it was worth.' Taking a breather, he drained his mug of tea in one long gulp before resuming.

'Having heard all that, we'll not know anything concrete until we get that letter. But one thing we do know is that we'll have to get a good solicitor if we want to keep our Harry out of jail. I've heard that the food in there is bloody awful,' he said, with a broad grin in an effort to alleviate the cloud of gloom that had descended on them.

None of the family appreciated Johnnie's attempt at comedy and stood quietly together but it seemed as if they were miles apart, digesting Johnnie's words.

At last Louise spoke up. 'Well, as far as I can gather from what you've told us, Johnnie, all is not quite as bad as was first thought. We'll all have to pray really hard that he gets off without charge and hope that he has learned his lesson.'

26

Louise dragged herself into bed beside Peggy with an exasperated sigh. She felt wretched. Today had been a long, tiring experience and although her body was crying out for rest, her mind was too active to allow sleep to claim her. Once again she went over in her mind every detail that needed attention. Kennedy's had been notified and Johnnie had phoned Eason's from the shop to let them know about Harry's *accident* to explain Louise's absence from work. Her thoughts shied away from what Harry had done. How could he be so stupid? How could he? *How could he?*

To her relief, Mr Murray had said that he was sorry to hear about Louise's brother and that she could take as long as was necessary. She had been inclined to let Dick Patterson know too but had refrained. If Harry was charged, perhaps Dick wouldn't want to have him look after his estate. And who would blame him? Best let sleeping dogs lie until it was all sorted, she decided.

Her memory still nagged at her. Had she forgotten anything? She was sure that there was something she had neglected to do but couldn't put her finger on it. Again she went over everything step by step in her mind and suddenly reared up in bed, dragging the bedclothes off Peggy who was just dropping off to sleep. Peggy propped herself up on one elbow and gaped as her sister scrambled out of bed, her bare feet making a loud slapping noise on the linoleum. 'Shush!' she warned her. 'You'll waken me da. Then there will really be ructions and nobody would get any sleep.'

Louise's agitation bewildered Peggy. Surely it wasn't morning already? Peggy sat up straight, struck by a thought. Were the police at the door to take Harry away? She watched her sister pace the floor.

'What's wrong, Louise? For heaven's sake, what's wrong? You're scaring me.'

Louise was distraught. She leaned over the bed and whispered fretfully, 'We forgot to let Hannah know about Harry. I can't believe I forgot all about Hannah. Her above all people. She's the cause of all Harry's troubles, you know. Why didn't she come down to the house? Eh? Do you think Liz wouldn't let her?'

Peggy was now wide awake. 'Today was Hannah's day off,' she reminded her sister. 'She won't be in until one tomorrow afternoon, so she wouldn't have any way of knowing that anything was wrong. So no sleep will be lost there. Lucky her.'

Louise replied, 'Still, I'm surprised Harry didn't ask one of us to fetch her down.'

'We don't know in what state of mind they parted. Perhaps Harry finds he can't forgive her. Eh? Do you think that's the reason?'

'No!' Louise was abrupt. 'No, Harry isn't like that. He loves Hannah. He wouldn't do anything to hurt her or cause her any embarrassment, even if they have fallen out. I just can't make it out. I wish I'd remembered to ask Harry if we should send word up to her.'

'If he loves her all that much, why not just forgive her and let things be. Eh? After all, I'm sure she didn't ask to be groped. Anyway there's nothing you can do about it this time of night, so get back into bed and let's get some sleep while we can.' Peggy plumped up her pillows and turned her back to her sister, determined to get some shut-eye.

Louise, however, sat on the edge of the bed, still worried. Why had Harry not got in touch with Hannah? She gently eased herself back between the sheets so as not to upset Peggy again. She need not have bothered. Peggy was already sound asleep, soft snores coming from her open mouth. How Louise envied her. She tossed and turned for some time before eventually falling into a fitful slumber.

As Harry was a lot better on Friday morning, Louise decided to broach the subject of Hannah. He had come downstairs to go to the toilet and when he came back inside and was washing his hands at the sink, Louise offered to bring his breakfast upstairs to him. He assured her that he felt well enough – if his mouth permitted – to eat in the kitchen. Sitting himself down at the table, he reached for an old newspaper to read, probably to avoid having to answer any questions that were bound to be forthcoming.

Boiling two eggs, a bit on the soft side, Louise spooned them into a cup. Adding salt, pepper and a knob of butter, she mixed them together and put the cup on the table with some buttered bread and a cup of tea. 'I've been wondering, Harry. Does Hannah know what happened yesterday?'

He threw her a dirty look. 'How could she?' he growled.

Louise reared back, offended. 'Here, there's no need to take that attitude. For all I know she might have been with you and you sent her off home.'

'Do you think she'd have left me in this condition?' His tone mocked the very idea, as he pointed at his face.

'Not really. However, neither would I have thought that you would ever end up in the state you were in, and all through your own stupidity,' she retorted curtly. It seemed that she couldn't do right for doing wrong.

Harry, wincing every now and again, with great difficulty slowly ate his breakfast and carrying his dishes into the scullery apologised to his sister. 'Sorry, sis. It's just that I don't know what to think about Hannah. Didn't any of you call up to her house and tell her about me? Mind you, I don't want any pity from her. She must come off her own bat. And sis, you didn't need to make a special breakfast for me. Porridge would have done fine. But it was lovely. Thanks a lot. Is there any more aspirin?'

Louise nodded towards a cupboard. 'In there. Remember it was Hannah's day off yesterday. How would she know about the fight? We were too worried about you and never thought of informing her. You two didn't happen to fall out when she admitted the truth to you, eh?' She was filling a glass with water as she spoke.

'I honestly don't know. But it's the least of my worries at the moment. What is Dick Patterson going to think of all this? That's what I'm worried about. This could spoil my chances of that job.'

'You should have thought of that before your lifted your fists to that lad. What on earth got into you?'

He shrugged. 'Do you think I don't know that? I'm away back to bed for a while. Give me a shout if I'm needed.'

While Harry was climbing the stairs Tommy came out of his room. 'Did I hear Harry talking a minute ago?' An abrupt nod was his answer, as Louise hurried back into the scullery.

'Sit down, Da, and I'll lift your porridge.'

Tommy did as he was bid and soon Louise placed a bowl of porridge on the table in front of him.

'How is Harry this morning?'

'Something the same. Stiff and sore and his face is in an awful state. At least his mouth seems a lot better. He managed to get some breakfast down him and that's a good thing.'

'I couldn't help notice that there was neither hide nor hair of Hannah McFadden last night. Was she running about with this other lad? Is that what started him off? Did he dump her?'

Silently Louise ranted, *So you mean you heard us talking*. She somehow managed to control her tongue. 'Not to my knowledge he hasn't. And I don't think she was out with him last night, so she wouldn't know anything about the scuffle.'

'I wouldn't blame him if he had dumped her, mind you. He could do a lot better than that one.'

Louise was so angry that she thumped the table with enough force to make her da jump.

'Look here, Da, our Harry could do a lot worse

than Hannah. He dotes on her and I believe she loves him. And she'll make him a good, loving, caring wife. So don't you go voicing your concern where it's not wanted. Keep your opinions to yourself. Do you hear me?'

Tommy drew back from her, a startled look on his face. 'Hear you? I'm sure the whole bloody street heard you.' He glanced upwards. 'And I'm sure Harry heard you too. But tell me this, if you're so clever, if she loves him, why isn't she here?'

Dismayed at her lack of sensitivity, Louise too glanced up at the ceiling and lowered her voice. 'I have no idea. But . . . it's none of our business, so it's not. So hold your tongue,' she cautioned. 'I'm sure they can sort out their own problems without any help from us.'

Dick Patterson learned of Harry's predicament when he ran into Al Murray in Lower Donegal Street. He had been seeing his solicitor on business and was leaving his office when Al hailed him from across the street.

He crossed over and shook Al's offered hand in greeting. They had met each other often over the years as Dick's books came out and signing sessions were arranged, becoming good friends. They enjoyed each other's company, although with Dick now spending a lot of his time in Dublin they had returned to being mere acquaintances.

'I thought you'd have been away back to Dublin by now,' Al chided him.

'I'm in the middle of something here at the moment so I'll be up and down on a regular basis for a while.'

'Have you time for a drink or . . . a cup of tea as the case may be?'

'As a matter of fact I am feeling a bit peckish. Can we go somewhere I can have a sandwich as well?'

Al nodded and with a slight bow Dick gestured for him to go first. 'It's your territory, lead the way.'

A few minutes later and they were sitting in a café with a plate of sandwiches and a pot of tea in front of them.

'How's the book doing?' Dick enquired.

'Very well. Very well indeed. We are very pleased with the sales. As I'm sure you'll be when the royalties start pouring in.'

Dick just nodded his head saying, 'Good, good.' Trying to keep tabs on George Carson, he ventured casually, 'How's that young nephew of yours doing?'

Surprised at his interest, Al replied, 'George? He's doing very well at work. He's now with some structural engineering company down the Shore Road and has managed to work his way up to junior contracts manager.'

Knowing full well that George was fancy-free, Dick asked, 'Is he married or engaged yet?'

'Heavens, no. I've only heard lately that he used to go out with one of our sales ladies, Louise McGuigan. I think you know her.' Dick nodded to let Al know he already understood this. 'Well, it would appear that they are going out together again and as a result he doesn't show much interest in anyone else. Mind you, I'm not keeping track of him or anything. After all, it's none of my business what he gets up to. I only know all this because my sister is worried about their association. If he should continue seeing Louise and they discover it's the real thing, I shudder to think what will happen, her being a Catholic and all that. His career could be ruined and his parents wouldn't be too pleased about it, especially his father being a staunch Orangeman. Neither would hers, for that matter. But I believe in letting things take their course. No good can come of interfering. It will only get George's back up and make him more determined.'

This was news to Dick. 'You mean he was involved with her before?'

'So I'm led to believe, but it was some time ago. But look, it's a long story. You'll only be bored stiff.'

'Well, we have all these sandwiches to get through, so fire away.'

* * *

Thus Dick learned a lot about Louise and how, in spite of the troubles, she and her friend Cathie somebody or other had gone out with two Protestants. It had created a lot of trouble at the time as the other girl had run off to Scotland with George's best friend, Trevor Pollock. They had left a lot of bigotry and bitter resentment in their wake for both their families.

'At that time it seemed that Louise had been dumped by her childhood sweetheart and was just making up a foursome to please this friend of hers. When Conor came back on the scene, to my sister's relief George faded out of the picture and everything was fine and dandy. Then, when Louise came to work for me, George showed a lot of interest in her again and I know that he has taken her out some.' Al picked up a sandwich and sat back. 'That's enough said. I don't usually talk about my employees' private affairs. You'll be thinking me a right old gossip-monger.'

'No! Nothing of the sort, Al. Indeed I could write a book about this,' Dick said mischievously.

Al laughed. 'Well, if you do, for goodness' sake don't mention my name in it. And while you're at it, there might be another chapter for this book. It seems that Louise's younger brother was in a fight on Wednesday night. I heard on the grapevine that he was arrested for assault. Louise's older brother rang me to say that his brother Harry had

had an accident and Louise was staying at home on Thursday to care for him. Now when anyone is arrested here at the moment it's usually something to do with the troubles. Someone unable to hold his tongue would start a fight, you know how it is.'

Dick was silent, turning this piece of news over in his mind. How come he hadn't been told about this?

Wolfing down the last sandwich and draining his cup, Al rose to his feet, once more thrusting out his hand. 'I'll have to be leaving you now, Dick, but do call into the shop whenever you're back in Belfast.'

'I'll do that, I promise. Thanks for lunch. My turn next time.'

Long after Al had gone, Dick sat for some time deep in thought. Why hadn't Harry let him know that he had been involved in an altercation? Was it because he thought that he would not understand? There was only one thing for it. He would have to pay the McGuigans a visit, see how the land lay. Glad of the excuse to see Louise sooner than expected, he hurried to where his car was parked in the grounds of St Anne's Cathedral, and some minutes later he was turning into Springview Street.

*　　*　　*

443

Louise was busy in the scullery cooking when Dick knocked on the door. Harry was on his way downstairs and shouted that he would see to it. He looked shocked when he opened the door and saw Dick Patterson standing there.

'Come in. Come in, Dick.' He stood aside to let Dick into the kitchen and closed the outer door behind him. 'This is a surprise.'

Hearing Dick's name mentioned, Louise slowly came out of the scullery, drying her hands on her apron.

'Hello, Dick. I didn't expect to see you today,' she greeted him.

Harry said, 'Sit down, Dick. Can we offer you a cup of tea? I'm afraid we haven't got much of a selection.'

'No, thank you. I've just had lunch with Al Murray and he told me you had an accident on Wednesday night. I just wondered if you were badly hurt, so I thought I'd call in and see how you were. You certainly look as if you were on the receiving end of something.'

Harry's face reddened with embarrassment and he tried to make a joke of it. 'You should see the other guy.' To get it over and done with, he admitted, 'Yes, I've been a stupid eejit. I got into a scrap with another lad and was arrested for assault.' He pointed to a chair and Dick sank down onto it.

'You started it, Harry? That surprises me.'

'It's a long story. Sure you won't have a cup of tea or maybe a cold drink?'

'A cold drink would be fine, if it's not too much bother, thank you.'

Louise retreated to the scullery and Harry sat on the chair facing Dick. He smiled ruefully. 'I'm ashamed of myself. I can't explain what drove me to it.' He grimaced and Dick could see that it hurt his mouth to speak, but he gamely carried on. 'Well, I can and I'm aware that it should never have happened in the first place.'

Louise returned and handed them each a glass of lemonade. 'I've things to do, so I'll leave you both to it.'

'You can stay if you like, sis. I'm sure Dick won't mind.'

'Not at all,' Dick agreed with a warm smile.

With a wave of dismissal Louise went back to making her stew, closing the scullery door to give them some privacy.

Louise didn't make any attempt to hear what was being said out in the kitchen. She closed her ears and concentrated on chopping carrots and onions while keeping an eye on the simmering mutton. She did, however, ponder on how the news would affect Harry's new job. A handshake was their only bond and nothing had as yet been signed. Harry had told her that he was prepared to turn down Dick's offer if he thought for one minute that Dick began to regret making it once he heard about the trouble Harry had been involved in. Harry probably hadn't expected for Dick to hear quite so quickly. But it's a small world.

Some time later, there came another knock on the door, a very loud one this time that didn't sound as though it would take no for an answer. Louise opened the scullery door to see what was going on.

Harry was already on his way to answer the knock and Dick had risen to his feet in anticipation. He sent her a reassuring glance and she shyly smiled at him.

With the police very much to the fore of their minds, it was a relief to discover that Hannah was the culprit.

They heard the front door closing and her high-pitched voice close to tears as she asked Harry over and over again whether he was all right. Was he sure he was all right? Why hadn't he sent for her? They came into the room with their arms around one another. With a shrug of the shoulders, Dick joined Louise in the scullery and closed the door.

He smiled at her as she edged closer to the door, ears strained. Taking her in his arms, he eased her away from the door and further into the scullery, whispering assurances that everything was going to be all right. She lifted her face to his, 'Did Harry tell you about Wednesday night and how foolish he's been?'

'I am aware that he was arrested but I don't think he'll be charged. I think with a good solicitor he'll get off with just a verbal warning. I'll get my own man on to it today.'

She made no attempt to get free of his embrace. 'You're such a comfort, Dick. You always seem to know just what to do and when to do it. Harry is very fortunate to have met you. In fact, we both are.'

She sniffed and a tear slid down her cheek. He brushed it away with his thumb and pulled her close against his body. Lowering his head, he brushed her lips with his. It was meant to be a reassuring caress. He didn't want to alarm her but she parted her lips and moved them hungrily against his. He was unprepared for such a spontaneous response and reminded himself how vulnerable she was. Nevertheless he gathered her closer still and lavished all the love and affection he felt for her on her willing mouth and neck. All the while he was muttering words of endearment and promises that if she could only learn to care for him a little, he would do all in his power to make her happy.

They lost all track of time and it was a tap on the scullery door that brought them back to reality.

'You can come out now.' Harry's voice was tentative. He had reassured Hannah that everything would be all right, now that Dick knew the full facts. It was so quiet in the scullery that he was unsure what was going on behind the closed door and didn't want to push his way in unannounced.

Opening the door, in spite of himself Dick couldn't keep the wide grin from his face. He glanced over his shoulder at Louise and couldn't believe her expression. She looked like a woman in love. His heart raced and he couldn't tear his eyes away from her.

Knowing that, unless Harry was blind or else a complete idiot, he must be aware what they had been up to, Dick waited for Louise to speak first. She stepped towards Hannah and took her in her arms. 'How can you ever forgive me, Hannah? Not knowing whether or not you had dumped our Harry, I neglected to send for you.'

Hannah swung round and flashed Harry a worried glance. 'It's Harry who should be dumping me. I don't deserve him. He's so good to me.'

'Is everything all right between you two then?'

'I think so, yes. I love him so much that it hurts when we're apart.'

Harry drew Hannah gently away from his sister and, cradling her in his arms, kissed her. 'I love you too, Hannah. Louise, we have some good news for a change. We're going to get engaged. I'm taking

Hannah downtown tomorrow to buy her a ring.' He was beaming from ear to ear and Louise was afraid he might burst his stitches. 'What do you think of that?'

Louise gave her a tight hug. 'I'll be proud to have you for my sister-in-law, Hannah.'

'Congratulations, that's wonderful news.' Dick grabbed Harry's hand and vigorously pumped it up and down. He then kissed Hannah on the cheek. 'Look, I'll have to be going now. I want to catch my solicitor before he closes up for the day. He will look after you from now on, Harry.' He paused. 'Tell you what . . . on second thoughts, why don't you come with me now and he will advise you what to do. It will be better if he speaks to you in person rather than me acting as a go-between.'

'That will be great, Dick. I'll just change into my best clothes. I'll be quick as I can.' He hugged Hannah, then said, 'Hannah, you had better go back to work, love. We don't want Johnnie to think we're taking advantage of his goodness, do we?'

'Of course we don't.' With a quick farewell, Hannah left the house and Harry raced up the stairs to change.

Alone with Louise and afraid to touch her in case he had read all the signs wrong, Dick moved until he could look into her eyes. 'Are you all right?' he said softly.

She smiled shyly and blushed. 'Never better.'

'Sure?'

'I'm sure.'

His eyes spoke volumes and hot colour stained her cheeks at the memory of their antics in the scullery. She couldn't believe how she had returned all his caresses without a second thought.

'I'll look forward to when we next meet. If I don't see you beforehand, I'll pick you up at seven on Saturday evening. OK?' He cupped her face in his hands and kissed her softly on the lips. 'Goodbye for now, my love.'

When they had all gone and glad for a few minutes to herself, Louise sat in a dream until with a sudden start she jumped to her feet and darted into the scullery in a panic. The stew would be ruined. She had forgotten to turn the light out under the pot. Although there was no smell of burning she expected to find it at least stuck to the bottom of the pan. However, Dick must have noticed it and turned off the gas. He was a wonderful man, always on the alert. A girl would need her head examining to turn down someone like him. With a smile she relit the gas and returned to finishing her preparations for the stew, wishing it was Saturday already.

James Hamill, Dick's solicitor, told Harry that it looked like an open-and-shut case and that he would deal with it. It would probably be a few days before anything happened and they were to try not to worry about it in the interim.

Tommy was truly delighted at Dick's generosity and when Dick called to collect Louise on Saturday evening, Tommy told him so in no uncertain terms, urging him to stay for a chat if he had any time to spare.

Sensing Dick's embarrassment, Louise came to his rescue. 'Dick will have already made the bookings and we mustn't delay, Da. We don't want to be late now, do we?'

Tommy was quite literally fawning all over Dick, apologising and telling him he was welcome to visit any time he felt like it, even coming to the door to see them off. When the door had closed on Tommy, in the privacy of the car, Dick turned to Louise. 'Wow! That was some welcome.'

Reluctantly Louise agreed with him. 'I've never seen me da act like that before. Believe you me, you've started a new trend as far as Tommy McGuigan is concerned.'

'Actually, I quite like your dad and I'll be glad to have him in my corner.'

Louise became flustered. 'Dick, I'm all confused. Everything seems to be happening too quickly and I'm not sure how I feel about you. I like you very much, but you'll have to give me some space, some time to myself to try to figure things out.'

He gripped her hand. 'You can have all the time in the world. I promise not to hassle you. Now I have a nice treat in store for you.'

Comforted that he wasn't going to rush her into anything, Louise beamed at him. 'Well, what are you waiting for?'

27

Dick had been reticent about where he was taking Louise, saying that he wanted to surprise her, although he thought she would be delighted with his choice of venue. However, when he parked the car and, taking her by the elbow, led her across High Street, she had a fair idea just where they might be heading. She felt sure that it had to be the club that George Carson had introduced her to. She knew nowhere else about here that Dick would think new to her. But then again, it was only recently that she had learned about the club, so who knew what else might be hidden in the other entries running between High Street and Ann Street? Not being one for going to such establishments, she was really quite ignorant of what nightlife was available in central Belfast.

When they turned into Joy's Entry, sure now that it would be the same club and not wanting him to be disappointed when he discovered she had already been there on previous occasions, she said tentatively, 'Are we going to a private club down here?'

He stopped mid-stride and looked at her in surprise. 'Don't tell me you've been here before?'

Thinking how handsome he looked, standing there with a slight smile on his face, she smiled back at him, confessed that she had and, at the same time, admitted, 'And I loved it.'

By now they had reached the club and, suddenly enlightened, Dick made a guess. 'I suppose George Carson brought you here?'

She was thoughtful as they paused at the large entrance door. 'Yes, George did bring me here a few times. Will that spoil the evening for you? We can always go elsewhere if you so wish. As a matter of fact he asked me to accompany him tonight but I told him that I had already made other arrangements, never dreaming that we would be coming here.'

'No. No, not at all. I just wanted to surprise you. I'll have to try harder next time.' He grimaced. 'Now my only fear is that George might be present tonight with his cousin and fiancée.' He opened the door and ushered her inside. 'I couldn't bear their company for hours on end. I'd be bored out of my boots.'

'If they're here, we'll ignore them.'

'That would be easier said than done, I imagine,' he replied drily. The expression on her face told him that she was in total agreement with him.

Recognising her, Joe hurried forward to greet them, a wide smile on his face. 'Good evening, Miss Louise and . . .' His glance passed over her head as he made to greet her companion. He hesitated but regained his manners right away and said, 'Nice to see you again, Mr Patterson. It's been a while.'

'Hi, Joe. Glad to see you still work here, but, mind you, you're wasted in this place.'

Joe tapped the side of his nose and confessed, 'Actually, I'm doing very well. I've been promoted. I am in complete charge of the club now. Will you be joining friends?' he asked tentatively.

This alerted Louise to the fact that George must be there already or was at least expected. She flashed a quick look at Dick.

He immediately said in a low conspiratorial voice, 'Miss McGuigan and I have some business to discuss. I know there's a cabaret on tonight, but I wonder if you have a vacant table somewhere where we can enjoy the show but still hold a private conversation. You know, between turns. I'd be obliged if it could be arranged.'

Joe nodded in understanding. 'I'm sure we already have a table reserved for you, Mr Patterson.'

He produced a sheet of paper as if by magic, gave it a quick glance and led them to a table with a reserved card placed on it. 'Here it is, sir. It's in a great position to see the whole of the floor show.' Seeing Dick hesitate, he raised his eyebrows enquiringly. Joe, being the understanding type from years in the business, came to a swift decision. 'No matter, sir, if you're not happy with this table, I may have just what you're looking for. Come this way, please.'

The usual helpers who travelled with artistes were bustling about. Lads were already setting up stands for lighting and sound boxes, taking up a lot of floor space. Beyond them stood a concertina-type partition that Louise had not noticed before. It was folded back, disclosing another smaller room, which also had subdued lighting and was organised to allow space for additional tables. With a friendly smile and a flourish of his hand, Joe said, 'Take your pick.'

Dick chose a table for two close to the wall beside a large plant that afforded partial privacy but still had a clear view of where the cabaret would be performed. Once they were seated, Joe took their order for drinks and Dick released a long sigh of relief. He turned to Louise. 'I take it George must be coming then?'

'I'm not sure, but Joe was surprised to see me with you, so I imagine he thought at first we would be sitting at George's table. At least that's the way it seems to me.'

'Will he mention to George that we are here, do you think?' Dick was regretting not taking Louise up on her offer to go somewhere else. The idea of enduring Gabby's prattle for three hours did not appeal to him.

'I wouldn't think so. I'm sure Joe has been in this business long enough to use a bit of discretion at times like this. After all, it's no skin off his nose that I'm here with you and I don't think he and George are all that close.'

Feeling comfortable with Dick, Louise chatted away as if she had known him a long time. She was so in tune with Dick, she could enjoy his company. When he spoke of foreign affairs, Louise discovered that she was not as ignorant of the state of the world as she had thought. She must have unconsciously stored in her memory bank the things she had read in the newspapers and heard on the wireless without realising it, and she was able to talk freely about certain current events. She relished their intimate conversation whilst waiting for the floor show to begin.

The lights dimmed further and the compère introduced the first act, a comedian. He was a small, portly built man dressed in outrageously coloured clothes that appeared to be two sizes too small for him. Just minutes into his stint, Louise caught sight of George by the light from the hall as Joe ushered him and his female companion into the lounge.

She made Dick aware of their arrival and informed him that there was no sign of Gordon. To Dick's delight, Joe showed the couple to a table at the far end of the room from where Louise and Dick sat. It was out of their line of vision.

'Maybe we'll be able to avoid them after all,' Dick said gleefully.

Louise was beginning to feel a bit guilty. She had been here a few times with George and had had a thoroughly good time. It didn't seem right to spend the entire evening avoiding him. But if, as it appeared, Gordon wasn't with them perhaps George wouldn't want to join them anyway. He might prefer to be alone with the lovely Gabby.

She voiced her doubts. 'I feel awful mean, Dick, ignoring them. If they see us and just wave a greeting or something like that, that would be fair enough. But I think we should play it by ear and go whatever way the dice fall. Will that be all right with you, Dick, should they ask us over to their table?'

Glad that Louise didn't appear too eager to make a foursome with George and Gabby, he agreed with her. Smiling, he patted her hand, saying, 'So be it. We'll play it whatever way you like, Louise.'

* * *

The comedian brought blushes of shame to Louise's cheeks, with his risqué jokes and crude remarks. She squirmed with discomfort in her seat and didn't know where to look for the best. Everyone else seemed to find him funny. For the life of her she couldn't understand most of the innuendoes they were laughing at. When she noted Dick eyeing her apprehensively, she made her excuses and escaped to the ladies' cloakroom. No need to spoil his night out by being so prim and proper.

As was the way with things you disliked, the act seemed to go on and on for ever with the audience giving the comedian great acclaim. Unwilling to listen to such filth, as she thought it, Louise delayed in the cloakroom until thunderous applause told her the comedian had at last finished his act and it was safe for her to return.

She had been gone so long that Dick quickly rose to his feet looking anxious when she came back to the table. When they were seated again he leaned across, took her hand and said, 'I'm sorry, Louise. There wasn't a comedian on some other cabaret nights I've been to here. Or if there was, they were a lot easier on the ear than that one. Believe me, I wouldn't upset you for the world.'

She grimaced and shrugged. 'It's not your fault. Here was I, thinking I was broad-minded, but it turns out I'm nothing but a prude.'

'I'm so sorry, love. You are not a prude at all,

far from it. In fact I'm glad you don't like blue jokes as they are known. If I had known a comedian was on tonight I wouldn't have brought you here.'

Keeping her voice down, she quickly reassured him, 'Don't be daft. It's me who's at fault here. I need to grow up, see the bigger world. No one else seemed in the least bit annoyed.'

'Do you want the truth?'

She nodded cautiously, not knowing what to expect. Was he going to tell her that she should get used to it? Because if he did, he would be wrong! And she would tell him so, in no uncertain terms, not mincing her words when she did.

Instead he confessed, 'I was squirming myself at how filthy he was.' It was his turn to grimace. 'I was trying to look like a man of the world. There's no need for that sort of thing, especially in mixed company. I brought you here because the top turn is a singer and she is one of the best I've heard in a long time. I heard her down south a couple of times. She has a beautiful voice. I'm sure you'll enjoy her singing. If, however, that guy comes on again, we'll leave, OK?'

She relaxed and, nodding her agreement, settled down to enjoy the rest of the show.

The waiters had been unobtrusively serving drinks to the customers. Now that there was a short intermission, the men, glad to stretch their legs, went to the bar for their own orders while the women headed for the ladies' room. That was when George spotted Louise. He was standing nonchalantly, one arm on the bar, surveying the clientele. His gaze passed aimlessly over Louise and then slowly returned. His attention swung to her companion and she saw shock register on his face. A sideways glance at Dick revealed that he also had been watching George.

Relinquishing his place at the bar, George made a beeline for their table, and before Louise had time to speak to Dick, he was there gazing down at them.

'Well, well, well. Look who's here.'

Dick rose to his feet and offered George his hand, which he absent-mindedly shook without taking his eyes off Louise.

Dick spoke first. 'Didn't know you were here, George. Are you with company?'

'Just Gabby. Gordon has a bad toothache and cried off tonight but Gabby wanted to go out. How come we didn't see each other sooner?' He went on without waiting for an answer, 'All right if we join you?'

Dick glanced at the small space around them. 'I don't think we could get any more chairs in here, do you?'

'Oh, folk won't mind shuffling about a bit.' George was scrutinising their neighbours, who were

461

pointedly avoiding eye contact with him, but when he opened his mouth to ask them to make space, Dick quickly interrupted him.

'That won't be necessary, George. I don't like being cramped myself, so I'm not going to impose it on these other people.' He looked hard at George, willing him to get the message that he wasn't welcome and back off.

George's shoulders visibly slumped and all the arrogance left him. With bad grace he said with a slight sneer, 'I understand. Goodnight to you both.' He turned abruptly and made his way back to join the queue at the bar.

Feeling a bit apprehensive, Dick looked Louise in the eye. 'I hope you didn't mind me putting him off?'

'Not at all. I only hope Gabby doesn't insist on coming over.'

'I don't think she would dare.'

'Wanna bet?'

After the interval, Cathlin Brennan was introduced by the compère and a hush fell as everyone paid attention. Cathlin was in her early twenties and as pretty as a picture in a full-length dress of a dark green, silky material that clung to her slim body. Her wavy red hair tumbled over her shoulders and down her back. A shy nod acknowledged the smattering of applause from those who had obviously

462

heard her before. With a glance at the pianist who was accompanying her, she nodded and waited for her cue. The clapping died away as the pianist played the intro and a voice as clear as crystal filled the hushed room as she began to sing a beautiful rendering of 'Has Sorrow Thy Young Days Shaded' followed by 'When You and I Were Young, Maggie', 'Believe Me if All Those Endearing Young Charms', and 'Moonlight and Roses'.

Tears pricked at Louise's eyes and as if aware how the songs were affecting her, Dick reached for her hand again and gently squeezed it. You could have heard a pin drop and when the last song finished there was thunderous applause. Cathlin bowed and thanked the audience, then left the floor, promising she would be back after a short break.

Louise let out a long contented sigh. 'That was wonderful. She does indeed have a beautiful voice.'

Pleased at her reaction, Dick edged his own chair closer and put an arm across the back of hers. 'I agree, she has a terrific voice. I felt sure that you would enjoy listening to her.'

'"Danny Boy" is my favourite song. Do you think that she might sing it? It always makes me want to weep, but I love it.'

'Mine too. I'll put a request in for it and we just might get lucky. Another drink?'

'If you don't mind, Dick, I've had enough orange squash to last me a week.'

He grinned. 'Me too. They won't let her go without singing another song or two. Then if the comedian finishes the show off, we'll leave. Is that all right?'

Dick excused himself and went to the Gents. Not long after, Cathlin came back to loud applause. Thanking the audience for their kind appreciation, she started off with 'I Dreamt that I Dwelt in Marble Halls', then 'The Last Rose of Summer'. She finished off her performance by singing 'Danny Boy', which was greeted by a standing ovation and calls for an encore.

Afterwards, they left the club but not before Dick sought Joe out to thank him for looking after their needs. Louise saw money exchange hands and a very happy Joe bade her 'Goodnight.'

'I have really enjoyed myself tonight, Dick. Cathlin singing "Danny Boy" was the icing on the cake as far as I was concerned. She was fantastic.'

As they turned up Springfield Road, Louise asked Dick to drop her off at the corner, saying her da would be waiting to grab hold of him and they wouldn't have a chance to say goodnight. To her surprise he carried on up past Springview Street and turned into Malcomson Street.

'He's not likely to come round here, is he? So can I kiss you goodnight.' She nodded and turning in her seat leaned towards him. His left arm went round her shoulder and his right hand tilted her chin until he could see into her eyes from the light of the street gas lamp. 'Louise McGuigan, I love you and I won't rest until you marry me.' Then his lips claimed hers and she became lost in his embrace.

With a sigh she pushed away from him, glad that the gearstick had been between them; his hands were starting to stray and that would never do. She wasn't prepared to go that far. 'I'd better go, Dick. Thank you again for a lovely evening.'

'Can I see you after church tomorrow?'

'Sunday is a busy day for me. I'd rather see you later in the week, if that's OK with you?'

'Monday night? I'll be away down south from Tuesday until Friday.'

'I'm sorry, Dick, but Monday I do the family wash, so I'm afraid it will have to be next Saturday.'

She turned to open the door but he was out of the car in a flash and quickly around the front of it to assist her out. He made to take her in his arms but her slight withdrawal warned him not to push it. Taking her arm, he walked her to the bottom of Malcomson Street and around the corner into Springview Street. He stood watching until he saw her go into the house. His heart was light as he returned to the car. He felt that he was in with a chance.

But he had better not let himself get carried away, trying to touch her. He could wait until they were married.

28

On Tuesday, George Carson put in an appearance at the shop. He wandered about a bit before selecting a magazine and some writing paper and envelopes.

Bringing them to Louise's counter, he handed them to her and asked, 'Did you enjoy the show on Saturday night?'

'I loved it. That Cathlin girl has a wonderful voice.'

'She has that. I intended taking you to the club on Saturday. Why did you go with him and not me?'

'Because Dick asked me first, that's why. I hope Gordon recovered from his toothache?'

'He had the tooth extracted yesterday morning. Any news from Cathie Morgan lately?'

'Yes. As a matter of fact I got a letter from her yesterday.'

'Then you already know that Trevor has been offered that job he was interviewed for?'

Louise smiled happily at him. 'I do. Cathie was full of it in her letter. I'm so pleased for them.'

'So am I. I'm thinking of going over to visit them soon. Would you consider coming with me?'

She looked at him blankly. 'Me! Go over to Carlisle with you? You must be joking.'

'Why not?' He couldn't conceal his anger. 'Cathie and you are best friends. I thought you would be glad to take a few days off to visit her.'

'Oh, I would. But not with you. My da would have a heart attack if I mentioned going over to England with you. Besides, it might give some people the wrong idea.'

'People? Who? Like Dick Patterson, for instance?'

'Yes, him and others.'

'Look, I need to talk to you. Will you meet me outside when you're free?'

She opened her mouth to say no, but he was insistent. 'Please?'

'OK.' She glanced at the clock. 'I'll be outside in about twenty minutes.'

Without another word, he paid for his purchases and left the shop.

* * *

She kept him waiting an extra ten minutes, hoping he would get fed up and go away. However, he was standing outside the shoe shop across the street and came to meet her when she left Eason's.

He smiled wryly to show he was aware of her duplicity and said, 'Can we go for something to eat? There's a bite in this wind that sweeps along Ann Street when you're standing about doing nothing.'

She smiled sweetly at him. 'I was hoping you would offer. I hadn't time to make up any sandwiches this morning. I almost slept in.'

They made their way in silence along Castle Junction to a café on Donegall Place. Louise had a fair idea what George wanted to discuss with her.

They talked about the weather and trivial things until their order arrived. Then she got stuck into one of the sandwiches he had ordered and was chewing away at it when he leaned across the table, his words stopping her in mid-bite.

'Louise, I know you have to go back to work so I won't mince my words.'

Putting what remained of her sandwich back on the plate, she swallowed what was left in her mouth, then taking a sip of tea, she replaced the cup on the saucer with exaggerated deliberation and raised a warning hand. 'Stop right there, George. I know what you're going to say, and it's none of your business who I go out with. So keep your opinions to yourself. I don't want to hear them.'

A sad shake of the head greeted these words. 'That's not what I was going to say. But since you have broached the subject, I'll tell you what I think. Dick Patterson is way, way too old for you. You're wasting your time on him, mark my words.'

'Let me tell you something, George. Dick Patterson has done me the honour of asking me to become his wife. No ifs or buts about it. He spelled it out so that there would be no misunderstanding what he wanted. Not like Conor who seems afraid to put a ring on my finger.'

To her dismay she detected a haunted look in George's eyes. Surely he couldn't really care for her? She needn't have worried; George answered in a scornful voice, 'Don't be silly, you can't marry him. You'd be a fool if you did. I'm trying to save you from yourself.'

'I don't need to be saved. I'm more than capable of taking care of myself and making my own decisions, thank you very much. And why on earth you should worry about me, I don't know.'

He clenched his fists in frustration and growled, 'Because I care.' Thrusting his face closer to hers, he said, 'Well, have you decided? Are you going to marry him?'

Getting more flustered by this harassment,

Louise tried to keep her temper. 'To be truthful I don't know what to do for the best. Dick has given me time to consider whether or not I'll accept his proposal, and that is what I'm doing. Can I eat my sandwich now? I'm starving.'

George could see that she was upset and knew he couldn't win her over in the short time left to him. But he could at least make her see that he was serious about her.

'Listen, Louise, I admit that seeing you with Dick Patterson on Saturday night gave me the shock of my life. It woke me up! You looked so at ease, so contented, like an old married couple sitting there sipping orange juice. I never saw you like that before. It made me realise you are getting too fond of him, relying too much on him. But you don't have to. I've only been hanging back until I was sure that Conor O'Rourke was out of the picture. You must have known that, surely?'

'Huh! I'm not a mind-reader, George. Why would I think you cared? Eh?'

'Why do you think there is no other woman in my life? When you first came to work in Eason's I was bowled over. I realised why I couldn't get interested in anyone else. I also sensed that all was not going too smoothly between you and Conor. I was giving you time to come to your senses, never dreaming that in the meantime Dick was worming his way into your affections.' He lowered his voice but she still heard him when he added, 'The sly old bugger.'

Louise could see that George was all wound up. His fists were clenched as he leaned across the table, his face screwed up as he endeavoured to make her understand how serious he was, but she wasn't going to let him talk about Dick Patterson like that.

'Don't you dare say that Dick is sly. He's the most decent and honest person I've ever met, so don't you denigrate him. Do you hear me?'

Embarrassed, George held up his hands as if to ward off a blow. 'Sorry. I'm sorry. I just want you to know that I care deeply for you. You know that I never did think that Conor was good enough for you, don't you? Look, let's you and me, for the moment anyway, forget all about religion. I do believe that you have feelings for me. In fact I'm sure of it. I've been thinking lately, if Trevor and Cathie can make a go of it across the water . . . why not us? Eh? Could we not give it a try?'

Louise's grunt showed her exasperation. He was beginning to get on her nerves. 'Why are you rambling on like this, George? Cathie and Trevor are head over heels in love with each other. No one could have stopped them. They took a chance and for a while it looked as if they were wrong to run away. But so far their love has won through. They are bound to feel isolated but they're in love and that's all that matters. It's enough that they are together and the baby will bring them even closer. That's the reason it would never work for us. We were just mates, friends.' She shrugged. 'Whatever you want to call it. But we were never in love. That's the difference between them and us.'

'I think you're wrong. The only thing that held me in check last time was Conor coming back on the scene and you fell right back into his arms, without a single thought of how it would affect me. I took it very badly! I thought that you had been using me to win Conor back and I was angry and hurt and in a foul temper. Told myself that I was well rid of you. If things had stayed like that I would have eventually admitted defeat, wished you and Conor all the best and got on with my life. But can't you see? I was proved right!'

'I beg your pardon? I don't know what you're going on about.'

'I mean I was right all along, that Conor isn't the man for you. But don't you expect me to hang around waiting while you lead Dick Patterson up the garden path.'

Face ablaze with colour, her words coming out harsh and bitter, she hissed, 'I expect nothing from you! I want you to leave me alone. Do you hear me? Besides, you're not being fair. I never ever used you, not once. We had agreed to be friends.

A platonic friendship, you said. Remember? Nothing more.' Her chest was heaving with the exertion of her outburst.

'Are you saying you didn't know that I was attracted to you, eh? What about a particular day spent on Cave Hill, eh? Are you saying you didn't enjoy yourself? That you didn't want me as much as I wanted you? I know you did, although you backed down. Then shortly after that Conor came back on the scene.' She started back as if he had slapped her face and he knew that he had hit a raw nerve. 'Don't tell me you've forgotten about it?'

She felt her face blanch and cowered away from him. She remembered it well; the day she had seen her mother and Bill McCartney on Cave Hill kissing and cuddling like a pair of teenagers. The day she realised her mother was in love with another man and if her father found out murder would surely have been done. That was what had made her turn to George Carson that day. Not love, as he had thought. It was because she hadn't wanted her mother to catch sight of her. If her mother had seen her, she would have known that Louise must have seen her as well and be aware of the antics she got up to with Bill. Her mother hadn't lied when she said that she was going out with a work-mate that day. Nora just hadn't revealed that the workmate was none other than Bill McCartney. A fitter who, at the time, worked in the Blackstaff mill maintaining the machinery. Some workmate, Louise thought. At that time she hadn't the slightest inkling that anything was going on between her mother and McCartney.

George continued, 'I was so sure you cared but I was a mug. I was waiting until you got Conor out of your system before I showed my true feelings. Then Conor upset the apple-cart by coming home and telling you some cock and bull story and you chose to believe him. But look how he has been acting since you got back together.'

Shame made her bow her head. She had guessed that George had deep feelings for her but, wanting to renew her friendship with Conor, she had convinced herself otherwise. If Conor hadn't told her the truth that he was illegitimate and had thought she wouldn't marry him because he was a bastard, who knows how her relationship with George would have progressed? She had found herself very attracted to him and had returned his kisses on Cave Hill with fervour. But it had been all lust and passion! Hadn't it?

'It's too late for us, George,' she protested. 'Too much water has passed under the bridge. There's no going back.'

'Just let me take you out again, Louise,' he pleaded. 'At least give me a chance to try and change your mind about me.'

'I'm sorry, George. I may not marry Dick Patterson, but I always knew that I couldn't marry outside the Church. My religion means too much to me. You knew that. I never tried to tell you otherwise. That's something I really would live to regret.'

'What if I converted to Catholicism?'

Taken aback, she gasped, 'Don't be silly. You'd never do a thing like that. You're talking rubbish now and you know it. There are stacks of girls out there you can have. Girls your family would approve of and welcome with open arms, so don't pretend you care about who I marry.'

She picked up her sandwich and started to eat as if her life depended on it. It tasted like sawdust in her mouth, but she had to get out of the café and away from him without making a scene. George Carson had certainly given her food for thought.

They finished lunch in glum silence. He stopped to pay the bill and she was already on the edge of the kerb, waiting to cross Donegall Place, when he eventually left the café. Catching up with her halfway across the road, he apologised. 'I'm sorry, Louise, if I have upset you. I never meant to, but I haven't given up all hope just yet. You will soon grow tired of an old man's affections. When you change your mind you know where to find me. Just don't leave it too long. It's time I was married and starting a family.'

The conceited pig, she thought as she broke into a run along Cornmarket to escape any more of his babbling.

The rest of the day dragged by and it was a relief when it was time to go home. Deirdre was in a huff because Louise had been so offhand with her but Louise couldn't care less. She had enough on her plate without worrying about her friend.

She had been kissed and caressed by three different men in her lifetime, each one so different from the other. Four, if she counted the assault by Liam Gilmore on Johnnie's wedding day. Had any of them definitely been 'the one'? Was she so naive that she wouldn't know love if it jumped up and bit her on the backside? She hadn't the foggiest idea.

Hurt at the time, she was now glad that Conor had rejected her when she had indicated that they should carry their romance a stage further. Imagine her encouraging him to commit a mortal sin? She should be ashamed of herself! She had been so sure back then that he was the one and only man she could ever love. Her first love in fact. How wrong she had been. And now Dick had joined the equation. A trilogy of love. It sounded like some Greek tragedy, she thought with a whimsical smile. It would be laughable, so it would, if it wasn't so bloody serious. Imagine her, of all people, having a choice? Louise McGuigan, ex-mill girl with three handsome men striving for her affections. But how did one know when it was the real thing?

The letter she had received the day before from Cathie had been a lot more cheerful than her previous ones. It had been a pleasure to answer it and rejoice in her friend's joy at the way things were panning out for them. Louise had quietly sent up a prayer to her favourite saint, St Theresa, thanking her for granting her her petition and asking her to keep a watchful eye on Cathie and Trevor and their unborn child. She tried to imagine George and herself married but failed. No, she couldn't take George Carson seriously enough to entertain the idea of marrying him. He was well and truly off her list of options. But what about Conor? Was it because she hadn't seen him for some time or even heard from him and knew in her heart that it was all over between her and Conor; was that why she was finding so much pleasure in Dick Patterson's arms? Or was she falling in love with Dick? Only time would tell. A shiver of anticipation slid down her spine at the thought of seeing Dick again.

Harry had returned to work on Monday. His face was healing well and, with Hannah promising to become his wife, his cup was full. But . . . he had yet to hear from his solicitor, James Hamill, as to how his case was progressing.

Peggy, not being shy, had asked Hannah if she could be her bridesmaid. Louise, who was present at the time, saw Hannah cast a furtive glance in her direction and guessed that she had intended asking Louise instead. Now she was tongue-tied by Peggy's audacity.

Louise came to her rescue. 'Peggy, you're supposed to wait until Hannah asks you to be her bridesmaid. You don't just take an honour like that for granted, so you don't. Can she, Hannah?'

'I'm just letting her know that if given the chance I'd love to be her bridesmaid. I do, however, realise that she will probably ask you.'

'No, I think you're wrong there. I imagine Hannah will ask you. You two were so close until Harry caused a bit of an upset between you by falling for Hannah. Of course Hannah will want you to be her bridesmaid. Not me.'

Glad of the opportunity that Louise had given her, Hannah said, 'You won't mind, will you, Louise?'

Louise gave her a smile of approval and Hannah turned to Peggy. 'Will you please be my bridesmaid, Peggy?'

Peggy sprang at her as if released from a catapult. 'Oh, I'd be delighted to be your bridesmaid, Hannah. Very much so,' she cried, hugging her friend close.

'Of course it will be some time before we can get married. We'll have to start saving for a start. Louise will probably be away long before me.' Hannah cocked an eyebrow in Louise's direction, but it was Peggy who answered.

'Oh, I doubt that. Conor O'Rourke is still dragging his feet. There is no reason in the world why they can't get engaged . . . but,' she shrugged her shoulders in resignation, 'looks as if she's going to be left on the shelf if she's not careful.'

'Look, you two forget about me. I wish you all the best, Hannah, I really do. The way I feel at the moment I think I'll be spinster aunt to your and Peggy's children.' To close the subject she headed for the scullery, throwing over her shoulder, 'Anyone fancy a cuppa tea?'

On Wednesday, Harry got a letter from James Hamill requesting him to attend Belfast magistrates court on Friday. The solicitor wrote that the hearing was scheduled for eleven o'clock. He said he would be there at half past ten to confer with his client and would wait outside the court until Harry arrived.

It was with trepidation that Harry set off, dressed in his Sunday best, to meet James Hamill. The solicitor took Harry to a room where he explained what the procedure would be, assuring him that he was confident of the outcome and that Harry had no need to worry.

Harry's case was the third to be heard. He listened in trepidation as one young man was released on bail until a future date and the next man, middle aged, was remanded in custody for being drunk and disorderly and resisting arrest. Then it was his turn. It was as James Hamill had predicted. It was all over in five minutes. Harry was given a nominal fine and released with a warning from the magistrate that the court would not be so lenient should he ever appear before the bench again.

Outside the court Harry stood in a daze. He couldn't believe that he had got off so lightly. James gripped his hand. 'I wish you all the best, young man. In future, you make sure that you keep your temper in check.'

'Thank you! Thank you very much, Mr Hamill. I have certainly learned my lesson today.' James made to move off and Harry grabbed his arm. 'Wait. You haven't told me how much I owe you.'

'It's all right. Mr Patterson is seeing to that. He'll probably dock it from your wages when you start working for him,' he said with a smile. 'Well, goodbye, young man, perhaps if we ever meet again it will be in more pleasant circumstances.' At that James Hamill strode off swinging his briefcase and looking every inch how Harry thought a solicitor should look in his black, pin-striped suit.

* * *

After dinner on Friday Louise couldn't get the house to herself quickly enough. She waved her da off to the pub, lent her best cardigan to Peggy who was meeting someone, to hasten her departure, and waited patiently for Harry to leave.

Harry eyed her suspiciously. 'Doesn't Dick come back from Dublin tonight? Is that the reason you're on tenterhooks?'

'He does, but I won't see him until tomorrow night.'

'Then why the big rush to get rid of us all?'

'Because I want some time to myself to get this place tidied up. Look at it, it's like a pigsty. Then I'll have a good wash-down and shampoo my hair. Is that such a crime? Is it?'

'Ah. Seeing as how you put it like that, I'll take myself off then and leave you to it. Unless you want me to give you a hand with anything?'

'No, thanks. But it was very kind of you to offer, Harry.' To make sure she meant it she handed him his jacket and opened the vestibule door. 'Make sure to shut the big door on your way out.'

With a laugh he was on his way.

Louise fussed about, tidying the kitchen and scullery, and dusting the furniture. When she was satisfied that everything was presentable she climbed the stairs to her room. She wanted to look at her wardrobe and decide what she would wear for her outing with Dick the following night. She wished she had something new, something real classy. With a sigh she took her green suit off the rail and held it up for close inspection. It was the nicest garment she possessed and she loved it, but she had worn it when out with Dick twice already.

She examined it minutely. There was no sign of smudges around the neck, no marks at all on it. It still looked new to her. Why was she being so fussy? On other outings many was the time she had gone out without worrying what her clothes looked like as long as they were clean. So why worry about what Dick Patterson thought of her? Because she cared. Just how much, she didn't know. She couldn't really fathom their relationship.

A knock at the door brought her to the bedroom window. She frowned as she peered down through the nets. She saw the car first and then, moving closer to the window, Dick Patterson gazing upwards. With a gasp of dismay, Louise turned sharply away from the window and in doing so caught sight of her reflection in the wardrobe mirror. She was a right mess: still in her work skirt and blouse covered by a pinafore that was stained by her labours downstairs. Her hair was straggly and limp from the steam in the scullery while she had been boiling potatoes and frying sausages and bacon for dinner.

Her heart sank and she thumped the wardrobe

with her fists in frustration. In spite of all the great plans she had made to look her best when she met him tomorrow night, he had to come now when she looked the worse for wear. If she didn't answer the door, would he think the house was empty and go away?

That's what she would do: pretend no one was at home. After a restive ten minutes she cautiously approached the window and peeped out again. To her horror the car was still parked there and she could see Dick sitting in it. Well, so be it. There was nothing else for it. She would have to let him in to see her as she really was, warts and all. Taking the apron off, she threw it none too gently into the wash bag. Straightening her shoulders, she headed for the stairs.

The second the door opened Dick was out of the car in a flash and quickly crossed the pavement. Without further ado he was in the hall and closing the door behind him. He appeared upset.

'Why didn't you open the door when I knocked? I guessed you were inside and didn't know what to think. Didn't you want to see me?'

'Yes, but you weren't supposed to come here until tomorrow night. Look at me, I look a right mess. That's why I didn't want to open the door.'

He grabbed her by her upper arms. 'You look beautiful. You'll always look beautiful to me. I only wish you were a bit older or I was a bit younger. I know what they will be saying. He's a cradle-snatcher. He's an old sugar daddy. But a man is in his prime at my age, and I love you so much. I know that I can make you happy, Louise.'

Eyes wide, she gazed up at him. 'I've never thought of you as being too old, or a sugar daddy. I just thought I wouldn't reach up to your expectations. I mean, I imagine you will soon get bored with me. I'm still wet behind the ears, you know, while you're a man of the world.'

He shook her gently. 'You silly, silly girl, I love you. More than you'll ever know. I couldn't wait until tomorrow night to see you again. Once I was in Belfast I had to come straight here. I have missed you so. Did you miss me at all?'

'Much! So very much. Did you really mean that? You think I look all right like this? You're not disappointed to see me at my worst?'

'Not in the slightest. If this is your worst, I'm very happy with it. You'll always look lovely to me. Has George Carson been trying to lure you away from me? That was my biggest fear while I was away.'

Louise laughed and pushed him into the kitchen. 'He doesn't come anywhere near how I feel about you.' Without thought she said, 'I love you, you big goon.'

He pulled her close and gazed at her in awe. 'Do you really mean that, Louise?'

The warmth and emotion that radiated from him engulfed her and she was certain, there and then, that he was indeed the one she wanted to spend the rest of her life with. This was how she had wanted to feel: snug and secure, sure that he would never let her down. The feelings that swamped her made her suddenly realise that she had no doubt whatsoever about his love for her – warts and all. Smiling and happy, she paused and looked at him in wonder.

'Yes . . . I do. I really do. I've been trying to deny it, but . . . but, yes, I love you very, very much, Dick,' she said softly. The joy of it made her glow with happiness.

Dick hugged her closer still. 'Thank God and all His saints for answering my prayers,' he whispered with a slight tremor in his voice.

Throwing back her head, she gaped at him. 'I never thought of you as being the religious sort.'

He grimaced. 'When I was a young man I was a good, practising Catholic. I don't mean a goody-goody type. Huh! Far from it. But I did go to church regularly and received the sacraments. Then when my wife died, I lost all interest in the faith. But lately I've started going back to church down in Dublin.'

'You never said.'

'I was afraid that you would think that I was returning to the faith because of you and that you wouldn't believe that I was serious about you. And in a way I suppose it's true. I've been on my knees a lot lately, asking God to let you be my wife. And it looks as if my prayers have been answered.'

She offered him her lips and he covered them with his. His kiss was deep and she was aware of the passion he was controlling and she loved him all the more for it, sure that he'd always put her feelings first.

He eased his hold on her. 'Can we get married soon?' He laughed. 'Me being older than you, I'm impatient to start married life with you. And I may not have much time left to enjoy your company,' he joked.

In the safe hollow of his arms she whispered, 'Yes. I'll marry you any time you like. I love you, Dick Patterson.'

Closing her eyes, she nestled her head against his chest, a small bubble of laughter escaping her lips.

'What's so funny?'

'I've just realised that this will come as one hell of a shock to my whole family. My mother hasn't even met you yet. Peggy thinks I'm destined to spend the rest of my life on the shelf, a confirmed old maid. I'm sure that Johnnie will be pleased for us. Harry will be delighted of course. You're his hero at the moment. And as for me da, I think he likes you, but I don't think Cissie O'Rourke will be too pleased. She had these big plans for me to marry her Conor so that me da could move in with her.'

'Well, to tell you the truth, Louise, I couldn't care less what Cissie O'Rourke thinks. All I know is that you have made me the happiest man in the world, and I love you too much to start worrying about what other people think. You, and only you, are all that matters to me from now on.'

Louise hugged him close and gave out a long, contented sigh.

Acknowledgements

To my son, Con, my ever grateful thanks for his unselfish help solving the many computer problems that I encountered during the course of this book.

To Sue and Billy for assisting me in my research across the water.

To Séan Caughey, my grateful thanks for his help with local knowledge.

To my copy-editor Celia Levett, my sincere gratitude for her editorial input.

To my desk-editor, Hannah Green, for her patience in dealing with my many queries.

And last but not least to my husband, Con, who was always there at my side with his support, advice and pearls of wisdom.